'This book kept me up half the nigh[t...] down, and read it in one spellbou[nd...] novel should be: compassionate, unpredictable, and questioning. *Haven* is Donoghue at her strange, unsettling best.'

Maggie O'Farrell, author of *Hamnet*

'Brooding, dreamlike ... it's in descriptions of the physical world that Donoghue's prose soars ... Likewise, among themes that include isolation and devotion, its ecological warnings are its most resonant.' *The Observer*

'Donoghue excels in creating not just a world but a worldview that is far removed from our own ... this is a bold, thoughtful novel.' *Financial Times*

'Donoghue wrings unlikely psychodrama from such everyday chores of monastic life as copying a manuscript or building a drystone wall. But if that doesn't grab you, rest assured that the devastating denouement amply repays the reader's patience – and has a thing or two to say about modern-day moral panics, too' *Daily Mail*

'I read it in a couple of sittings with a growing sense of foreboding and desperation to know their fates. A powerful story, brilliantly imagined.'

Clare Chambers, author of *Small Pleasures*

'*Haven* creates an eerie, meditative atmosphere that should resonate with anyone willing to think deeply about the blessings and costs of devoting one's life to a transcendent cause.'

The Washington Post

HAVEN

Born in Dublin in 1969, and now living in Canada, Emma Donoghue writes fiction (novels and short stories, contemporary and historical, most recently *The Pull of the Stars*), as well as drama for screen and stage. *Room* was a *New York Times* Best Book of 2010 and a finalist for the Man Booker, Commonwealth, and Orange Prizes, selling nearly three million copies in forty languages. Donoghue was nominated for an Academy Award for her script for the 2015 film adaptation starring Brie Larson and her theatre adaptation is coming to Broadway in 2023. She also co-wrote the screenplay for the film of her 2016 novel *The Wonder*, starring Florence Pugh. For more information, visit www.emmadonoghue.com.

ALSO BY EMMA DONOGHUE

HAVEN

EMMA DONOGHUE

PICADOR

First published 2022 by Little, Brown and Company
a division of Hachette Book Group, New York

First published in the UK 2022 by Picador

This edition first published 2023 by Picador
an imprint of Pan Macmillan
The Smithson, 6 Briset Street, London EC1M 5NR
EU representative: Macmillan Publishers Ireland Ltd, 1st Floor,
The Liffey Trust Centre, 117–126 Sheriff Street Upper,
Dublin 1, D01 YC43
Associated companies throughout the world
www.panmacmillan.com

ISBN 978-1-5290-9116-8

1 3 5 7 9 8 6 4 2

A CIP catalogue record for this book is available from the British Library.

Printed and bound by CPI Group (UK) Ltd, Croydon, CR0 4YY

Visit www.picador.com to read more about all our books
and to buy them. You will also find features, author interviews and
news of any author events, and you can sign up for e-newsletters
so that you're always first to hear about our new releases.

For Anne Schuurman and Zoë Sinel

What, then, consoles us
in this human society full of calamities,
but the unfeigned faith and mutual love
of true and good friends?

—Augustine, *City of God*, AD 426

CONTENTS

MONASTERY

TRIAN'S STOMACH GROWLS. He's not twenty yet, still growing, and always hungry.

The first fast-day after Easter, and the hall is crammed with more than thirty monks and their Abbot, as well as the families who serve them and work the land. Even the Abbess is here, though not her nuns, who dine in their quarters at the other end of the double monastery. Also half a dozen strangers, come to Cluain Mhic Nóis to study with one of the celebrated teachers, or for a few months or weeks of respite from the grasping world.

The Abbot's led the congregation in saying grace in Latin, and is eating already. Trian gestures to his neighbour to help himself to roast swan and onions from their platter. Then Trian spoons what's left onto his own trencher. He makes himself chew slowly, and rations out his ale in sips. The rich meat's gone down all too soon, and then he lets himself eat half the round of three-day-old bread, saturated with savoury juice.

His red-faced neighbour downs another cup of ale, belches, and looks sideways at Trian's remaining bread.

Trian pushes it towards him. Sits still and tells himself that he's had enough, *Deo gratias,* thank God.

Chatter, argument, laughter; the hubbub of Gaelic rises and fills the hall like smoke. Out of the corner of his eye Trian catches a shape looming in the doorway: the stranger called Artt, who walks along the wall now, away from the Abbot's table, and lowers himself onto a bench at the back of the hall.

Trian's fascinated. This Artt has the bearing of a warrior king, but he behaves like a scrupulous monk working out a long penance. It's been a fortnight since Trian took the boat across the river to ferry this man over to the monastery, carried Artt's meagre possessions to the guest hut, washed his broad feet (cracked nails, a sign of hard travels), and brought him food, and Trian hasn't dared address a word to him yet.

Of course the monks have shared every scrap of information and hearsay. Scholar, priest, hermit, Artt is the most famous visitor to Cluain Mhic Nóis in the six years Trian's been here, and possibly in the half century since its founding. From a clan of judges in the West, fostered out to a holy man at the age of seven—as soon as Artt knew more than his master, he sought out another, and another, but outshone them all. Now in his prime, familiar with many tongues, the sage is said to have read every book written, and has copied out dozens. Artt can work complex sums in his mind and chart the tracks of the stars. One of the band of solitaries who've been carrying the light of the Gospel from Ireland across a pagan-gripped continent, this soldier for Christ has converted whole tribes among the Picts, the Franks, even the Lombards.

Still, Artt looks to Trian as fresh as if he's just returned from the Land of Youth. Brown-haired, grey-eyed, the man is as brawny as some hero who can toss with one hand a boulder twice the size of his head. Artt's single blemish—the blackened stump of the little finger on his massive right hand—is rumoured to be a mark of God's favour: proof that he's done the impossible by surviving the plague.

Now Artt is sitting with his trencher dry in front of him, shaking his head no matter what he's offered. As Trian watches, Artt breaks off a piece of the bread and chews it. He ignores the ale flasks and fills his beaker with water.

At the top of the hall, a monk is speaking into the Abbot's right ear, their eyes on the honoured guest as the boy refills their cups with wine.

The Abbot smacks the table. When the noise quietens, he calls out, 'Brother Artt, are none of our dishes to your taste?'

Artt answers in his deep, melodious voice. 'Thank you, Father. I keep the fast.'

'As do we all, every week, to mark the day our Lord Christ was put to death.' The Abbot smiles stiffly at the heaped remains on his platter. 'Don't waterfowl count as fish, since they feed only on fish and weeds?'

Artt's sharply incised lips press together. 'By custom more than by logic.'

Too little air in this stifling hall. Trian feels sick, thinking of how greedily he gulped down his own portion of swan, and still longs for more.

The Abbot's flushed now. 'Will you take eggs or cheese, then?'

Artt sips his water while the whole community waits. 'No thank you.' The silence stretches. 'Nor butter, milk, nor whey. Whatever comes out of an animal is of the same nature as its flesh.'

The Abbot's jowly face shuts tight.

If one of Trian's brother monks said such a thing, it would be insubordination and earn a beating. But this Artt is a living saint, and can't be wrong, can he?

Then is the Abbot wrong about the rules of fasting?

But for Trian to judge his own master would be disobedience, so he'd better turn his thoughts aside this minute.

Maybe Artt's come among them to stir up their souls, he tells himself; to inspire them to live more cleanly.

The Abbot gestures almost violently to Cormac, a few places away from Trian: 'Entertain us, Brothers.'

The humped old monk is on his feet at once, lyre in hand, and nodding to the other musicians. Trian's already pulling his pipe out of the narrow bag that hangs from his belt. They all hasten around the tables into the middle of the hall, blocking the Abbot's view of his guest. They wait for Cormac to pick a tune—something familiar and cheerful—then hurry to find their unison.

Hours later, Artt lurches out of sleep. He finds himself on his feet, one hand pressed against the wattle wall. The other visitors are still snoring, but his heart is going so hard he feels he'll never sleep again. His dream, so close he can taste the salt on his lips.

He throws on his sheepskin cloak over his nightshirt. He remembers to get the little roll of painted linen out of his satchel before he leaves the hut.

Halfway between Nocturns and Vigil, Artt would say by

the way the fat moon sits on the tips of the yews guarding the church. He turns the other way, seeking out the Abbot's quarters. It's the most handsome building after the church—all in wood, with a carved lintel. When Artt bangs on the door, a yawning servant comes to turn him away.

'I'm aware it's the middle of the night. Rouse your master.'

The groggy whimper of a child, several rooms back; a light voice, protesting. Artt steps to one side, for fear of laying eyes on the woman in her nightclothes. It's not strictly against the laws of the Church for an Abbot to have a wife—*Better to marry than burn in lust,* the apostle Paul conceded—but it disgusts Artt. Like most abbots, this one comes from the clan that gave these lands, so clearly his concern is to maintain his kin's grazing rights as much as to govern his monastery. Artt believes monks should be ruled by one committed to the way of Christ, who spends his days praying, fasting, and working, and his nights alone.

Wrapped up in furs, rubbing his swollen lids with a hand that's never done manual labour, the Abbot appears in the doorway, holding up a taper.

Artt cuts off the tetchy greeting. 'Father, I have had a dream.'

'Couldn't you tell me about it in the morning?'

'A vision,' he clarifies. 'An island in the sea. I saw myself there. As if I were a bird or an angel, looking down on the three of us.'

'Three?'

'I was with an old monk, and a young one.' The Abbot shows no sign of understanding him. 'The dream is an instruction to withdraw from the world. To set out on pilgrimage with two companions, find this island, and found a monastic retreat.'

The Abbot's mouth opens and shuts, a fish gasping. 'Artt, Brother—'

Through his teeth: 'I saw it. I was *there*.'

'On this, ah, island? Which is...where, do you believe?'

'Far away, in the western ocean. Away from everything.' Artt holds up the map in his hand, and lets the linen unroll. The letters HIBERNIA float beside the jagged silhouette that resembles an oak leaf or a wolfskin.

The Abbot peers at it, bringing his flame close. 'Where's our abbey of Cluain Mhic Nóis?'

Is he ignorant, or are his eyes weak? 'Here, in the very middle of the country, halfway down the Sionan, our greatest river.' Artt points to the heartland. 'Our men of God who go into the wild places—since there are no deserts in our Hibernia, of course, many establish houses in forests or glens, or on lake islands.'

'Indeed, isn't Ireland a byword for such holy hermitages?'

His host's smug tone sticks in Artt's craw. Standing there swaddled in embroidered linen, reeking of Gaulish wine. How many times the Abbot must have recited Christ's call—*Sell all you have, give it to the poor and follow me*—without ever hearing it.

But Artt hasn't come here in the middle of the night to preach to the Abbot, only to get his permission. He pushes on. 'Those who hate the world most have to go even farther to escape its seductions, right out to sea.' He moves his finger to the right. 'See, in the waters between us and Albion? Blessed Nessán and Colm Cille each landed on his allotted rock there.'

The Abbot nods at the familiar names.

'Then this large island off our north coast,' touching a dot on the map, 'sainted Comgall's claimed that one for God.

But it is in the great ocean on our western side that the water's most richly seeded with refuges.' Artt taps to the left of Hibernia with one nail. 'The blessed Ríoch discovered his here, for instance, and Macdara to the south of him. Farther south again, holy Éanna, Brecan, Senán and Caomhán—they set up their monasteries among the isles of Aran, like beacons on the frontier of Christendom, manned only by the best fighters, keeping the devil out by the power of prayer.' Artt's finger slides down that coast. 'For all my researches, I haven't yet learned of any monks south of there,' he admits. 'But there must be more islands that way. Empty ones, even less tainted by the world's breath. That's where I'm to go, with one old monk and one young one, and the message of my dream tonight is that I must waste no time.'

The plump lips purse. 'Three men—that's few, Brother. Twelve would be more usual, like the apostles. When holy Ciarán settled on the site of what would become this blessed foundation'—the Abbot gestures grandly at church, hall, library, scriptorium, dormitories, workshops, shelters for livestock—'he had eight with him.'

Stone-faced, Artt quotes the Lord: '*Where two or three gather in my name, I am there.*'

A small sigh. 'In your dream—did you recognise this pair of monks?'

He nods. 'The first was the hunched fellow with the dented head, who played the lyre tonight.' Artt's seen him all over Cluain Mhic Nóis, doing repairs, tending the plots, slow-moving but dogged.

The Abbot's mouth turns down in surprise. 'Cormac? He was a late convert. Nobody knows his years.'

'A pious man?'

'For all I know.'

But the Abbott should know; a master is supposed to look into the naked hearts of his men.

'He can certainly turn his hand to anything. I suppose he'd be useful to you.'

Artt wonders cynically if the Abbot will be less willing to spare him a monk with a life's worth of work left in him. 'Also the gangly, red-haired one, the piper.'

'Oh, Trian? He's a strange boy all right.'

In the guest hut, Artt has watched this Trian rush to meet needs before they're mentioned. Earnest-looking, not one of those messers with their shoves and jokes. A *ciotóg*, of course, an awkward left-hander; some call that trait the devil's mark, but Artt doesn't blame the young man for his misfortune. He noticed that Trian ate only half his trencher tonight, giving the rest to the fat fellow beside him. '*Strange* how?'

'Hard to say. Nothing bad,' the Abbot assures him. 'A bit of a daydreamer.'

But Artt has to trust his heaven-sent vision.

The Abbot puts his head on one side. 'For such an uncertain voyage, wouldn't you be better off choosing strong, seasoned men of middle years?'

His anxiety sounds genuine. But would he really be ready to give up such men? Besides, the decision is not Artt's. 'It's God who's chosen these two.'

'And if they refuse? I must tell you, I won't compel any of my sworn monks to leave.'

They won't refuse. Artt knows it in his bones.

As the monks in the church sing Vigil, later that night, Cormac sways. Vigil's the hardest of the six holy hours, for him; the rags of sleep cling to his legs, his tongue, his mind. He takes a big breath of the rich beeswax scent and straightens up.

His shoulder twitches; he glances down at the seam and picks out a louse. When Cormac first came to Cluain Mhic Nóis he found himself scratching all the time, and tried various preventives to keep the pests out of his bedding and clothes. Gradually he came to understand it as part of monastic life, like the bells. *God's messengers,* some of the brethren call the lice; once you make your peace with them, the bites hardly itch.

Cormac feels watched, somehow.

Across the golden pool of light from the candelabra, their famous guest has a hawk's gaze fixed on Cormac.

He drops his eyes. What awful error could he have made, to draw down on himself the attention of this extraordinary man? Maybe it's just his almost-bald, bockedy skull; strangers often stare. He buries himself in the prayer.

When Vigil's over, they all file out, yawning, under a sky still diamonded with stars. Cormac heads towards the cell he shares with just one other old-timer, looking forward to the luxury of his straw-and-chaff pallet, sheets and blanket and pillow, a few more hours of sleep before dawn.

A heavy hand grasps his shoulder. The holy man.

There's no doubt in Artt's bass, sonorous tones, only author-ity, and an urgency that speeds Cormac's pulse. He begins as if taking up a previous conversation. 'In our country, Brother, lovers of Christ have been called not to the red martyrdom of violent death so many on the Continent of Europe have endured, but to the pale martyrdom of world-renouncing.'

Cormac nods helplessly. Why is the visitor preaching arcanely, to him alone, in the middle of the night?

'The fact is, Cluain Mhic Nóis has lost its way.'

He flinches, to hear that put so baldly.

Artt's wave takes in the starlit grounds all the way to the palisade that rings them. 'This monastery has sat on rich land so long, safe from starvation and raiders, that its brethren have lowered the shield of perpetual prayer. Greed has crept in, and laziness, and spite, and lust.'

Cormac can't deny a word of that. He's seen monks come to blows, and suspected some of fornicating with the women or each other. But the thing is, he has lived so many years that the varieties of human weakness have lost their power to shock him.

'Will you leave this place behind and come with me, Brother?'

The question makes Cormac stare.

'Sail to the west in search of a far haven where we can live purely,' Artt asks, 'working and giving glory to our Maker?'

Picked for such a mission, at Cormac's age?

Then again, he remembers, the most celebrated of travellers, holy Breandán, lived past ninety, and voyaged till the very end.

Cormac hasn't felt discontented at Cluain Mhic Nóis, only bored, on occasion. He's assumed this is the effect of a routine, undemanding life. Or of old age itself; a certain slackness in the rope. Suddenly to be invited to join a brave band venturing into unknown waters . . . He tries to speak, but finds his throat too dry.

Artt's voice goes deeper: 'What I must know is, are you strong enough in faith?'

He hasn't asked if Cormac wants this. More a command, then, like that of Jesus to the fishermen: *Come, follow me.*

Cormac swallows. It doesn't occur to him to refuse. 'I think so.' Then, more firmly: 'I believe so. I'm tough old meat.'

A rare smile lights Artt's face like the moon through cloud.

Excitement prickles in Cormac's soles.

'Your Abbot tells me you were baptised only fifteen years back.'

He nods, sheepish; he was a wizened apple among the harvest offerings. 'Before that I worked our kin's land.' He gives himself a moment to find the words. 'I had a wife and three children by her. The next time the plague came, I lost them all.' He glimpses the tangle of those small limbs, creamy skin spotted blue-black. Their daughter had just taken her first steps.

'But you survived.'

'It so happened the infection never touched me.' After that he hung around as an uncle to his brothers' children, a ghost at the feast.

'Don't credit happenstance,' Artt rebukes him. 'God in his wisdom saw fit to spare you, so you could come to Christ.'

'That happened only many years later,' Cormac admits, 'and by accident.'

One thick eyebrow jumps.

Cormac's fingers go up to the little crater above his left ear. 'A slingstone stove my head in.'

'In battle?'

That seems too grand a word for it. 'Well, we were disputing with another clan. The blow sent me out of my senses.

But my brother's wife had heard the Christians had strong medicine'—he almost said *magic*—'so my people brought me to Cluain Mhic Nóis. A monk called Fiach, he saved me.' Gone now, along with most of the folk Cormac's ever known, all his elders and many far younger.

'How?' Artt asks.

'Cut the scalp and peeled me like an apple. With a hand drill he bored holes until the smashed piece came right off. Then he sewed the skin back over the hole, and poulticed me with herbs, and prayed till my fever broke.'

'You were quite well again?'

'Better than before, in fact, *Deo gratias.*' Cormac makes a cross on his forehead. 'Wits a bit sharper and memory roomier.'

'See what the Lord can accomplish? *I was a stone lying in the deep mud,*' Artt intones, *'and he who is mighty came and in his mercy lifted me up.*'

Cormac nods. 'I told this Fiach I owed him my life, but he said he was Christ's bondman, so now I too belonged to Christ. I was baptised and taught to read, and took vows.' He remembers sending word to his kin to divide up his fields and cattle.

'You were preserved so you could join my pilgrimage,' Artt insists.

Might all that's happened to Cormac have been leading to this? 'May I ask…why would you want me?' He glances down at his gnarled knuckles, the pearl swellings around his fingernails. 'I had skills and powers in my prime, but these days—'

Artt cuts him off. 'I care nothing for your skills or powers.'

Cormac looks away, embarrassed.

'God put you in my dream.'

That disconcerts him. 'And how many of us do you mean to bring?'

'Two.'

It hits Cormac then, the full honour of it. In the twilight of his days, he has heard the call to arms; his Lord has need of him.

The rising sun's sharp in Trian's eyes as he stands outside the hut he shares with three other young monks. He's still in his nightshirt; the knock at the door has roused them early. Pulse pounding, so he can hardly make out the holy man's words. 'I was...in your dream?'

Artt nods, impatient. 'Ours will be a sacred wandering.'

A chance for Trian to trade his mundane existence for an adventure, like a heroic deed out of a song.

'Then, once we find the island,' Artt warns, 'it will be a hard life.'

'That'll suit me,' Trian manages to get out.

Artt squeezes his shoulder till it almost hurts. 'A small brotherhood—you and I and Brother Cormac—but mighty in faith.'

Cormac? Trian's startled only because of the monk's age. They've played music together for years, rarely exchanging a word. Cormac is a fount of lore, of course, and skilled at gardening and building, whereas Trian is unaware of possessing any special talents. Ungainly and odd, and he knows it; knowing doesn't help it.

'Did you grow up on the river?' Artt asks.

'At the sea'—he gestures east—'many days from here.'

'You've no family, I understand.'

'My parents gave me to Cluain Mhic Nóis when I was thirteen.'

'In payment of a debt?'

Trian shrugs; no one ever said so.

'Jesus told his followers to hate their own fathers and mothers, wives and children,' Artt remarks. 'You are already free and clear of those ties.'

Trian frowns, trying to call up the faces of his father, mother, brothers, sisters. Need he go so far as to hate them, since he's almost forgotten them? There was a time he did miss them sorely, but over six years they've receded to the far back of his mind. He imagines it is the same for them. He tries to remember the words his mother said at the gate, before handing him over. 'They thought I'd be safe here. *My soul,* I suppose they meant.'

Artt puffs his breath. 'A safety of the body only. This place is riddled with sin, as a book with worm tunnels.'

Trian looks down, mortified.

'I've caught a whiff of the same rot in even more-celebrated abbeys,' Artt tells him. 'Monkish life is one long war against the devil. And when dozens of men live together ... well, where better for wolves to hide than in a great flock of sheep?'

Trian broods over the times he's seen the rules broken but turned a blind eye. He's never felt it his place to cast blame; just kept his head down and worked harder.

'Well, I mean to pull you out of this mire,' Artt says. 'A couple of brethren, that's all the fellowship a man needs.

Besides, three is the most sacred number.' Putting his thumb to the third finger of his left hand so the other three are left standing: Father, Son, and Holy Spirit, threefold God.

Trian stares at the dark stub on Artt's other hand, living proof that this man can survive all trials. A confessional impulse opens his throat. 'Thank you. A thousand thanks. But I must warn you, I am not worthy.'

Those bright grey eyes narrow. 'Brother, which of us is *worthy*? We all stink of sin.'

Trian blinks.

'What matters is, we three have been chosen.'

Four days later, on a cloudy spring morning, Artt carries an ironbound wooden chest down to the riverbank where the narrow boat waits.

Curled up at bow and stern, this craft—the larger of the monastery's two—is the length of two men. Like a frail tent inverted in the water, it strikes him; nothing more solid than a dozen oxhides bark-tanned, puzzled together over an ash-wood skeleton and pulled drum-tight with leather thongs. The vessel has been freshly curried with wool grease to keep out the water, the joins pasted with pine pitch one last time. Artt takes it as a sign that the single mast in its socket and the flat yard with its sail furled make the shape of the cross on which Jesus was nailed. *Christus,* he murmurs silently, *Christus, Christus.*

Their cowled, unbleached robes hitched up to their knees, Cormac and Trian are packing the boat. Artt takes off his shoes and wades into the cool water to help. He glimpses the whole party as if from a vertiginous height. Himself, brown hair still unsilvered; one bent man with only strings of grey hair; one bony redhead. Beards freshly cropped; long hair tied back at the nape and tonsured at the crown in a triangle (strongest of forms, sign of the Holy Trinity).

Right where the mast meets the hull sits the grooved anchor stone, wrapped about with thorny branches for added traction and attached to the gunnel by coils of nettle rope. Beside it the old monk and the young one are putting the heaviest things: three yew buckets; a stack of earthenware crocks set into an iron cooking pot; a wicker creel crammed with griddle, tripod and hook, chisels and hammers. But the grassy bank is still covered in baggage.

'Brothers,' Artt objects, 'if we bring all this, we'll founder at the first hard wind.' *And deserve it, for their greed.* 'We don't need half of it. Here, let's start by putting the holy chest in the very middle.' He makes room and sets it against the base of the mast. 'It holds all I'll require to celebrate Mass, as well as two codices—my own work—with supplies to make more.'

The figure stuns them: two whole books, out of the dozen or so that hang in satchels on the library's pegs. 'The Abbot has been generous,' Cormac murmurs.

Artt juts out his chin. 'Ah, but when we set up our outpost of prayer in the ocean, the copies we produce will increase the honour of this monastery and the whole Church, as saplings glorify the tree from which their seeds blew.' He passes Trian a tiny leather flask. 'Holy water, blessed by the Pope in Rome—this will guard our boat from danger.'

Trian kisses it and tucks it under the bow.

Artt scans the litter of goods. 'Now, what's that great roll?'

'Hides for mending the hull if it were to get holed,' Cormac says.

'One will do, surely?'

Trian hesitates. 'In case of spreading rot...'

'Hold on, here's more.' Artt points at another roll.

'That's our spare sail, in case the wind were to rip the first.'

'Then we'll bring the spare instead of the three hides,' Artt decides, 'and cut patches from its edge if needed. If our hull moulders *and* our sail tears, it'll be a sign to halt our journey and settle there.'

Without a word, Trian heaves the other skins back onto the bank.

Artt unrolls the spare sail and folds it into a great square to lay flat over the laths at the bow end. Behind the mast he stacks charcoal, candles, oats, and wheat flour for Communion bread, all in linen sacks waxed to keep out water. 'Now, absolute necessities only.'

'Food for the journey, and water.' Trian holds up a basket and three goatskin flasks.

'Seeds and herbs.' Cormac shows a small wooden box.

'Of course. But what can we do without?'

The old man discards their whetstones, and also the scrapers for defleshing skins, as the monks can fashion stones as they go. But he argues for a spade (ash, tipped with iron) and a mason's dividers and L-shaped square.

Artt throws a crowbar back onto the bank. Cormac points out that if they lever rocks with the spade, it could crack in two. Artt can't know what conditions they'll face on their island, so he allows the crowbar. But he says no to the rest of the ironmongery: billhook for brush-clearing, pitchfork, trowel, spring shears. He tosses half a dozen pegs back, then decides they may be needed for attaching pulleys for heavy lifting, and wades around to pick them up again. He rejects a fishing spear—*can't the monks sharpen branches, as required?*—but allows nets.

'We could leave this big axe,' Trian offers.

Cormac grimaces. 'For felling trees, though—'

'Won't the small hatchet do us?'

True, if the arm's strong enough and works long enough. Artt nods approval. He challenges the older monk: 'Brother Cormac, what else?'

Cormac squints around. 'We could share one spare set of clothes, maybe—not likely we'll all get soiled or soaked at the same time?'

'Excellent.' Artt casts the other robes and shoes onto the bank.

Similarly, he decides that one set of fire-starting gear will do.

'The blankets?' Trian suggests. 'Our cloaks could serve to cover us.'

'That's the spirit.'

The young monk is jettisoning items as if they burn his fingers now: a flask of whey, a skin of ale, three leather mugs, a chopping board.

Artt finds a jar of honey to put back, and another of pickled cabbage. But the pile around the mast still seems too high. 'What's in this bag?'

'My lyre.' Cormac corrects himself, 'I mean, the Abbot's entrusted it to me.'

Artt weighs up the matter. 'I'm not one of those zealots who believes the sound of instruments to be sensual or barbaric. But what I would say is, we'll need nothing but our own

18

mouths to make music. Plainchant is so pure, it flies directly to God's ears.'

He notices Trian bite his lip, and readies for the first hint of insubordination. But no, the young man's stepping over to lay a slim pipe with the other discards.

Here comes the Abbot in his vestments of white striped vertically with purple, flanked by his favourite advisers. With every second step he leans on a crozier with a hook of riddled ivory—more like a king's mace, it strikes Artt, than the humble crook of a shepherd of souls.

Artt steps up onto the bank with the two monks behind him. He guesses the Abbot's relieved at the prospect of seeing the back of this troublesome guest, for all it's costing the monastery.

'Still barely half-packed, I see,' the Abbot calls.

'No, it's done. The rest you may take back, with my thanks.'

He's gratified by the Abbot's surprise.

'Your austerity puts us to shame.' Doubtfully: 'You're still fixed in your purpose?'

'Quite fixed.'

'And you, Brothers?'

Artt's eyes move between the two monks, who nod.

'There can be no turning back,' the Abbot warns them.

Is that true concern for their welfare, Artt wonders? *Or does this man not understand that no one turns back from a sacred mission?*

'Amen,' Cormac says gruffly.

'Amen,' Trian echoes.

'Well, then. I release you from your vows.'

Despite his muddy feet and his wet-edged robe, Artt matches

the Abbot's formality: 'Brothers, will you now pledge your-selves to me?'

The two drop to their knees on the soft ground, Cormac more heavily.

'For the second time in your lives, do you vow poverty?'

They say it in unison: 'I vow, Father.'

'Again, do you vow chastity?'

'I vow.'

'And will you swear fealty and obedience to me?'

'I vow.'

The men sound out that new promise with as much convic-tion as the familiar ones, even though five days ago Artt hadn't yet spoken to either. He lifts them up. He kisses the old monk's whiskery mouth, the youth's soft one.

'Monks should be steady as rock, and humble as slaves,' the Abbot intones sanctimoniously. 'Cleave to your new Superior, your Father and soul-friend, your Abbot for the rest of your days.'

Artt finds he balks at the title of *Abbot;* it smacks of land-deeds, somehow, fur robes and roast swan. 'I believe I'll be their *Prior* instead. *First among equals.*'

Cormac and Trian exchange an uncertain glance. The younger asks, 'May we call you *Father,* though?'

An odd shiver of delight. 'Of course.'

'Thank you, Father.'

'Thank you, Father.'

It's the first time Artt's ever been addressed that way.

Other monks have trickled down to the Sionan now, in ones and twos. He notices some fond smiles and bows of farewell. Cormac's embracing many of the monks. 'Brother Conall,

20

Brother Lugaid! Brother Ercc, would you give me your blessing?' Several of them are weeping to see him go. Trian hangs back, but does bow to several.

Among this crowd, Artt supposes some must be gripped by envy, wondering what can have marked out the concave-skulled ancient and the gawky youth as fit candidates for such an honour. Others may be weighed down by a purer longing to join in this pilgrimage. Abler men than Trian and Cormac, for all Artt knows, better men perhaps; why didn't any of them appear in his dream?

But he must trust what was shown to him. *The last will be first,* he tells himself. *Blessed are the humble, for theirs is the kingdom of heaven.* It is too late for doubts now, and besides, three is the holiest number, even were there room for a fourth in the crammed boat.

A beam of sun spears through the clouds; several monks murmur and remark on that as a sign of divine favour.

The Abbot leans on his crozier. Waiting for further thanks? True, the man has surrendered some of his most valuable goods, as well as two monks. But it's God who has asked it, after all; God who's given a flawed leader a chance to back this holiest of ventures, and (as the Gospel puts it) *lay up treasure for himself in heaven that no moths or rust can eat.* So all Artt says is, 'Ready.'

The three take up their walking staffs—those of the monks plain blackthorns, simply curved at the top, Artt's topped with a T-shaped bronze cross.

'Well, go in peace.' The Abbot sighs the words.

(Is that worry in his voice, Artt wonders? *Or envy?)*

'Bring glory to our Mother Church.' Raising his crozier, the

21

Abbot dedicates the boat, the journey, and the men to Christ. Behind him, dozens of voices rise in a psalm.

Artt steps down into the water and over the side of the hull, Cormac after him. Trian gives the boat a great shove off the bank before he gets in.

RIVER

Hours later, Cormac kneels facing backwards, gripping a narrow oar. Even with their reduced load, the shallow craft is so weighed down that its sides rise only a foot above the water.

Cormac's heard of boat sickness, but never knew it could rack a man so fast and so hard, like a malign spell cast by the motion of the river. The reek of wool grease and pine pitch isn't helping. Reaching dizzily for the nearest goatskin, Cormac takes a sip of water, then drives the wooden stopper back in with the heel of his hand. He rows on, his knees numb where they press on the slats. He swallows hard, breathes through his nose. But his throat emits small noises in spite of himself, and twice he has to thrust his head over the side to spew up his breakfast. Each time he begs pardon of his brethren.

On the other side of the bow, Trian's pivoting his oar with much more precision and power than Cormac. Of course, the young monk's well used to taking this boat up and down the Sionan, trading for the monastery. From the small bench in the stern, Artt—no, Cormac reminds himself, their *Prior* now—commands the steering oar, staring past his monks at what lies ahead. The slow but steady current is doing much of the work, sliding them south.

But how long will it take to get down the river to its mouth? Then how long at sea? How many days of this racking nausea?

The third time, when Cormac gags, all that comes out is a string of silver, as delicate as a spider's web.

'Should you lie down, maybe, Brother, and shut your eyes?' Trian suggests.

Through clamped teeth: 'I'll be all right.'

The Prior rises to his feet, and the boat wobbles. 'I've seen stronger men laid low for days, Brother. You're no good to us like this. Give me your oar.'

Cormac swallows sour humiliation.

Great frame bent low, the Prior steps around the sacks, making sure to stay on the laths so his feet won't hole the boat's hide.

Cormac ships his oar, and ducks out of the way.

'Sit in the middle, now,' the Prior orders.

So he hauls up his robe till it billows above his roped waist, and clambers past the stools, the creel, the cauldron full of crocks. He huddles on the piled dry goods, digging his fingers into the waxy sackcloth. He crosses his legs under him and leans leadenly against the mast.

To distract himself, he watches Trian's propelling strokes piercing the water in the shadow of the hull. Under the faint red beard, Cormac can still see the pimpled boy. Limbs too long for his body, spindly as willows; elbows and knees given to bending too far back.

Now that the Prior's taken up Cormac's oar and the boat's speeding along, no one is in the stern to steer her. Sick or not, Cormac should at least keep an eye out for hazards—mudbanks, logs, whirlpools, rocks, or rapids. If the boat were to capsize, they'd all drown. Also Cormac really should be scanning the banks for hostiles. He's lived behind the stockade of Cluain Mhic Nóis for so long, he's forgotten what it's like to roam through strange territory.

He squints hard at the water ahead, then at the land on both sides. But he's realising on this journey that his sight's not what it used to be. Mostly he sees gorse, to north and south, vast sheets of the prickly stuff blooming butter-yellow already. The occasional silhouette of a farm defended by a round ditch and fence or blackthorn hedge. A blur in the distance must be a man with an ox ploughing crisscross, dragging a wooden spike to break up the winter-clogged soil; Cormac remembers doing that, how his forearms shook from the strain.

After a while, another fellow, riding, and leading one—no, two—packhorses. Cormac's never been on a horse. He imagines how lofty it might feel, and precarious. He wonders whether it's harder for a wellborn man such as the Prior to vow poverty; how rough a woollen robe must feel to smooth fingers. But their new master seems zealous for all hardships, as if dearth is sweet to him.

Jaw clenched, Cormac can't stop himself from retching again. Nothing comes.

'Try fixing your gaze on the horizon, Brother,' Trian offers under his breath.

The Prior's voice booms: 'Have you always had this weakness?'

'I . . . have never been in a boat,' Cormac admits.

Trian gapes at that. 'But you've lived so long. Been to battle, even, I heard.'

'I walked, that time,' Cormac tells him wryly, 'and got a javelin through me, so my kin had to bring me home on an ox-cart.' Touching his waist, where his skin bears two puckers still. Beside him on the cart, in a tangle of guts, his third brother had died sometime along the way. That's twice Cormac's life should by rights have ended: the slingstone above his ear and the javelin in his side. Three times, if he counts the plague that took his wife and children.

The Prior tips his face back to reckon the dazzling point of white in the clouds. 'Noon.'

Time to recite the holy hour of Sext.

The Prior lifts his oar into the boat and lays it down. On the other side Trian does the same, and jerks his head from side to side to relieve the muscles of his neck with loud creaks.

Cormac realises the Prior doesn't intend to moor; drifting south on the current, this trembling vessel is their chapel now. Though he longs to get off it and be still, even for half an hour, he says nothing.

The Prior unbuckles the pouch on his belt and takes out a quadrangular bell by its loop, making its bronze-coated iron plates ring to ward off bad spirits. He rears to his feet in priest's pose, elbows by his sides and hands turned up. Trian follows, and then Cormac, staggering. The boat tilts, rights again. Cormac swallows hard, commanding himself not to spew during prayers.

The Prior switches from Gaelic to Latin for the plainchant: *'Morning and noon and evening I pray and cry aloud—'*

Cormac joins in, and Trian after him, repeating the clear line of melody. '—*and God will hear my voice.*'

The Prior leads them in the three psalms. Having been a storyteller, Cormac didn't find it too hard to commit the whole Psalter to memory once he became a monk. Whereas Trian, even after his six years of training, still stumbles over words and loses track of the phrases. The young man's not stupid, Cormac knows, just shy, with a wandering air at times.

At the top of each psalm they genuflect by going down on the right knee, which makes the boat lurch and Cormac's stomach heave. When they've finished the service, they kneel again and murmur in Latin, '*God save me.*'

Trian digs out the holy chest and passes it over to the Prior. Of the two volumes inside, their master selects the Old Testament, drawing a small cross on its wooden cover and bending to kiss it. He reads aloud a passage from the Book of Isaiah. Since neither Cormac nor Trian knows more than a little Greek, afterwards he puts it into Gaelic for them.

God's word in their mouths, then their ears, then their hearts, that's the order; every holy hour of the day ends with quiet contemplation. Cormac sits very still, pressing his chapped lips together and locking his throat. He prays to God to mend his stomach.

Afterwards, as they float on, Trian doles out food from the basket. Cormac makes his best effort, chewing on a piece of oatcake, and taking tiny bites of a slice of dried pork. He still has his teeth, even if they are worn short.

'Any better, Brother Cormac?'

'It'll pass, Father,' he says. 'I'm sorry for being a hindrance on this journey.'

The Prior shrugs grandly. 'Between the helplessness of the cradle and that of the deathbed, hasn't every man his times of frailty?'

Cormac nods gratefully, though the motion brings up another sour wash in his throat.

'*The old may be weak, but the young are ignorant.*' Trian quotes the proverb in such a stern tone that the older men both burst out laughing.

The river is more easily navigable than Trian expected. In places it's under two feet deep, but the boat's draft is even less, so with a push of the oar in the mud she slips on by. The heart-shaped leaves of aspens rattle, giving off a sweetness that makes him snuff the air with pleasure. Downy birch and willow are woven thick on both banks in the first haze of Eastertide green. Tall alders dangle reddish catkins against glossy ovals that have only just opened.

When evening draws in, the Prior directs them to moor under a spreading oak tree. Trian takes off his shoes to spare them a wetting. Robe bunched in his fist, he jumps off the hull and wades to the muddy bank, hauling the boat like a stubborn cow. Once he's tied her up—the rope hitched around a half-submerged willow—his elders climb out, though they still get wet to their shins. Cormac helps Trian pull her up a few yards more until she's well wedged in the rushes.

The Prior presses his right thumb and first two fingers together to stand for the Holy Trinity, and makes the sign of the cross over the place to banish any evil, calling out, 'In the name of Jesus!'

The men all stretch their arms and roll their shoulders to ease them. Trian and Cormac already have leathery palms from working with oars and spades, but the Prior's are swollen and blistered—not that he says a word of complaint.

Trian tops up the waterskins in the river before he fills their wooden bowls with pork and cheese. Cormac, still green in the face, barely touches it. Trian eats fast, then waits for the food to reach his belly and give him that lovely feeling, not of fullness, exactly, but at least the lulling of his savage hunger.

Cormac brushes off the crumbs. 'Where's your home, Father, may I ask?'

'I have none.'

That throws the old monk. 'I only meant—'

'I was born in the West,' the Prior concedes.

'And your people?'

Learned judges going back generations, Trian's heard.

The Prior's mouth twists. 'They hoped I'd make an arch-bishop, for the clan's advancement. It's been a long time since that word *home* has held any earthly meaning for me, Brothers. I am an exile for God, and I love nothing here below.'

Trian has never met anyone like this. Where others speculate, the Prior knows; when others merely say, he does. Somehow he's cut himself free of the ropes that keep lesser men bound to the world.

After the Prior leads them in reciting Nocturns, they roll themselves up in their sheepskin cloaks. Trian finds he's not missing his old hut at all, with the three other young monks always chattering, the stink of feet.

'A spell cast over the senses,' the Prior murmurs.

Trian tries to puzzle that out. 'What is, Father?'

'Sleep.'

'A necessary evil though, no?' Cormac asks out of the dark.

'Unfortunately so. Really we should succumb only when we're dropping with exhaustion, and break our sleep to pray at least once every night, and get up early, still a little weary.'

'Amen,' Trian makes himself say. He's an awful gorger of sleep, but he still hopes to grow out of that. Right now he finds himself wary of dropping off, in case the three of them won't manage to wake for Vigil without the bells of the night watch.

But hours later, when the Prior's big voice rouses him, Trian realises that their new master always knows the time, even in his sleep. Or maybe—he wonders as they settle back on the ground after their psalms and brief prayers—a man this holy never closes his eyes, but lies all night interceding for the weaker souls on either side of him. Still brooding over that, Trian plummets back into the dark.

In the morning, they row for hours. When they stop to eat, Trian notices Cormac's managing his apple and oatcake. 'You've a better colour today, Brother.'

Cormac produces a smile. 'I suppose I must be getting used to the motion.'

'It's a matter of humility,' the Prior tells him. 'Once your senses stop fighting and accept the constant bobbing, your suffering lessens.'

Trian frowns. He's been taught that suffering is good, since it lets you enter a little into the agonies of Jesus on the cross. But so is humility; a monk should be *humble as a slave*. If humility happens to lessen your suffering, is that allowed, so long as that wasn't your aim? Trian's head wasn't meant for wrestling with such abstractions.

The boat glides past a few river islands today, occasionally even a peopled one. 'This sea island we're seeking, Father,' Trian ventures to ask, 'it will be quite empty?'

'More than that: untouched.' The Prior jerks his head with scorn at the huts they've just passed. 'If an island's ever been settled, that means it's too fertile for us. No, our gleaming rock will be set apart from men and all their wiles. Bleak and harsh—a desert place in the ocean.'

All Trian knows is the coastal farmstead where a dozen of his people scraped a living by fishing and birding, and then the crowded monastery. He tries to picture this sea island; to smell the cleanness of it.

Gradually the Sionan opens out into a long lake the Prior calls Loch Deirgeirt. They pass a fragment of land with a small wooden rectangular structure that Trian recognises as a church, and a cluster of round wattle huts sending up trickles of smoke. He half-expects the Prior to moor here and speak with whatever saint's claimed the lake island for God. But no. And after all, they're in search of solitude; Trian supposes they will be stopping only when they need to trade.

So the laden boat floats on down the endless water. On low green slopes, far off, black cows and brown sheep with curly horns look to Trian to be the size of flies.

That evening they rest on a hummock of dry bank fringed with marsh. A great thumb of stone has the name of this territory's chieftain notched in ogham script down one side. Or its onetime chieftain, rather, given how thick a coat of moss has grown on the stone. Trian wonders why men vie to amass possessions, when they can't even hold onto their own skin for longer than God allots.

He watches the green glistening head of a mallard parting the reeds, drab brown mate behind. A white-masked coot cuts between the ducks, leaving a rippled line in his wake. Why are all other creatures born knowing how to swim, whereas most human beings sink like stones? So few men trust the water enough to learn how to lie flat and stay afloat, but Trian—he knows this is one of his oddities—doesn't remember a time when he couldn't.

A pair of silent swans glide around the bend, their white shine catching the last of the setting sun, their beaks orange rimmed with black. One dips and comes up bearded with weed. The other arches and spreads gleaming frilled wings. Five grey cygnets chirp along in their wake. Trian remembers the rich, lingering taste of swan meat. He thinks of the swans in the legend who were king's children under a spell, imprisoned in feathers. He would not much mind being a bird, himself. This family pays the boat no attention, he notices. Do they mistake her for a hulking dead tree caught on the bank?

On the third day, Artt takes a turn at rowing and sets a faster pace; he can't bear how long it's taking to get to the western sea. Lake narrows into river again, the stretch known as the Luimneach—the last before the estuary.

He watches herdsmen, tiny at this distance, moving their flocks upland for spring pasture. He thinks of something to tell

Trian. 'Pádraig, the holiest of our saints—he who was the very first to bring the Gospel from Albion to Hibernia—when he was young, he minded sheep and pigs.'

'Captured by pirates as a boy, and made a slave, so they say,' Cormac adds in his storytelling voice. 'Six years Pádraig endured herding on the hills, but the rain and the frost did him no bit of harm.'

'*Ora et labora*,' Artt rhymes. 'Work and pray. Young Pádraig recited a hundred psalms a day and the same number at night, and the love of God was a fire inside him. His prayers revealed to him at last that his shackles were made not of iron but of sin—something every true Christian must learn.' He can almost feel the metal chafing; he rubs his wrists. 'It was through solitary meditation in the wild that Pádraig won that wisdom. As Jesus told his apostles, *Come away to a quiet, remote place*. That's what we're looking for, Brothers: our own lonely hill.'

Both monks nod and say Amen.

But Artt wonders whether the brethren truly grasp the nature of their quest or are only paying lip service. That's the problem with a vow of obedience; it tends to make sheep of men. He'd almost rather monks with the fiery natures of wolves, who've harnessed their forces to follow him in all things.

Around a bend, the Sionan splits now and a fortified island looms in the middle of the water; an earthen circle topped with a palisade, lines of smoke rising. Fisherfolk, Artt guesses. Huts, but nothing that looks like a chapel. This could be one of those pagan holdouts where they still brew potions and cast charms. He mutters a prayer in Latin: '*Against the spells of druids and blacksmiths and women, I summon your aid*.'

Artt thrusts the steering oar straight down, then braces it against his torso and rotates it, slowly angling the boat into the wider west channel, as far from the island as possible. His monks don't need to be told. Trian seems more excited than afraid; he gouges the water with his oar to hurry the boat on.

Close to, the riverbank is webbed together by fibrous roots. Alder doesn't rot even in water, Artt finds himself remembering; it makes the hardest shields and the sharpest spears. Not that his party is carrying any shields or spears, only the small iron knives in their belts. They're men of God, after all. They come in peace, though that doesn't mean they'll find it. Artt rows faster. The boat rocks. What if the monks capsize their heavy craft and go down with her?

Cormac mutters a protection: *'Gabriel, be my breastplate. Michael—'*

'Be my belt,' Trian intones.

'Raphael, be my shield.'

Artt glimpses no faces through the island's blank palisade; no movement. Is the boat more than a spear's throw from the line of stakes? He pictures the three of them through enemy eyes. The triangular tonsure marks them out as monks, as does the wooden four-armed Greek cross on a thong around each neck. Are these marks likely to help or hurt their chances, if they're captured? Their vessel and all its goods seized, the holy chest cracked open and its treasures ripped out, the monks kept chained for labour here, or sold on?

Artt berates himself for his scuttling thoughts. He prays, like Jesus to his Heavenly Father when the soldiers were coming, *Not my will be done, but yours.*

A whizz, a splash.

Another.

Someone behind the fence whirling a sling, shooting stones at them. More than one attacker?

Cormac huddles down, clutching his skull.

Panic, a pebble in Artt's throat. He swallows it down and steers even more sharply away from the island, almost driving the boat into the rushes on the bank. His monks stab the water. 'Are you hit, Brother Cormac?'

'I'm not,' the old man gasps.

And now they're out of range of danger, gliding fast and beautifully. This broad channel joins up with the narrow one again. The whole skirmish has lasted no more than a couple of minutes. The river widens, stretching its greedy mouth, as the fortified island diminishes in the distance.

Cormac keeps his head down, ashamed.

Trian's panting a little, exhilarated.

'See?' Artt demands. 'Fear nothing. We travel under God's protection.'

Sun reddens in the west. Cormac's knees are raw and his shoulders ache, but he's still dizzy with relief that they weren't caught, or even injured. His hand keeps going up to his misshapen scalp to marvel that it's intact. Also, his stomach's quite sound now, for which he thanks the Lord too. To travel is to turn the pages of the great book of life.

The bank is interrupted by a silty creek, where water thrashes behind a weir of woven willow. Cormac's suddenly ravenous for something fresh. 'Fish, Father?'

Trian frets under his breath: 'Unless that would be thieving.'

The Prior shrugs. 'As no one's come to pull them out of the river yet, they still belong to their Maker, and the riches of creation are for all to share.'

He steers them to the right, and the others work their oars to bring the boat to a standstill. Pinned, she resists the current.

Cormac rummages around for the hand net and passes it to Trian. The young monk leans overboard to dip it into the busy water behind the weir, and brings up a salmon right away. Stuck to its flank, a long silvery lamprey has already gnawed a red hole. He stuns the pair against the gunnel. Cormac watches with interest as Trian inserts and jiggles his knife behind the salmon's eye, then dispatches the lamprey the same way. He stabs each fish in one gill to bleed it, cuts off the fins, slits it from jaw to vent, and pulls out the guts to drop in the water. Then he sets down the gutted fish and rinses his bloody hands over the side.

Cormac can see that the *ciotóg* is deft with all water matters, even if those dangling arms have a clumsy look to them; Trian handles the fish as fluently as he used to touch the holes of his pipe. Cormac's reminded of their last time playing music at the monastery—the night of the roast swan, though neither of them had any idea it would be their last time. He considers that he may never have an instrument again, and it hits like a blow to his gut. Only his ragged voice to lift in song as best he can. *Well,* Cormac reminds himself, *all treasures must be left behind in the end.*

The Prior gestures to him to push them off from the weir.

They row on till the sun's edged behind a hill a little to the left of them. 'Time to moor.' The Prior points out a flat place under trees.

When they get out and genuflect on dry land, Cormac's knees almost buckle. It's dim and faintly fragrant under the lower branches. His arms tremble as he starts collecting twigs for kindling—but the bell recalls him. First, Vespers.

'Three foes attack me: my eye, my tongue, my thoughts,' the Prior teaches this evening. 'But the Psalter'—he holds up the bigger of their books—'is armour against them all.'

Making camp, Cormac lifts arches of bramble out of the way, but a stinging nettle gets him; he sucks the heel of his hand. He finds enough stones to ring their fire and stacks the twigs inside this circle, with tinder of dry leaf mould at its heart.

Meanwhile Trian's rinsing the two fish. He sets them down on a flat stone, in the last of the twilight, and scales them with the blunt edge of his knife, scrape after patient scrape. Soon he has the salmon and lamprey spitted on two iron skewers to set across the rocks for roasting. He whistles as he works.

Cormac smiles, recognising a snatch of a dance. He takes the fire gear from his belt pouch and uses a fingernail to lift out the horn's fitted stopper, made of clay, pierced with holes to let the flame inside breathe. He shakes out the grey ash that blankets the glowing embers from last night, then scatters them lightly on the tinder; he cups it with his hands, and blows the flame to life. He feeds the new fire with a few lengths of charcoal from their sack; once it catches properly he adds twigs. The green wood smokes and fills the dusk with hissing.

The fish finally start to sizzle, and the six damp shoes Cormac's put by the fire release their steam. He drags over a rotting log for the Prior to sit on, then skinnier ones for himself and Trian. He stares into the blue flames, grateful for this respite.

To be at rest, steady on the motionless ground. Alive, and free, too, when they might well have been chained up on the island of the fisherfolk, or floating facedown in the river.

The fish spit like live things as Trian turns the skewers. 'You put me in mind of the hero Fionn Mac Cumhaill,' Cormac tells him, 'when he was a boy, and in the service of the poet Finegas.'

The familiar names make Trian look up as he sets out their bowls.

Cormac glances to make sure their master doesn't object to heathen legends. But the Prior says nothing, so he goes on. 'Now Finegas—all his study and thought was to catch the magical salmon in the well of wisdom that's the source of this river Sionan. The well was ringed by hazel trees whose fruit dropped into the water and soaked up its powers, and the salmon that ate those hazelnuts absorbed all the wisdom. Learned Finegas dipped his hook in that water every day for seven years, until the hour came at last when he landed that magnificent king of fish!' Cormac lets the triumph have its moment. 'So Finegas set his young servant to roasting it, forbidding him to taste a bite. But a drop of fat leapt out of that pan, and onto Fionn's hand. It was burning the boy's skin, so he licked it off.'

'Sure who wouldn't?' Trian asks sympathetically.

But the Prior shakes his head. 'Rebellion, our downfall, ever since Adam.'

'In a trice,' Cormac hurries on, 'young Fionn was filled with all the wisdom there is.'

Trian's eyes flare. 'His master must have been furious.'

'He was, of course, having worked and waited all those years, but it couldn't be helped.' Cormac finds himself wondering whether the poet beat his boy. He pictures Fionn bruised, hungry, aglow with what he'd learned, what could never be taken from him now.

The Prior grunts. 'As if knowledge is a treasure that can belong to only one man, and must be stolen or fought over!—when the truth is, God pours out his wisdom like honey.'

Cormac feels a flicker of resentment that the Prior's scorning his story. But he says Amen along with Trian.

The salmon and the lamprey look flaky now, so Trian doles them out with stale oatcakes. (Cormac remembers with a pang that jar of pickled cabbage they left behind.) Trian sets down the Prior's bowl, with a deep bow, and then Cormac's, with a little dip.

The Prior makes a cross in the air and asks a blessing on the food and on their voyage and fellowship.

Head down, Cormac mulls over that word. The three of them hold their goods in common, like the first Christians, and share according to need...but the Prior commands. Is there a word for a fellowship of unequals?

Now that he's recovered from his boat sickness he eats with relish, stopping every now and then to pick a fish bone out of his teeth. It's not true that old men always lose their taste. Or rather, he thinks, *What they have left of it they prize all the more.*

The Prior, though—Cormac hasn't yet seen their master finish a portion. He sets aside his bowl now, with a good piece of fish still in it, and wipes his hands on the grass. 'There's a different legend told of the same mysterious well,' the Prior remarks. 'Some say the river is named after a maiden called Sionan, who longed to get all the well's wisdom for herself.'

Cormac's never heard this one.

'So one night she dared to approach the water, in fear and trembling, since it was forbidden to her sex.'

Trian asks, 'Why was it forbidden?'

The Prior answers with a hint of exasperation, 'The wisest Church Fathers, and the ancients before them, all agree that a woman is a botched man, created only for childbearing.'

Cormac wonders what his wife would have said to that. A contraction in his chest, like a muscle ripping. After all these years, he has trouble calling up her lovely face.

'Well, this perverse daughter of Eve, Sionan, lifted the lid of the well,' the Prior goes on. 'She sucked up the sacred waters, and gobbled all the hazelnuts too.'

Cormac imagines the thirsty, ravenous girl.

'Trying to coax the great salmon into her grip, she tickled its belly with her finger, but it began to lash about in fury, till its gigantic tail raised the waters so high they swallowed Sionan up and drowned her.' The Prior's arms shoot out. 'The flood spilled right across the country, as far as the western sea, and when it subsided at last, what was left was this vast river.'

Trian nods in rapt appreciation.

Something's rattling and squeaking in the trees overhead: a sedge warbler, maybe? Cormac recognises a magpie and a quarrelsome robin; the repeated phrases of a song thrush. Also the soft rise-and-fall whirring of a nightjar. The darkness thickens around their fire. A whine in the distance, then another. Some farm's watchdogs, set free to roam now that the cattle are stalled?

A howl.

No, not dogs, he decides. Wolves. The countryside is rife with them. Pray God these ones aren't too hungry.

Trian's dipping the bowls in the river and rubbing them clean. Each man goes a little way into the woods to crouch and wipe himself with leaves. Then Cormac gets down stiffly on his knees to bank the fire, using a piece of log to scoop the embers into the middle, between the charred branches, and swaddle them in ash for the night.

TO SEA

On the fourth morning of their voyage, Trian wakes in grey twilight and lies still. Only when light prises open his lashes does he force himself to his feet. It still feels odd to sleep in his clothes; he brushes down the dishevelled layers. But he likes thinking of himself as a traveller, hardy, ready for anything. Making the sign of the cross, he whispers, *'From the rising of the sun to its going down, praised be your name.'*

The Prior's on his knees already, of course, locked in prayer. Around the snoring Cormac stretches a carpet of bluebells, sprinkled with dog violet and small suns of coltsfoot, the odd spike of red plague-flower.

Trian leans over the river to splash his face. The water tastes green, with a tang of vegetation. He smoothens his hair, reknotting the leather that ties it back. He gets a scrap of cloth out of his pouch to rub his teeth and gums.

A repeated whistle makes him look around for the kingfisher. There's the gaudy thing, motionless on a low branch, watching the water. It's good luck to spot a kingfisher, the first creature with nerve enough to leave the Ark, which was rewarded with the blue of the sky daubed on its back and tail and the orange of the setting sun on its breast.

Trian tightens the rope around his waist. *Gird me, O Lord, ready to serve.* He tugs on the three knots at the end to remind him of his vows: poor, chaste, obedient. Loyal to his master without reserve, like Christ who died hanging from nails through his hands and heels, without murmuring against his Father who ordained it.

The Prior's ringing the bell for Terce, so Trian hurries to fit his feet into his shoes and pulls their thongs. Cormac lurches off the ground, haggard. By the lapping water's verge, they kneel and sing three Latin psalms: *'See how good it is when brothers live together in harmony.'*

After the Prior reads a passage in Greek, he switches back to Gaelic for the prayers. Protections always go in threes in honour of the Trinity. The last one starts, *'Christ shield me today against poison.'*

'Against burning,' Cormac responds.

Trian finishes: *'Against drowning.'* Which always reminds him of his uncles.

He passes out two roasted eggs apiece, and a few soft apples. His share barely takes the edge off his appetite.

With his sleeves doubled over his hands to ward off stings, Cormac's ripping up a patch of nettles. Trian goes over to help, and asks, 'Are these for eating?'

A nod. 'One good dose and we'll keep our health all year.'

'God willing,' the Prior corrects him.

'God willing,' Cormac echoes. 'Mortar and pestle, Brother?'

Trian reminds him, 'We left them behind.'

So Cormac crams the serrated leaves into a bowl, and pulps them laboriously with a wooden spoon.

They each take the waterskin in turn, to wash the stuff down. The nettle mush tastes so sour, Trian knows it must be doing them a power of good.

He watches Cormac pack up the fire now. The older monk beckons him close to show him how it's done. 'Take touchwood—' He picks a big flake out of a rag from his pouch.

'What is it?' Trian has to ask.

'Fungus off a fallen tree, boiled in urine.' Cormac lights it from last night's embers, tucks it deep into his fire horn, and adds crumbs of moss to keep it smouldering. He scoops in some soft ash before he stoppers it up, then puts the horn in his leather pouch.

'Doesn't it burn you?'

Cormac grins and pats his belly where the pouch sits. 'I keep a thin board behind the fire horn, to save my skin. I fear I'll never make a saint.'

The Prior speaks up from the boat, where he's fitting their baggage snug against the mast: 'The blessed ones aren't greedy for pain for its own sake, only for its teaching. Holy Brigit's pupil Darlugdach, for instance. When one night she was tempted to go to a man, she sprinkled embers in her own shoes.'

Trian's startled. 'So that she wouldn't put them on?'

'Oh, she did anyway.' The Prior's tone is grim.

'And went to him?' On sore, smoking feet? He tries to imagine a want that strong.

'No—once she felt the burn, she ripped her shoes off again,

and went back to bed. She needed the pain to keep down her lust, see?'

Trian wonders who the man was, and how long he'd waited in vain for the holy woman.

Cormac's kicking dirt over the embers and stirring them with his staff. Trian dips a bowl into the river and dowses the ashes.

He holds the boat steady for Cormac to get in, then shoves her off the sucking mud and out into the current before leaping in.

The banks recede, as he and Cormac row, and the Sionan keeps widening. 'We're in the estuary now,' the Prior remarks. 'That was our last night on land.'

That thrills Trian. He wonders if their master has a map of the whole world in his head that unscrolls as he travels, showing the landscape from overhead as angels must see it.

Cormac kisses the cross on his thong, and mutters a protection.

'Just wait till you set eyes on the sea, Brother,' Trian tells him.

Plunging his long oar into the river, Trian notices all the signs of spring. Swallows wheel and cavort overhead in shrill numbers, the odd little brown flier dipping low enough to beak an insect off the water between one wingbeat and the next. Now the whole mass forms a spiralling, swirling cloud, speckling then darkening into a winged shape that smears like ink, rips and dissolves again. So many! What can drive them to flock in such urgent numbers, to form one great bird shape of their countless pointed bodies?

Long-legged herons stand frozen in the shallows as if hoping the monks floating by won't see them. A godwit ignores the boat and stabs its bright head over and over into the water. Trian spots a few wading snipe. One of them flies overhead in a display to its mate, swooping downwards and making a loud drumming with its tail.

'Brother Trian, are you dreaming?'

How long has he been kneeling, letting the oar drift in his hands and the boat go askew? 'Pardon, Father.' He whacks his chest.

'*Age quod agis,*' the Prior reminds him. 'Keep your mind on what you're doing.'

Trian nods, hot-cheeked. He rows on.

The estuary is so broad, now, the monks seem to Cormac to have shrunk to the size of three ants on a floating leaf. But in the afternoon, when they stop to sing None, their voices spill across the water.

As they set off again, Trian yelps, 'A boat!'

At this distance Cormac can see only a smudge.

'Traders, maybe,' the Prior speculates.

Cormac sniffs the air, sensing something unfamiliar.

Trian leans over the edge of the boat and lifts some water to his mouth. He grins as if it's fine wine. 'Brackish—half-salt. That means we're getting close.'

'A man who takes a sip of one sea tastes all of them,' the Prior says from the stern.

That mystifies Cormac.

'The various seas of the earth touch and form one ocean,' their master explains.

Really? Cormac inhales the strange saltiness. As he and Trian row on, he begins to feel the incoming creep of the sea, the turbulence as it tussles and mingles with the last sweet outpouring of the river.

A while later they pass a different vessel, close enough that this time Cormac can make out figures on board, working their nets, indifferent to the monks.

Slim gulls fly overhead with unnerving grace. Cormac and Trian are beginning to have to put their backs into the rowing. Salt stings in the oar-blisters on Cormac's hands. He sees blue veins stand out on Trian's sunburned forehead and arms.

Now the sea is a vast surge coming down the throat of the estuary. The wind against the current kicks up a real chop. 'Shouldn't be long, Brother,' Trian assures him. 'The tide's at its height, so in a little while it'll reverse and pull us with it, outerly.'

'God moves the very waters for us,' the Prior says.

Cormac frowns. Doesn't the tide turn twice a day, heedless of who floats on it?

He reminds himself that their master sees deeply into things and discerns the secret ways of heaven. Maybe both things are true; the tide always turns, but today God's making sure it'll lift his monks just when their arms begin to fail.

Sure enough, soon the oar work eases. The mainland slips away behind them.

Are they at sea now? The blue vista widens and widens, alarming Cormac. The boat is starting to revolve; a slow skimming one way, then back again, a leaf-dance under darkening clouds. He grips the gunnel with one hand. 'Is it always like this—the spinning?'

'She's a river boat, not made for seafaring, a round-bottomed dish,' the Prior says without concern. 'Hard to sink, but with no keel to help her hew a path through the waves.'

Cormac's distracted by a slopping sound under the slats. He keeps talking to soothe his nerves. 'Here's a saying I've heard but don't understand: *Never turn your back on the ocean.*'

'Even on a calm day, Brother, a roller can come in without warning and lick a man off the shore,' Trian tells him. 'Our mother had two brothers taken that way.'

Cormac winces.

'*So keep watch,*' the Prior quotes, '*for you know neither the day nor the hour.*'

Trian licks one finger and holds it up to the wind. 'Our island will lie to the southwest, you said, Father?'

The Prior nods.

Trian eyes the heavy yard above their heads. Diffident: 'We'd catch this bit of a northerly if we let out the sail.'

'Do it, then.'

It occurs to Cormac to wonder how much their Prior knows of navigation. For all the man's voyages, maybe he's always been a passenger. Whereas the young monk has seemed to grow in confidence from the first day he stepped into the boat.

Trian clambers onto the sacks of supplies, now, to tug at the yard's thongs. As the ties come loose the great square of leather drops with a loud snap. Trian's pulling a line from the bottom to an iron loop on the gunnel and tying it taut. On the other side, the Prior follows suit. The sail bellies, filling; four brown hides pieced together.

The boat straightens and speeds along, fast enough to grip Cormac with dread. To distract himself, he squints at the line of the coast to their left. There's a huge bay, like a giant's wet foot giving the countryside a savage kick. Then a sprinkling of tiny pieces of land, flat and green, dust shaken off the mainland.

Trian asks the Prior, 'Is it true what they say, that no pestilence can travel over nine waves?'

A shrug. 'When is man ever safe from contagion? God visits ills upon whomever he chooses.'

Trian dips his head. 'I didn't mean—'

'This much is true,' the Prior tells him, 'that when folk huddle together in numbers, for fear of cattle raiders or slavers, death can still find them out in their comfortable beds. Every settlement I've visited has its plague-grave outside, where the people leave small stones as they pass.'

That's to honour the dead in the old pagan way, Cormac remembers, but keep down the rot too. He can't turn his thoughts away from his own beloved four, whom he laid out and keened all in the one night, half a lifetime ago. He remembers lighting candles and setting a full bowl on his wife's flat chest, and one on his little daughter's, and on each of his sons'. Foolish, Cormac knows now, to try to provision the dead with food for wherever they might be going—but it was some comfort. He didn't hold the traditional feast in their honour, not even for his kin, because who'd come to a plague-struck hut? In the morning he laid his wife on the ground outside with her arms wide, her three young gathered back into her, and then he piled on rocks until he couldn't see them anymore.

He doesn't say a word of this, for fear he'll weep.

But as if reading Cormac's mind, the Prior turns to him. 'Whatever lands or houses, parents or wives or children a man loses, he has Christ's word it'll be returned a hundredfold.'

The image bewilders Cormac: hundreds of unfamiliar sons and daughters and wives waving to him from unfamiliar fields. Frankly, he'd rather have back the ones he had.

Then he rebukes himself for taking the Gospel too literally. It's like a song; the meaning comes roundabout. Cormac's no scholar, only a tired old man, and he doesn't need to fathom the depths of scripture, only follow and obey.

'Is it true you came through the pestilence, Father?' Trian asks.

A calm nod from the Prior. 'My case was the choking kind. Great swellings all over me, leaking, and my fingers and toes so black I expected them all to drop off, not just one.'

Cormac stares at the tarry stub on the man's mighty right fist.

'I was sure my time had come, and I didn't fight it. Hadn't I pledged myself to God as a child, and stood ready for the call to heaven, all those years—almost longing for it?'

Joy, Cormac hears in their master's voice; an eerie joy at the prospect of dying.

The Prior stretches his marred hand now, as if it pains him. 'My Maker took only an inch of me, as an earnest of his love. And here is a miraculous thing—I've never been sick a day, since.'

Trian marvels at that.

'Of course he may come back and claim the rest of me whenever he likes.'

Trian crosses himself and mutters 'Amen,' and Cormac does the same.

'Remember, too, Brothers'—the Prior turns his gaze on them like a flaring torch—'in seeking out this island, we're fleeing not contagion of the flesh, but of the spirit. We're taking refuge from the nine evils: pride, vanity, anger, envy, avarice, lust, gluttony, apathy, and sadness.'

'We are,' Cormac agrees.

Trian almost shouts: 'Let's get nine waves away from them!'

Trian feels as lively as a dog who jumps and whines for a scrap of meat. The salt scent is making a child of him again. He remembers how he used to pick his way along the foreshore to find the food the sea scattered for free. Shinning up tufted, slippery cliffs for eggs, and for the glee of it.

He undoes the line nearest him to angle the sail a little, keeping the boat scudding due southwest. Hundreds of little kittiwake gulls are settling on the water, letting out quacks and yelps, plucking up small fry with no effort. Birds always seem to stick to their own kind, even if they sometimes squabble over a scrap or a place to land; strength in numbers, Trian supposes. The kittiwakes' movements chime together like bells; one flutter will prompt another and another till the whole flock's shifted from water to sky. He can't spot a leader among the kittiwakes; at any one moment, he wonders, how do they decide which of them to follow?

Up ahead, an island with a long, rippled silhouette, almost like a man lying on his back. As the boat nears it, Trian makes out a few thatched huts plumed with smoke. People cutting and stacking turf, none in monks' habits that he can see. A couple of knobbly-legged cows.

A whole cluster of islands reveals itself behind the first. What looks like an old cliff fort. On the next island, a chapel cobbled together from boulders, swaybacked under the weight of time. Built of rock for lack of trees, Trian realises. *Who prayed in this now-slumped chapel, and when? And how did they come to abandon it—bad luck, sickness, pirates? A faltering in faith?*

The Prior leans on his steering oar, setting course to thread through the cluster.

Trian points out an outlying island on the western edge. The waves are gradually gnawing an arch through it, and it's crested with circling seabirds. 'What about that one, Father?' His voice comes out half-choked with excitement.

'What about it?'

'Might that be the one in your dream? It's bare and bleak.'

The Prior's tone is almost contemptuous. 'Not half a mile away from its neighbour? No, no. The farther from men, the closer to God.'

Trian subsides.

They're passing close by the black slope of the nearest island, where turf-cutters are working. A woman straightens up. A man does the same, and raises a hand. Friendly? None of them seems to be raising an alarm, or running for a weapon. Trian waves back.

In a little harbour below the turf-cutters, three boats lie at anchor. Cormac voices what's on Trian's mind: 'Father, should we maybe pull in for a few provisions?'

'I see no need. We still have drinking water.'

'We're nearly out of cheese, though, and we're low on pork.'

A magisterial shrug from the Prior. 'We have enough.'

For the first time it strikes Trian that even if they stop, they've nothing surplus to offer in trade for provisions. Although those folk, if Christians, might offer hospitality in exchange for nothing more than the holy man's blessing. But the Prior's right that there's no real need to break the journey yet.

On they sail, and the cluster of islands shrinks behind them till it's gone. High on the coast to their left, Trian spots the occasional farmstead, ringed by a stockade. But no more islands. The ocean is an empty, sparkling dish.

The boat spins again. The steering oar is slack in the Prior's hands.

'Father?' Trian prompts him. 'Still southwest?'

'Who knows?' The Prior says it so low that Trian's not sure he heard right.

He tries again. 'Which way?'

'We are off the map now.' The Prior lifts the dripping oar out of the water and rests it. He opens the pouch on his belt and unrolls a piece of linen. 'See, this is Hibernia.'

Trian twists his neck to make sense of the image.

'We've come right down the Sionan and out its great mouth, and some way farther down the west coast.' The Prior fingers the line. 'Now, west or south—from here on, it's all a blank.'

Trian looks at Cormac, who meets his gaze with unease.

'Oh, our island is out there,' the Prior assures them as he rolls the map up again. 'But we cannot find it by ourselves. God is our pilot now, and we'll go wherever his breath blows us.'

That sounds incongruous to Trian, not to plot course; to let the currents seize the boat like any detritus. But he sits back on his heels quietly, and watches the sail plump with wind. *God's breath,* he tells himself.

So they are blown on, still more southerly than any other direction. A raft of hundreds of great black cormorants stains the water ahead. Thousands, more like, foraging busily. The boat drifts right through the indifferent birds. Guttural grunts: *Ark ark ark!* One cormorant pops out of the water beside Trian with a big fish, and sucks it whole into his throat pouch. By some collusion a gang will suddenly take off, running along and kicking the water till they gather enough momentum to heave into the sky. Another group swoops down to take its turn forming a dark raft on the sea. One cormorant—a good four feet long, Trian would say—stands on a protruding rock, snake-necked, holding out its angular, powerful wings.

'Like some demon carved on a pillar,' the Prior mutters.

'Just drying its feathers, could be,' Trian suggests.

'What's that bird?' Cormac asks.

'A cormorant,' Trian tells him.

'Ah. Famous for greed, aren't they?'

Trian shrugs. 'My folk said they brought good luck.'

The Prior huffs his breath. 'Those sinister creatures?'

'Luck for the catch, anyway, Father. They know where the fish are.'

The boat lolls, rotates. Trian says prayers in his head to pass the time.

When he first came to the monastery, he found it almost unbearable. He was always roaming off or shinning up trees, which earned him beatings. Gradually he learned the knack of sitting still, but it's against his nature.

His knuckles and wrists feel tight now, so he has to crack them. But when he catches himself whistling a tune, he stops at once, because his people always said whistling in a boat could wake rough wind.

The invisible force of air curves the sail one way, then another.

The boat spins. God's breath will blow them where they're meant to go, Trian promises himself. Wherever that may be.

The three psalms of None float out over the waves. Seabirds of various kinds that Artt doesn't recognise interrupt the singing with raucous coughs and honks. He's never liked feathered creatures, especially in numbers. They seem like harbingers to him, bad omens. Not that he would invent meanings for their flights or cries, practising divination like some druid. But there is something uncanny about creatures that won't confine themselves to land, water, or sky, moving at liberty through all three.

Artt calculates it will take his monks a week to complete the full cycle of one hundred and fifty psalms. The Desert Fathers used to go through the whole Psalter over the course of each day, but he must be patient; this is a softer generation.

By the time he has finished saying the Scripture passages—from memory this time, so as not to risk a wave spraying any of the two precious books—the afternoon sky is dark blue overhead and a northerly's sprung up and filled the sail.

Cormac is bracing himself against the gunnel, clearly rigid with nerves. A wash slops over the side now, wetting their feet. Trian takes up his bowl and starts bailing out, and Cormac copies him. The young monk murmurs a reassurance: 'She's balanced nicely, Brother. We shouldn't be swamped.'

But as each wave smacks the side, the boat skids. Stirred by greater swells and chopped by the new wind, the sea forms a lumpy gruel. Artt feels no panic, only uncertainty, which he finds rather harder to bear. He demands silently, *What now, Lord?*

'Father, could we . . . maybe I'll turn us face-on into each wave, at least,' Trian suggests, 'so her prow can ride the crests?'

'As you like.' Artt's voice is almost blown away. He swaps places with Trian to let him take the steering oar.

The young monk twists it to straighten up the boat a little, but she's still bucking at the whim of the wind. Cormac is breathing as loudly as a horse, nostrils flared. Artt supposes he should give the old man something to do. Feeling a drop of rain on his jaw, he tells Cormac to unpack their waterproofed leather hats, and the cloaks. The three put them on oiled side outwards, fleece inwards. Artt fastens his cloak with an iron brooch, a simple pin piercing up through a ring, and the monks use thorns, which work just as well.

Soon the smoke-grey clouds let down their burden. Quick-thinking, Trian sets out the bowls.

'See, God's gift to us of fresh water.' Artt has to shout to be heard.

A shaft of low light spears through. The scudding clouds take on a reddish tinge to the west. The boat drifts on more smoothly. Once the shower's over, Cormac shakes diamonds off the cloaks, and rolls them up.

Artt gazes west, then south. The view's appallingly open now, empty of even a fragment of land. What if there are no more islands?

What if Artt's dream, which seemed like a true vision—

These are doubts, the foul whisperings of demons; he should know better than to lend his ear to them. He punches his fist against his chest so loudly, his monks startle like sparrows.

Artt despises himself for his momentary lapse in faith. A priest owes a greater tariff than a mere monk for the same weakness; more is asked of him. Should Artt do penance by standing in cross-vigil now, arms out? But the boat's moving too fast; he might topple, which would be undignified. Instead he kneels down on the slats, shuts his eyes, and mutters the 119th Psalm, the one used to atone for sins, as it is 176 verses long. In a harsh whisper: *'I am a stranger on earth; do not hide your commands from me.'*

When he has finished the last verse, Artt sits back on the bench in the stern, avoiding the others' glances. An absurd vanity—he'd rather they didn't know when he sins. But he must be an example for his flock, both in avoiding error and in atoning when he fails. How lonely it is to be the leader; to stand as his own soul-friend, his own confessor, his own guide.

Thirsty now. Artt picks up a bowl, with its puddle of rain, and allows himself a sip. To their right, the sun is sinking in scarlet fire. He takes the bell out of his pouch and rings it for Vespers.

They all work to keep their balance, standing, in the slowly pivoting boat. Cormac sways and lurches, and grabs at the yard. As a concession, Artt lets them kneel instead.

Afterwards, before the evening meal, he lifts his robe and undoes the drawstring of his woollen braies to make water over the side. He notices Trian avert his face sharply. Some youths just can't shake off that squirming shyness about the base needs of the body.

Sitting, they pass around their half-bare joint of pork, chipping small pieces into their bowls with the very last of the cheese.

A dusky face rises behind Cormac in the twilight: big-eyed, womanly. Artt jerks backwards.

Trian lets out a whoop.

Cormac spins around, but there's nothing there. 'What? What?'

'Only a seal, Brother,' Artt says gruffly.

The creature reappears a minute later, nosing the hull with interest, then sinks away.

Artt is reminded of a story. He jerks his thumb north. 'One of those old chapels on the estuary back there was founded by holy Senán.'

'Blessed be that saint's name,' Cormac murmurs.

'Now Senán was so strict,' Artt goes on, 'he laid down as a rule that no female should ever set foot on his island to tempt his monks.'

'An act of kindness in him, to spare them,' Trian comments.

Artt thinks, with a flash of revulsion, of those sinners back at Cluain Mhic Nóis. 'Senán came from a devout family, and his own sister was a nun.'

'Conainne, I believe her name was,' Cormac puts in.

Artt would rather not be interrupted, but he knows the old monk's used to being the storyteller. 'Well. On her deathbed the nun asked to be buried near her dear brother. Her sisters in Christ rowed Conainne's body to Senán's island and made humble petition. Now what was he to do?'

Trian squirms. 'Surely, Father, especially once she'd departed this life...'

Cormac fills in, with a little chuckle: 'A corpse could hardly be an occasion of lust.'

'That's neither here nor there,' Artt snaps. 'If Senán had broken his own rule, it would have been rank hypocrisy. Once the track is marked out, there can be no wandering.'

Trian sounds confused. 'So Senán turned away the body of his own mother's daughter?'

'Not that either,' Artt says with satisfaction. 'He told the nuns to wait till low tide and bury her in the wet sand of the foreshore, because that wasn't part of the island. The saint was as clever as he was clean-hearted, see?'

His monks are nodding in the thickening dark.

'Father,' Trian asks, 'maybe we'd furl the sail now?'

Artt should have thought of that; otherwise they might run onto rocks in the night and be wrecked. He gets to his feet and finds his balance before loosing the cord. The leather is sticky with salt spray. Trian does the same on the other side. Between them they roll up the square of skin and bind it tight against the yard.

Now the boat's movement slows, becomes aimless again; it's a toy for each wave. 'Drop anchor,' Artt tells Trian.

The young man grimaces.

'What is it?'

'This far out, Father…I doubt the anchor would come near to reaching the seabed.'

Artt peers at the grooved stone in its tangle of thorny branches. Its looped rope can't be more than a dozen fathoms long; why didn't he think to ask the boatwrights to add more? 'Well, let's try.'

Trian gnaws his lip.

'Speak,' Artt snaps.

'It's only that...the weight of the rock might tip us over.'

Artt can see that now. There's a lesson in that: the very thing they have lugged along as a safeguard could be what capsizes them. As the Gospel warns, *Whoever seeks to save his life will lose it.*

So. In open ocean, drifting blind now, and with no way to stop moving through the dark. It is Artt who's brought them to this extremity, and it's too late for doubt. 'Never mind. We won't founder,' he assures them. 'We travel in the palm of God's hand.'

He retrieves one of their beeswax candles from the holy chest. 'Your fire, Brother Cormac?'

Cormac gets the gear out of his pouch and unstoppers the horn.

Artt leans across the boat and pushes the taper down into the embers until the wick flames up.

The boat dips and sways, pivots, circles. Silence stretches. The candle in Artt's hand gutters, leaking hot wax. He registers the pain in his fingers; waits as it fades. He had better recite Nocturns soon, before either of the monks drops off or the flame goes out.

BECALMED

CORMAC GETS BARELY a wink of sleep. The relentless creaks and whirlings of the boat, the screechings of birds, the bell summoning the monks for Vigil by the light of a candle stub, Cormac so groggy that he slurs his psalms like a drunk...

At dawn he wakes and reckons in his head. The fifth day of travelling, but it feels endless. At the moment they don't seem to be moving at all. White in his eyes, white all around: fog.

The ocean is all the more disturbing now that Cormac can't see it. The appalling breadth of it, one maw eternally drinking and spewing. He shivers, rubbing his arms and legs through the wool. Greenish-white spatters on his robes, on all their robes, he sees; the birds have fouled the monks in the night as if to say, *The sea is ours.* Still, though, being shat on is said to be good luck.

The Prior prays: '*I arise today through the strength of heaven.*'

'*Through the light of the sun,*' Cormac answers.

'*Through the swiftness of wind,*' Trian finishes.

The bell for Terce. Cormac staggers to his knees, clears his throat, and joins in the psalms. (Seven rather than three, at each of the hours, since today is the Sabbath.)

Afterwards they munch on very dry oatcakes. Cormac thinks it's just as well the fog has come, because there's not a breath of wind to fill their sail, and they're not allowed to row. No lifting, no cooking, no work of any kind; what would count as idleness another day is virtue on the Sabbath.

A bird flaps by, yelping almost in his ear. 'I'm put in mind of the voyages of holy Breandán and his seventeen companions.'

'I hope they had a bigger boat than this,' Trian says under his breath.

Cormac grins, nodding. 'They found one island made of clear, shining crystal, and another covered with grapevines that were heavy with fruit.'

'Ah,' the Prior says with an odd tenderness, 'I don't suppose either of you has tasted a grape? I ate them right off a wall, in Gaul. They burst in the mouth like balls of juice.'

It's the first time the Prior's shown the slightest enthusiasm about food.

Cormac goes on with his tale. 'Another island had a well whose soothing water put the monks to sleep. But the next, now—the next actually rained fire. Spurted it upwards, shot flames into the sky.'

Trian's mouth hangs open.

'The holy man and his followers sailed on and on till they came to a rock with no human mark on it at all,' Cormac continues. 'Birds were perched all over it, singing praise to the Creator day and night. Breandán called that place the Paradise of Birds.' It's quite clear in his mind, the tufted embellishment of every crag. And the polyphonic chorus: not ordinary, shrill birds, but a heavenly choir. Maybe they were the souls of the blessed dead in disguise. Or sinners' souls, more like, Cormac thinks now—encased in feathers as a penance, to work off their crimes by singing hymns for hundreds of years.

'The island in your dream, Father.' Trian's peering into the fog. 'May I ask, what did it look like?'

The Prior sounds nettled. 'It was not drawn like a picture, or illuminated in colours. It was more the idea of an island.'

'Somewhere out there in the ocean.' Cormac means that as confirmation, but it comes out almost sceptical.

'It's out there, all right,' the Prior insists. 'Since God has given me—given us three—this holy mission of serving him in absolute seclusion, he will have prepared a fit place for us.'

'Amen,' Trian murmurs.

Cormac's thinking, it will have to possess a spring or a well, to supply them with water. So, a scrap of land far from the mainland, and well south of all the other islands. Capable of cultivation ... but where no one is living, nor ever tried living. For the first time, Cormac registers how unlikely that sounds.

'It will be defended by waves against the world's encroach-ings,' the Prior goes on. 'All we have to do is wait for a wind, Brothers, and let it take us there.'

This is sounding to Cormac less and less like an actual island. As if the three of them have stepped out of everyday life into a magical boat, and their journey is a fable.

Trian asks warily, 'If we go on and on, Father, over the ocean ... won't we come to the rim?'

The Prior laughs a little. 'Aristotle teaches that the earth is as round as an apple.'

'Round?'

Cormac has heard the same thing, though he's always had trouble picturing it.

The Prior explains, 'Hibernia is called by some *Terra Finalia*, the far or final country, but that only signifies the last before the great western ocean. If we crossed this whole water,' gesturing into the thick white, 'we would come to unknown lands, and beyond them the Indies, and Africa, and the European continent again, and on its edge, Albion and our Hibernia—as if we'd thrown a rope around the globe, you see?'

Trian's clearly straining to follow.

It's not the risk of sailing over a rim that's worrying Cormac, but a much more mundane prospect: death by thirst. Their food will not last a week, and their fresh water—unless more rain falls—only a matter of days. His throat contracts at the thought. He has an impulse to reach down for one of the goat-skins, but stops himself.

'And how will we recognise our island?' Trian wonders.

'By a sign of some kind.'

Cormac realises something: the Prior doesn't know.

Trian hesitates as if about to say more, but doesn't.

It comes to Cormac that maybe it's their fault the boat hasn't reached the island yet, his and Trian's. *We of little faith*.

He speaks rapidly, to hide his treasonous thoughts. 'Didn't holy Ciarán's bell begin to ring, all on its own, the moment he reached the site where he'd build his monastery?'

The Prior rewards him with a nod.

Cormac lowers his eyes.

Say the island in the Prior's dream is real, but even when the monks get a wind, they don't pass close enough to spot their destination, because two of the three are having trouble believing it's there? Say they slide right past it in the fog tomorrow, and blunder on into open ocean, and starve and parch and die in their own ignorance? Fit punishment, Cormac supposes: they will be lost, for lack of conviction. *Christ, my true friend,* he prays, *strengthen my faith. Cherubim lift me, angels support me, archangels bear me up.*

Artt sits quite still, trying to forget the fact that his robe is bedaubed in droppings. The fog is as thick as ever; the sun's only lit, not lifted it. The boat stands as if the water's thickened and congealed around it. Becalmed, not a breath of wind; everything is motionless, except for the flocks overhead keeping up their complaint.

He rebukes himself for his itch to be sailing on, even on the Sabbath. Isn't it enough that he has time to sit with eyes shut and contemplate the holy island that God has set aside for them? *Pray without ceasing,* Paul told the Thessalonians. That's the only true urgency.

A peculiar rumbling makes him open his eyes. Birds floating all around the boat; black and white plumage and snubbed beaks of riotous orange, red, grey, and blue. Such a deep growl for such little creatures.

Trian's watching them with interest. 'The puffins have put on their gaudy faces already, to find mates.'

Yes, now Trian's said it, Artt can spot pairs of them rubbing bills, like any man and maid: the endless, predictable rhythm of it. 'Time for Mass.' He pushes himself to his feet and the boat shakes.

Cormac blinks and stirs from his doze. Trian scrambles to open the holy chest.

Artt unrolls the narrow white linen stole—the mark of priesthood—and hangs it around his neck, crossing the ends over his breast and fixing them in place with his belt so they hang down to his ankles. He lays the linen cloth over the flat lid of the chest, as a tiny, makeshift altar table. He unwraps the cloths that hold the chalice and dish—not gold, but the best the Abbot could spare them, a small bronze cup and a thin stone plate inlaid with amethyst.

'Holy water,' Trian remembers, and leans over to retrieve the little flask from the bow.

Artt takes it from him, pulls out the stopper, sprinkles the draped chest, and makes a cross in the air over it: 'The sign of the living Christ.' He picks up one of the beeswax candles.

But when Cormac opens his fire gear, he tuts. 'Gone out, Father.' He gives his chest a token smack. 'Beg pardon, I should have kept a closer eye on it.'

Such disrespect to the Mass. Artt breathes out his annoyance.

The old monk fusses about, unwrapping a rag and choosing three big flakes of touchwood. He sets them into the horn, then uses his grooved flint to strike against the back of his knife over and over. He makes sparks, but none of them land on the dried fungus.

Artt catches himself grinding his teeth.

At last, a spark flares up. Cormac blows on it gently and feeds it some moss.

Finally Artt can light the taper. Palms pressed together, heads down, the monks pray silently, preparing for the sacrament.

Artt fills the little gilt jug with fresh water, and pours some over his hands, murmuring, 'Lord, wash away my crimes. Cleanse me of my sins.'

No need of a book; he knows all the parts of the Mass by heart. For want of a deacon, he nods to Cormac to sing the antiphons in his hoarse voice. 'Now let us offer each other peace,' Artt says, 'and when your lips approach those of your brother for the Pax Tecum, do not let your heart shrink from him.' The boat lurches under their feet as they embrace each other in turn.

Taking up the wine jar (bound in coils of rope), Artt pulls out the wax plug and pours a trickle into the chalice. As ever, he adds some water from the jug and the blood-red pales to pink. It is not yet clear to him how he's to get any more from Gaul, but he pushes that qualm aside. Now he opens the silver box which holds the Host—three small rounds of wheat bread, the *Chi Rho* symbol baked into their tops to mark them as Christ's. After the Greek blessing he goes on in Gaelic.

Trian is already ringing the bell to mark the beginning of the Consecration. In Latin Artt says the words of power: 'On the night before Jesus died, he took bread and gave thanks, broke it and gave it to his followers, saying, *Do this to remember me. This is my body.* He took the cup and gave thanks, and said, *This is my blood.*' Artt elevates the Host in both hands, as high as he can reach. Squeezing his eyes shut, he stares past the treachery of appearances, to the very substance of the bread and wine transformed into the flesh and blood of Jesus. As always, the miracle makes him shake.

Next Artt raises the chalice so the monks can adore the Presence in that form too. He breaks the Host into three roughly equal triangles and puts one into each mouth, the last in his own. He passes the chalice around. When he swallows, his throat is sour with ecstasy. 'We three are made one.'

As Trian washes the holy vessels afterwards and swaddles them in the chest, the glare of sun intensifies behind the fabric of cloud. The white thins, lightens, finally tears. At last a spring breeze starts up. The boat slides broadside to it and lolls and rolls. Relieved to be moving, even if only uncontrollably, Artt watches the fog meandering off and leaving a sky only ribboned with cloud.

Is that shock on Trian's face? He turns to look where the young monk's staring. On the horizon to the southwest of them, two islands side by side, thrusting up from the sea. One larger, both weirdly pointed. 'What a pair of skelligs,' Trian marvels.

Cormac skews around and shifts his head from side to side like a bird. 'Skelligs?'

'Spikes of rock in the sea—sheer, sharp islands. I suppose our eyes were on the setting sun yesterday,' Trian adds uncertainly, 'so we didn't look any farther south.'

'It's not that.' Artt's voice comes out like a lion's roar. 'Christ is revealing them to us only now. Our island—it must be one of these two.' He makes a cross on his forehead, his mouth, his chest. *'If God is for us, who can be against us?'* he sings out. *'Ask and you will receive. Seek and you will find. Knock and it will open.'*

'Amen,' the monks chorus, catching his fervour.

He watches the islands in a loud silence; his gaze eats up the distance. The boat rotates and drifts, more or less in the right direction but with a languor that racks his nerves.

Trian must feel the same way because he begs, 'Can we go faster, Father?'

'The Sabbath,' Cormac reminds him gruffly.

Artt stares at the two great jagged outcroppings. The small pyramid floats beneath the level of the clouds; the broader, higher one rears up, wrapped in vapour. It seems ungrateful not to harness this bit of heaven-sent wind. 'Well, I don't suppose it would count as work to drop the sail, at least.'

The others rush to follow his lead, unfurling the great square and stringing it to the sides of the hull. A light puff fills it at once and speeds them south, just where they want to go.

Closer, the great shards of grey are dabbed with green, as if a pair of mountains slid off the land into the sea and sailed away. Like some desert mirage; a miracle worked on a floating altar. Little by little the skelligs grow. Their crazed cones seem to Artt to be merging, the lesser slipping in front of the greater, two becoming one. He wonders aloud, 'Could that be snow on their tops?' Well past Easter, so surely not. Unless these unique rocks have their own rarefied weather.

'Bird droppings, more like,' Trian says.

'Ah, yes.' With misgiving, Artt jerks around to reckon how far these extraordinary islands lie from the mainland. Seven miles, eight, no more; will they have been claimed by impure folk long since? 'I see no signs of settlement yet.'

'Nor I, Father.' The young man's voice is shrill with excitement.

'Maybe they're uninhabitable.'

Artt glares at Cormac.

'I only mean...they seem all up and down. But my eyes aren't what they were,' the old monk admits.

It strikes Artt that the combination of the light current and breeze is going to take the boat right past the skelligs, too far south. He grabs the steering oar and pushes it deep into the water, just to nudge them west. He wouldn't call this work, only sitting, holding on, feeling the pulse of the sea, his gaze on the islands' splintery silhouettes. His throat is locked as the boat inches nearer the smaller one, and the greater one looming behind it. They are like nothing he's ever encountered in all his travels, two broken fists of rock held up in prayer. He sings out, *'Be before me, O Lord.'*

'As a bright flame,' the others chant back.

'Be above me, O Lord.'

'As a fixed star.'

'Be below me, O Lord.'

Cormac and Trian finish: *'As a clear path.'*

As they approach what Artt is thinking of as the Lesser Skellig, it reveals itself as entirely possessed by an army of birds. He can't hear anything like a hymn of praise in the screams of these vermin. Nor can he see any spot to moor around this whole stained crag. Could it be too steep to land on?

The boat is past already, gliding slowly, straight towards the bigger island, which is still a mile or two off. Its rough cone is veiled in cloud, but the breeze is already beginning to wipe it clean.

Now the Great Skellig is revealed in all its strange glory. Twice the height of its neighbour, sharply fingering the sky. Eroded by wind and water; littered with rockfall, smeared with emerald vegetation. Its crags are capped with the droppings of the wheeling flocks who keep up their harsh cacophony.

'This is the place,' Artt proclaims. 'The higher up, the closer to heaven. On this island's peaks, our prayers will be halfway to God's ears already.'

'Amen, Father.'

'Amen.'

The Great Skellig is an abandoned fortress, awful in majesty. No, Artt tells himself, not abandoned, just lonely, waiting for its commander. The most gigantic of cathedrals, ready for its priest.

Belatedly he realises that the boat is getting close enough to run aground. 'Furl the sail!'

Trian and Cormac hurry to bind the leather against the yard.

'Now drop anchor.'

Trian heaves the thorny stone over the side. Its rope slithers, and slithers, and finally stops.

They kneel there, in the bobbing boat, pinned in the shadow of the island. Artt demands, 'Any signs of occupation?'

'Not from this side at least,' says Trian.

No possibility of landing today; it would be too late to make a start, even if it weren't the Sabbath.

As the sun goes lower, his neck aches from staring up at the Great Skellig, which takes on new colours in the dying light. Seabirds wing by, shedding the odd acrid spatter. Trian hands him a bowl with some salt pork and an oatcake. Artt makes himself eat; the body is a beast of burden that must be fed and watered.

'Our second evening without a fire,' Cormac remarks.

Artt narrows his eyes; is the old monk complaining?

'A fine, mild night it is too,' Trian hurries to say.

'Holy Éanna and his men lived in caves, on their island, and never lit a flame,' Artt points out.

Cormac nods apologetically. 'And one of our strongest saints, blessed Comgall—he too preferred to deny himself that comfort. Though one time, in the deeps of winter, his companions broke down and begged him to make them a fire.'

Trian asks, 'Did the holy man take pity on their weakness?'

'He did, in the end. He picked up a few dry sticks,' Cormac says, half-laughing, 'and kindled them with his breath.'

Artt pictures that: a puff of warm air sparking to red life. The weaklings—ashamed, but grateful—holding out their hands to the flames, their renewed faith glowing inside them. Well, he supposes there are times mercy may do what strictness can't.

Evening is drawing in; he shivers and reaches down for his cloak. Around the boat a flock is gathering to preen and bathe, thousands strong, glossy black on white, pure white underneath. 'Brother Trian, do you know what these creatures are?'

'Shearwaters, Father. My people used to call them night birds, or devil birds, for the awful racket when they visit their burrows after dark.'

A pair of them come in stiff-winged now, scraping the water and leaving a fine wake; like gliding crosses, to Artt's eyes. Everything is a sign if you look at it hard enough.

The water laps; the tethered boat bobs. After a while the first lights stand out in the sky.

Trian asks, 'Are they holes, the stars?'

'Bodies of cold fire,' Artt corrects him, 'fixed in a sphere around the earth. God spins it westwards every day. That's what makes the air and the clouds move.' He cranes up, a little dizzy, imagining that giant hand flicking the globe.

The dark shape of the Great Skellig looms above them, blotting out half the sky. Staring up at it, Cormac asks, 'Has either of you spotted any marks of a spring on this island?'

Trian doesn't answer, meaning no.

Nor has Artt, not yet. But he doesn't like the question's implication—the sneering hint that there may be no fresh water here. He'd like to crack their two heads together for doubting him, the haw-red one and the grey-wisped one. He bites his lip, tasting salt. 'Trust me, the island must have water, since we need it to live. This place was set aside for us when the earth was made.'

LANDFALL

Curled up against the skin of the boat, Trian breathes in pine pitch and wool fat, but behind it all, the savoury sting of the sea. The long night's paling at last. The air above and around him is awhir with birds. He makes tiny crosses on his forehead, mouth, and chest and says his dawn prayers silently, so as not to disturb his elders: *From the lures of the world, protect me. From bad men and demons, protect me. From plagues and accidents, protect me.*

The mainland lies like a black smear to the east; light rises over its low hills, tinting the sky pink. *From the rising of the sun to its setting, praised be your name.*

The sea is quite glassy, as if God's poured oil on it. As the red berry of the sun floats up into the sky, Trian can see everything: the silken fabric of the ocean, stretched out smooth with barely a ripple; flocks of voracious cormorants and moaning puffins working the waters.

Looming over the boat, the Great Skellig's sharp magnificence. To Trian it almost looks as if its rock was formed in flat layers, then the whole thing tipped sideways. *Every valley shall be lifted up,* Isaiah promises in the Scripture. This is a tiny, perfect land, stood on end; a bridge to the sky. *O bringer of good news, go up on the high mountain.*

The Prior's bright granite eyes are fixed on the peak. 'A perfect day for making landfall.'

Trian's heart leaps at the word.

With his bell, the Prior summons them onto their knees for Terce.

Afterwards they share a few eggs, roasted flesh gone rubbery. Then the Prior takes his place at the stern, with the steering oar. Trian eyes the northernmost headland. 'Which way around the island, Father?'

'Sunwise, of course.'

He feels foolish for having asked, since that's the luckier direction. He heaves at his oar, to angle the boat to the left of the protruding spit.

The Great Skellig looks to Trian to be not much longer than its sister, but twice as wide across and twice as high. Greener, too; grey scree patched with vegetation. On its eastern side the rock slopes rather more gently down to the water, but he sees no landing place to moor the boat. They pass a cove like a little bite. Then a deeper one.

'Might this do for an anchorage?' Cormac asks.

The Prior shakes his head.

'The walls are too sheer, Brother,' Trian points out.

While they circle the ragged pyramid, it seems to unfold and come apart. Two great breasts of rock, divided by a cleft, as if the Great Skellig has been cracked almost in half. The south side's quite different; cliffs tower above the little boat. But on the other side of the headland, a gigantic cove opens up.

The Prior leans forward. 'Now this is more promising.'

Trian doesn't like the look of the open sea to the west. 'Maybe too exposed, though, Father? No shelter at all if a breaker were to roll in while we were landing.'

He can't help thinking of his kind uncle and his mean one, plucked off the shore in the same moment.

They row on, sweating in the still air. A splash to the left, a flurry of water. 'Dolphins!' Trian hasn't seen one since he was a child.

The old monk's eyes bulge at the sight of the sleek creatures leaping along in the boat's wake.

A pair—*or is it mother and infant,* Trian wonders? They speed up to come alongside and pass the boat, then double back, clearly curious.

The Prior stares past them. He steers farther out to give a wide berth to a reef of islets and sea stacks that trails off to the west of the Great Skellig.

Trian watches the water, wary of any rock that could hole their hull. Stroke by stroke, they work their way along to the northern face. This side is just as steep—incongruously, impossibly jagged. No hint of human presence; no level ground except the tiny ledges crowded by kittiwakes and guillemots, hundreds of feet in the air. Trian spots another great cove without any flat ground to get out on. Stone walls lean over, becoming precipitous overhangs.

A while later, he makes himself speak up. 'Father...isn't this where we started?'

The Prior nods, frowning. 'Keep on, Brother. We'll moor in the first cove we saw, just to the east of this point.'

'The little one?'

A nod.

At least it's sheltered there; with no swell at all, they should manage to scramble onto the rocks. As the boat moves in, Trian asks for the sounding line, and Cormac passes it to him. Trian heaves the lead, tossing the pointed plummet well in front of the prow. It sinks a surprisingly long way before it finds bottom. He pulls it up, counting by the leather ties that each mark off the height of a man. 'Still more than five fathoms, right here, but I'd expect off-lying rocks.'

The Prior gestures impatiently for them to close in on the island.

Next time Trian heaves the lead it sinks only two fathoms. He scrutinises the shoreline for any level perch at all. In the shadows, what looks like a sea cave. Beside it, a descending diagonal of rock, almost flat at the base, washed by the surf. 'There, Father?'

'That's it.' The Prior leans forward, using his steering oar to push the boat.

Trian eyes the slippery platform and the boulders around it, slick with rotting kelp. Twenty feet of water between them and the Great Skellig, he guesses.

Just then, a bump, an awful lurch.

The Prior lets out a groan.

'What is it?' Cormac asks.

'Aground,' Trian whispers.

Just the bow, maybe. The boat's skin is four layers deep, a full inch of cowhide. But the baggage she carries must be weighing her down, and if the spike of rock presses hard enough to pierce her...

Trian toes off his shoes and leaps over the side.

Cold water closes over his head. The shocking brine in his eyes makes him splutter and laugh.

When he comes up blowing like a whale, the Prior's barking: 'Brother Trian!'

Trian churns the sea with his legs and grabs the gunnel with both hands. Gasps, 'Just trying to shift us off the rock.' He flails at the stony knuckle the boat's wedged on, till his soles hit slimy stone; he plants them, heaves and pushes.

'Get back in,' the Prior's ordering.

'I nearly have it,' he protests. But what if his efforts to dislodge the boat only push her harder onto the sharp point?

The outcropping under his feet seems to move, or rather the boat's pulling sideways, slipping free at last. Trian heaves himself up on the gunnel, panting.

Cormac pulls him into the boat. 'Well done, lad.'

First thing, Trian checks under the laths. All the water there seems to be running off his own soaked robe; no sign of any rips in the hide.

But the Prior's voice is steely. 'You should have asked before you leapt into the water. I thought you were drowning.'

Trian's thrown. His master didn't know he could swim. 'I...I beg pardon, Father.'

'Impulsiveness *and* insubordination.'

Cormac looks wide-eyed from one man to the other.

Trian's eyes brim. *No excuses,* he reminds himself.

'This is our testing ground.' The Prior speaks through his teeth. 'In the face of new difficulties and dangers, I ask you again, can you hold to your vow of obedience?'

'I can. I will.'

'Our mission depends on brotherhood. Divided, we'll fall.'

'Father,' Trian weeps. He slams his fist against his chest, a dozen times.

After a long silence, the Prior moves his oar and the boat inches forward. Cormac pokes the water ahead to make sure there's room to pass. The hull touches the platform at the base of the rock—scored with fissures, encrusted with limpets—and bumps away.

Shoes off, staff in hand, the Prior steps forward, edging around their goods. Trian doesn't dare move until he's told. Cormac offers a hand but the Prior ignores him, gripping the edge of the prow instead. (Is he still angry?) He springs forward like a much younger man. The boat recoils as his feet find purchase on the wet slab.

Trian has the mooring rope ready to throw. Catching the coil, the Prior hitches it around a shard of rock and pulls, drawing in the boat as close as he can. He makes a tight knot. Then he reaches out to Cormac.

The old monk grasps his hand and uses his staff to get up onto the platform.

Trian hangs a waterskin around his neck by its horsehair strap before he joins them. He ventures to say, 'We might be the first men ever to set foot here.'

The Prior's voice booms, exultant: 'Like Adam in the Garden.'

Three Adams, one of them drenched, two of them caked in dried bird droppings. Trian shivers a little. He tips his head back and scans the cliffs, which are thick with clamouring birds.

The Prior quotes, *When they had brought their ships to land, they forsook all, and followed him.*

'Well now.' Cormac squints upwards, looking daunted.

The Prior's almost chanting: '*Neither height nor depth nor any creature can keep us from God.*'

Trian crosses himself. 'Amen.'

Their master gives him the nod. 'Brother, lead the way.'

And like a rabbit gratefully released from a snare, Trian is off up a ledge that offers just enough purchase for his feet. He's left his staff in the boat, along with his shoes; he prefers to rely on the grip of fingers and toes. His wet robes cling to his limbs, but he springs from rock to rock. Finding one handhold and foothold after another, he spider-dashes up the slope, setting course towards the bump he thinks of as the North Peak, the slightly lower of the Great Skellig's two.

Greasy, weed-scummed rocks give way to cliffs covered in nests. A reek of bird droppings, fish scraps, sea. The dusting of white reveals itself, up close, as fragments of eggshell. Left over from last summer, Trian supposes.

He glances over his shoulder. Cormac's hunched, grasping each rock as if in hand-to-hand combat. Trian calls, 'Close one eye, maybe, Brother?'

'What's that?'

'Shut your seaward eye and look only at the rock beside you.'

Cormac nods.

Below them, the Prior climbs with neither trouble nor grace.

Wherever Trian can, he picks his way along the carpet of cliff plants. Only low, hardy things seem to thrive on these salt-sprayed patches. Tufted fescue grass; low-growing mayweed, splotched with white daisy-like blooms already. Dense tussocks of thrift, sending up the odd stem of pink. Mounting higher, he spots more and more spurrey with its little pointed leaves, as well as tiny yellow buds of vetch, and white sea campion that some call *dead men's bells* because it seeds in unreachable niches. Where there's no vegetation, Trian follows firm slants of bedrock, rather than the scree that's so treacherous underfoot. Once or twice his step dislodges something and he shouts, ''Ware rocks!' so his elders below can shield their faces.

Puffins poke gaudy beaks out of burrows. One launches itself into the air in front of Trian, then returns to the hillside with a crash of feathers. The squeaks and screeches of kittiwakes rise above the other cries; in their grass nests mudded to inaccessible perches, they face inwards and display their forked tails like knives. High ledges bristle with guillemots—duck-sized and upright in their black and white plumage. Some massive birds of a similar kind, too, that Trian's never seen before, bigger than geese.

The Great Skellig's feathered inhabitants are all so tame, they may shriek in surprise but they don't so much as flutter out of Trian's way. No, not tame, he realises: wildly innocent. They don't know enough of men to fear them.

His robe's beginning to dry already, and he's warming up. On the next turn, he passes a bizarre rock formation like a woman looking out to sea—her jaw jutting in grief, her hair blown behind her, her hand gesturing at the Lesser Skellig. Could the wind and the rain really have carved this? It's only a trick of perspective, Trian tells himself.

His mother wasn't crying when she and his father left him at the monastery, or not that she let him see.

Trian goes on, till he comes out onto a narrow plateau. Such a relief to stand on a patch of flattish ground and let his arms hang. He crosses to a rowan no taller than himself, growing out of a crevice in the rock. Three wizened red berries from last autumn cling on, but new toothed leaves are showing already, and the first blooms coming.

The Prior catches up, breathing heavily and swaying a little oddly as he stands surveying the island.

Shyly Trian asks, 'Does the earth feel like it's moving under you, Father?'

A guarded nod.

'You may be a touch landsick, then.'

The Prior stares at the word.

'When a man comes home from sea, and it takes him a day or two to get his land legs again.'

A shake of the head. 'So many varieties of frailty of the flesh.'

Here comes Cormac. He drops to the ground beside them and lets out a wheezing laugh. 'Good to take one breath at least without fear of dropping off a cliff.'

'You're a strong enough climber,' Trian says.

'Ah, but I haven't the balance anymore. It leaks away with age.'

Behind the little rowan, bare bedrock stretches up diagonally—no more than forty feet, Trian would guess—to the island's North Peak. The Prior's already heading up the slope. Trian and Cormac follow him to where the land drops away as if a giant's sliced it with a battle-axe.

Cormac lurches back from the brink. 'Too close for me.'

Trian keeps an eye on the Prior, ready to grab hold if need be.

Below them, birds arc and dive. Farther down the delicately etched water spreads out as far as Trian can see. No more islands. The three men have reached the edge of everything.

'There must be a spring here somewhere.' The Prior turns and strides down the hill.

Cormac struggles to his feet again. They head inland, towards the cleft in the middle of the Great Skellig, down a slant steep enough that once or twice even Trian has to sit down and slither, grabbing at the rock. This landscape is pathless, quite untrodden—because it has no four-footed beasts, he supposes. A great blank page, and these travellers are the first pens to touch it.

A grassy depression is opening up—a U-shaped saddle between the island's two high points. In the very middle, the Prior stops and spins in a circle. To north and south, empty sky, empty sea. 'Still no water,' he complains. 'Besides, this part is too exposed to build on. The winds would whip right across it.'

Cormac gives no opinion, only bends to examine a tiny flower.

Trian goes ahead, working his way up the conical tusk of the South Peak. He swings himself between narrow ledges. He supposes it is dangerous, but aren't they here on God's orders?

At some point he realises he's left the others behind, or they've dropped back. But he has to find water. Not out of vainglory, just to prove himself of use, despite his failings. To make the Prior glad, after all, that he brought Trian along.

So much seems wrecked about this island: stone shattered or worn, with deep vertical cracks, stained with droppings and lichens, rank with decaying seaweed. But in another way it feels quite new. As if Trian is being permitted to see a piece of creation at the very moment the world was made, more than six thousand years ago.

The valley's far below him now, an emerald patch with two tiny sitting figures. He moves on, without effort, without doubt, weightless, as if in a dream. The risk buoys him up. He follows a ledge that twists around a blind corner where he finds himself above a pure drop of hundreds of feet. The only way forward is a cleft in a great wall; he squeezes through. It's narrow enough to claw at his damp robe, and he thinks of Jesus's parable about it being easier for a camel to get through the eye of a needle than for a rich man to reach heaven.

Trian stands at the very top of the island now, where a horizontal spit of rock leads forward. He steps along it, then drops to a crouch. The spit's several times his length, thrusting into the sky. He crawls along, out into the blue. The rock slopes down a little; now it's no wider than his hand. He's inching on his belly, his hip bones hanging free. Where the spit runs out, Trian lies still, not even holding on; his hands rest on the air. His face floats in open space. Like flying. The hugeness, the glory.

A screech behind him.

Trian spasms and nearly rolls off. Gripping the needle of rock under him, he cranes up over his right shoulder—

And an enormous bird screams down, blotting out the sun. *Jok-jok-jok!*

The eagle's deep-fingered wings are as big as a pair of doors. It grips a crag and settles its bleached brown feathers with its hooked beak. Gripping a large, twitching fish in one yellow foot, it makes no move to swallow it. Its crop is bulging, the size of a fist, Trian notices; maybe it's gorged itself already. These seas must be one great board spread for this king.

Nearby, a different cry: *Krau-krau-krau-uik-ik!*

The eagle goes on the alert again, throwing back its pale head and answering more shrilly: *Kri-kyi-kyi-kli-kliek-yak!*

His mate. Of course, this male must be warning Trian away from their eyrie. With a single flap the eagle wings away, out of sight.

When Trian stumbles back down to the central valley he's dubbed the Saddle, he expects a rebuke for having been gone so long. But the Prior only asks, 'Anything to our purpose?'

Rock. Air. Eagles. 'No water, Father, sorry.'

The Prior looks up at the bright clouds. 'Noon.' He opens the pouch on his belt and takes out the iron bell.

The other two press their palms together and follow him in chanting the three psalms.

Trian's belly growls. They brought no food up from the boat, since they were so keen to explore. He contents himself with a drink of water.

'Father.' Cormac sounds troubled. 'Can this really be the place? Without a spring...'

Trian stiffens at the hint of dissension.

For answer, the Prior flings his huge arms wide. 'Does God not visit those who love him in the wildest wastes?'

'He does,' Cormac acknowledges.

'This is an island unlike any other on earth. Do you doubt that?'

Both monks shake their heads.

'Then it must be meant for us, Brothers. It must have water, if only we have eyes to see it.'

Trian doesn't know what to say to that.

Leaving the grassy Saddle, the Prior retraces his steps up to the little Plateau below the North Peak. The monks follow. Out of the corner of his eye, Trian watches the Prior stare past the spiked pyramid of the Lesser Skellig to the gauzy country they've left behind, with its hills that look like low tents. A small fishing boat is rounding a headland; there must be a settlement around there.

Is their master waiting to be guided by a vision, Trian wonders? An angel who'll come down and make sweet liquid shoot up out of this bony ground? *Water, water, water.* His thick tongue presses against the ridged roof of his mouth.

The stunted rowan is the only tree they've seen here, and trees live longer than anything. Trian goes over and reaches down beside her roots, fingering gently, prodding. Is he imagining it, or does it feel a little damper? He scans the huge inclined surface of rock and pictures it during a rainfall, trickling, streaming. If there were a way of collecting that water...

In one slab, Trian finds a slanting fissure. In the next, a crack that runs to join the first. A shallower groove that looks like it's been worn by water. Where the lines drop out of sight, he pokes his left hand into the darkness, cramming it between the rocks. He wriggles, scrapes, struggles to decide what he's touching... When he pulls his hand out, one knuckle's bleeding, but the end of his middle finger's wet and clear. He examines both liquids, the scarlet and the see-through. Puts his tongue to his fingertip. 'Father!'

The other two come hurrying.

The Prior's eyes flare. 'A well!'

'Not water springing out of the ground,' Trian hastens to say, 'just a basin that seems to hold rain.'

They each dip a hand deep into the crack and taste it. 'Fresh water at such an elevation—a miracle,' the Prior pronounces, sketching a great cross in the air.

'We could dig it out to make a proper cistern,' Cormac says.

The Prior thumps down onto his knees. *'You who makes a way in the wilderness and streams in the desert,'* he recites, *'praised be your name. You who told Moses to strike the rock so water gushed out for all the Israelites to drink—'*

Trian joins in, with Cormac: *'Praised be your name.'*

'You who splits the mountain and gives us drink—'

'Praised be your name.'

'And blessed be the rowan,' Trian adds, 'for leading us to the water.'

'Isn't she known as the quicken tree, for how fast she grows?' Cormac is almost gabbling. 'And as for her fruit'—he strips the three gnarled red balls from their yellow stems—'they're famous for cleaning the blood.' He hands them out, one to each man. Trian chews his; it's tart enough to make his mouth pucker.

'Right here is where we'll camp, and then build,' the Prior decides. 'This flat part has the well, and the peak to our backs to keep off the wind. Of what, maybe fifty acres of land, only this one's level enough for us to live on without rolling into the sea in our sleep. I could wish we were facing away from the world we've escaped, not towards it,' he adds with a scowl at the mainland, 'but that should remind us to stay on guard against its temptations.'

'We'll get the warmth of the southern sun here, too,' Cormac points out. 'We could terrace our garden to make it flatter and more sheltered.'

The Prior raises both hands. 'Lord, I beg a blessing from heaven on this Great Skellig, and on us who'll live out our days here.'

'Amen.'

'A home for whatever time we may be granted, where our bones will lie.'

That gives Trian a shiver. Of course he knew, when he said yes to this great man outside the dormitory less than a fortnight ago, that there'd be no going back. But somehow it unnerves him to think of dying here, on this gargantuan sea-hill.

Descending the slippery cliff after they've sung their psalms for Sext is harder. Trian's stomach rumbles and he finds his legs wavering under him.

When they're nearly at what Trian thinks of as Landing Cove, Cormac stops short in fright. 'The boat's not there!'

The Prior lets out a bark of mirth.

'The tide's gone down, that's all, Brother,' Trian murmurs, 'and the boat with it.'

Cormac's quick to laugh at his own mistake.

Reaching the shell-pocked platform, they find the boat sitting a fathom lower, her rope pulled taut. 'Will I jump down and pass things up?' Trian asks.

But the Prior's already sitting down on the slithery edge. He lands on a lath with a loud creak, and the boat wallows. He heaves each item over his head to Cormac, who passes it to Trian: the holy chest first, then the stools, the great iron pot, the creel full of tools. 'Set everything down farther up the rock. Keep this flat place clear.'

'Mightn't the tide wash them off, even up there?' Cormac frets.

Trian points out the seaweed mark below. 'Unless there's a storm, Brother, the water won't come up any further than this line here.'

As they unpack, he finds he's almost sickened by their

quantity of stuff. So unlike the birds and the beasts, who accumulate nothing, have nothing but what they seek out when they need it.

Their one spare robe Cormac hands to the Prior, who puts it on in place of his spattered one. Trian drops his eyes while the Prior's changing. He knows himself to be modest to a foolish degree. In all his years at Cluain Mhic Nóis he never took off his clothes in front of anyone, and washed only under them. On the rare occasions when the monks bathed in the river, Trian hung back until he could do it alone.

Now Cormac pulls his own tunic over his head and kneels down in his braies, trying to reach the water. Trian can't help noticing a blue-grey marking—an animal?—tattooed on his wrinkled back. 'Let me, Brother!' Eyes still averted, Trian takes both men's filthy robes, moves lower and crouches to rub them together in the sea. He gets the bird muck off and wrings as much water as he can out of them before handing Cormac's back up for the old monk to put on wet, since they have no other. The one the Prior was wearing, Trian stretches over a boulder to dry.

Joining in the chain of hands again, he passes up the sacks of charcoal, oats, wheat flour...

Cormac catches him staring at the food basket. Trian looks away, sheepish.

'Father,' Cormac asks, 'might we take a bit of nourishment to strengthen ourselves?'

'Very well, but don't waste the daylight.'

After an apple, Trian finds his hands are steadier. Cormac eats even the seeds and stem of his. The Prior only takes a drink from a waterskin. Trian's curious—is their master fasting as penance for some minor offence, or just caught up in the work?

From the rocks above, a derisive quack from one of those great waddling birds, the size of a child. Trian asks, 'Has either of you ever seen the like of that creature?'

The Prior shakes his head impatiently.

'Such comical white circles around its eyes,' Cormac points out.

Some sort of auk, Trian supposes, a hugely overgrown cousin to the guillemots and puffins. It rattles its stumpy little wings, then flops to its belly and slithers away. How odd—a bird born landlocked, like a goose with one wing clipped by a farmer's wife to stop it from flying away.

The Prior heaves himself out of the boat, onto the platform, and considers the rocky slope.

Trian is worried about how Cormac's going to manage the journey back up, heavily laden this time. 'Father, maybe I could go up first and rope the steepest spots, for us to hold as we climb?'

The Prior gives permission with a wave.

So Trian rummages around to find their iron pegs, the mallet, and a long, thin skein of nettle cord.

By the time he comes back down the cliff, Cormac is ready, with a sack slung evenly, front and back, over each shoulder. He grips his staff for balance. The Prior has lifted the wicker creel onto his own back, sliding his arms through the straps. What's more, he's got a stack of earthenware crocks under one arm. Trian wants to say something—to suggest their master is carrying too much—but it's not his place.

So he crams the iron cauldron with as many tools as it will hold, and leads the way.

It's slow, precarious work, even with the rigging he's pegged into the rocks. They pant and sweat; they kneel on rocky knobs and cling to wiry plants. Looking down, Trian spots a faint pale line in Cormac's wake. 'Brother, you're shedding flour!'

'Ah, no...'

A puffin runs over to peck at the trail. Cormac staggers, struggles to find the hole in the half of the sack that hangs down his back and lift that corner before—

The bottom rips loudly, unseams, and sheds a choking cloud. Released, the heavy front half of the bag falls through Cormac's flailing hands and scatters itself across the rocks.

This stock of ground wheat is all they have for making Communion bread.

Cormac's frozen, chalk-faced. 'Father,' he coughs. 'I beg pardon.'

'Nothing to be done,' the Prior says disgustedly. He turns back to the cliff with such furious momentum that the stack of crocks he's holding sways and the top half-dozen crocks fall, rebounding and smashing in pieces below.

Puffins flap away in outrage. Neither of the monks says a word.

The three push on, the Prior gripping the rest of the crocks with white-tipped fingers, Cormac clutching his remaining sack as if it's a baby.

When they've finally mounted up to the Plateau, they're all in a lather. Cormac folds up the ripped bag dolefully and begs pardon again and again.

They make a great pile of their stuff. Anything light, they

weigh down with stones. But they can leave it all sitting here without fear of theft, Trian realises, because there are no enemies. The monks have the place to themselves, and the birds pay them no attention. The whole island's a royal treasure house, locked tight by the sea.

The Prior scowls in the direction of the cliff. 'If only there was some better way to get the rest of our necessities up here.'

Cormac's eyes brighten in their nests of wrinkled skin. 'What if we hoisted them?'

An hour later Trian is kneeling with him at the top of the cliffs, beside a protruding rock. Cormac's leaning all his weight into the pulley they've pegged into a cleft. Sweat stands out on his forehead as he winds the handle.

'I can take a turn, Brother,' Trian repeats.

Cormac ignores that. Trian waits for the lumbering bundle the Prior's attached down at the shore—stools, cloaks, nets, the spare sail; he leans over to haul it in and untie the rope.

By the time the monks have winched up three bundles, the sun's low in the enormous sky. Trian guesses the job must be almost done by now; he can't think of anything still missing. 'Stay up here, Brother, while I go down to the Prior.'

Cormac objects: 'It must be nearly time for Vespers.'

'This is a hard climb even in full daylight,' Trian tells him. 'Say your prayers and get a fire going for us, maybe?'

Cormac nods and lets himself down on the ground.

Trian finds the returning tide has lifted the empty boat closer. The Prior breaks his pose of contemplation and looks up. 'Help me lift her out, Brother.'

This puzzles Trian. Won't they be needing to set off on a trading trip soon enough—to a farmstead on the mainland, or that island where they saw the turf-cutters? But he holds his tongue. He supposes it might be safer to store her on dry land for now, in case a spring storm breaks her on the rocks before they go to sea again.

First the two of them lift out the oars and the anchor stone. They draw the heavy mast out of its socket and lay it along the landing platform.

'The sail,' the Prior orders. 'It could come in handy.'

So Trian unwinds it from the yard, undoes its laces, and rolls it up.

Then they heave the hull out of the water, the effort nearly knocking him off his feet. 'Upside down,' the Prior grunts, 'to keep the rain out.' They tip it over, inverted like a gigantic shell against the rock wall.

The Prior pants with stern satisfaction, 'Nothing's won without pains.'

The sun's already slipped below the cliffs overhead, making a black jagged line. Trian shoves the anchor stone and the oars under the hull. He wedges the folded sail under his arm and goes up the cliff in the dimming light, on all fours this time.

He remembers to take a few eggs from a ledge as he passes, and tucks them into the pouch on his belt. Where the path turns left, there's that outcropping he thinks of as the Wailing Woman. Trian's starting to feel almost at home on this weird mountain. He mouths the old prayer to Mary the Virgin: *We fly to take refuge under your wing, Mother of God. Don't ignore our pleas in times of trouble, blessed one, but rescue us from danger.* Then he catches a whiff of smoke from above—what must be the first fire ever lit on this island.

THE CROSS

THE GREAT SKELLIG reminds Artt of Jacob's dream, in the Book of Genesis—a ladder planted on earth and reaching up to heaven, angels going up and down it all the time. This must be the most pointed place on earth; horns, spears, spikes, and blades of rock as far as he can see.

He walks at dawn. The sheer relief of being alone, after the week in the boat packed in so closely with the young monk (who seems to have no sense of how loudly he cracks his joints) and the old one (with his endless stories).

My island: Artt tries out the phrase in his head. Here he and his followers can live sequestered from the corruptions of society, and have some breathing space from each other too. But the heavy yoke of authority sits on Artt's shoulders. *The first shall be last;* a truly Christian master must serve his men. It's Artt who bears all the responsibility for lighting a beacon of prayer in the ocean, now. A waymark pointing up, one that will stand till the Last Day.

Rays of light sword out from the east, illuminating patches of glowing lichen on the grey rock. Birds spread their wings to catch the dawn's warmth. Artt would wish the Great Skellig not already occupied by so many feathered pests...but they're a useful reminder that there's no perfection to be found this side of heaven.

Artt takes out the iron bell and jangles it hard and fast now. He calls on Michael the Archangel, to whom all high places belong ever since he cast Lucifer's rebels into hell. 'By the power of Michael, I expel and banish any evil from this place!'

Silence, except for the odd yip from the birds.

This island's mine, Artt reassures himself. Meaning, his to hold in trust for his own Master. *'You bring them to your mountain, Lord, your own dwelling, the sanctuary made with your own hands.'* He rings the bell as he walks, drawing a musical line of blessing along every scaly rise and dip. *'His rule will be from sea to sea, and from the river to the ends of the earth.'*

At the south end of the island, where Artt finds he can go no farther, he kneels and kisses the ground. Its thin skin of green; its hard skeleton of stone. He shuts his eyes and quiets himself. Becomes as firm as rock. Begs to be as clear as crystal, so God's light can shine right through him. *Christus, Christus, Christus,* over and over more times than Artt can count, calling on his beloved.

When he emerges from his daze of prayer, he turns back, heading towards the green Saddle. One of those gigantic auks waddles straight across his path and stops, giving him a stupid, round-eyed stare.

Artt's reminded of a purifying rite from his childhood in honour of holy Martin—the blood-sprinkling. For lack of a cockerel, won't this creature do? Shaking off squeamishness, he walks up and takes the great auk by the neck, which is as thick and warm as a baby's arm. He says aloud, 'I dedicate this bird to sainted Martin and to our Lord Christ.' He gives one hard yank, hoping that will do it.

But the huge creature still struggles in his hands. Artt has to kneel on it. Pulling the knife from his belt, he lops off its head, and the thing is done. Having no bowl with him to catch the blood, he lets some spill into his left palm and asks Christ's blessing. He dabs a wet X on his own forehead with his right hand.

Carrying the heavy auk under his arm, Artt makes his way back to the camp on the Plateau, sprinkling the dark liquid to cleanse the land, the sea, the air.

Waking, Cormac's bewildered. Last night he was glad to stretch out on the ground after so long cramped in that wretched boat. But in his dreams he found himself crazed with vertigo, pursued up and down pinnacles by honking birds. His back's aching, this morning. He has salt in his mouth, the air's so strongly flavoured with it.

No sign of the Prior. There's Trian, back turned, hunkered down; a trickling sound. Cormac himself has to crouch to make water, these days—easier to get out the last dribbles that way—but he's never known a young man to do it that bashful, girlish way, and it makes him grin. 'Good morning, Brother.'

Trian straightens and pulls down his robe before turning to bow. 'Can you believe it, Brother? We're like the lords of the great ocean!'

For Cormac, the immensity of the sky seems to shrink them to the size of insects. 'I'm just relieved to be on dry land that's not wobbling about,' he tells Trian, searching for a pair of socks. He works them onto his feet, then ties on his shoes; the wool and leather should keep off the chill and soothe his aching toes.

A gull flies past so close, Cormac feels the waft on his face. He stumbles aside; laughs under his breath. He remembers sayings about birds being in-between creatures; maybe the souls of the dead, hovering above the land of the living for days or years before they'd drift west to what folk called *the other land*, or *the land of youth*, or *the land under the wave*? Since his conversion to Christ, Cormac knows all living things are simply part of God's creation, but birds still give him the odd shiver.

Breakfast. He pokes last night's embers and feeds the little flames with charcoal from the sack. He sets the three-legged griddle over the fire to heat up. In a bowl he grinds oats with a roundish stone till they're smooth enough to mix with a lump of butter, salt, and water, and form into a ball.

Cormac's head is crowded with practical concerns. The party is down to less than one full waterskin, so they really must start gouging out that crack in the rocks above to catch the next good rain. By the time the weather turns, they should also have put up some rough shelter, because getting soaked through is a recipe for illness. But their garden, shouldn't that come first? Every day they haven't put the seeds into the ground is a lost day of growing.

Cormac shoves the oatcakes around on the hissing iron with his finger. 'Such a fool I was to spill that wheat flour.'

'Ah, come,' Trian says, 'something must have torn the sack in the boat. And which of us makes no mistakes?'

'True, we're all cracked vessels. God must make the best use of us he can.' Cormac uses a wooden spoon to press together a crumbling oatcake. 'Now blessed Molua was so celebrated for his hospitality, God granted him a remarkable power.'

Trian always pricks up his ears at a story. 'What was it?'

'The saint could sow common grain—oats and barley—and have fine wheat spring up in its place.'

Trian laughs at that.

Cormac leaves the oatcakes to cook. He folds away the three cloaks. He takes the three long ticks and looks for something to fill them. There's fescue grass; he rips out handfuls. Cushions of thrift, too, its first pink tufts feathering, its grey-green blades sharp enough to cut any hands less leathery than his. He thinks he recognises a sprawling mass as spurrey; its hairy foliage leaves his fingers sticky. Sea campion, too—the small waxy oval leaves look rather softer for lying on.

As he forms the mattresses, Cormac fills a pouch with any greens that seem edible. Spinach-like goosefoot, even spoonwort with its heart-shaped leaves that make the eyes water with their mustardy pungency. Until he can grow a few potherbs, he must gather any healthful forage he finds.

'Brother Trian, do you know this succulent one?'

'Sea beet. That's good eating.' Trian drops to his knees and starts helping to sort food from bedding.

'You didn't take a chill yesterday, from going in the water?'

A shake of the head.

'Your uncles who drowned, God bless them. Had they not learned to float like you?'

Trian shakes his head. 'My people thought, if the waves were going to take you, better to die fast than slow. And they had a saying: *The sea must have its share.*'

'Its share of . . . people?'

'Right. If you saw someone struggling in the sea, you'd make a grab for him, how could you not? But you knew if you managed to haul him out, you'd owe the sea a life—yours.'

Cormac murmurs, 'What our Prior would call a heathen superstition.'

Trian's abashed. 'Of course it's God who decides, not the sea. My people were baptised, but they still held to some of the old ways.'

Who understands that better than Cormac? Even though he's been Christ's man for a decade and a half, those ways still flow in him like an underground stream.

It occurs to him that if Trian's family lived far off on the east coast, they can't have been serfs of the Abbot's clan. 'Your parents, I wonder why they made an offering of you at thirteen—was it in thanksgiving for an answered prayer?' Like Brother Ronán, a quarrelsome character; his parents gave him to Cluain Mhic Nóis at eight, Cormac remembers, and kept the other twin.

Trian shakes his head. 'Our priest spoke about the monastery on the great Sionan, and how it was famous for the teaching of the young.'

'Had you a longing for education?'

A shrug. 'My mother told me I was made for a monk.'

It doesn't sound to Cormac as if the boy balked at the prospect, though. Trian seems to have a natural talent for working, obeying, and doing without. 'And how did it—how did we seem to you, when you first came?'

Trian grasps for words. 'So many men, cheek by jowl.'

Cormac chuckles. 'The stink.'

'And the noise.'

He remembers finding that a shock, himself, when he woke up after the surgery with his astonishingly mended head. But he stayed anyway, out of gratitude, and embraced a second life. Cormac never imagined, all these years later, that he'd find himself beginning a third one, on a great rock in the ocean.

The three ticks are stuffed with foliage now. Misshapen, bulging oddly, but they'll do for sleeping on. Cormac unrolls the leather that holds the bronze needles, which are among their most irreplaceable tools. He chooses a small one, handling it with great care so as not to drop it. He cuts off a length of strong wool thread and sets to tacking up the ends of the bags to hold in their scented green.

Trian's head is up, his eyes on the skinny rowan that led them to water yesterday. Buds just on the verge of blooming. A small brown bird perches on one of her branches, then wings away.

Cormac thinks of the tree in the Scripture, a mighty cedar where birds of all kinds nest and find shelter—not like this puny bush. Still, rowan's known for warding off evil spirits. 'The hardiest of all trees.'

'Is she?'

'Some call rowan *the lady of the mountain*,' Cormac tells him, 'for her skill at rooting herself in the rockiest places.'

'I wonder how big this one will get, when full grown.'

'Oh, she's old already.'

Trian looks confused. 'But she's still only child-sized. *The quicken tree*, you called her, because of how fast—'

'They thrive in good soil, but this one's stinted and stunted. No, you can tell her great age by the bark.' Cormac puts his finger to the scaly, cracked black. 'It starts out smooth, with a tinge of yellow to the grey.'

Trian strokes the furrowed rowan.

'Trees were so precious in the eyes of holy Colm Cille, when he heard that to build his church facing east in the customary way would require cutting down a stand of ancient oak, he laid out the foundations facing north instead.'

Trian smiles and crosses himself. 'What an act of mercy, to spare those trees.'

Cormac spots the Prior coming towards them, bloodied on head and hands. Has he had a fall?

They jump to their feet and make their bows.

But the Prior's unhurt, and exhilarated. He drops a great dead bird on the turf and steps up close to mark Cormac's forehead, then Trian's, with its warm blood. 'The blessing of Christ on you.'

'Amen, Father.'

'Amen.'

The Prior takes the jar of soap and the goatskin of water, to wash his hands.

Cormac hopes their master doesn't use up too much of their drinking water, but doesn't dare say so.

Then the Prior rings the bell for Terce.

After the service, they share the browned oatcakes, and the Prior tells Cormac to put the great auk on to roast. 'Fat and flightless—could we have more plentiful or easy prey?'

The notion seems to make Trian uneasy. 'We shouldn't take more than we need, though, surely Father?'

The Prior looks at him, one eyebrow tilted. 'What else are they for?'

'I only mean...they were here long before us.'

He corrects Trian: 'Ready for our arrival. This whole island's like one great banquet table that God's spread for us.'

Trian's tongue-tied now.

'Didn't he give man *dominion over the fish of the sea and the birds of the air*?' the Prior quotes.

There's no arguing with that. Cormac offers a story, to ease the mood. 'I'm put in mind of a tale told of holy Columbán that's known as the Manna of Birds.'

The Prior nods.

'One winter, our blessed countryman's followers hadn't eaten for three long days, but he told them to fear nothing because God would surely feed them. And sure enough,' Cormac goes on, 'on the fourth day, the monks woke up to find an abundance of birds covering the ground, as white as snow.'

'Were they singing,' Trian asks, 'like the ones on the paradisical island you said holy Breandán discovered?'

Cormac shakes his head. 'Frozen, as if under a spell. Or rather, held by God's command, so they wouldn't startle and flee. Meekly those birds offered themselves up for the famished monks to wring their necks.'

'Of course, God offers us all the like abundance,' the Prior points out.

Cormac looks at the limp great auk. 'You mean...'

'The one nourishment that truly sustains? That feast that all may approach, without one man's share reducing what's left for his brethren?'

'Oh! Holy Scripture,' Trian guesses, before Cormac can say it.

When the Prior goes off to pray, Cormac wakes up the fire, putting on more charcoal. Since there's no timber or even peat here, before this sack runs out they'll have to sail in search of more. Well, leave that worry for another day.

He concentrates on plucking this bird. A great auk can't be so different from a goose or a hen, surely? He starts by yanking out the primary feathers—the tail ones he pulls directly, but for the wings he goes against the grain. He wishes he had shears to snip off the last joint of each wing, but the big knife will do. Anchoring the auk's legs in the grip of his right fist, with his left thumb and knuckles he grabs the breast feathers and rips them upwards, towards the missing head. He moves on to the smaller feathers farther down the belly and the undercoat of fine down. This grown bird's tough, and even though the body's still warm, the plucking proves such hard going that Cormac begins to think he should have skinned it instead, especially as a sea bird will have a rankly fishy skin. Ah well, he'll finish what he's begun. Legs, then wings, the hardest spots to pluck. The auk's naked skin is yellowish and looks coarse-woven; he has to dig into the armpits to tear out the little feathers. Finally, the back, where the feathers come out almost as easily as from the breast.

Trian's collecting them before they can drift away on the spring breeze. 'Separate out the down for trading, would you?' Cormac asks. Trian nods and opens a smaller bag for that.

Cormac feels around inside the auk's limp neck and digs out

the crop with its mess of undigested stuff: shells, bones, scales, and beaks. Two fingers in one end of the bird, he wrenches out a tangle of entrails; two fingers in the other, the rest. The little heart he snips off. It's a tidbit that some prefer raw, but that seems savage to Cormac. He spikes it on an iron skewer and sets it almost in the flames, so it begins to sear and juice at once. After a minute he holds it out to Trian.

The young man waves it away.

'Aren't you hungry?'

A half-smile. 'Sure I'm always hungry, Brother.'

'Go on, you're still growing. A bit of heart meat will do you good.'

Trian thanks him and takes it off the spit with his teeth, blowing to cool it; he swallows it in one gulp.

Cormac reaches for the knife again to hack off the auk's feet. He adds a very sparing slosh from the goatskin to rinse the bird through. He'd use salt water for that if he had it, and for washing hands and implements. 'Brother, could you ever haul us up some water from the sea?'

Trian grabs two of the buckets, and sets their straps over his shoulders. He heads off without a word.

Cormac pulls the leather stopper out of their big jar of salt and takes a gritty handful to rub over the carcass. He spears the great auk on two crossed iron skewers. Under the skin, the meat's a dark red. Cormac knows little of the arts of the kitchen, but he doubts the Prior would approve of fine cookery anyway. He sets the spitted bird across the stones to roast. He goes over to a patch of fescue and rubs his bloody, down-flecked palms on it.

The Prior comes back to the fire. 'I've never seen so many

birds,' he complains. 'Huddled in their thousands, or tens of thousands.'

'I suppose they must like the company,' Cormac says.

He puffs out his breath. 'Each jostling for his foul few inches of ground, more like. Like those stinking cities, on the Continent. I suppose you've little grasp of what a city's like, or even a town?'

'Only from books,' Cormac admits, feeling ignorant. He's pored over drawings of towers, amphitheatres, buildings tall and uncountable, all packed with people living like grubs in a log.

The Prior shudders. 'Charnel pits, I call them. Sin spreads there as fast as infection. The noise and filth I witnessed in Autricum, Cenabum... or poor ruinous Rome, where refugees drop down starving in the streets.'

Just then Trian staggers back into camp with both buckets half-full of seawater.

Cormac points along the Plateau. 'Father, I was thinking I might tackle a proper cistern to catch the rain for us, even before I start on the garden, or some kind of shelter—'

The Prior puts up his hand, silencing him. 'Does it not strike you that these are low concerns?'

Cormac's face heats.

Their master's tone is serene. 'Having landed on this holy island, should our first thoughts be for the body's wants?'

The rising aroma of the meat seems to mock him. He finds himself wishing Trian weren't there to hear him put to shame.

'Instead,' the Prior says, 'our very first task will be to claim this Skellig for Christ with a great cross.'

Cormac's carved high crosses before, of wood with metal ornaments, but that's impossible here. 'Incised on a boulder, you mean?'

The Prior shakes his head, his smile gleaming. 'Freestanding. A tall cross-slab chiselled out of the bedrock, so it can be seen from all directions.'

Seen by whom, Cormac wonders?

'Like a standard carried into battle, a banner to mark this as sacred ground.'

All he can say is, 'Right, Father.'

Soon the great auk's blackened, so Cormac takes it off the fire and sets it on a flat rock. He carves pieces off it, still bloody at the centre. He turns the third bucket over as a seat for their leader. He and Trian sit on the grass and wait for the Prior to bless the meat. Each man makes a cross over his own bowl and thanks God before he eats.

'Liverish?' the Prior wonders aloud.

'Beefy, more like,' Trian suggests. 'Or gamey, maybe.'

'A bit fishy, but not as much as I was expecting.' Whatever about the taste, it's rich, fresh meat; Cormac tries not to bolt his too eagerly.

When he's cleared his bowl he feels more solid; more able for whatever will be asked of him today.

'Come,' the Prior says.

Cormac and Trian follow him down the Plateau to where an outcropping more than the size of a man thrusts up, almost like a thick pillar.

The Prior touches an indentation on one side, at the top.

'See this piece of our cross, Brothers—already cut out, as if God's begun the work for us?'

Cormac nods, less certain. 'We should test the stone for soundness, first, I'd say.' He goes back to fetch the short-handled oak mallet, which is less likely to damage the rock than their iron hammer. He taps the pillar all over.

Trian asks, 'What are you listening for?'

'That ringing, like a bell. If there are fissures inside, they'll suck in the sound, deaden it.'

The Prior persists: 'But this pillar sounds right?'

Cormac nods. 'To be quite sure, though, we'll need water.'

Trian's already hurrying off to get one of the buckets.

Cormac trickles seawater all over the great rock, a drip at a time. He can detect no cracks. He runs his leathery hands over the grain, from top to bottom. 'The wet shows the bed lines, see?' He points out the pattern to Trian. 'Every rock's strongest along its bed. Where we cut across it, that's where we'll have to take most care.' Turning to the Prior: 'Is it a Greek or Latin cross you want, Father?'

'Latin, with a long leg, to suit such a tall slab.' The Prior picks up a shard from the ground and begins to scratch out his design on the rock: the pyramidal base, the giant cross rising from it. 'Sturdy enough to stand until the end of time.'

Cormac's relieved to see that a thick ring will connect the short arms and bear their weight; they'll need to protrude only a few inches past that.

'The circle symbolises the heavens, the celestial sphere,' the Prior declaims. 'The heavens turn, but the cross stands still.' He steps back and considers the pale lines. 'You can start blocking it out now, Brother Cormac.'

A few mornings later, in faint drizzle, Trian's fowling.

This island is one great festivity of birds—more of them every day, swooping in and scrambling across the rocks, which are increasingly whitened by a snowfall of creamy droppings. Each bird seeking out its kind, he supposes, longing to pair and breed little copies of themselves.

A funny thing he's noticed—once shearwaters land, they have to drag themselves across the rocks, because they can fly but not walk, which is the other way around from great auks. Maybe each creature's granted only the powers it needs to live? The Creator doles out talents at his pleasure, Trian supposes, and brooks no argument.

He remembers how his kinsmen used to go out roped together in pairs for some measure of safety. They pursued the birds all over the cliffs with their nets, or three men would dangle a fourth from an overhang so he could pick a whole basketful of eggs out of the nests. The most talented cragsmen scorned the ropes; they claimed to scrabble up and down cliffs better that way, knowing one misstep would be their last.

On the Great Skellig the hunt is so easy, it troubles Trian. He's already caught a kittiwake by holding the hand net under a ledge and knocking the bird in with his staff. And the bright-faced puffins, in their burrows, like juicy turnips waiting in the ground. He chooses a dark hole now and inserts his left hand, all the way to his armpit. Nothing but the smooth blockage of an egg. In the next, a peck at his finger; Trian pulls back, to check he's not bleeding, then goes in again fast, winding his wrist around a corner, and at the very back lays hold of a puffin on its egg. He pulls out the bird, calms it by stroking, and says a quick thanks to God before he twists its vivid head.

With his knife he cuts a slit right through the puffin's limp neck and pushes its head under his belt and through its own neck gash, pulling it into a knot.

Should he leave that egg in case the other parent comes back to sit on it? It seems unlikely; he's only ever seen a pair manage to raise young. (Not like the she-cats at the monastery, who rear their litters alone.) Trian decides he'd better take the egg, so it won't be wasted. Pure white, and oddly big for such a neat little bird. He holds it up to the morning sun; no sign of anything growing yet, only a little spot darkening the oval. He places it at the bottom of the cloth bag tied to his belt. An egg and two birds—that seems more than enough to feed three monks for a day.

Another puffin walks past Trian, toting a feather the size of itself into its burrow. He's struck by how industrious they are. Another picks up a little dried root of some plant and scratches its underbelly with it. This impresses him, that a bird can make something into a tool. Trian's learning to distinguish a neutral greeting from an alarm call, from a boast to attract a mate. Now a cormorant flies by low with its neck stuck out, a long ribbon of seaweed in its beak. All these different birds, on the same mission of nest-building, and with such energy and inventiveness.

Time slides away from Trian, here on the cliffs. The cross-winds flare his rain-damp robe and he finds himself wondering what it would feel like to be equally at home on land, in water, and in air. To be powered by the breeze, wheeling and soaring, free from the weight that keeps other creatures shackled to the earth. Could a man make a cloak of feathers that might bear him up, gliding over the sea?

When Trian gets back to the camp up on the Plateau, he takes the birds off his belt and sets them by the fire with the egg. He follows a clinking to where Cormac's toiling on the stone cross. Its right arm is already emerging from its shielding ring, as if the shape's always been hidden inside, ever since God first formed the rock.

'Your carving goes well, Brother.'

'So far.' Cormac wipes his rain-slick forehead on his grey-fuzzed arm. 'Well, as the saying has it, work as if all depends on you, but pray as if all depends on God.'

'Amen.'

'Maybe it's time you learned to cut stone. Come here.'

Taken aback, Trian goes to stand at Cormac's side.

'Always carve towards the centre of the rock. The edges are thinner and can sometimes break off without warning.'

Trian flinches at the idea.

'First we rough out the shape with the mallet and the pitcher'—Cormac shows a flat-ended tool in his left hand. 'I hold this pitcher halfway down its length, and tuck my thumb into my fingers so I won't hammer it with the mallet. Though you being the way you are, I suppose you might wield the mallet with your left, for more force?'

'If that's allowed,' Trian says uncomfortably. 'My two hands are about the same in strength—it's just that the right isn't as nimble.'

Cormac sets the tip of the pitcher tool to the spot on the cross's arm where he's been working. 'Keep the tool coming in low, nearer to flat than upright.' He hits it with his cylindrical mallet, and the stone chips. He moves on half an inch and does it again. 'If your tip gets stuck, it means you're digging in too steeply. And don't strike the stone head-on, or you'll leave a shiny bruise, and nothing can rub that out.'

Trian's trying to commit these warnings to memory.

'Nor too shallow either, or your blade will skip right off. If you find yourself sliding about on the surface, go deeper.' Cormac cuts on, every move clean. 'Now, keep your tip pressed to the stone all the time, no jiggling about.'

'Right.'

'Here's the rule: *pitch, punch, claw, chisel*,' Cormac tells him in a singsong voice. 'After you've roughed it out with the pitch, you'll need the punch—the pointed one—for clearing away all the leftover stone, but don't get carried away and take too much.'

Trian fears he's muddling up the various tools already.

'The claw is this toothed one,' Cormac says, 'it'll level the surface nicely. The last is the chisel, with a narrow flat end, for the fine details.'

He's finding it hard to imagine he could ever do such subtle stonework.

'What's the rule?'

'*Pitch, punch, claw, chisel*,' he repeats back. 'Let me try? I pick things up better in the doing.'

Cormac hands over the tools. 'Get above it, and carve down—that way you'll have more force.'

'Like in battle, bringing a spear or sword or axe down on an enemy?'

A shrug. 'Fighting goes by in such a blur, it's hard to recall.' He pats Trian's right hand on the mallet handle: 'That's a fierce grip. Looser, looser. You'll be keeping this up hour after hour, so if anything's a strain it'll wear you out in no time.'

Clutching the punch, Trian chips the stone away.

'Oh, and guard your eyes from motes and specks, they could blind you,' Cormac warns. 'Veil your eyes with your lashes.'

Trian nods, half-shutting his lids, and hammers again.

Cormac stares at the tiny puddle on which their hopes rest. Now that Trian's taking a turn on the cross, at last the Prior has given Cormac permission to dig out a cistern.

He's already pried up three boulders with the crowbar to find the precious rainwater, which fills a depression only the size of his palm. A bullaun, that's what such a hollow's called. When Cormac was young, you'd drop a pebble into the puddle in a bullaun stone and turn it rightwards first thing in the morning to work a cure, or leftwards for a curse. Now he makes a cross in the air with his thumb and first two fingers, blessing the water in the name of the Father, Son, and Holy Spirit.

He starts with the wide punch and a rounded rock the size of his fist, since he's left Trian the lump hammer for carving. Cormac gouges delicately, widening the rut; when the water's thick with stone chips he pauses to rake them out with his fingers. If in a careless moment he cracks this strong base, the liquid will trickle away into the hill, and they'll have to resort to setting out bowls to catch the rain.

But the hollow grows, little by little, and Cormac's mind leaps ahead. He'll make the basin as deep as his forearm, with small scoops out of its base to catch any sediment that settles. Then he'll start cutting shallow channels down the rock wall above, to feed the cistern. The whole bare scarp, he could cover with grooves like a spiderweb. No, more like silver snail tracks, many trickles joining in a thick flow.

And if the cistern works so well that it fills up in heavy rainfall and brims over? Cormac will make a notch in the side, and hollow out another basin underneath to catch the overflow. What's more, he can raise and reinforce their sides with thin slabs of slate. His arms are throbbing now, but he works all the faster. He repeats the Scripture in his head for encouragement: *So lift your tired hands, and straighten your shaking knees.*

When the bell for Sext summons Cormac back to the fire, Trian already has a great auk sizzling. He shows what he uses to noose them: a loop of string stiffened with beeswax and tied to the end of his staff. 'Though it hardly seems fair,' he says under his breath, 'when they can't fly away.'

Cormac nods ruefully. 'Every kind of creature needs to eat, I suppose, and we're no different.' He hurries to grind some meal, to make oatcakes on the griddle.

The Prior comes up, ringing the bell for silence. The monks stop what they're doing and stand to recite the holy hour.

As Cormac joins in the psalms, his mouth is watering like a cavern behind a waterfall. He'd forgotten how fierce a hunger a man can get from hefting stones. At Cluain Mhic Nóis, he had a hand in many tasks, but there were always younger men to do the heavy lifting. Cormac hasn't felt so tired, or so needed, in long years.

After their prayers, he takes the charred oatcakes off the griddle. He watches Trian poke the auk's blackened breast. The juice runs clear at last, so Trian wraps a cloth around his hand to yank the bird out of the fire.

At last, the day's come. Artt's stone cross stands as tall as him, and beautiful.

His followers are blistered and sore. They've stood for hours on upside-down buckets to shape the top arm where it pushes up from the ring like the branch of a petrified tree. They've bevelled the edges with the claw tool. They've scrubbed the droppings off every time a bird dares to dirty it.

The rock faces are still nibbled, but Artt's decided that is as it should be. 'There's nothing smooth about this Great Skellig,' he muses aloud, 'so it should be a rugged cross, to command a rugged place. No, there's only one spot that needs a touch more work.' He sets a chisel to a darker lump that blurs the lovely line, where the ring meets the protruding right arm.

Cormac grimaces. 'There seemed a weakness in the stone there, Father, so I was afraid to go any deeper.'

'Oh, it only needs a stroke or two.' Artt taps once with the mallet—

He doesn't hear a crack, or see it grow, but the whole arm of the cross drops away.

Artt recoils. The white-dusty wound; the lump on the grass, like any fallen rock. He thuds to his knees and the tools drop from his hands. 'God forgive me!'

Trian crosses himself and mutters a prayer to avert evil.

Cormac speaks hoarsely. 'Not your fault, Father. Pure accident.'

'There are no accidents.' Inadvertence, inattention. Worse: the reckless arrogance of a priest who insists on going one better than his simple monk brethren; the devilish pride of a man fonder of his own judgement than God's.

Artt's mind races. If he could cement the piece back on...but how can he make mortar with no slaked lime, with no sand even? No, his awful blunder can't be fixed.

He reaches out and hefts the fallen arm; fingers the jagged point where it fractured. He could bring that down on his own fist right this minute; he longs for the blow. But which hand is the sinful one—the left, which set the blade to the weak point despite the old monk's warning, or the right, which must have landed the mallet too hard? Artt should smash both his hands, and his eyes for misjudging, and his ears for not listening, and his brain for its willfulness—

No. He reins in his rage. Founding this monastery is going to take all three of them, and all their limbs, and all their powers. Even with all their weaknesses.

'Father?' Trian whispers.

Artt finds he can't speak yet. He gets up and stumbles away.

What penance should he set himself to make satisfaction? He could roll in nettles, except that he's seen none here. Lie in cross-vigil? No, stand—that's harder. Or kneel—that's even better punishment. Artt crashes down, in the middle of the Plateau, and holds his arms straight out from his sides, the position of Jesus on the cross. He starts his prayers of contrition. He waits for discomfort to ripen into pain.

The man who masters himself rules a mighty kingdom. Pain is one way to do it. Those who love Christ, he grants permission to suffer for his sake. Pain's a privilege, a gift, a grace. The more Artt's knees hurt, the more he'll be atoning for his sin—albeit never quite enough, because every wrongdoing leaves a faint mark. Isn't every child born bearing the smudge of Eve's sin of eating the fruit the serpent offered, and Adam's sin of letting her persuade him—that deep-dyed human tendency to stray from the loving Father?

Sever me not from your sweetness, Artt begs.

He straightens his aching back and stretches out his arms. Remembers Moses, who was already eighty years old when God called him. During the battle against the Amalekites, didn't Moses hold up his hands to encourage the Israelites? When his strength began to fail and his hands sank down, the fight started going against God's people. So Moses asked his elder brother Aaron to hold up one of his arms, and their companion Hur to support the other. With his comrades' help, his hands stayed high till sunset, when the Israelites triumphed. Artt clings to the image of those three men, bearing each other up. So few, but indomitable.

A puffin walks right up to him now, motley-coloured, like some jester jeering. Artt squeezes his eyes shut. Holy Cóemgen, who lived in a glen in a hollow tree, knelt in cross-vigil for so long, one time, that a crow made a nest in his hand. The saint didn't move a muscle all the time the bird was laying her eggs and brooding on them; didn't let his arms down while the chicks were breaking out and cheeping to be fed; never moved from his penitential posture all those long weeks until the fledglings flew away.

Artt will be as strong as Cóemgen. He chants, emptying himself out so he can be filled with God: *Sanctus, sanctus, sanctus, sanctus, sanctus.* Truly hurting now. He opens a door to the pain. Penance is balm to the soul; it releases sorrow,

119

softens the hardest heart. God teaches by tears, and he wounds only to heal.

The next time Artt feels his hands failing a little, he imagines himself held up by a long nail hammered through each palm. He recites fiercely: *I am crucified with Christ.* He tries to be the man on the cross—not Jesus, but one of the lowly thieves by his sides, the penitent one.

Artt will stay in cross-vigil all afternoon, all evening if he can, until the sky's quite black. God is all he strives for, all he thinks about, his very breath. He'd like to level the botched high cross, first thing tomorrow, but he won't. Let it stand as a warning to himself and his monks, a sign of their imperfection, the crippling weight of it. That's the lesson stone teaches: even after it falls, it endures.

SEEDTIME

THE HEIGHTS ARE mysterious with cloud, today, and Trian can't see a thing. Fog makes an island of every man. Trian can find his brethren only by calling out, as he picks his way around the Plateau, and he has to restrain his usual lope so he won't fall. He pops his neck muscles in loud frustration; he prays; he waits.

Then a breeze clears away the wreaths of white, and the Great Skellig dazzles like an emerald.

The Prior asks Trian to catch them some fish.

So it must be the weekly fast, the day Christ was put to death. (Trian's lost count. Time runs differently here; sometimes when he hears the iron bell, he's bewildered, because it seems only minutes since the three gathered for the last service.)

What he doesn't mention to the Prior is that he's far from sure how to fish here. He remembers his father and uncles rowing in to their coastal farmstead with nets full of shining catch, but the monks' boat is upended on dry rock below, in Landing Cove. He knows better than to suggest putting her to sea again to catch fish in quantity; the Prior would call that greed. Instead, Trian will have to cast a line from the rocks. But where to begin?

He knows he'll need juicy bait, anyway. So he climbs down the cliff, carrying the fishing gear. The tide's going out; it looks like a massacre. It's only gaudy red kelp fringing the rocks. Small pools hold opaque spills of white, lumps of startling green that wave in the water like hair, and little air sacs of bladder wrack. Smears of foam are drying out already, and the seaweed's begun to decay in clumps and twists, tiny flies leaping and biting.

He leaves his shoes near the upturned boat, above the tide line, and scrambles over giant boulders across the strip of cove that gets wetted and dried twice a day. This is a good time to harvest shore food, he realises; any shellfish still clinging to the rocks should be healthy, now the weak or dead have been washed away.

Looking for limpets, Trian finds dozens of the oval cones with their blue rays and pearly sheen. Approaching quietly, he slides his knife tip under one to prise it off its rock. Such strength for a little thing! It gives in at last, revealing its snail-horns and puckered gripper, as round as a baby's mouth. It comes back to Trian that you can knock a limpet off its perch if you hit it sideways, so he tries that on the next few. It works only when he surprises the creature; if the first blow doesn't do the trick, the limpet takes fright and clings twice as hard. He supposes it's a sign of life if it resists being seized. Like a mussel, which claps its two shells together when it feels a hand.

His bag's starting to fill. Would the Prior consider it a sin to eat between meals? Distracted by hunger, Trian decides to allow himself one limpet. He makes a cross over it and pulls off the head and guts before he bites the meat off the shell. Deliciously salty and chewy, though he has to spit out the grit.

When he opens the next it smells wrong, and he's about to throw it aside before he remembers that fish find the tang of decay irresistible. He unrolls the fishing gear and takes out a short line—no more than three times as long as he is tall—with tiny iron hooks knotted on at intervals. He scrapes and yanks the rank limpet out of its shell and pushes it onto the first hook. He baits the next, and the next.

He finds himself wondering what makes it permissible to eat fish on a fast-day. Is it because fish are less like men than pigs or cows are, so less likely to rouse the baser appetites? Trian's never understood why, in the Garden, at first Adam and Eve ate only fruits and nuts, but after the Flood God told his people, *Everything that lives and moves will be meat for you.* Well, the important thing's not to grasp the rule but to obey it.

He's hoping for bream, today, maybe, or pollock. Wrasse? Whiting or scad, even? Unless the fish on this coast are quite other than the ones of his childhood. When he's loaded all his hooks with bait, he scans the water. There's a good rock out there, though its furry green patches look slippery. Trian wades out and clambers on, finding a spot where his toes can get purchase. The sea's calm enough that a rogue breaker is unlikely to roll in. He ties a pebble onto the bottom of the barbed line to weight it; he whirls and casts it out, well away from him. He loops the end around his left hand and waits.

Trian perches there for what feels like hours, watching the tide shrink away from the foreshore. The sea stacks seem to be rising, and his own little pedestal too, like a hill budding out of the sea, but that must be an illusion. He shifts his weight from left to right and back again, over and over, like dancing. He whistles a tune under his breath. He misses his bone pipe, the one he carved with the guidance of Brother Blathmac. That's something Trian did love at the monastery: making music at dinnertime. Here on the Great Skellig, when the birds sing out their different calls, Trian would like to be able to answer them with human tunes.

No flicker on the line yet, no feel of anything alive at the other end, only the gentle fluctuations of the sea. The fish aren't there, or they're sleeping, or not hungry enough to bite. The water's too low; it must be slack tide now, the hour before the turn, when nothing's moving. Is it too bright for fish at this time of day, the water too riddled with light, despite the gauze of clouds? The air's sprinkled with gliding birds; puffins land on the water with a splash or an undignified roll. Divers occasionally duck under and come up with fat fish, effortlessly, as if taunting Trian.

A light shower of rain begins. His stomach creaks; he's tempted to pull another limpet off a hook and eat it, but what if that's the one bit of bait that might catch their noon meal? And he doesn't know which is the graver offence: to miss Sext because he doesn't hear the bell down here, or to get back on time but empty-handed.

Cormac hurries to help the Prior cover the baggage. They push the stuff most vulnerable to wet (the chest of books and writing supplies, the sacks of oats and charcoal) into the middle of the pile, then drape it with the two sails and fasten down the edges with rocks.

As the rain thickens, he's excited at the thought of his cistern being put to the test. It's drizzled on other days, but this is the first heavy shower since he's had the cistern dug out. He hopes the elaborate grooves he's carved will direct the little runnels down the rocks and into the pair of basins. Foolishly, he finds he can't bear to go and check.

Without a word, the Prior withdraws to the edge of the Plateau, head down over clasped hands. Cormac marvels at the man's ability to immerse his mind in silent meditation for hours on end; he himself finds manual work more prayerful.

Cormac is tempted to find somewhere to shelter, but if their leader won't hide away from the rain, nor will Cormac. It's high time he broke ground on their garden, he decides.

The turf is slick. No matter where he tries it by prodding, it's no more than a fingernail deep, a thin green cape thrown over bedrock. At least there are plenty of stones lying around. Hood up to keep the water out of his eyes, he starts by gathering a great pile on the south-facing part of the Plateau. He lays them out in lines: the small, the middling sized, the large. He'll stack them three courses high, to make an oval enclosure around his plot; not a proper drystone wall, only a rough rim to shield the seedlings from being scoured away by the wind, and to catch and hold the sun when it shines.

First Cormac pulls out the ground cover. Quantities of spurrey, great hummocks of thrift so dense at the base he has to fetch the hatchet to hack through. He can't remember which severe saint it was who wouldn't let his followers use any tools to clear the fields. What Cormac wouldn't give now for the sharp billhook they left at Cluain Mhic Nóis! *Never contented,* he teases himself. No matter what the monks brought with them, even in a boat twice the size, he supposes there'd always be some so-called necessity he'd find himself hankering for.

A low mat of stonecrop. Under its multitude of fleshy leaves, its wiry stems grip the wet ground so hard that when Cormac tugs it out, he bares a patch of bedrock. He shakes and rubs each clump to make it cede its crumbs of soil. He takes the tiny leather pouches out of the herb box. He hasn't opened them till now; hasn't wanted to risk it. He hunches over to keep his shoulders between the seeds and the rain.

If only he had an iron trowel, or even a bone one. And a dibber—Cormac thought he could make do with a sharpened stick, and never imagined he'd be somewhere there are none. He supposes he could break a twig off the solitary rowan, but he hates to do any harm to the only tree on the island, and such a thin old one. He wipes water off his nose, and tells himself to stop griping.

Cormac begins with the onion sets—orange scaly bulbs from last season, dried and saved—which should be much quicker to grow than seeds. He uses his index finger to dib each hole a handspan apart; it should be a full inch down, but the dirt's barely half that. He drops the onion sets in, one by one, and paws up the soil to cover their brightness, though only barely. The gardener monks at Cluain Mhic Nóis would shake their heads to see him grubbing around in such inhospitable dirt, like a small child at play.

The rain's stopped, he registers.

Next he puts down sorrel seeds, and the smooth brown pods of fat hen. That's all he can chance, this early in the spring. He fears he may be throwing the precious specks away. Never in his life has he sown in such a poor skin of earth.

Whatever about potherbs, this scanty soil will never be able to grow grains. The monks will have to barter for those, offering the mainlanders—what, down? Bird meat? This little monastery will also need more charcoal, candles, wine, salt, soap, butter...How will they ever be able to afford it all?

That's the Prior's concern, Cormac reminds himself. He kneels outside his oval garden and starts setting the enclosure's first course of stones. This patch, stripped bare, harrowed and rock-ringed—it's hard to believe it'll bring forth anything to feed three men.

Next time Cormac looks up, to stretch his neck, Trian's ginger head has appeared against the grey sky. Then the rest of him, as he comes up onto the Plateau; what a long-legged, spindly bird.

Cormac straightens up, brushes down his wet robe, and goes over. Trian has a heavy bag dangling from his belt. Feet wrinkled from the sea, he wipes wet strands of red out of his eyes. 'I see you covered the dry goods, Brother.'

Cormac nods.

'If we hung the sails from that overhang over there, could we maybe make a bit more of a shelter?'

He looks where Trian's pointing. 'There's a notion.'

Trian drapes the wet leather squares from the rock, while Cormac finds four heavy boulders to pin down the top edges. Now they move the baggage behind the hide curtains. 'Room to spare,' Cormac says with satisfaction.

Trian comes over to examine Cormac's plot. 'I thought it would be a bit bigger.'

'Better to do less this first season, but do it well, than take on too much and fail,' Cormac tells him. 'Do you know the story of holy Brigit's cloak?'

Those pale blue eyes light up. 'I forget how it goes.'

'Well, the holy woman had a vision telling her to found a convent, so she called on Christ to convince the King of Leinster to give her land for it. When that bad lord refused, Christ put it into Brigit's mind to ask for just a tiny patch, then, only as much as her cloak would cover. That made the King laugh and say yes. So clever Brigit put the corners of her cloak into the hands of four of her nuns.' Cormac spreads his arms. 'One ran to the east and one to the west, one to the south and one to the north...and her cloak stretched and stretched, till it covered a fine estate of land, and that's where the holy women built their convent.'

Trian laughs. 'Could our little garden grow in all directions like that?'

'God willing. Now, what have you caught for us today, Brother?'

He empties out his bag by the steaming, hissing remains of their fire. 'I had a wrasse twice the size of this one, but it dived and ripped the hook right off the line.'

Amid the scattered limpets and mussels, Cormac recognises the wrasse's long fin, its scales shimmering between green and orange. And a ray beside it: bat-winged, diamond-shaped, with its gasping mouth on the upturned underside. As for the third—'What's this huge flat-faced fellow?'

'A sea devil, we used to call it, or a frogfish. There's good eating in that thick tail,' Trian assures him.

Brown, warty; the jaws are agape. 'Is that seaweed stuck to its head?'

'No, bits of the fish itself.' He lifts one of the fringed filaments to show him.

Suddenly the Prior's behind them. 'Throw back the shellfish.

We're told in the Book of Leviticus that every water creature without scales and fins is unclean.'

Cormac frowns. He's come across that passage in the Old Testament, but never thought it a rule; river mussels were often served at Cluan Mhic Nóis.

The Prior flicks his finger disgustedly. 'The ray too, and the devil.'

Trian's jaw drops. 'They're fish, though.'

'But the flesh of these kinds is well known for stirring up lust.'

'I never heard that,' Cormac remarks, so Trian will feel less foolish.

A hard gaze, turned on Cormac. 'Are you contradicting me?'

'Not at all, Father! I only meant—there's so much you know that I don't, for all my years.'

The Prior nods, mollified. 'Well, inquiry is the beginning of knowledge.'

'Pardon my ignorance.' Trian snatches up the sea devil and the ray by their tails, and starts scooping the shellfish back into his bag. 'I'll get rid of the dirty creatures.'

Cormac puts his hand out. 'I wonder could I cut up the fish for planting?'

'Planting?' the Prior asks.

'I've heard of sowing seeds with the heads, to nourish poor soil.'

A shrug, which Cormac takes as permission.

As Trian starts scaling the lone wrasse for their meal, Cormac picks up the spurned ray and sea devil. He hacks them into bits on a rock. He tries to find each spot where he buried a seed; he fingers the earth open, and pushes in a chunk.

When Trian slits the wrasse's belly, a whole fish slithers out, smooth and unchewed. Cormac jokes: 'Jonah, returned!'

Trian grins. 'A sprat. We'll roast that too.' He rubs the backs of his hands as if they irritate him. 'Extraordinary little things, scales.'

'Are they?'

The young man comes over and puts a palm right up to Cormac's face. The tiny discs speckling his skin are transparent but dabbed with silver. 'Soft and thin, but they form a coat so strong a knife can barely cut it.'

'Brother, what else do you think you could find me to dress my beds—to cover the seeds against the first stiff wind, then rot down fast?' Like a shivering patient who can't get warm, Cormac thinks; you pile on the blankets and spoon broth into his mouth.

'How about...bird droppings? That's the most plentiful stuff here.'

He makes a face. 'Too harsh. The smell of it makes you blink, so it'd scorch the seedlings.'

'Seaweed, then?'

'Too salty, surely.'

'It'd just need a wash. If I spread some out,' Trian suggests, 'and we wait till it's been rained on a few times...Maybe green from the tide pools, and brown thongweed? Maidenhair, that'd shrivel down fast for you.'

'That sounds good.'

'My folk made soil out of nothing but seaweed and sand and time.'

Yes, a midden, that's what Cormac really needs, with its promise of richer earth for next year, at least.

He's chilled from standing still in these rain-soaked clothes; best to get moving again.

Just outside the low garden enclosure he chooses a midden site. He wishes he had some brown gold—cow dung—to get it started. Instead he undoes his braies, lifts his robe, and squats down. *Lord, thank you for all the food you grant us. May our dirt carry some of its goodness back into this earth.*

To his brown pile Cormac adds the ground cover he ripped out earlier, spade-chopped. In the creel he carries over all the stinking scraps from their meals so far: birds' wings raw or cooked, bones, heads, feet, stray feathers, and eggshell. The sea may nibble away at the land, he thinks, but she feeds it too.

Now, what can Cormac add? He fetches a spadeful of wet wood ash from beside the fire. The mix could do with some grit as well. He goes to collect some fine stone dust, scraped up from around the base of the high cross. (*The poor cross,* he calls it privately, ever since it lost its arm.) He mixes it all together so the light stuff won't blow away. This should rot down together into good earth, given enough time.

Time, that's the thing. The old are meant to be more patient than the young, but sometimes those who've lived as long as Cormac sense the sand in the hourglass running out.

Trian has the wrasse cooking aromatically on skewers. Cormac goes over to the fire and points out his midden in the distance. 'Throw the fish guts on there, right? And the skins, after we've eaten. And whenever we make water or move our bowels, it should be on the midden, if we're close enough to get to it. Our hair-clippings, even.'

That amuses Trian. 'The parings of our nails, too?'

Cormac nods. 'Everything that was once alive has a bit of goodness left to give back.'

'The rain's filled your cistern nicely,' Trian mentions.

He'd forgotten his cistern. So it worked; they won't go thirsty.

'I set a pot for washing beside it, with a dish of soap.'

They can even clean their hands whenever they want. Cormac straightens up as if he's done some deed that will go down in the annals.

Next morning, the spring light blinds Trian as he stands chewing a rubbery tangle of dillisk from the seaweed he's hauled up the cliff for Cormac. He's considering the sails hanging from the rock over their most valuable goods; is there a way he can weigh them down with stones at the bottom so they won't flap?

'Brother Trian.' The Prior's at his side.

Trian swallows the seaweed, choking a little.

The Prior brushes the sail aside and digs their holy chest out of the pile. It looks unmarked. 'Today we begin the sacred task of copying.'

Trian blinks. 'Already? I mean—before we've built our monastery?' Surely they'll need a dedicated hut to work on the precious manuscripts?

The Prior's gesture takes in the whole sweep of crags and sky. 'This is our monastery, composed not of stone buildings but of our little family, our faith, and our works. And what could be more urgent than copying the Bible?'

Trian makes himself nod.

'Every day now the light lasts a little longer, which is a clear sign we should be using it for its highest purpose. Time to up and wage war on the devil with pen and ink, Brother.' The Prior lifts a thick leather pouch out of the chest. He takes out the Psalter and kisses its wooden covers before he opens it. 'This book here is a great sword of the spirit. Do you know its lineage?'

Unsure what that word means, Trian shakes his head.

The Prior touches one fingertip to the black markings on the first page, the elaborate initial capital letter of the psalm. 'Since God guided my hand, I think it no boast to say that my lettering was well done here. I was the humble midwife only—every codex is the child of the mother manuscript from which it's copied, as calf to cow.' He goes on, reminiscent: 'The one from which I took this was itself written out long before my time, in a Coptic refuge at an oasis in the desert mountains of the Red Sea.'

Trian's thrown by the image of desert mountains. Made of sand? 'You said—*oasis*?'

'A life-giving spot in the wilderness, where God reveals an unexpected well.'

'Like this Great Skellig, then?'

'Only much hotter and drier,' the Prior tells him. 'The Egyptian psalter I speak of was the calf of a codex made long before, in Constantinople, known then as Byzantium. The Byzantine book was smuggled into the desert by Melchite monks fleeing the persecutions of the Persians.' He smooths the Psalter tenderly. 'The text of all these copies is holy Jerome's own revision of the Latin version of the Septuagint, which he corrected against the original Hebrew.'

Their master speaks as if of absent, beloved kin. For himself, Trian wishes he was still down on the shore, fishing.

The Prior fingers the page, making a rasping sound on the vellum. 'And now this calf, grown to a cow, will bear her own calf, on this lofty island, and so the light of Christendom spreads in glory.'

Trian says shortly, 'God be with the work.'

The Prior's eyes glitter. 'I'll take charge of the Old Testament, as you know no Greek, Brother, but you'll copy this Psalter.'

Trian is shocked; he thought he'd only be assisting. He clears his throat with a ragged gulp. 'You're the famed scribe, Father. I can prepare parchments, and ink, and pens, but—'

'The two of us will write side by side, but each on a different book.'

He shakes his head hard.

'Come, false modesty is no virtue. I know they trained you well at Cluain Mhic Nóis.'

'But I've no particular talent.'

'Then you must improve.' Steel in the Prior's voice.

'Father, for all the care I take...you know my hindrance.' Trian holds up his left hand, which is trembling. 'My own fingers obscure the letters they've just written, and cast a shadow over the one they're forming next.'

The Prior nods. 'Just as our sins overshadow our lives.'

Parables are no use to Trian right now. 'Also the side of my hand sometimes blots or smears the ink. I have to push the nib ahead of me rather than pulling it, which can make it trip or fray.'

'Many a scribe has struggled with your burden, or others. What matters is purity of heart.'

Trian gnaws his lip.

The Prior says, 'Go find us something to use as a desk.'

Trian manages to nod before he stumbles away.

Roaming the Plateau, he remembers his first teacher, the withered, unsmiling Brother Óengus. The scribe handed Trian a stone the size of a loaf with the Roman alphabet chiselled on it, and ordered him to carry it everywhere. Trian found this humiliating, like the millstone in the Gospel that's hung around the neck of the sinner to drown him. But gradually he became fond of that incised boulder. Having nothing else of his own at the monastery, he guarded it like a lamb from the wolves. Trian used to finger those letters at idle moments, and their shapes cut deeply into his mind. His teacher set him to practise forming them on wax tablets and slates. He made a straggly mess with his right hand for long months before Brother Óengus accepted defeat and let him use his left.

His teacher died of a cough that winter. In spring, when a little boy came to the monastery—Ronán by name—Trian was told to pass on the alphabet stone to him. He cried for it in secret, or maybe for Brother Óengus.

Right now he tries to keep his mind on one worry at a time, the desk rather than the book. He and the Prior will need a spot near enough to their camp that they won't waste most of the day coming and going. (And what if they're carrying the books up or down one of the steep slopes, and drop one like the Prior dropped half their crocks on the day they landed? What if its irreplaceable pages were to be scattered or lost?)

Trian searches everywhere for a rock surface smooth enough that it won't pock the vellum. Ideally it should slant towards the scribe, too, so the nib can meet the page at a right angle. After a quarter of an hour, he finds one outcropping that's almost flat enough to write on, but far too low; he tries to fit his legs under it first by kneeling on his heels, then by sitting cross-legged in the Eastern style, but either way the stone scores and grinds his thighs through his robe. He could dig out a hollow underneath, maybe...except that under the grassy tufts of fescue, his fingers meet hard rock.

Trian spots Cormac adding another course of stones to the oval around his garden, and goes over. 'What've you planted lately, Brother?'

'Now the days are warming a little, I've put in two long rows of turnip seeds'—Cormac points them out—'and nettle and spinach will be next.'

'I miss parsnips.'

'Ah, yes,' Cormac says with a laugh. 'What else?'

'Curds,' Trian murmurs. 'Blood sausage.'

'Beef. Fresh butter!'

The butter they have left is getting rancid. 'The Sunday gruel,' Trian says, 'all milky, with nuts and berries and honey.'

Cormac chuckles. 'I liked getting a clean pair of socks every week. And my lyre, of course.'

'Yes!' A pang in Trian's chest. 'My swan-bone pipe.'

'Ah, we're still allowed to play the five-stringed harp, though.'

He's at a loss.

'You never heard of that harp? What you hear, see, smell, taste, and feel.' Cormac touches his ears, eyes, nose, and lips, then wriggles his leathery fingertips. 'Though I must admit, a couple of my strings are frayed,' he adds ruefully. 'I barely noticed at the monastery, but my far sight's failing.'

Trian comforts him: 'You seem to see what's in front of you well enough.'

Cormac nods. 'My weak eyes keep my attention trained on the matter in hand, I suppose. *Age quod agis,* as they say— concentrate on the task!'

Which reminds Trian that he's supposed to be finding a desk.

He wanders farther up, towards the North Peak where there's a horizontal slab he remembers. But no, it turns out to slope away instead of towards him. He examines another, which proves too small to fit the exemplars, the copies, and all the supplies the two scribes will need. Yet another is huge but very uneven.

Finally Trian's eye lights on a slate surface that's smooth... except it's too high, sticking directly out of an outcropping at the level of his ribs and sloping ever so slightly towards him. The scriptorium hut at Cluain Mhic Nóis was furnished with a long-backed chair with rungs for the feet; here Trian and the Prior would need very high stools, and all they have are upturned buckets. Or they could always stand, he supposes.

Trian goes in search of his master and finds him deep in prayer, the Old Testament in his lap. He waits until the Prior looks up, then asks his question.

'Why would there be a rule against standing up?' the Prior demands.

'I just thought... it isn't the usual way.'

'We've left behind all the usual ways. No doubt our legs will ache,' the Prior adds with a smile, 'but we'll offer that up to our Lord.'

Now that they have a makeshift stone desk, Artt decides they will begin the sacred copying tomorrow.

He can't hold a candle to a legendary scribe such as Colm Cille, credited with some three hundred codices, but Artt has copied more than a score. He thinks of his manuscripts as his children, the only trace of him that will be left on earth once his bones have rotted. He has deposited at least one at every monastery where he's stayed, including Cluain Mhic Nóis. But the two they've brought with them are among Artt's best, the script elegant, without a blot. The Old Testament in Greek he made in Wales, from an exemplar he'd carried from Gaul, which in turn had come all the way from Egypt. When Artt turns the pages he imagines he's touching paper reeds, three times the height of a man, which once swayed in the Nile.

The fittings of these two books are metal, but unjewelled; only the words inside are treasure. To the ignorant, Artt supposes, all this ink would be so much soot scratched into kidskin. If the sling-whirling inhabitants of that river island on the Luimneach had seized him and his monks, they might have tossed these volumes on the fire; months and years of Artt's life, fuel for an hour. There's a lesson in that: man's flesh is grass, and often his works too. Artt shouldn't be too proud of these copies, or too confident that they'll outlive him.

But his exhilaration bursts out when he's speaking to the brethren in the evening. 'Think of it! God's words breathed into King David's ear, entrusted from scribe to scribe for centuries, unaltered, unadulterated, passed all the way down in unbroken descent to Brother Trian here.'

The bump in the young man's throat writhes as he swallows.

'Angels will guide your hand,' Artt promises him. 'Now, we're all looking a little ragged, so let's shave.'

He's the first to kneel, so Cormac—having sharpened his knife on a whetstone—can make his master's cheeks, chin, and upper lip smooth. Then Cormac blows away the tufts, and finger-combs and reties Artt's ponytail before he tidies his tonsure with the blade. Artt knows his hairline's receding somewhat, though not much for a man in middle age, so his forward-pointing triangle is more of a trapezoid.

Next Trian works on the old monk, who says a cropped beard will do him. 'And since I've only a few wisps left up top, Brother, just shave off everything in front of my crown.' So Trian rasps away. The arc of Cormac's skull is curved like an axe-head. Artt notices that Trian skims lightly over the shiny hollow where there's no bone beneath the scar. Cormac's long strands, pulled back tight, make a skinny rat's tail.

Artt passes the time trimming his fingernails. Finally Cormac and Trian swap places and Cormac shaves the young man's beard, which is reddish, but nearer to brown than the plentiful, bright hair tied back in a ponytail. Cormac scrapes the tonsure into Trian's sun-weathered scalp, making the line clean over the hill from ear to ear, the point of the triangle coming forward almost to his hairline.

Finally Artt nods approval. 'We look like proper monks again.'

Cormac's on his knees, gathering up their detritus to add to his precious midden. 'While you and Brother Trian are at work on the books, Father, could I start on a hut for us? Just a simple stone cell?'

Artt needs to be firm with this old monk. He reminds himself that Cormac must have grown accustomed to following his own path, all those decades before he took vows. 'No, Brother. God has ringed us with his sea—set the waves like shields around us, keeping attackers at bay whether animal or human. The air grows milder every night, too, so we won't freeze, lying on the ground. It's not our bodies but our souls that need protecting. No, what you must make us first is an altar on which to celebrate the Mass.'

Will there be any resistance?

Cormac says nothing, only bows.

Artt rings the bell for Nocturns. In the dancing circle of firelight, he leads them in the first psalm: *'Morning and noon and evening I pray and cry aloud, and God will hear my voice.'*

After they eat, they sit on their buckets by the last of the fire as the darkness grows and the shearwaters cackle and howl. They sound more like wolf pups than any flying thing Artt's known. 'The devil birds seem even louder this evening.'

'I suppose they're calling out to their mates on the eggs, as they fly in,' Trian murmurs. 'Otherwise they'd be hard put to it to find their own burrows.'

Artt wonders whether he could stop up his ears with some beeswax from the little jar. Then he reminds himself that the sound is a small trial to bear—one he should welcome. 'Well, they're here to try our patience, so we thank them for their service.' A different thought strikes him. 'Unless they're hell-sent? Antonius the Egyptian—the first holy man to go into the wild—even in the cave where he lived, he was tempted by demons in the form of animals.'

Trian asks, confusedly, 'Isn't this Skellig a refuge from temptation?'

Artt clicks his tongue. 'We're out of the clutches of the world of men, Brother, but we've dragged along our heavy carcasses'—he gestures down at himself—'with all their low cravings.' Such as, in Artt's case, a longing for peace and quiet; for five minutes' relief from the feathered pandemonium. 'Aren't our souls as frail as ever they were?'

Cormac nods glumly at that.

'Besides,' Artt goes on, 'we've journeyed here not to escape from Satan like cowards, but to fight him off like soldiers, with prayer as our weapon.' He likes that; he warms to his theme. 'We're sentries standing guard on the outer frontier of God's empire—the last outpost of Christendom. We must expect attack. We're halfway to heaven here, and if our enemy snatches at our heels we must kick him off.'

'So...the shearwaters are the devil's messengers?'

Artt lets out a small sigh. This young man seems shackled to the literal. 'They're birds, Brother Trian. But Satan might be inspiring them to new heights of horrible noise, to see if they can chase us away.'

'Not us,' Cormac says.

'That's right,' Artt says. 'We stand fast.'

The fire crackles. Cormac remarks, 'I heard the tormentors of Antonius came in the shape of wolves, bears, lions, leopards, bulls, snakes, and scorpions. Imagine that hullabaloo of howling and hissing!'

Trian sucks in his breath.

'They hurt the saint terribly, too, with their claws and horns and fangs. But Antonius only laughed through the pain and told them, *Come on now! If you'd any power over me, a single one of you beasts would be able to tear me to shreds. The*

141

proof of your weakness is that you have to gang up in such a hell-horde. Then'—Cormac pauses for effect, and pokes the charcoal to make the flames flare—'there was a bright light and the animals disappeared like smoke.'

'The devil called them home?' Trian asks.

Artt corrects him: 'God banished them.'

Cormac nods and goes on with the story: 'So Antonius cried out to the Lord, *Where were you when the demons were ripping and gnawing on me?*'

A child's cry, it strikes Artt; wounded petulance. What reason has any mortal man to expect to be spared pain?

Trian asks, 'How dared he? I mean—wasn't that a dreadful thing to say?'

Cormac shrugs. 'That's the story as I heard it. And God told Antonius, *I was here all along, but I wanted to watch you fight.*'

Artt finds himself wondering if perhaps tales will be told about him. Is it arrogance to think it? The legend of how the priest and scholar Artt set off, with just two humble companions, in a small boat. The extraordinary pair of islands he found in the western ocean; how he claimed the higher one for God, and founded a great retreat in the clouds. The glory of the books reproduced there, and then generations of the copies' offspring. The ceaseless hum of prayer always rising from that little hive.

When in time to come Artt is buried in a rocky hole on the North Peak—Brother Cormac before him, presumably—will other pilgrims be miraculously drawn to sail this way, he wonders? To join Brother Trian, and live on together on these heights like unquenchable candles, forever blessing the name of their founder, holy Artt?

TO WORK

A DAY OF SUNSHINE and shadow, alternating as the clouds scud overhead. Cormac's gathering stones for the altar. It's to be a plain drystone square, knee-high. He's made walls before; a flattened cube can't be any harder, surely?

He collects mostly sandstones and slates, gritty to the touch. Sandstone is good stuff for building—soft enough to work, but stands up bravely to weathering. When Cormac peers at the shimmering greys, he finds hints of tan, yellow, green, brown, even red and purple. Many of these boulders have wavy layers, as if they were liquid before they hardened to stone.

He seeks out the flattest rocks, for stability. He pries up heavy ones with the crowbar, but leaves any that are too big for him to lift alone. He sets them all out in rows according to size. Drystone can stand for generations, if you take the trouble to pick the right rocks and give thought to how they'll sit together.

A mason at Cluain Mhic Nóis taught him that every stone has six faces—front, back, left, right, top, and bottom—though it often takes a few blows to reveal them. Cormac starts to shape his first rocks with the lump hammer, knocking off corners and humps flake by flake, always hitting away from the centre. Occasionally a stone cracks in two; if the break makes a smooth face on each half, Cormac keeps them both, but sometimes there's nothing left but debris.

Patience, he reminds himself. If he rushes the work, and cobbles together boulders that don't fit, the altar's own weight will make it sag or topple. But if he can remember where just the right shape is waiting in the gritty rows, he can pluck it up and set it in place like a key in a lock.

Cormac's calmed by the clink of rock on rock, the dust between his swollen knuckles. He mutters protections as he works. *'From temptations of vices, God's hand to steer me. From snares of the devil, God's shield to guard me. From all far and near who wish me ill, God's hosts to save me.'*

The dense, creamy flowers of the nearby rowan are sending out a musk that reminds him of the monastery church at night, crammed with sleepy-breathed men just out of their sheets.

Trian's making pens. For lack of geese on the Skellig, the great auks will have to do.

The flight feathers he needs for his own writing will have to come from the right wing, because those have a slight curve to the left, to fit his better hand; he'll use the left wing feathers for the Prior's pens. He finds a few in the sack that seem fit for the purpose: long, glassy quills below the soft plumes, as bendable as his own fingernails.

When God created men and women and set them apart from the beasts and the fowls, could it be that he made all of them from much the same stuff? It occurs to Trian that the difference isn't in the raw material, so much as in the making.

He'll prepare four pens for a start. With his whetted knife, he strips all the soft barbs off the shaft of the first right-side feather, and slices off the thin end. Then he does the same to a second. Then two left-siders for the Prior. They're all too soft, of course. Better if they could be left to dry out for months or years... At Cluain Mhic Nóis, the scribes sometimes set Trian to tempering and hardening quills with heated sand. But here there's only silt, down at the shore. And if he holds them over a fire, he's likely to singe them to a crisp.

He goes to find Cormac, whose square altar's looking firm and true, a handspan off the ground already. The old monk seems preoccupied, fiddling with a bob that hangs from a crossbar.

'What's that for?'

'If my surface is level, this string should hang plumb against the vertical mark on the bar.'

Trian remembers his own problem. 'For hardening quills, Brother, would boiling water work, do you think?'

A shrug. 'Why not put them right into the hot ashes?'

Trian thanks him and hurries off.

Once the quills are half-buried in the bed of grey ash, he gets the vellum out of the holy chest. The parchmenter entrusted three whole rolls to them, fully prepared, so Trian's spared the long and nasty work of purging them of flesh and hair in a vat of human excrement, pegging them out and scraping them.

He undoes the first roll now, counting a dozen bifolia. Good skins, soft and velvety, from white calves unmarked with shadowy brindles.

So as not to waste any of this, Trian decides to cut each page to about a quarter of a hide—bigger than the exemplar from which he'll be copying. For a start, he'll prepare just one gathering for himself and one for the Prior. He cuts three full sheets in two, chooses the five best half-sheets of the six, and lays them on top of each other, folding them over, with the calf's spine as the book's spine, making ten leaves.

Trian catches himself already fretting over how long it'll take him to fill up these twenty pages. How much of his life will be enclosed in hard oak by the time he's finished this book? (He makes a mental note that the monks will have to trade for the boards to make covers for each codex.) He soothes himself with Scripture: *Take no thought for tomorrow, for each day has trouble enough.*

He fetches the ball of thread and takes out of the roll the biggest bronze needle, the one with a triangular point for gouging leather more easily. He threads the eye, presses the whole gathering against his rock desk, and starts sewing the five skins together. Soon his fingers are marked with painful red lines.

The parchment has too much of a glassy shine left on the hair side, so he gives it a rub all over with a pumice stone, then adds ground chalk from a bag. This is the skin of two and a half calves he holds in his hands; by the time the new book's finished, it'll contain a whole unseen herd. Trian imagines them nudging and bumping each other, lowing in the dark. He touches the first page. Its owner had no chance to grow into a great bull and sire others, and never fed a crowd with his vast haunches. All so a clumsy *ciotóg* can scrawl on his back. The fear of botching this makes Trian feel sick.

When he's formed the second gathering—a little more sure

of his movements this time—he goes back to the fire to retrieve the stripped, opaque feathers from the ash and scrub off their greasy coating. What if there's some inherent weakness in the wings of a flightless bird? But when he clips off the very end of one quill, it doesn't shatter. He scrapes and cuts it gently, and uses the tip of his blade to clear old honeycomb out of the shaft. Now to shape the nib, ever so carefully. He cuts, splits, presses, cuts again, slanting ever so slightly to the left to suit his grip, shaping the two tines. A finishing touch: a tiny slit to channel the ink.

As he's cutting the last of the pens, the Prior's shadow falls across him. 'Have you everything ready?'

'I believe so, Father.'

His master takes the Psalter out of its leather pouch. 'If there's the least smell of rain, put it back in the bag before a drop can fall on it.'

'I'll guard it with my life.' Though this volume could be said to be worth a lot more than the life of one young monk. Trian gestures over at their improvised desk. 'Should I...'

'You go on the left.'

So Trian's writing hand will be out of the Prior's way.

As soon as Trian sets the Psalter on the slate outcropping, a new problem occurs to him: how to hold it open to the first page without one of those scribe's strings with a pyramidal weight at each end? He looks around until he finds two walnut-sized pebbles, then binds them to the ends of a length of twine from the ball he keeps in his pouch. If he had a real desk he'd hang one weight over its back. Instead he tries looping the twine over the wooden cover of the Psalter, but it threatens to drag the book right off the slab. Trian sweats under his master's cool gaze. He wrenches the stones off the string and goes to look for smaller ones. On the third try, a bee-sized pebble at each end of the string proves just heavy enough to hold the page open.

'Three things to bear in mind,' the Prior says musically. 'The first two will make your copy even more beautiful than the exemplar.'

Trian swallows. That sounds almost heretical.

'First, as an illumination, you must start each psalm with a large and complex capital'—

Trian knows how to do that much.

—'and outline it with red dots.'

He's never been allowed to use colour. 'The capital letter only?'

'With tiny dabs all round the black. Also, embellish with diminuendo—form each letter after the capital a little smaller than the one before, until by the fourth or fifth they've shrunk to the size of the ordinary script.'

What if they shrink too much, till they're no longer legible? Trian's armpits are running with sweat.

'And finally, at the top of each psalm, in Gaelic, you'll interpret the Latin Scripture below.'

Trian shakes. 'Ah Father, I couldn't think of making up words to—'

'Don't be ridiculous. I'll compose the headings.'

He lets out a long breath. The Prior will tell him exactly what to put, much as God blew his thoughts into the minds of David and the other Psalmists.

'You may rule the guidelines, now.' The Prior walks away.

Trian feels calmer now that he's not being watched. Alone but for the wheeling, crying birds.

With the ruler and his knife tip, he measures and pricks the margins around the square that will contain his text, with bounding lines to stop the words from spilling. Twenty-seven lines, he decides, just under half an inch each. He rules them in hardpoint, scoring firmly with the back of his knife. (In training, he cut a page right through; Brother Óengus called it an error every scribe makes once, but that didn't ease Trian's guilt when the page had to be thrown away.)

Now he uncorks the wide-necked stone jar to make up the ink. He takes the stopper out of the sheep's horn that holds the oily soot and scoops some into the jar, mixing in water a few drops at a time. For a thickener to bind the ink to the parchment, he supposes white of egg will do. At the end of a snaking burrow Trian finds a little egg, pale, under the caking mud; shearwater, he'd guess. Having held it up to the sun to make sure there's no chick—why kill without a reason?—he cracks it delicately over a bowl. He asks a blessing on the dark yolk and tips it into his mouth so as not to waste it; stronger and wilder than a hen's egg. Then he beats the white hard with a spoon till it's foaming, and adds a little of the liquid underneath to the ink.

He does the same with vermilion, in a smaller jar.

Now at last Trian has all their supplies to hand. His desk is thick, irregular, stony; he feels the cold pressure from heart to gut. But the top is almost miraculously flat. *Like a table spread in the wilderness,* he tells himself—*made ready for the Word.*

He doesn't want to interrupt the Prior's prayers, so he stands and waits, trying to remember the perfect position for holding the pen. Quite high up its shaft, gripped between the tips of his left thumb and first two fingers, with the other two curled out of the way. He cocks his wrist a little to the left; he mustn't let his hand form a hook or he won't be able to see what he's writing. He sets the nib head-on, at a right angle to the parchment.

With no warning, the Prior is beside him, dictating: *'In this first of the Holy Psalms, God promises that the good man will endure and be blessed, but the evildoer will be blown away like chaff.'*

Trian whispers the entire line under his breath, and then again, so he won't have to ask his master to repeat a single word.

It feels strange to spell out the plain Gaelic words of the Prior's preamble, when Trian's only ever written in the language of Rome. He's using the one script he knows, with a flat nib and wedge-shaped serifs. Rounded and distinct, with short ascenders and descenders, his letters don't touch even though they form one continuous track of black. (Like himself and Cormac and the Prior, it occurs to him—living close, but separate.)

The Prior inspects his work, squinting a little, and nods. 'Now the Psalm itself.' And turns away, to begin his own copying of the first page of the Old Testament—those curling Greek letters which are gibberish to Trian.

Large capital, Trian reminds himself (a great double-bellied black *B* for the start of *Beatus vir,* happy the man), red dots, diminuendo. He must faithfully replicate what he sees, splitting his attention between exemplar and copy, so as not to get lost in the gap. He dips his nib again. The ideal is a controlled flat flow, a gliding stream with no waves, no rocks, no gaps. Downward strokes are smoother, following the natural pull of the ink; upward ones are precarious. Lift the pen, reposition, as precise-footed as a wading bird. The key is never to let his own unworthy skin touch the surface. His left hand must hover in the air; only the arm moves, so lightly that a watcher mightn't notice. Trian should barely even put nib to page, transmitting the ink like the lightest of caresses.

The Prior's writing away intently, to his right. *It's not a race*, Trian tells himself. *Nor a contest*. The Prior's a famed scholar and scribe, as holy as he's wise. Trian's nobody. He repeats a different psalm in his head: *O Lord, hasten to my help*. He dips his nib again.

Sunday, and Artt's standing at the completed stone cube, which is draped in linen—a proper table to bear the Mass dishes at last, a fit altar for the sacrament of Communion. In a ringing voice, he blesses the tiny flasks of water and olive oil (carried all the way from Rome): 'May all fevers, maladies, and evil spirits be banished from him who drinks or is anointed with these liquids, in the name of Christ Jesus.'

The Great Skellig falls away below the Plateau like green silk, and Artt's suddenly filled with triumph. To think that he and his monks have travelled all this way, to the hidden haven saved for them since Creation. They've begun their work, and God looks on it and calls it good.

When it's time for the Consecration of bread and wine, Artt opens the silver host box and sees at once that the last wheat loaf is spoiled. Pale blue mould flares around the *Chi Rho* symbol.

He goes rigid, but only for a moment. Then he sets the loaf on the jewelled stone plate and carries on with the ritual. Trian rings the bell, and Artt intones, *'On the night before Jesus died, he took bread and gave thanks, and shared it with his followers, saying, Do this to remember me. This is my body.'* He elevates the Host over his head and his monks bow to it. This is not a loaf rife with mould, but the Bread of Life, the actual flesh of Christ. Breaking it in three, he puts the bluest piece in his own mouth and washes it down with the strong wine, which is not wine at all but the blood of their Lord. He hands out the rest, his eyes daring his brethren to say a word about the mould.

Each monk swallows his third.

Afterwards, at their midday meal, Cormac asks Trian, 'How goes the copying?'

Trian lets out a gloomy breath. 'Practise doesn't seem to improve my script.'

It seems to Artt that the young monk's letters are getting more awkward, if anything. But he fears that reproof will only make Trian's grip more cramped. 'Prayer can do wonders.'

'I hope so, Father.'

Cormac's face brightens. 'I remember a story about a novice scribe.'

Artt pulls a string of something rubbery from between his teeth. This stream of tales rather gets on his nerves these days, but he reminds himself that any company would be grating by now. That's the nature of congregation, he supposes—like the grit in a millstone that gradually smoothens down the soul.

'This young monk's writing was slow and ugly,' Cormac begins, 'like chicken marks in the soil.'

A chuckle from Trian.

'But he prayed to God to bless his eyes and hands and give him time enough to form the words gracefully. He set to work on the Four Gospels the next morning. Well, the hours passed, but the sun never set, so that scribe never put down his quill—and when the book was done, he thought it had been a single day, when in fact forty had passed!'

Artt dislikes these legends in which God takes away all his followers' troubles. Mere wishful thinking, like pagan stories of magic by another name. How do such fantasies fit men to live in this world, or find their way to a better one?

Trian doesn't seem fooled. He gnaws on a thigh bone without a word.

'Father,' Cormac says with no warning, 'of the supplies we need, I'd say charcoal's the most pressing. Maybe a couple of sheep to graze on the clifftops too? Soap, wine,' he lists. 'And wheat flour, of course, to replace the sack I so stupidly spilled down the cliff.'

So that's what this is about, the mouldy Host.

Trian puts in, 'I believe we'd reach the mainland in five or six hours, with the right wind.'

Have his monks planned this artless conversation, Artt wonders now—plotted behind his back? 'I thought you both understood. Our travels are done.'

Cormac meets eyes with Trian. 'Only a brief journey, I was thinking, to trade with fellow Christians.'

'What have *we* to do with other people?' Neither of them dares answer Artt. 'We've looked our last on the filthy world.'

Trian speaks up, childlike. 'But how are we to manage for supplies?'

Artt almost growls it: 'God will provide.'

153

'God will provide...charcoal and wheat?' Cormac asks.

Artt rears up, on his feet. If he can't instill conviction into this pair of Doubting Thomases, at least he'll put them to shame. 'Brother, do enlighten us, why was it wheat bread that Jesus shared at the Last Supper? Because it's a holier grain than any other?'

Cormac hesitates.

Artt knows the convert can't debate theology. 'No, it was merely the common bread of the Holy Land. So if we've no more wheat flour left, we'll use what we have.' He pushes on. 'Next Sunday, make us oatcakes.'

Cormac's grey eyebrows go up. 'For Communion? Ordinary oatcakes?'

This may not be what Artt was taught, but it's what God's telling him now. 'Whatever we offer at the Consecration, with clean hearts, will be turned into Christ's flesh.' As he makes this guarantee, he feels his wrath fall away and he's their guide again, their soul-friend.

Trian's blue eyes are wide; Cormac's are lowered to the ground.

'Come now, pray with me.' Artt gets out his bell and rings it melodically. '*Christ be my shield.*'

'*My sword,*' Trian answers.

From Cormac: '*My stronghold.*'

'*Christ be my wealth.*'

'*My meal.*'

'*My delight.*'

Artt sings out, '*O arms of Christ, be around my shoulders.*'

HATCHING SEASON

TRIAN WAITS, PERCHED hundreds of feet up over the southwest corner of the Great Skellig, the line between his fingers. He's caught wrasse before, under this overhanging cliff, and lost hooks to them too; they're hard fighters. Sometimes a bream, the odd mackerel or gurnard. But it's too calm today. He's found that sea fish show themselves only in lively weather, something that ruffles or darkens the water, or a strong tide at least; he supposes it makes sense for them not to approach the island unless they have a reason.

He looks down, all the way down. There are days when the ocean's a playful, bubbling cauldron. Trian's seen wonders. A school of porpoises cavorting, unless they were great dolphins—he couldn't guess their size. A basking shark, lolling and rolling to the south of the Skelligs; when it surfaced, with black fin and long snout, water poured out of its gills. Trian calls the indent below him Seal Cove, because seals often haul out there, to keep company and squabble on the rocks. Their big eyes are so childlike, they remind him of tales of mermaids.

Trian is beginning to be able to interpret this sea. At low

tide, the swirl of a sunken reef troubles the water. Farther out, currents meet, scribbling a message that he tries to read before it melts away. Even on a day this quiet, an ocean breaker can flash white as it rolls in to take a chew of the island. He stares at the horizon now and tries to grasp what the Prior's taught him, that the earth is a ball with the stars and heavens spinning around it.

Stray beams shard through gaps in the vast sky. The clouds shift, the light tints the Great Skellig brown, then grey, then green, as if God's nib is inking in an illustration. Land and sea like opposite pages, intricate and bejewelled with colour, in a book laid open for all to read.

Scrutinising the rock faces below, Trian counts eggs, just out of curiosity. He's found that a kittiwake will lay two or three, in a tiny nest. Whereas a cormorant has a huge nest with as many as four, pale blue; those are the only eggs the monks agree are inedibly foul. Anytime Trian's delved into the burrow of a puffin or shearwater, he's found only a single egg. Once he encountered a shearwater, in the daytime, and it spat a stinking oil at him. Great auks and guillemots, they too lay one pointed conical egg, left carelessly on a ledge—the guillemot's egg a dark-blotched green ovoid, the great auk's marbled white and a good five inches long. As for the new eagles on the South Peak, they've hatched already, though only one chick seems to have lived.

'Brother.' Here's the Prior, panting a little.

Trian leaps to his feet.

Is their master a little leaner than when he first came to Cluain Mhic Nóis? But the outline of his shoulders seems even stronger, grey eyes more sparkling in his weathered face.

The whole island spreads out behind him like holy Brigit's magical cloak.

'Were you in a trance?' The Prior stands, catching his breath.

'No, Father.'

'Remember the dangers of idleness, Brother. Any moment not filled with work or prayer is a chink left open to the cold winds of hell.'

If Trian says he was contemplating the glories of creation, but that comes down to mere daydreaming, is he doubling his error?

'What have you caught for our meal?'

He hauls up the twine hand over hand to check: the hooks have nothing on them but winkles and whelks, his tiny scraps of bait. 'Sorry, Father. I'll try casting from another spot.'

The Prior frowns. 'Well, don't stay much longer—I need you to work on the Psalter. And while you're waiting for a bite, let your head be bent, Brother. No one can pray with his eyes open.'

Trian nods. The Prior's hard on him, but only to mend him, he reminds himself.

Cormac makes sure to keep his garden moist under its mulch, now that the weather's getting warmer. When the seaweed shrivels down, he asks Trian to bring up more and spread it on rocks for the rain to rinse. The midden, too, he tends so it won't dry out and be scattered by the wind; after washing the bowls and spoons in a bucket he always throws the water onto the rotting pile, which he slices and turns with the spade every day. He's glad to see it is alive with little springtails, those jumping flies that swarm on anything damp or rotten. Earthworms, now, they'd be a big help, but he's found none on the Great Skellig; he supposes they've no means of crossing the water from the mainland. If only he'd thought to bring a few, alive in a jar; if he'd had the slightest idea what it would be like on this island.

Cormac's far sight is going fast now. In the distance he can make out coloured shapes, that's about all. He's reminded of the blind man in the Gospel. Jesus spat on his eyes and touched them, asking whether he could see anything now, and the man replied that he saw people but they looked like walking trees. So Jesus touched him a second time, and then he could see perfectly. It's the other way around for Cormac. The gift of vision is being taken from him in stages, maybe so he'll grasp what he's had and be grateful he's had it so long, since many folks' eyes turn milky long before they're old.

And sure what does it matter, really, when Cormac's sight at close quarters remains as sound as ever, for a chisel or a leaf or a needle? Everything he needs to see and do is contained on this small piece of high ground.

Today he makes a stew of fish heads and tails, just for a change from the endless roast birds. He throws in handfuls of bitter greens, and lengths of seaweed: translucent frilled green, fronds of carrageen, red leathery dillisk. He can't say what good the monks will get from each food, but he knows they need variety, or they'll sicken.

'Brother Cormac.' The Prior, standing at the altar. Has he been beckoning for a while?

Cormac adjusts the pot on its tripod over the fire, and hurries to him.

'This altar was well built, Brother.'

'Thank you, Father.' Their master's less stern, today. Might this be a good moment for Cormac to admit what's weighing on him? 'I must tell you something. These days, anything far off...it's a blur to me.'

The Prior nods, unsurprised. 'Well, no one picks an old companion for his sharp eyes.'

Cormac bows deeply.

'We all have flaws, Brother. Some that may be hidden from us, even.'

Since the Prior's in a benign mood, Cormac chances it: 'Maybe now I could start on a hut for the safekeeping of our goods from rain and wind, and for us to sleep in, when winter comes?'

A shake of the head, inexorable.

Cormac should have known.

'We can lie on the ground for many months yet. God must be housed before man,' the Prior tells him. 'What we need next is a chapel around our altar.'

To Cormac's mind, the whole Great Skellig is a church; can't the three of them pray undisturbed on every inch of it? And what more glorious windows than the ever-changing sky?

But as the reed told the oak tree: *Better bend than break*. He says, 'Right, Father.'

'A plain rectangle, I think, with sides sharply pitched.'

Cormac pictures this chapel as a sharp-bottomed boat turned upside down—a sign of their pilgrimage being complete, he supposes. 'Triangular gables at the ends?'

The Prior nods, sketching it on the air. 'And the door here at the west end, of course, and a triangular window opposite, to let in light over the altar.'

Because Christ will come again from the east. Cormac nods. He's resigning himself to the task of building this church. It would be a simple enough plan if they only had timber, but Cormac must work out how to do it with loose stones. 'How big would you want it, Father?'

'It's not my desire you must satisfy, but God's.'

He suspects whatever number he proposes will be wrong. 'You'd have the best idea what proportions he'd like, though. Maybe you'd mark them out for me?'

The Prior finds a boulder to set down. 'Around here, perhaps, the southwest corner. This'—a vein zigzagging across his broad, brown forehead as he cradles and sets down a bigger rock—'the northwest.'

Twelve feet by eight, Cormac guesses. 'And how thick the walls?'

A hesitation. 'A handspan? A foot?'

He can't help making a face.

'Thicker, then? A cubit?'

Cormac explains, 'There'll be nothing keeping it together but the rocks' hold on each other. If the walls were more like two feet wide, at least at the base, to make it stable...'

'As you say, Brother.'

'That means there'll be less room inside,' he warns. 'Only about this much.' He holds out his hands to make a span of four feet.

The Prior nods. 'Enough for the three of us to kneel in front of the altar.'

In his day, Cormac has worked with teams of men, and heavy equipment—oak tripods three times his height, compound pulleys to winch up tree trunks or boulders, and log rollers to move them. Here he has only a crowbar, a mason's level, dividers, and an L-shaped square. It'll do; it'll have to.

He fetches the dividers now and uses their pointed wooden feet to measure out the distances. He marks the inner and outer corners of the chapel with pebbles. 'I'd corbel the roof from about here, Father?' He holds his hand just above his head.

'Corbel...'

Cormac hides a smile; he knows one word his master doesn't. 'Set each course of stones a little farther in, so they overlap each other and make a closed vault.'

The Prior nods.

Cormac admits, 'I've never done it, myself, but I've watched it done.' If he can get it right, the stones will kiss, press and hold together. 'It takes two men to snap the lines—to mark out the walls. Father, would you mind helping me with that?'

'Certainly.'

Cormac digs out of a bag the little box in which he keeps the thin cord half buried in chalk. He hands the Prior one end. The Prior holds it firmly to the ground, under the pebble that's marking the inner northwest corner of his imagined church. Cormac stretches the string taut with one hand, all the way over to the inner northeast corner, while with the other he plucks it, twanging an imprint of white onto the rocky ground. It'll have to be redone after every rainfall, of course, but it helps him to picture the whole shape laid out.

The Prior murmurs, as if he already sees the walls rising in his mind's eye, '*On this rock I will build my church, and the gates of hell will not prevail against it.*' When they've chalked out all the lines, he leaves Cormac to start the building.

First Cormac collects and sorts all the biggest stones he

can find—except for round-backed ones, which would be too wobbly to build on. (He wishes he hadn't used up so many good flat ones making the garden wall and the altar.) Usually he'd start by digging a foundation trench and setting the first course into it. But he's working on bedrock here, so that would be backbreaking labour. This chapel will just have to hold itself down by its own weight. All Cormac has is hammer and chisel to make each rock a level place to sit.

He starts the first corner with the biggest, squarest lump he can find, for strength. The stones should be heaviest at the bottom, lightest at the top. Moving along, setting the first course, Cormac places each so its longest length goes into the wall. He's lucky enough to find a couple of through stones that thrust right across the two-foot span, locking it together. But mostly he lines the inner and outer edges of the wall with face stones, leaving a gap in the middle that later he'll fill up with smaller shards and pebbles, the hearting stones.

Whenever he finds a wedge-shaped rock, he sets its thicker end towards the inside of the chapel, so the wall won't bulge outwards over the decades. He's seen a building swell like a woman with a great belly, until it cracks and sheds its load. It occurs to Cormac, too, that each wedge should tilt ever so slightly towards the outside, for the structure to shed rain as beautifully as a duck's feathers. He almost talks to the rocks as he puzzles over them by twos and threes, looking for the angles that tell him which ones will be able to support their neighbours, so this chapel can root itself into the Great Skellig as if it's stood there since time began. So it can last for the ages.

Standing at the stone slab he calls a desk, Trian registers his neck twinging whenever he turns his head to his right to check each run of letters. Five is about as many as he can hold in his mind while he's transcribing. His knife tip stays on the exemplar, pressing down the springy parchment and anchoring his eye to the right spot in the psalm. Imagine if Trian were to skip one of God's words, or a whole line—he remembers a scribe at Cluain Mhic Nóis who did that, and was given a penance of no meat for a week.

The Prior writes on, with unnerving steadiness, a few feet away.

In recent days, Trian has found his gaze sliding around on the page, so the Prior's made him an eye-guard: a page with a slit cut out of it that reveals no more than one line at a time. The Prior calls it a window into heaven, though to Trian it feels more like a dark cell.

Crisp, clean. Keep the bows plump. Give each finial the same claw. Don't go too fast or the verticals will slope. Don't relax the hand too much, or the headstrokes will be too long.

Yesterday the three of them celebrated Pentecost, which means seven weeks have passed since they set off on their pilgrimage. Pentecost is the day the Holy Spirit came down on Jesus's bereft followers in a strong wind and flames that didn't burn, granting them the ability to speak in unknown tongues and cast out demons in his name. Trian wishes he'd been there; wishes he had such powers. The grace to keep copying for forty days and nights, for instance, like the spellbound novice in Cormac's story on whom the sun never set until his whole book was written.

Ink pools in the base of Trian's letters before it dries; all things incline downwards, from a dropped egg to rain and hail, and he wonders why, but that way lies distraction. He peeks at the sky, because if a shower is threatening, he should put the manuscripts safely away in their chest. Or wind—that's a threat too. Even a kittiwake passing overhead. (The birds have already fouled the cistern once, so Cormac's made a thin slate cover.)

For all Trian's efforts to concentrate while he's copying, doubts swarm about him like biting flies. If he doesn't grasp what an abbreviation mark or suprascript line means, he reproduces it by sight, as best he can. But sometimes he can't tell one word in the Psalter from the next. If only there were marks between words, to keep them apart—dots, or spaces even—those would make the copying so much easier. It shouldn't matter whether Trian knows the word, so long as he copies the letters in the right order. But the downstrokes of *i, u, m,* and *n*—how can he be sure he's not confounding them and making a jumble of holy writ?

Already he has to interrupt the Prior's flow of work at the end of each psalm, to ask him to check Trian's copy before dictating a preamble to the next. Or whenever there's a passage Trian can't puzzle out because of cockling—the wrinkling and pleating of a page, as if a demon's breathed on it in the night. Then occasionally a word will make so little sense to him that he wonders, *What if an error crept into one of the earliest copies of the psalms and has been faithfully reproduced by every scribe (including the Prior) since?* But then, who's a young monk to voice such a suspicion?

Mostly he tries to keep his mind on his pen. So many things blunt a nib; so many times a day that Trian has to sharpen it or cut a new tip. And always he's tormented by the stunted unevenness of his script. Will the perfection of God's meaning be able to shine through this clumsy fence? His left palm cramps and his flexed wrist aches; his right hand feels bruised where he grips the knife handle too hard. *Three fingers write,* the saying goes, *two eyes read, one tongue speaks, the whole body toils.*

When at last he hears the Prior's bell marking the end of the morning, he lets out a grunt of relief, which earns him a sharp look from his master. Head down, Trian puts away the books and writing things in the holy chest.

After psalms, readings, and prayers, it's time to eat. Almost always great auk — Trian catches one every two or three days. (He tries to spare young ones that haven't had the chance to see the wheel of the seasons go all the way round.) But Cormac does his best to vary the fare. Their little plot's doing remarkably well, a sign of God's favour; it's producing a few green onions already, and saw-toothed seedlings of fat hen, as well as narrow arrows of tangy sorrel. Trian relishes every leaf.

At today's meal, Cormac lets out a satisfied belch. 'How's the scribing?' He must be able to read Trian's face, because he chuckles and quotes the Scripture: *'There is no end to the making of books, and much study wearies the flesh.'*

Trian mustn't complain, so he changes the subject. 'I see our chapel's rising.'

'Slow work. I'm only on the third course of stones.'

'What matters is the quality of the effort,' the Prior says, 'however long it may take.'

Is their master praising Cormac's stonework, Trian wonders? Or rebuking him for his concern about its pace?

Cormac's eyes are on the translucent flames. 'By the way, Father, we've only bits and pieces of charcoal left.'

Trian's alarmed to hear that, but the Prior chews on.

The tension between his elders sours the last bite in Trian's mouth. He thinks of Abram's plea to Lot: *Let there be no strife between us, for we are brethren.* He jumps up. 'I'll look for something else to burn, then, will I, Father? Driftwood, maybe?'

The Prior eyes him. Trying to decide whether this is some pretext for taking an afternoon away from the copying?

It is, of course. But still, they do need fuel. Trian brushes his greasy hands on his robe. 'I'll go this minute.'

The Prior releases him with a small nod.

For hours Trian scrambles around the edges of the Great Skellig. No driftwood anywhere. He notices that footfall has scored and wrinkled the ground with faint paths wherever he or the Prior has gone exploring. (Cormac, distrusting both his balance and his eyes, stays close to their camp.)

Trian gets down to points on the foreshore he's never visited before. One rock floor has swellings like breasts; many coves he finds choked with rotting tangles of wrack. And after all this exploration, he's managed to gather no more than a handful of waterlogged, splintered sticks.

He's hungry. He finds himself eyeing mussels and limpets on the rocks. *Unclean,* he reminds himself. The Prior knows these things.

Trian's mind is racing through the alternatives to wood. Plants ripped out of the ground? No, they'd burn up in seconds. He seems to remember his folk throwing dried seaweed on the fire, but even if the monks could sun lengths of the stuff on rocks during a spell of fine weather, they've no building to keep it dry in after.

Bird droppings? No, those sticky white-green spatters are nothing like cow pats, which dry out into grassy discs; even if they weren't too wet to burn, they'd send up a choking smoke.

It has to be wood, but there's none to be had. Trian's mind goes in tired circles. If the Prior's unwilling to leave the Great Skellig even briefly, couldn't he give his monks permission to take the boat off in search of land that has trees to cut down, charcoal or turf to trade for? Can he really think they'd be lured back into the world by a single journey, corrupted as fast as apples in a barrel?

But the point of a rule is to put self aside, Trian reminds himself. To answer, *Your will be done,* as Jesus did when his Father sent him to die on the cross.

Breath harsh in his chest, he sits on a high ledge and shuts his eyes. If he was a piece of timber—a fallen trunk drifting down the great Sionan and out into the sea, or a mast off a wrecked vessel—where would the currents carry him? He pictures the knobbly outline of the Great Skellig, its protrusions and folds.

His eyes pop open. The day they moored, where the flat platform came down to the sea, didn't he glimpse a cave tucked behind? If flotsam happened to drift in there, it might well get stuck. It's worth a look, at least, because Trian can't present himself on the Plateau to chant None with no more than these few wet sticks.

Down at Landing Cove, he cranes around the rock to his right, but can't see a thing from here. He'll have to go in. He lifts off his robe and sets it, with his shoes, high enough to stay dry. He wouldn't chance this on a rough day, when a roller could smash him on the rocks. In nothing but his woollen braies he steps down into the motionless water, his toes feeling for sure footing—but it's all slithery with weed, and he slips, and bangs his elbow, and is in over his head, loose in deep water, splashing to the surface, gasping from the cold.

Trian paddles on the spot till he gets used to it and his breathing steadies. He fixes his gaze on the shadowy space at the back, under that overhang, and he makes his way towards it, into it. Yes, a cave, and choked, clogged with driftwood! Is this the hoard of years of waves carrying snapped branches and lost logs, fallen huts and broken boats to their last rest, tucked under the Great Skellig?

Much later, halfway up the cliff path, snake-haired and salt-crusted, bloody-knuckled, Trian pauses to adjust the long branch resting on his shoulder. Then he carries on dragging it up the hill. The driftwood is walnut-dark, heavier than it looked when he decided to haul it up, but he can't stop now; he wants to present one great log to his master the moment he tells him the news. He heaves hard, and walks on. Tries to remember the name of that good man who carried Jesus's cross for him for a while.

The Wailing Woman faces due west, as if watching for the sunset. Mary, sorrowful mother to them all. Trian stands still long enough to heave a breath, and prays: *We fly to take refuge under your cloak.* He eyes the descending sun, and hurries on.

The Prior's magnificent face broadens into a smile at the sight of the wood. 'Well done, Brother Trian!'

Trian aches with gladness. 'There's lots more,' he says, eyes down so as not to seem boastful. 'Though it'll be too water-logged to be much good for burning yet.'

After chanting None, the men work together to bring up the driftwood. Cormac attaches ropes to the winch that's been pegged into the rock since the day they made landfall, and positions himself there, on winding duty. Trian follows the Prior down to the platform of rock where he left all the flotsam. Together they rope it in a great dripping bundle, and Trian scurries up the path to help Cormac draw it up the cliff. They set it in a great pile on the Plateau where it will catch sun at almost any hour; the breezes should help dry it out too.

That evening they rest by the fire, where Cormac's already added a few of the sticks to the charcoal. Still aglow with sweat, Trian picks splinters out of his white-sponge fingertips. The flames leap blue and purple, and the wet in the wood hisses fiercely. He smells salt; the smoke catches a little in his throat.

The Prior, dishevelled but magisterial, sits down on his bucket. 'Did I not say God would provide?'

'You did, Father.'

'You did,' Cormac admits.

'I tell you, Brothers, what seems impossible to us is easy to him.'

The hottest day so far, and Artt's temper is rising. Writing out-doors, standing at their rocky desk, means the light is usually wrong—stabbing his eyes or casting heavy shadows—and his back, still so able for hard feats of lifting, responds to standing still all day with a dull ache.

He's groggy from lack of sleep, too. He's woken by the dawn every morning and drags himself off his tick right away. His soles slip on the dew as he makes the circuit of the Great Skellig, walking the pattern, keeping the devil from getting so much as a toehold on their holy mountain. Everything glitters, that early; wet spangles the small leaves and the exposed veins of crystal in the scarp. The relentless beauty exhausts Artt.

Summer's under way; their pile of driftwood is drying fast. All over the island chicks are breaking out of their eggs, shrill little reminders of the passage of time. The copy he's making of the Old Testament is on its third gathering already, but Trian's Psalter limps on, maddeningly slow. Artt has preached to the young monk as eloquently as he can; urged him to run to the Scriptures as a gasping fish returns to the waves. To shelter in these words, cling to them, mount up high on them. Writing, Artt teaches his young follower, is praying with both hands, fighting the devil with pen and knife, each word a deep wound in his side.

Trian does everything he's told, but sluggishly and cack-handedly.

'Excuse me, Father, but would you look at this hole?'

Artt narrows his eyes as he examines the curl of thread from where the parchmenter mended the tick-bite into a pucker, not well enough. 'Did you stretch the scar, or finger it?'

'I did not.' Trian wipes his nervous fingers on his robe. 'I just turned the page and saw where it'd opened up.'

Flaws can creep into vellum at any point: scabs on the living calf, a careless cut during the slaughter or flaying, specks of rot during storage. Much like sin, it strikes Artt: the kind that men are born with, the kind they blunder into in childhood, the kind they walk into as men.

Trian offers, 'I could sew on a little patch, maybe?'

'That won't hold,' he snaps.

'Should I just write around it, then?'

'Pretending it's not there?' Almost a shout. 'No, Brother, an eyesore only gets worse. With handling, this tear will widen and gape like a woman's part until it swallows up holy writ.'

Trian blinks like an idiot.

'Cut out the page,' Artt tells him. 'Bind in a fresh one with no faults.'

He nods miserably. 'Oh, and Father? I'm running out of ink.'

Artt turns a deaf ear to any whining about supplies.

'I was only wondering what I might use for black, instead of charcoal melted with pine pitch.'

He sighs. 'Any soot will do. Char an oily bird—a puffin or shearwater.'

'I will, thank you.' Trian goes back to his text.

But the next time Artt takes his gaze off his own pen and glances to his left, he finds Trian absorbed in watching a great auk shift about on her nest. 'Brother!'

Trian jumps. 'Sorry, Father.'

Artt leans over and raps the paper eye-guard. 'Look here.'

Dark clouds have gathered over the sun, he notices.

'Weather's turning,' Trian murmurs. 'Should I pack up the books just in case?'

'Work on,' Artt barks.

The rain holds off for the rest of the afternoon, but the warm air thickens.

At their evening meal, chewing on roast puffin, Artt registers that the island is oddly silent. 'Have our feathered tormentors given up plaguing us?'

'Storm's coming,' Cormac predicts.

Trian nods. 'They always hunker down in crevices beforehand.'

Sure enough, soon the wind's rising so fast that Cormac has to put the fire out. Artt takes the little bottle of holy water and sprinkles it in all four directions, reciting prayers for calm weather. Trian rushes to move their three lumpen ticks into the shelter behind the hanging sails where the monks' goods and tools are secured, together with the sacks of down and feathers they've been amassing. He runs back and forth to the driftwood pile, collecting armfuls of branches to stash away from the coming rain.

Feeling the first big drops on his face, Artt throws on his cloak. He picks up the holy chest and swaddles it in the cloak like a child. He folds himself into the shelter, picking his way over piled sticks. 'Get in, Brothers.'

Cormac squeezes in behind the flapping hides.

'Brother Trian!'

A faint reply; something about the firewood.

'Get in here!'

Trian appears, lugging a great log.

The three of them huddle together uncomfortably behind the sails like chicks in a too-small nest. Rain is coming in at the bottom, drenching them to the knees already.

'*A wise man built his house on the rock,*' Artt recites, though he's not sure the other two can make out his words over the rising wind. '*The floods came, and the winds blew and beat against that house, and it did not fall.*' His eyes are watering in the pummelling air. Something out there crashes and whirls by: what's been lost? *Things, only things,* Artt says silently, with a shiver. *Let go of them all. Let the storm rage; let the demons bite.*

He's hit by a memory of sitting in clean linen in the hall at Cluain Mhic Nóis two months ago. A civilised, respected guest, whose name went before him. And now look at Artt: a fishy-smelling vagrant in wet rags. He and his monks like kinless men, outcasts.

But they washed up here by God's design, he reminds himself as the wind screams and the sea batters the cliffs. Castaways by choice, marooned on purpose, gladly imprisoned beyond the reach of men. This island is a ship to heaven, and they won't founder no matter the weather. '*The Lord is my rock, my fortress, and my deliverer.*' He howls the words with wet lips. '*A shelter from the wind and a refuge from the storm.*'

The night's one long sleepless tempest, to Trian, till just after dawn, when the wind finally drops and their wet sails stop lashing. He seems to remember the Prior chanting Vigil at some point; Trian wasn't able to distinguish the words, but he hummed along—unless he dreamed that?

He staggers out of their cramped shelter, rubbing his eyes.

The wicker creel is gone, and so is all the rest of their precious driftwood, no doubt swept into the ocean or smashed on the rocks below. Trian thinks of how much work it took him to collect it, and sets his jaw so hard a tooth throbs with pain.

As he wanders along the clifftops, his frustration begins to ease. The air smells new, and cool. How well the bird flocks seem to have come through last night's lashing! Some nests must have been blown into the void, but there's no visible gap in the bristling ranks along the cliff ledges. Trian does happen on one kittiwake in the fescue grass, apparently unharmed but stone dead, eyes open, stiff on its back. He picks it up, remembering the Gospel line about sparrows: *Not one of them falls to the ground without your Father knowing*. The kittiwake's shorter than Trian's hand, and as light as a drawing of itself. Was it worn out by the bruising wind, or struck against a rock?

A tiny life, he thinks, lived according to God's instructions. Such poised, still feet. The kittiwake has only three toes instead of the four most birds have, he notices, and they end in tiny sharp claws. Did God give it those for clinging onto its nest? But then...what purpose might the little line of red around its eyes serve? Or the bright drip at the corner of the beak, and the same red on the long tongue-dart inside? Trian can't puzzle out the divine intention behind the painting of these details. Maybe the Creator's fond of variety for its own sake, and takes delight in all the ways his creatures differ from one another?

Best not to eat this bird, Trian supposes, in case it was sick before the wind knocked it down. He goes to set the airy body on Cormac's midden. The decaying stuff hums with the play of insects. He calls, 'What are you doing, Brother?'

'Thinning out the spinach,' Cormac pants, bent over his plants. 'If I keep only the stronger seedlings, a handspan apart, they'll have more of a chance.'

'How're the turnips?'

'Swelling nicely.'

'Any of them ready to eat?'

'Why don't you be the judge?' Cormac rubs the dirt off one the size of a walnut and tosses it to Trian.

He crunches the white flesh between his teeth. He mumbles, 'That's the best turnip I've ever had.'

Cormac chuckles and finds another for himself. He's harvesting leaves of fat hen, Trian sees, and sorrel too. 'At least whatever we grow here is safe from goats and rats and mice. And from men too. Remember the time holy Comgall caught some thieves?'

Trian shakes his head. 'I don't think I ever heard that story.'

'Well, those curs had the cheek to plunder vegetables right out of the saint's plot. So Comgall lifted his holy bell in his left hand and cursed them—asked it as a favour of God, who struck the lot of them stone blind.'

Trian laughs, before it occurs to him that Cormac mightn't find the notion of going blind so funny.

But Cormac doesn't seem offended. 'Though some say, once the thieves begged forgiveness and did penance, Comgall cured them, and even let them join his monastery.'

Repentant sinners could make the best monks, Trian supposes, since they'd be under no illusions about themselves.

He notices that the kelp dressing on the vegetable beds has

shrunk right down. 'Would you like more wrack, Brother? A gale often washes up quantities of the stuff.'

'I would—if Father can spare you.'

He goes off to ask.

'Very well,' the Prior says grudgingly, 'but catch a bird for our meal too. And then get back to the copying.'

On the path down to the shore Trian nearly trips over a pair of rainbow-faced puffins. From their burrow he hears a faint cheeping: their egg must have hatched. He goes down on his knees in the mud to peer in, but can't see that far into the dark. Farther down the cliff, though, in a crevice, he glimpses another, grey and fuzzy, looking like no relation to its spectacular parents. Imagine having emerged from your cracked white shelter last night, into such a storm-tossed world.

There's still a heavy swell left over. The waves push into Landing Cove one by one. Like grandparents and then parents and then children, it occurs to Trian, each generation taking its turn. Tangleweed lies thick on the rocks above the tide line, like Joseph's coat-of-many-colours in its intricate luxuriance, tiny insects jumping through the tangle.

He remembers the foreshore in the story where holy Senán's sister had to be buried because her brother wouldn't allow her any closer, not even when she was cold in death. That was harsh. Do saints have to be so harsh, to be so holy? No, that can't be true. Trian frowns over the stories that give it the lie. Comgall forgave the thieves in the end, didn't he? Cóemgen let a crow nest in his own hand, for forty days, and wouldn't disturb her; Colm Cille spared a whole grove of oaks the axe.

An armoured thing crawls over the pebbles; thin, waving feelers and two huge dark blue claws. *Lobster*—that's the word. Trian remembers them from his childhood. Boiled, they turn red, and you smash them open to get the luscious meat. He never knew it was forbidden.

His stomach growls at the sight of the shellfish clattering down into a rock pool. He wishes he still didn't know it was forbidden; wishes he was innocent and could cram his belly with whatever dirty, delicious stuff he found.

Trian thumps his chest hard, and tells himself to get on with his work.

For lack of a hook or even a rake, all he can do is gather the reeking clumps of seaweed in his arms and wrench them off the rocks. He wishes he had the lost creel, or had thought to bring down one of their sacks, even.

Mounting the cliff, he can't see where he's putting his feet; at one point he trips on a ribbon of kelp and slips onto the pile. He bursts out laughing at the notion that if he's to fall to his death, after months clambering up and down the Great Skellig, it'll be for the sake of some maggoty seaweed.

Craning up, Trian's disturbed by something about the silhouette of the clifftop. Didn't it bulge out before, just there? When he climbs nearer, the hollow is fresh; he realises a whole chunk of the cliff must have been broken off in the storm. Strange to think that a landscape can be transformed, just like a man's face. Are wind and waves and rain God's fingers, then—still tinkering with what he made more than six thousand years ago?

That prompts Trian to gaze over his shoulder at the Saddle, the island's thin waist. Will the Great Skellig itself be eaten away over time till one day it breaks in two? Maybe everything wears down in the end.

As he deposits the seaweed on Cormac's midden, Trian registers the Prior standing at work at their desk in the distance. He hurries off in search of dinner. Many kittiwake and guillemot are still sitting on their eggs, and don't budge even when Trian works his way within arm's reach. It's love that dooms them, he supposes; they won't leave their clutch, not even to save themselves. He takes just one of each kind, today, and tries to break their necks before they know their time's up.

'I only mean one sleeping cell between the three of us,' Cormac pleads. 'Just for bad weather. We saw the other night that the overhang's not half big enough for us and our things.'

The Prior's dry lips purse.

'Now we have less driftwood left to feed the fire at night, it takes days for our robes to dry out, and our mattresses are damp too. We could catch our deaths.'

'*Whoever seeks to save his life will lose it,*' the Prior quotes, '*but he who would lose his life for my sake will save it.*'

Cormac can't argue with the Gospel, but doesn't quite see how it applies to the hut he wants to build.

'All these daily protections we say,' the Prior adds—'why do we snivel so?'

'Snivel?' Cormac repeats.

'What are these poor bodies of ours, that we should expect Christ and his angels to shield them? Why dread sickness and death at all, when we should rather trust God to do with us what he will?'

Cormac never considered it that way; never felt the need

to justify his preference for survival. A quick thought flickers: *This is nonsense*. Doesn't every creature on the earth, water, or sky want to stay alive?

But he dips his eyes and makes himself mutter 'Amen.'

The Prior's tone is calmer now, as if he's solved a theological conundrum. 'From this day on, I say we'll beg no further protection, except against the assault of sin.'

Cormac doesn't answer. If their master says it, then that's how it'll be.

But the sleeping hut, that's why Cormac rashly began this conversation. He tries again, going roundabout. 'Really we were lucky we didn't lose more than the creel and half the driftwood, Father, and that was only a summer storm, not a real winter gale. The water that blew in under the sails—what if it had soaked the holy chest, with the books and writing materials inside?'

Is that a shift in the Prior's expression?

'I'm only proposing one little hut to shelter our treasures as well as us. A simple hive shape, to keep it watertight. Aren't bees the most virtuous of insects, always working for the good of their brethren?' Cormac pictures the beautiful curve of the cell—like an egg half-buried in the ground. 'No need for windows—or a smoke hole, even, as we'd keep our fire outside.'

'All right,' the Prior says reluctantly. 'But as soon as this hut's done, you'll return to the greater work of the chapel.'

Hiding his grin. 'Of course.'

'And the hut will be built faster by two of us, so you must teach me.'

Cormac winces. 'Oh, but Father. You're a man of deep inquiry—'

The Prior shakes his head. '*Ora et labora.* Prayer and manual labour are equally noble.'

The man's no mason, that's what Cormac meant. Well, there's no point in arguing.

He chooses a flat spot on the Plateau, on the other side of their fire from the chapel, and uses the dividers to chalk a wide circle, nine feet across. The space inside the round hut will be a square, he decides; he and the Prior snap those four lines.

Next they gather stones, and lay them out according to size. Cormac starts setting the first course, between the outer circle and the inner square.

The Prior lifts a rock and holds it. 'Just here?'

Cormac hesitates.

'Too round? Should I take some off the side with the mallet?'

'Ah...That crack in the middle, see, Father? I fear there's a frailty there.'

The Prior tosses that rock aside.

It feels disrespectful to treat his master like a novice—but it would be disrespectful to the building to use the wrong rocks. 'If we find a long one, like this, we'll use it for a locking stone, to go right across the full width of the wall.' Cormac lugs it into place.

'Excellent. Every stone we add takes us a step closer to heaven,' the Prior says.

Cormac nods. 'And we should try to cover every joint in the first course with a stone in the second, so there's never two joints on top of each other. The rule is, *Every stone must lie on two*.'

The Prior nods. 'Like us.'

'What's that?'

'Three men, Brother. Each one leans on two, and each two on one.'

HARVEST

DURING SUNDAY MASS, when Trian receives a piece of the Host on his tongue, it smells and feels and tastes like plain oatcake. He has to gather all his forces to make himself believe that it's truly the body of Christ.

He lives for the Sabbath, but for a shameful reason: because it's the one day in seven when he's freed from the copying. At the week's end, Trian's cramped hands can loosen and uncurl; his neck can straighten. In between the holy hours, he's allowed to go and pray anywhere he likes.

Today after the noon meal he heads straight down to the sea. On the cliff path, puffin chicks cheep from every crevice. Trian does pray as he walks, but with his eyes wide open. *O winds and clouds, bless the Lord. O mountains and hills, bless the Lord.*

In Landing Cove he leans against the boat that's resting like a gigantic creature's discarded shell. Idly he checks that her joins are still tight and sealed with resin, her greased leather not showing any cracks. Does the Prior mean to leave her here as a sign of their old life, like a curiosity from a past age?

In the rock wall behind, a purple patch has a darker splotch in it. Trian puts his face closer. It looks like a piece of fern caught in the slate, but when he scratches it with one black-rimmed nail, it's hard. How did a leaf get trapped in the rock? Such divine handiwork. The book of the earth has enigmatic passages that Trian can't interpret, but still he loves to read it. It seems to him that nature is God's holiest language. Everything created seems to express its Creator; everything cries out, *You made me.* Trian wonders whether these birds wheeling over-head, even these rocks, might be his sisters and brothers.

He sits down at the waterline, now, dipping his feet in up to the knees. The tingle is delicious. A sleepy afternoon, the water barely lapping. On impulse, Trian pulls off his robe over his head and folds it up. Who's to say a man can't pray in the water?

In up to the neck, gasping from the chill, he holds a big breath and dips his head under, pushing his eyelids open. It's a green, flickering world down here. Two kicks power him off from shore, and the seabed's falling away from him, as if he's gliding like a young eagle over this silent, glowing landscape. The boulders below have turned weird, some coiled like worm casts, others forming columns of mauves and emeralds: *corals*, that's the word. And the bright waving things: anemones? Trian rears up to let out the old breath and take in another. Facedown, he swims faster, farther off. The clarity on every inch of his skin.

O rivers and seas, bless the Lord. O creatures that move in the waters, bless the Lord. So deep now; the floor's shelving sharply to black as he moves farther offshore. Trian kicks his feet and shoots away. The sense of height is dizzying, yet he can't fall. He's floating along on the skin of the water, like a passing cloud.

High on the Plateau, Artt's ringing the holy Hour of None.

No sign of his monks. They're too far off to hear, though they're supposed to stay within range of the bell that keeps them all tied together with its invisible threads. Could they be so deeply immersed in prayer that they don't hear? Artt suspects old Cormac of dozing his Sunday away, and Trian's distracted by every passing bird. So Artt rings again, and keeps ringing, and waiting, and his anger rises. Two such ordinary men, marked out in his dream so he could bring them along to an island at the ends of the earth. But godliness remains impossibly far out of their reach, because they can't be bothered to get on time to the holy service.

Here comes Cormac now, with a strange hopping gait. Artt calls, 'What's the matter?'

'I might have done myself a bit of hurt, Father.'

How, in the middle of a quiet Sabbath afternoon? Cormac's careful to avoid the vertiginous cliffs. 'Did you roll your ankle?'

Shyly he lifts his robe to the knee, revealing a bloody gash like a dog bite. 'I suppose I wasn't looking where I was stepping, and a rock slid and threw me down the slope.'

'Careless! Come, I'll wash and bind it.'

Ill at ease, Cormac waves his master away.

'Sit down,' Artt orders him. He goes to fetch water from the cistern, and the herb box. Once Artt's washed the rock dust out of the cut, Cormac takes the cloth and presses on it to stanch the bleeding.

'Is the bone broken, would you say?' Artt asks.

'No, no. I'll dress it with honey...' Cormac trails off.

Of course, they discarded the jar of honey on the riverbank at Cluain Mhic Nóis.

Cormac scoops a palmful of cobwebs from the box instead, and stuffs the wound with them. He uncorks a tiny flask and shakes some salve into his palm, smears it on. 'Aloe, powerful stuff. This'll heal in no time.'

But he's afraid; Artt can hear it in the tremble of his voice, see it vibrate in his hands. *Timor mortis conturbat me,* the fear of death is racking this old monk. He's survived perils, lived decades longer than anyone would have expected, and still he shakes to see his blood spill. Artt wonders, *Is life so sweet to these men that they want it to last forever? Like tired children after long play, racing away from the arms of the father who's come to fetch them home?*

To bolster him, Artt strikes up a prayer: '*Christ's wounds—*'

'*—heal us,*' Cormac replies, his voice faint.

'*Christ's pangs—*'

'*—ease us.*'

'*Christ's groans—*'

'*—our songs.*'

Here comes Trian, draggle-haired as if he's been in the water. He points at Cormac. 'Your poor leg, Brother!'

'Ah, it's nothing.' Cormac binds the cloth twice around his calf.

Artt calls out, 'You absented yourself from service.'

'I beg pardon, Father.' Flushed, Trian drops prostrate on the ground.

Trian's never tended a sick man before. Cormac keeps insisting it's just a cut, even when—after two days of limping around the chapel site, crouching to fit stones into place—his lower leg swells up and leaks through the bandages. The bruising's an extraordinary purple and yellow. The Prior won't let Cormac stand on that leg anymore; he's ordered Trian to keep the old man on his tick by the fire.

Trian doesn't really know what to do with the bronze probe, but Cormac talks him through each step. 'See, it'll let out the noxious blood. A touch deeper now,' he says through his teeth. 'That's right.'

How can Cormac speak as if it's another man's leg, not his own? Trian wipes away the green seepage. He adds more of the salve, and reaches for a clean cloth. 'You bear it well, Brother.'

A laugh hisses out. 'If you're spared to reach my age, you'll find you're glad of even the hard hours.'

Trian knows that anyone can die of a wound that goes from green to black. Still, at least Cormac has no fever yet. He ties the bandage tight.

'Now, how can I be useful?'

'Your job is to rest,' Trian reminds him.

'I am resting, but I need something to take my mind off this wretched leg.'

'Well...I have been thinking about salt.'

Cormac's wild eyebrows go up.

'We haven't much left in our jar,' Trian points out. He's been worrying about this for some time. *God will provide*, but sometimes isn't it up to the monks to seek out his hidden gifts? 'Down on the shore, I saw a white crust around the edge of a rock pool and tasted it, and it's pure salt, dried up.'

'Did you scrape some out?'

'Just a handful. But I was thinking we could make a lot more.'

'What, by setting out a pot of seawater in the sun?'

Trian shakes his head. 'That'd work only if we had many shallow troughs, and weeks of fine weather. No, I thought we could cook it down, maybe.'

'Well, if you haul the water up from the sea, I can stir the pot.'

Trian grins.

He staggers back up the cliffs with two mostly full buckets, their straps scoring his shoulders through the wool of his robe. He fetches the biggest iron pot and hooks it onto the tripod while Cormac, leaning up on his good knee, builds up the flames.

They boil the water all that day. Cormac leans over at intervals and works it with the big wooden spoon, until the liquid looks thick to Trian. By the time the fire's needed for cooking a pair of puffins for the evening meal, Cormac is stirring the sludge almost continuously so it doesn't stick. 'That should be enough.'

'But it's still wet.' It seems to Trian like waterlogged sand.

'If we keep it over the flames, though, it might scorch.' Cormac lets himself subside on the mattress. 'Sit it out in the sun for a couple of days, stirring it ever so often. That should finish it gently.'

Trian wraps his sleeves over his hands, then lifts the steaming pot and sets it down on the ground. The iron hisses and the low grasses smoke. 'I'm curious how holy Pádraig managed for salt, when he was a boy on his lonely hill. Would the pirates have given him any?' He mulls it over. 'To think of their faces when they found he'd slipped his bonds and escaped!'

'Hmm. I never pictured him tied up,' the old monk says. 'A herder needs to roam with his flocks, even if he's a slave, so as I saw it, the pirates just left Pádraig with their sheep and pigs in the wild, and he didn't know where else to go. Until the angel came down and told him about a ship, hundreds of miles from there, that could take him away to freedom.'

Trian's nodding; this story's one of his favourites. 'I've always wondered what form the angel took.'

'Sometimes they're said to appear as bright lights,' Cormac tells him, 'or borrow the shapes of young men like yourself.'

Trian snorts at the idea of such an angel—gawky, with a fiery ponytail. 'Is it true they can come as birds?'

'So I've heard. Whatever their outward forms, they're made of light, and they speak without tongues, shaping the air into words.'

'I'd say Pádraig was glad to get home to Albion, all right.'

'Ah, here's the thing, though.' Cormac holds up a finger. 'No sooner was he back among his kin than didn't he have another vision, instructing him to go back and preach the Gospel to the Irish—the very people who'd enslaved him?'

Trian shakes his head in puzzlement. Clearly there was no escape, not as long as God had a job for you.

He glances at the pot. Tastes the sludge with one finger. 'We did it, Brother. We made salt.'

He looks over his shoulder at Cormac, who's attempting to smile, his face contorted with fresh pain.

Trian's pulse thumps. He should have insisted on keeping the old man lying down today, as he was told. *No*, he roars silently. *Don't dare die on me, our first season. Don't leave me alone here with a saint.*

When Cormac's leg gets so bad he feels it might burst, he stops speaking. He keeps busy, darning their socks. He wonders how much time will pass before their robes and braies will fall to rags. Maybe the monks will end up in tatters of bird skin and feathers. The thought doesn't horrify him, somehow. After all, these days they're burning twigs of driftwood instead of charcoal, and taking Communion of oatcakes. There seems no limit to what they can do without.

Every morning Cormac urges himself to mend fully, or die, nothing in between; if he winds up with a crippled leg, he'll be a perpetual burden to the other two. He can't decide which is more likely, death or recovery. Cormac's seen sick men writhe and screech as if they're giving birth, and be back on their feet a week later. Or, of course, lie down for a rest and never stir again.

In the meantime, he sets his teeth and never bothers mentioning the pain. His latest task is making soap, so his brethren will be able to wash the fishy stink off themselves in the months to come, whether Cormac's with them or not. Where will they bury his body, he frets, given that there's no soil here more than an inch deep? Really he should be put in the midden, giving back all he's made of, except the Prior would probably call that sacrilege.

Age quod agis, Cormac reminds himself. Keep his mind on the soap. He spoons ash out of the side of the firepit, and puts it in water to boil till the grit settles and the lye rises to the top. For lack of beef tallow, he's collected a bowlful of fat drippings off a roast auk, and he pours in the lye now. He mixes it up, trying to avoid getting any burning splashes on his skin, then puts it aside to set. 'It'll be a bit harsh for a few weeks, before it cures,' he warns Trian.

'Brother, lie down,' Trian pleads, putting the back of his fingers to Cormac's forehead. 'You're burning up again.'

There are dried leaves in the herb box that might help the fever, but Cormac doesn't say so. Better to save the medicine for the other two in times of need, since they likely have so many more years left in them.

Inside his pounding head, Cormac's thinking of all his markings. The cat that was pricked on his back when he was a boy; that tattoo has stretched and faded with his skin, but the pigment's never washed out. The odd shiny pink mark on his hands from cooking, and nicks from chisels. A scar over his lip, where his wife scratched him in a quarrel once, before she was his wife. A bump of lead under the skin of his upper left arm—an inch-long sling bullet he got in a clash between clans, which he's carried ever since. The ugly pair of scars where the javelin went right through his right side in battle, and somehow didn't spill his guts. The little crater above his left ear, where his skull was smashed by a slingstone, then drilled open by deft Brother Fiach—there's nothing shielding Cormac's brains at that spot but red skin. The fact that he's still alive makes no sense; he's a walking miracle. He lives and breathes at his Lord's whim, and he can only say *Deo gratias*.

He knows Trian's working hard to nourish him back to health, cooking up handfuls of turnips, sorrel, the tender top three leaf-pairs of nettle, whole heads of spinach. But Cormac's stomach turns at the food; he shakes his head at the bowl. He's talking again now, because if he can't tell stories, what use is he at all? His gaze falls on the Prior's missing finger. 'The young hero Cú Chulainn,' he begins in a rasping voice, 'he was so favoured by the old gods, he could swim like a fish the day he was born. Small, Cú Chulainn was, but with seven raven-clawed fingers on each hand, seven toes on each foot, and seven pupils in each eye.'

'Favoured?' the Prior queries. 'With such deformities?'

'Well.' Cormac's lost his thread. 'The hero's beauty was legendary all the same—hair of brown, red, and gold, all threaded with gems.'

The Prior shakes his head at the gaudy image.

Cormac's mind slides off down another track. 'Holy Brigit, now, she disfigured herself on purpose, for the love of Christ.'

Trian looks bewildered. 'Why would Christ want that?'

'No, no, listen. Brigit's father was a chieftain who begot her on a slave woman. He planned to sell the girl off to one man or another,' Cormac wheezes, 'only she'd sucked in the love of God with her mother's milk, and meant to live a consecrated virgin. She tore her face and body so all men would be repelled by her. But once her father let her take her vows, her beauty was restored overnight!'

Cormac's thinking of the round cheeks of his little daughter. She comes back to him more, these fever-muddled days, than she has in twenty years. Sometimes her brothers, too; occasionally their mother. Is this a sign that Cormac's dying? Not that he has the least hope of seeing his family again on the other side. They were pagans, back in that other life. How he wishes he'd heard the Gospel before the plague came, and could have had them baptised too, before he lost them. If only there was a heaven with room for them all.

Artt's tried to stay composed, even on nights when the old monk's been tossing in delirium on the other side of the banked embers. He's kept up the perfect rhythm of the holy hours, dividing the chanting of the psalms between himself and Trian. But slowly, as the wet gash in Cormac's calf dries up and closes over, Artt allows himself to feel relief. No one's dying; not yet. It seems God needs all three of them on his sacred island.

Cormac's soon back on his feet, if hobbling a little. For all his hump, his inflamed knuckles, short sight, and old injuries, the man is invaluable. With Artt at his side hoisting each stone to head height, Cormac has the dome of their beehive cell corbelled tight in a week. They use it as a store for all their possessions now, as Artt sees no need for a roof over their heads at night until autumn.

Now that lesser task is done, the two of them will be able to get back to the greater one—raising the higher, thicker walls of the chapel, God's own house set on the heights of the island.

Tonight Artt watches Cormac roasting them three puffin chicks for dinner—his fingers turning the skewers with snatching movements, to angle the raw sides of the birds down so they sizzle and twitch over the flames.

'We've only a few bits of driftwood left,' Cormac mentions.

'Well, I'm sure Brother Trian will find us some more.'

Trian speaks up glumly. 'I've swum right to the back of that

191

cave, and gone some way into other openings, south of us and on the northwest side. Not a stick.'

These mopers, Artt thinks—always brooding over what's to become of them next month, next season, next year. Can't they hear the music of eternity?

One of the puffin carcasses rips off its spit and drops into the fire. Cormac reaches for the big knife to skewer the flaming bird.

Something occurs to Artt. 'Wait.'

The meat's flaring up like a great ball of fire.

'But it'll be burnt through—'

'Leave it!' They watch the bird in the ashes burn on greasily, steadily. 'There,' Artt says. 'There's your fuel.'

'A puffin?' Trian asks, bewildered.

'The young ones are so fat, they're balls of grease—why not build a fire of them?'

'To burn? Not to eat?'

'We'll burn some to cook others. These islands are so teeming with birds, I knew there had to be some purpose to their numbers.' Artt laughs. 'See how tenderly the Lord provisions his beloved children?'

These days of high summer, Trian's hands have a lingering reek of blood, even when he's scrubbed them with Cormac's soap. Even when he's bending over the Psalter, forming letter after graceless letter. The Prior releases him from the copying every afternoon, but only for killing the vast numbers of birds they need to stoke their fire.

The rowan has lost her flowers, Trian notices as he's passing, but her first fruits are coming, clusters of green berries that'll soon turn red. He stands stroking her bark with his stinking hands, and watches Cormac and the Prior toil on the chapel. He's only putting off the moment he must begin the slaughter.

His task is to wait on the cliff path for puffin chicks to emerge from their burrows. The fledglings lurch about, trying their flight feathers; ungainly, excited, feet too heavy for their bodies. The adults nudge them from above and call out encouragement from below. Some fledglings fall on the rocks; Trian retrieves them with the noose on his staff, if he can reach. Others he simply snatches off the slope to left and right. He breaks their necks at once, uneasy to be dispatching birds in front of their parents at the very moment when their airborne lives are about to begin. Taking birds in ones and twos to eat, that was one thing. But scores of young at a time, just to feed the flames...

It takes so little effort, that's another thing that appalls Trian. No snaring necessary, nor feats of skill; no danger. A hard yank on a fledgling's slim neck, then he loops it on his belt. Once the belt's full, he follows the path back up to the camp, their bodies swaying like some ceremonial skirt. He slides them off the rope, dropping them on the waiting pile. No plucking and jointing necessary; all he has to do is keep up the killing. The air stinks of burning feathers and flesh. Their heaven-sent manna turned to greasy cinders.

Cormac wrinkles his nose at the stench of the fire, but says it can't be helped, because they've nothing else to use for fuel. And what are the monks to do for light, in the dark months ahead, he wants to know? They're down to the last two beeswax candles and a stub; what'll they use to see by on long nights, when they get up to chant Nocturns, Vigil, and Terce?

Trian imagines the winter hours the three men will have to spend together in the stuffy stone cell, darkness pressing on their eyes. The puffin bodies in the flames spit oil; the back of his hand stings, and he licks it.

'Like Fionn,' Cormac murmurs.

'What?'

'Fionn Mac Cumhaill, when he was cooking the salmon.'

Trian nods. The king of fish, one drop of whose fat held all the wisdom in the world. He wonders if the poet Finegas ever brought himself to forgive his servant for the accidental theft.

'What about rush lights dipped in bird grease,' Cormac says suddenly, 'as we've no wax? Have you seen any rushes growing?'

Trian tries to recall. 'Mostly toad rush, but it's shorter than my hand, so it'd hardly be worth the trouble.'

That afternoon, down in Seal Cove, at the southwestern end of the island, Trian does find some sea rush—green stalks a good two feet long and sharp-pointed. He brings back a whole armful.

Cormac's been refining his plan. 'Puffins have that little bag of oil in their bellies, that would do for coating the rushes. Easier to drain out than catching the drippings little by little as the birds roast.'

'Shearwaters are bigger, so they might have even more oil. If we caught a whole batch at once...' Trian eyes the clear blue sky. 'We'd have to wait for a cloudy night.'

For now, Cormac shows him how to prepare the rushes,

soaking them in a bucket of water for an hour, then stripping them with knives, peeling off the hard green to bare the white pith. 'Leave on just a line of green to stiffen the stem.'

Trian's so grateful this old man didn't die of his infected leg.

Next Cormac teaches him to tie the rushes in handfuls to dry. They make half a dozen bundles in all. 'A stick down the middle of each bundle would stop them from curling up—if we'd any sticks,' Cormac worries.

They have a few branches kept by, for starting fires, as bird corpses are no good for that. Trian tries cutting a slice from a thicker log with the hatchet, then shaving it into thin sticks, but they either snap or curl up. Sometimes living on the Great Skellig is like an elaborate riddle, or one of those dreams in which Trian's charged with sewing nettles to make a shirt, weaving a rope of ashes, carrying water in a sieve.

He makes do without sticks; he binds the bundles tightly at both ends and hopes that the rushes will all incline to curl in different ways, so that in their diverging they'll keep each other true.

The next evening, the warm sky's clouded. Trian tells himself that if the hunt's going to happen, it has to be tonight. Their meal is two puffins, skewered over a fire in which five others are flaming and blackening. As soon as he's eaten, he asks, 'Father, may I go shining?'

'Go what?' the Prior asks.

'Fowling for shearwaters by the shine of a candle, to collect their belly oil for making rush lights.'

The Prior nods. 'That will work. But be careful not to trip, on such a dark night.'

'It's only when there's no moon that they fly in off the sea,'

Trian explains. (Could the birds be scared of the moon?) 'But if I may take one of our candles—just the stub—I'll try to bedazzle them with it, see?'

The Prior shrugs. 'Very well.'

'Let me help with the shining, Brother?' Cormac asks.

Even though the old monk's gammy leg might give under him, Trian nods.

'You should wrap your hands in case the shearwaters bite,' the Prior advises.

Trian finds two cloths for each of them to double around their knuckles.

First they recite Nocturns. *'From the rising of the sun to its setting, there is none like you,'* the Prior chants. *'From the great sea to where the sun goes down belongs to you.'* When they've sung the three psalms, heard the readings, and said the prayers, it's dark enough to begin.

Cormac banks the fire, mounding ashes over the blackened bird bones. Trian has the hand net ready, and a short taper; Cormac, a sack and a bucket. Overhead, stars prick out between drifting clouds. Once Trian's eyes adjust, there's enough faint brightness to let him pick his way over to the honeycombed part of the hill. When he steps in a hole, he decides it will be safer to go forward on his knees. Cormac kneels too and fumbles in his wake, dragging the bucket.

Trian listens for the shearwaters coming in off the sea, shrieking to their hungry chicks. He takes out the fire horn and uncorks it. He pushes in the tip of the candle, and moves it about till the wick flares up. 'Here, Brother,' whispering as he hands the candle to Cormac. He stoppers up the horn and puts it in his pouch. 'Hold it up—'

Bird eyes are leaping out already. Pairs of them, framed in dark holes; unable to look away or hide, disoriented by the glory of the light. Trian snatches one shearwater out of its burrow and breaks its neck with a flick of the wrist. Oil dribbles from its beak over his hand, smelling sweet and lightly fishy; precious stuff he mustn't let seep out in the sack. 'Give me the candle, Brother, and you squeeze the oil directly into the bucket, that'll be faster.'

Cormac seems at a loss.

'Turn it upside down and knead the stomach,' Trian orders, handing over the limp shearwater in exchange for the wavering light.

The old monk clutches the bird so hard with both hands, Trian hears oil squirting onto the wood.

Another and another and another. Trian rips the shearwaters out of their burrows and Cormac drains every drop out of them. There are so many fliers drawn to the light, Trian takes up the hand net and makes great swings with it, sieving the air. He reaches into the wriggling, flapping net and shakes the life out of each bird. Grabbing and snatching at the crumbling ground, at the sky, he deals out death like some monster. Down-flecked hands slippery with oil, fingers pecked (he's lost his bandages), painful knees, scraped ankles. The faster Trian kills, the sooner it'll be over.

The hours slither by. The candle burns very low. 'Enough,' Cormac says at last.

'But we need—'

'The bucket's full, Brother.'

They crawl back to the fire, Trian hefting the bucket with great care, a foot at a time, so none of the liquid gold will be spilled; so that no small death will go to waste. Cormac drags the sack of shearwater carcasses behind.

The Prior's awake, lighting a candle, about to ring the bell for Vigil.

Cormac wakes puzzled by the sticky stench of his hands. Then remembers the night.

Trian's crouched over the bucket, examining the oil. He seems limber, as if after a long, unbroken sleep. Cormac tries to remember being that young, as he walks over stiffly to peer into the bucket. The yellowish stuff—some amber and red mixed in—is cool now, forming a wax at the rim. It's separating well, the stomach oil floating above the more watery liquid that's flecked with fish debris.

The bell, again, for Terce, though it seems only a minute since they were chanting Vigil. Cormac hurries to wash his hands, but even with a lot of soft soap the cold water can't shift the grease, and drops race down his skin.

After their prayers, he griddles oatcakes; he's mixed chopped seaweed in to bulk them out. The sack of oats is less than a quarter full, but he doesn't mention it for fear of starting a quarrel. If their master's still dead set against a trading trip this season, he must have some other plan for their future, surely?

'To our book-labour, now,' the Prior tells Trian. 'Be sure to scrub those hands first, so as not to taint the parchment.'

'Will I get on with making the rush lights, then?' Cormac asks.

Trian pleads, 'Father, we've a whole sack of shearwaters that have to be plucked and jointed, or they'll spoil.'

The Prior sighs. 'Time is more valuable than any meat, Brothers, and you spend it like profligates.'

Privately, Cormac can't see why the tasks of chapel-building and book-copying are so much holier than food-preserving. And he's tempted to point out that if you stint men of nourishment, their strength for work will shrink accordingly, and their lives on earth will dwindle. Why can't the Prior see that this bird meat is a bounty of time in concentrated, fleshly form?

But he presses his lips shut. He gave up the right to argue when he vowed obedience. *Monks should be humble as slaves.*

'You may take until noon, just this once,' the Prior tells Trian.

So all morning the two monks work side by side by the fire, while the Prior toils alone at the chapel. The long reeds seem dried stiff enough, or so Cormac hopes. He warms a shallow pan of the bird juice till it liquifies again—without being hot enough to burn his fingers—then undoes a bundle and immerses the naked reeds. He spreads them on a rock to congeal, with another rock resting on top to stop them blowing away. When he's finished the half-dozen bundles, he goes back to the first reeds, which feel firm enough to take another coating. Mutton fat would form harder, Cormac knows, and even a little beeswax would make these rush lights burn so much longer. But this is what God's provided.

Beside him, Trian wrenches feathers and down off the birds.

'You'll be plucking for days. Faster to skin them,' Cormac advises.

Trian nods, and switches to pulling their skins off. Denuded, the lumps of white fat stand out against the pink meat. He uses the big cleaver to chop each shearwater in four. 'We can eat a few today and tomorrow. But I suppose the rest will have to feed the fire,' he says, staring at the pile of limp carcasses. 'Unless there's any way we can save some for winter?'

Cormac mulls it over. 'We could cook them down ever so slowly over a weak flame, all day and all night too.'

'That'll preserve the meat?'

'If we cover it with its own grease in crocks, sealed tight.' Not that they've many crocks left, after the Prior dropped half of them, but still, it's a start.

'Brother, there's no end to your knowledge.'

'I'm just old,' Cormac says with a chuckle.

Together they joint the birds and layer them with handfuls of salt in the biggest pot.

Brushing stone dust off his hands, the Prior walks over to the fire. 'What success have you had with the lights, Brothers?'

'I'll try one this minute.' Cormac kindles one of the rushes at the fire. The flame shrinks and smokes; that's because the rush is too upright, he realises. They have no iron nips here to hold these lights up slantwise. He tries laying this one flat on a rock, but that makes the flame race along.

'Stand it up in a jar?' the Prior suggests.

Trian fetches one from their stone hut, and Cormac tries that. In the jar, the rush lies diagonally and burns more steadily.

'Not bad at all,' the Prior pronounces.

Cormac's relieved.

The Prior turns to Trian. 'It strikes me that with your young eyes, and these lights, now we have a stone cell to work in, you could keep up the copying after dark.'

The young monk doesn't say a word.

But Cormac can hear Trian's misery, as loud as a wail. He intervenes: 'Oh, Father, by their nature these rush lights will spit and sputter. Imagine if one dripped on a manuscript, or a bit snapped off and set it on fire.'

The Prior's lips tighten. 'What about oil lamps—would they be safer?'

'Somewhat, but we packed no lamps.' Cormac thinks of those little earthenware ones at Cluain Mhic Nóis.

'Shells,' the Prior says briskly. 'Oyster, or scallop—I'm sure the foreshore's littered with them? You could add little wicks of cord, fill them with this bird fat and let it set. Keep them stacked up and ready.'

Cormac nods. He can tell by Trian's face that the young monk dreads the idea of copying all evening as well as all day, but he has to admit that shell lamps could work.

Trian writes and catches birds, slaughters them and writes. The days are getting shorter but feel endless to him. His fingers are sore from gripping pen and knife, and ripping feathers.

The puffin fledglings are fatter than their parents now. They stagger around the rocks like drunks, trying out their wings, and Trian, watching, seizes and slays them, because those are his orders. He hauls their bodies back by the dozen, to feed the flames. He expected to be used to it by now, but it seems to be getting harder by the day.

The Prior insists it was for this that God established birds on the Skelligs in clamorous crowds when he first created the world. But Trian struggles to believe that such a variety of lightsome and beautiful birds have formed in their translucent ovoid caskets, broken out of them, walked, cried out to their brethren, taken flight, over and over for these thousands of years...all so Trian can now fling them down to flame and char on a cooking fire.

At night he dreams of throttling books in a great feather-storm of flapping pages. He resents the Psalter the Prior made, for its matchless grace that he can never hope to reproduce. But he reserves his real hate for his own grubby copy.

Now that they've made lamps of shells, the Prior insists there need be no slackening with the approach of shorter days. He and Trian should be able to keep at their appointed task all winter in the hut, crouching on their upturned buckets with their manuscripts on their knees. It'll grow cold, of course, he says, but not enough to make their hands seize up.

The prospect of such a winter makes Trian want to run away across the cliffs.

Summer's not over yet, and the aching in his palms is already spreading through his body. Tightness in his knuckles and neck no matter how often he cracks them. He has trouble waking up, whether first thing in the morning or when the bell calls him to prayer in the middle of the short night.

He craves—above all things—his pipe. *Not needed,* the Prior said on the riverbank, but so many of the things they did pack because they thought them needful, and have since been used up or lost, the Prior now deems surplus to requirements, so what was the logic? Trian can't see why the tiniest bit of room couldn't have been made for his instrument. He remembers its light feel in his hands, and the holes, smooth to his fingertips. He shuts his eyes now and whistles, fingers playing the air, trying to conjure up those sweet notes.

It occurs to him that a great auk's wing bone can't be so

different from that of a swan. In his next free moment, he sidles off to dig a wing bone out of Cormac's midden and scrub it clean. When he chops off the two ends with the hatchet, he finds the middle almost hollow; he just has to clean out the yellowish sediment with a pointer chisel. Trian grinds the straight mouthpiece smooth on a rock. He recalls, more or less, where Brother Blathmac showed him to put the holes; he drills them gently so the bone won't split, and checks the note by blowing as he goes along. Piercing the first three openings a handspan beneath the mouthpiece, he leaves a little gap, then makes the last two, and finally a V-shaped end to taper the sound as it comes out.

Over their noon meal of oatcakes and blackened puffin meat, Trian lets out a huge yawn.

'Tired from writing?' Cormac asks.

But Trian can't answer that in front of the Prior; it would sound ungrateful, lazy, rebellious.

'I'm put in mind of blessed Ailbe,' Cormac goes on. 'That holy man had so great a soul-friendship for an abbess called Scíath that he lent her his best scribe to make her nuns a copy of the Gospels. But it happened that year, when the scribe had only two of the Gospels written out, he fell ill and went to his rest.' Cormac crosses himself. 'Well, Ailbe, paying the abbess a visit some months on, was mortified to hear this news. He marched to the scribe's grave and ordered him out, setting him to work again till the second half of the task would be done!'

The thought of being exhumed for book-labour squeezes a terrible honk of laughter out of Trian.

The Prior glares.

He drops his head and says, 'I beg pardon, Father.'

Artt finds he's thriving on hard work. Whether he's hammering stones for the walls of the island's chapel or copying the Greek Testament, he relishes that sensation of giving everything in the Lord's service. Squeezing himself out like a grape.

But after a long morning of pelting rain, writing in the hut by the faint daylight that comes through the entrance, jostling elbows with Trian, even Artt needs air before he can start again. He sends Trian off to catch them some fish, as it's a fast-day.

He restores himself by looping the Great Skellig, pacing out his territory. '*God's eye to look before me,*' he chants. '*God's ear to hear for me. God's hand to steady me.*' Crossing the Saddle, he lets his hood fall, welcoming the soft drizzle.

When Artt first registers the notes, he mistakes them for the yip of one of the eagles who haunt the South Peak. But no, that's a *tune* he's hearing. Could he be imagining it, or is it some trick of the devil's? As he mounts up towards the South Peak, the music gets clearer. He creeps along a ledge and leans around a great boulder.

Trian, cross-legged, piping. He stops and stares guiltily.

Artt walks up to him and holds out his hand.

Trian puts the instrument into it.

It's so well crafted, Artt thinks at first that it's the one from Cluain Mhic Nóis. 'Did you smuggle this in our baggage against my orders?'

'No, Father! I made it, just yesterday. From the wing of a great auk.'

It is a fine instrument, but everything depends on the purity of the intention. In this case, it's rank disobedience. 'So you've defied me by whittling this behind my back.'

'But I couldn't ask—'

'Because you knew the answer,' Artt says. 'You knew you were going astray. You were skulking—ashamed, perhaps, but not truly penitent.'

A sob.

Artt tries to snap the pipe in two, but finds it's too strong. So he lifts one leg and breaks it over his thigh.

Trian lets out a gasp as if he's been stabbed.

Artt tosses the pieces into the void. 'My son,' he says softly, 'a man's life may seem long to you, but it is like the journey of a single day. We are all hurrying towards heaven, and I'm only trying to lighten your load.'

The pale blue eyes are shiny with water.

He makes his voice ring out like a trumpet. 'We can't bring so much as the clothes on our backs with us, not even our own skin or bones—we must leave all that to rot. Each of us will be summoned to the gates at a moment's notice, perhaps many years from now, perhaps today.'

He waits for Trian's acknowledgement. But the young man sits stunned, bereft.

'I'm just trying to keep your gaze fixed above, so you'll be ready, you see? I must part you from everything but God.'

Trian weeps, then, as if finally convinced of his fault.

Artt steps forward to enfold him in a strong and merciful embrace.

THE LAST FIRE

THE GREAT SKELLIG'S emptying. The puffins and guillemots have gone south, disappearing practically overnight; a great exodus, Trian thinks, as when the Israelites were freed from slavery in Egypt. Will the kittiwakes and cormorants be next to head off, he wonders, or might they overwinter here along with the flightless auks?

The birds are spending these last mild days on the water. The sea's their true home, Trian's coming to realise—the island only a precarious, temporary perch where they lay their eggs. Without puffin chicks for fuel, these days, he has to eke out Cormac's cooking fire with the carcasses of great auks, which smoulder more reluctantly. He doesn't hear the shearwaters anymore, on these cooler evenings, and he misses their hullaballoo.

He remembers leaf drop, in the groves of Cluain Mhic Nóis; the whirling smokes of gold and brown on the autumn winds. Here he has to read the turning of the season in the departure of birds, instead. And in the drying up of the lingering flowers: little pinks of spurrey and white stars of stonecrop, crumpled daisies of mayweed and red-brown pillars of dock, even great purple blooms of tree mallow. Everything's hunkering down, turning back to grey-green.

The one exception is the little rowan tree on the Plateau. Her leaves are red but they cling on with a stubbornness that gladdens Trian, and still she puts out handful after handful of scarlet berries. How she pulls such riches of colour from the dull slabs she's rooted among, he can't tell. He's wedged a few bunches of berries in between the stones of the hut's round roof to dry alongside Cormac's strings of onions. The Prior's decided they should sleep in there now, on cold nights, anyway. They lie wrapped in their cloaks, as close as three bodies in a grave.

Trian sits under the rowan's contorted form, one dank foggy morning, and introduces his arms through her pliable branches. His fingers caress her cracked bark in thanks for her gifts, not only the berries but her persistence, her grace. He needs to learn how she bends and endures.

'Brother, what are you doing?'

He scrambles to his feet. 'Praying, Father.' It's true, though he couldn't explain it.

'Back to the books now,' the Prior orders.

Trian follows him to the desk in the distance, already feeling the cramp in his palms.

Cormac has no idea when he and the Prior will ever finish the chapel. The walls are so massive, and they've already used all the best rocks for the altar and the beehive hut. So he has to pick his way nervously down the island's steep paths in search of big boulders, and split them by dropping them. He hammer-shapes each suitable stone on the spot, and carries it back onto the Plateau so he or the Prior can slot it into one of the walls that rise so unbearably slowly.

His garden is past its best, now, the bloated turnips gone bland, the bolted spinach bitter, the great nettles knotty with fibre, but still he throws everything into the soup. Cormac never got many leaves of fat hen, but it did send up a quantity of big brown seeds for planting next year, as well as tiny black ones that he grinds by the fistful to improvise a sort of dark pancake. How he misses leavened bread baked in a pot, the brown crust hiding the pillowy inside.

On Sunday morning, as they eat, the Prior mentions, with a glassy serenity, that there's no more wine for the Mass.

Cormac's eyes meet Trian's in panic.

'Many of the Church Fathers, such as holy Cyprian, rejected the drinking of any intoxicants,' the Prior goes on. 'They offered plain Communions of bread and water, so we will do the same.'

Cormac's head hurts, trying to make sense of this. Oat and wheat are both grains, at least, so in the case of their blackened-oatcake Host, one kind of bread is standing in for another. But wine is the fermented juice of grapes, and water is something else entirely.

The Prior goes on as if he hears Cormac's silent objections. 'The original substance doesn't matter, Brothers. Through the miracle of Consecration, any liquid can be transmuted into the blood of our Lord Jesus Christ.'

Any liquid?

'Amen,' Trian mutters.

Cormac forces himself to echo 'Amen.'

Trian looks around, clearly searching for a new subject. His eyes fall on the unfinished chapel. 'That's coming along,' he remarks.

Cormac thinks of a story. 'I'm put in mind of holy Mochaoi. How he was in the woods cutting timber to build his church, when he heard a gorgeous bright bird singing on a blackthorn nearby, and realised it was talking to him.'

Trian asks, 'What did the bird say?'

Cormac puts on a high nasal tone. '*I am here to tell you your work is good, to encourage you and amuse you for a while with my singing.* So Mochaoi stood there in the wood, entranced and enthralled. It felt to him as if the bird's song lasted one happy hour. The fresh branches he'd gathered didn't wither, and the spiders paused in their spinning. Even the tireless bees left off collecting nectar from the flowers. All creatures were listening to the ravishing music.'

The Prior's eyes have lost focus, as if he's hearing that same song.

'What happened next?' Trian wants to know.

'The bird flew off,' Cormac tells him. 'Only then did the holy man realise it had been an angel in feathered form. So he carried his timber back to the site of the church—and there he found it already built. He didn't know the monks' faces, and none of them recognised his, because not one, not fifty, but a hundred and fifty years had passed.'

Trian marvels at the span of time.

It strikes Cormac now what a sad story this is. To be soothed with music and given a heavenly reward, but in exchange you've lost a century and a half in a blink, and all your friends

are dead and buried…If he'd been Mochaoi, he'd have preferred to sweat over every beam of that church than to dream
away his whole life in an afternoon. Once childhood is over,
don't the years pass too fast already, rolling over a man as
fast as waves? But then, the Lord never does stoop to consult
his people.

Trian's voice has tightened oddly. 'If the Church teaches that
hard labour is so good for the soul, why did the angel entertain
Mochaoi with sweet music instead of leaving him to work?'

The question takes Cormac aback. He looks to their master.

'Perhaps to show God's powers,' the Prior says. 'We should
never take too much pride in our efforts, since beside his, ours
are as feeble as thistledown.' He rises to his feet now and strolls
off towards the midden.

Trian says, very low, 'The great auks, Brother. I think they're
going.'

This startles Cormac. 'Going where?' He waits. 'They can't
be flying south with the others.' Feeling foolish for saying it.

'Going to sea, I suppose. They're fierce swimmers.'

'But they can hardly stay afloat for six months at a time,
can they?'

Trian shrugs unhappily.

Because the great auks were already on the island when
the boat made landfall, Cormac's been assuming they're year-
rounders. How stupid of him not to suspect that the monks'
best source of food and fuel might abandon them at the end of
summer. 'Have you told the Prior?'

'He'll only say what he always says.'

Cormac nods grimly: *God will provide.*

'He broke my pipe.'

Cormac's brow furrows.

'Not God.' Trian nods at the Prior, who's squatting over the midden. 'Him.'

Cormac's never heard this mutinous tone from the young monk. 'No, Brother, we left it behind with my lyre, remember?'

'I made another, and he broke it.'

'Oh.' Cormac's chest hurts to hear that.

They sit in silence, their eyes on the Prior as he straightens and shakes out his robe.

All Cormac can think to say, under his breath, is 'Saints can be hard men.'

The Great Skellig gets quieter by the week—eerily quiet, it seems to Trian.

The day comes when they're gathered at noon, and he has to tell their master that he can't find a single, solitary great auk. 'And I'm having no luck chasing down any other birds.'

The Prior frowns. 'Surely you can make shift to get us other food—fish, say.'

Trian empties his bag on the ground: a slim bream with a bleeding mouth. 'I can, but there's nothing fatty enough to cook it with.' He finds a small, strange pleasure in spelling it out.

In the silence, the Prior nods as if this was all part of his plan; God's plan. 'Well, no more fires, then.'

Cormac gapes. He says it before Trian can: 'What, are we to eat raw stuff?'

A magnificent heave of the shoulders. 'Jesus told his follow-ers to eat *whatever was set before them*,' the Prior quotes.

'Raw is how all nourishment comes, after all. It's only worldly affectation to improve its tenderness and savour by cooking. Our food will be itself now, undisguised.'

Trian looks away to hide his face. He watches the ashes that still glow faintly from last night. He should have paid more attention to fire, while they had it; should have memorised the warmth, the dance of light.

'Let's begin this minute,' the Prior proposes in an almost festive tone. Taking up the big knife, he sets the bream down on the rock and lops off its head; hacks the body into small red chunks. He pops one in his mouth. Chews, removes a bone, chews again. Retches. 'I ate too fast,' he gasps, beckoning for a goatskin.

Cormac passes it to him.

The Prior gulps water. Then he carries on chewing. 'Join me, Brothers.'

Trian's throat locks at the prospect.

Beside him, Cormac gamely tries a piece.

But when Trian does make himself bite into the raw fish, it mostly tastes of the sea: like tears with a trace of blood. He's eating like any bird, now, he tells himself; like all God's other creatures do.

As the autumn winds down, here's the paradox that troubles Cormac. Everything they eat is cold, uncooked and leathery now, from seaweed to the tiny helpings of raw oats soaked overnight in water to the odd fish that Trian manages to catch. But even as Cormac chokes this food down, his mind's whirring with the question of how to save some so that in a few months—by which time it'll taste even worse—it might keep them alive a day longer.

Their larder, a hollow in the rocks, is half a dozen crocks of fatted bird and three of salt-brined fish. They've no containers to store any more than that. Drying's been a failure. Cormac's cut two kittiwake carcasses into pieces and filleted a few large fish, rubbed them all with salt, and hung them up, but they've only attracted flies and gone mouldy. He thinks of all those eggs back in the early summer, beautifully encased in their thin shells; he should have thought to find some way to preserve these in fat or salt. He's heard of burying eggs to keep them, but for that he'd have needed soil more than a fingernail deep.

It's too late in the season to do much about this. The Prior told them to trust in God. Cormac holds to his vow of obedience. But he can't help thinking of the boat, inverted in the cove below; of how the world of men (their fires, their hearths, their fresh-baked bread) is only a few hours' voyage away.

Every day Cormac ducks through the low door in the unfinished chapel's western wall, careful not to clip his head on the huge horizontal lintel. He straightens his back, takes a long breath, and goes to work, raising the walls. Toil is all that keeps his mind off his belly. He works either with the Prior at his side or (when the Prior's copying) on his own. These great hollow walls, why did Cormac decide they had to be two feet wide? They'll eat up every rock on the island and never be filled.

He lived through half a dozen famine seasons before he became a monk. Curiously it's not the worst time that comes to mind, but the one when Cormac was a child. Well, everything's more vivid when you're young. Then again, you snatch at any feeling at all, when you're old, even the aching of hunger, as a sign that you're not dead yet.

He's worried about Trian. Blank-faced, the young monk hunches over his Psalter on the Plateau on milder autumn days, by lamplight in the hut when it's colder. Whenever the Prior releases him, he mopes around the island, looking for bits and pieces for them to eat. Cormac finds him almost impossible to rouse for Vigil at night and Terce in the morning.

The Prior's exasperation is beginning to harden into anger. He orders Trian to skip that day's noon meal as a penance.

Cormac finds a moment to speak in their master's ear, as soothingly as he can. 'Amn't I right in thinking that scribes are known for depression of spirits, Father?'

'Notorious for it,' the Prior says crisply. 'The gloom goes by many names—*acedia, apathy, melancholia*.'

Cormac nods. It's the repetitiousness, he'd imagine.

'The condition must be subdued through prayer and hard work. If the scribe gives way to his affliction, it becomes a sin, and a great one.'

Cormac sighs. 'Maybe Brother Trian just can't keep going on so little food and sleep?'

The Prior turns away as if he hasn't heard that.

Hunger is a rumble in the concavity between Trian's sharp hips, a high note. He's beset by half-formed, unruly thoughts: *Why did we three come so far to live a cleaner life, to quell all appetites, with the consequence that all we can think about is food?*

Well, all *Trian* can think about, at least. But who knows

what goes on behind their leader's broad brow? Cormac is looking gaunt and haggard these days, and Trian imagines he himself wears the same face. But the Prior's perfect features gleam the same as ever.

Today the fishing line, when Trian dangles it from the cliffs, brings up nothing but the occasional sea devil or ray. He knows the Prior won't touch them, but he chews on their raw flesh himself, illicitly. He has trouble believing that these fish could rouse any base desires in someone who longs for nothing so much as a hot stew.

He drags around the Great Skellig whenever the Prior lets him off copying for half an hour, but rarely catches a bird anymore. If he gets near a kittiwake he tries a smooth stone in his braided leather sling: set, whirl, release. But his aim is rusty, and the bird almost always wings away.

As a child Trian used to set snares in loops of twine. It took hours of watching from a hiding place, waiting for a bird to step into the baited loop. He remembers, what were they called, *gorge hooks*? A little bone sharpened at both ends, hidden in a lump of meat, and tied to a long cord weighted down by a nearby boulder; if a bird swallowed the meat, the hook would lodge in its throat. But for bait Trian would need meat, or fish at least, and right now he has nothing. He shouldn't have thrown away the last of that ray. Would a cockle do, or a few limpets? First he'd have to make the bone needle, anyway. And before that, he must catch something for the other men to eat. His mind moves in groggy loops.

The big black cormorants are very few, this late in the season, but there'd be plenty of meat on them, even if it tasted as rank as their eggs. There's a sea stack where a couple of cormorants stand and stretch out their wings to dry. If Trian swam out to it, he supposes the birds would flap away contemptuously long before he got there.

He binds wing feathers together with twine to make a long, pliable rod, and knots his waxed noose to its end. Creeping silently along the cliff, he lowers it down to slip the loop over a cormorant's head. But the bird startles and flaps away, ripping Trian's noose and stick with it.

His attempts get more brutish. With his staff he tries clubbing kittiwakes from the length of a man away; they easily skitter out of range. He lurches around with the hand net, but can't get close enough to bring it down over any bird.

One day Trian spots a cormorant on a ledge above Seal Cove, busy swallowing a fish. His hand net would be useless against such a giant. He crawls up behind the cormorant and hurls himself on it, arms out, hoping to pin its wings with his elbows and wring its neck—

But it snaps out its wings with an outraged honk and shakes him off. He slithers down the rocks, banging his hip.

Trian limps down to the shore at Seal Cove and rips up handfuls of purple and green weed for his bag. Only a couple of limpets on the rocks; he prises them off.

He remembers the rule even as he's breaking it; he gnaws their rubbery flesh and finds he doesn't care that they're forbidden.

What can he eat next? He sees no scallops or cockles or oysters. There's so little eating on a winkle, they're hardly worth it, but still he gathers the sea snails with his blade. He pulls up one tangle of mussels—blues, purples, browns, and blacks together—and sniffs at them.

His attention's caught by the cry of a baby.

He spins around and there, rolling in the surf, making something between a grunt and a groan, is a seal pup. A whitecoat, still young enough to be helpless in the water. Injured, sick? Or just lost? The pup's creamy coat is bedraggled. Hauling itself up the rocks to get away from the punishing waves, it works its flippers exhaustedly. Five claws, Trian counts, more like the paw of a dog, more like a hand. He wants it: meat, fat, pelt. But those big moist black eyes...

He approaches, and crouches to pick up a boulder. If the pup's lost its herd, it has no chance. To leave it to die would be waste, he reminds himself. To let it die slowly, eyes pecked out by birds, would be cruelty.

But what if its mother were to come back? What if she's out there past the breakers right now, waiting, roaring back at her pup?

The whitecoat gurgles and pants. It's plumped with its mother's milk, brewed from the fish she ate yesterday.

Trian stares into its bottomless eyes. It comes to him that he himself is made of all the birds he's ever caught, which in turn owe their flesh to the fish they've snatched. And the fish are composed of the plants they nibble on, and the plants take nourishment from the sun, which rises at God's command: so he feeds all his creation. Either Trian and the other monks will eat this seal and live another week, or Trian will lie down here on these slick stones and in time his body will feed the seaweed and the fish and the birds and the seals. Everything borrowed has to be returned. The Lord made them all and will swallow them up again. *God gives and God takes, bless his name.*

Trian brings the rock down on the seal's silky skull, hard enough that one blow should do it.

Artt's not satisfied. No more than a month now until the church year will begin again with Advent. How fast summer has withered into autumn, and how little he and his monks have to show for their months on the Great Skellig. *Man's days are as grass*.

Today Trian has hauled back a gutted seal pup; the dark meat is as dense as venison, lean yet oily, with a wild, gamey taste. The liver in particular—Artt tries not to relish it too much. The problem with hunger is that he can't simply resist it, saying an absolute *no*, once and for all, as he has said to lust. The stomach whines to be fed every few hours, and to ignore it for more than a few days would constitute the grave sin of self-murder; that's why even the desert saints took their locusts and honey. Hunger is a constant argument, and Artt wishes he could be done with it.

The three men eat seal at every meal until, two days on, they can't deny that it's on the turn. Artt supposes it's the oiliness that makes the stuff so quick to spoil. Cormac won't let them eat another bite, in case they make themselves sick, and takes the carcass—still heavy with meat—to the midden.

Late afternoon, and Trian trails up the path from the Saddle, the bag over his shoulder light, holding nothing but seaweed and a few small fish for his brethren. His own belly is full of mussels—dozens of them. Heavy with shame. *Unclean*, and he ate them anyway; stuffed himself with uncleanness.

There's the Prior on the Plateau, kneeling in prayer.

No. Kneeling in a mess of foliage. And where's the rowan?

Trian's mind refuses to accept it.

The discarded hatchet catches the last of the western sun. With his knife, the Prior's slashing off berry bunches and red leaves.

A screech rips Trian's throat.

The Prior turns and calls, 'Brother, see?'

Trian sees. Hears the cuts. Smells rowan juice and tastes the tang. Feels the severing in his own limbs.

The Prior holds up what remains. Racked and twisted, a slanted vertical and two crooked, half-stripped arms springing out. 'A mighty cross to fix to the top of our chapel.'

He roars it: 'She was the only tree on the island!'

'And how favoured, now, to form the holy image of that cross on which Christ won our souls from hell.'

Trian's so close now, within arm's reach of the hatchet. He could snatch it up in half a second.

The Prior's face is shining like an angel's.

Trian shuts his eyes and drops to his knees. But still he sees that triumphant smile, and still he wants to kill the man.

He hits his own chest so hard he winds himself. To long to do murder, to savour it in your heart, that's nearly as bad as to do it. Trian's in mortal sin and he can't escape. He batters himself again and again.

That evening Artt gives his monks—as a concession to their weak understanding—a homily on the rowan. How in the depths of his contemplation, he heard God demand a great cross to affix to the roof of his chapel when it's completed. How their Prior was inspired to shape it from the one thing already growing at the top of the island (by divine plan) in cruciform shape. Could there be any higher use of a plant than this?

Still the two monks remain sullen, especially Trian, who hasn't said a word since he saw the rowan felled. In silence they chew on their raw fish and seaweed, grinding it down. They crouch on their stools around the blackened hollow where their fire used to burn and a rush light now slants in a jar.

Sometimes Artt wishes he'd never set eyes on either of these stupid men; had set out alone in search of his island. Could he have managed the voyage on his own? It might have been better to make the attempt, and die trying.

Time for Nocturns. He stands, rings the bell, and leads the others in the psalms.

Halfway through, Trian breaks off and retches silently behind his hand. Artt ignores him.

But after the final prayer, Trian scrambles away into the twilight and vomits, hard and wetly. Instead of blowing out the rush as a signal to bed down on their ticks in the sleeping cell, Artt moves the light closer to the young monk, scrutinizing him. 'Are you ill, Brother?'

All Trian will say is, 'I beg pardon.'

'You'll feel better now it's out,' Cormac tells him.

But Trian keeps retching. Soon he scuttles away in the dark, in the direction of the midden. Awful sounds of the voiding of bowels.

Afterwards, the young monk throws himself down on the

ground outside the hut. He gasps, 'I'll sleep out here tonight, so as not to disturb the pair of you.'

Cormac brings him a beaker of water. Then he goes into the hut to fetch Trian's tick, and his cloak for a blanket.

Hours later, when Artt wakes in the black night for Vigil, he feels around for the fire horn, and kindles a rush in its hoarded embers. Cormac sits up, swaying groggily. Only two of them in here, the huge shadows of their heads wavering on the inside of the dome, and for a moment Artt's confused, before he recalls that Trian's lying outside.

After their psalms and prayers, he stoops over to go out the doorway and check on the young man. The cloak's been cast aside, and Trian—silvery in the starlight—is writhing about on the lumpen mattress.

Cormac's at Artt's side. 'Still not well, Brother?'

A grunt from Trian.

Sometimes the vileness of the body revolts Artt. Why could men not be composed of air? Why did God stoop to making a race out of stinking clay?

'Here's water.' Cormac kneels to put the lip of the goatskin to Trian's mouth.

A swallow. Another. But a few moments later Trian jerks his head to the side and spews again.

Artt leads Cormac back to the cell. Soon the old man's snoring, but Artt lies staring into the dark.

The next morning, Trian's worse. He lies limp and sweating, except when he suddenly curls up with a groan as if some demon's gnawing at his vitals.

They ate the same meal yesterday, but Artt and Cormac have been spared, and Trian's being punished. For which sin, exactly, Artt wonders? Why did Trian start beating his breast like some frenzied druid when he saw the rowan cut down?

Artt does all he can. He stands over the young monk and prays for his soul, hour after hour. He uses their tiny flasks of holy water and oil to anoint him. He cups water in the holy bell, for added power, and has Trian drink from it.

Artt has never been ill, himself, since he did the impossible and survived the plague. But his own mother was taken this way, with a flux of the guts that made her bleed at both ends. Artt was five years old; he watched it happen. He's always known how flesh can melt away in days; how no amount of crying will persuade the Lord to change his inscrutable mind. So he whispers: *'Not my will be done but thine.'*

Cormac's no doctor. He can't tell whether it's Trian's black or yellow bile or blood or phlegm that's overbalanced his other humours; he only knows that the young monk seems to be dying.

He tries mashing up vervain and coriander in water, to cool the fever. He gets most of it down Trian's throat, but then it comes back up. Sunken-eyed, shrunken, the young man lies curled up like a baby on a mattress in the stone cell. He has too little control of his limbs even to pick up a waterskin.

Another look in the herb box. Cormac's mind is racing. He could blunt the young man's suffering with henbane and poppy. Some who take those herbs sleep three days and wake up with their fever gone; then again, some don't wake. Trian is already so weak, what if the medicine kills him?

Cormac pleads silently, *Don't abandon us.* The three of them are like one body that needs all its parts. Trian has the most skill and nerve for climbing and fowling and egging and hunting and fishing, shinnying up and down the bony flanks of this island. And other qualities, too: an innocence, a sort of radiance.

Cormac lays a wet cloth over the dark red hairline.

A terrible squirting. Trian moans. 'My fault.'

'Brother! How is sickness your fault?'

'Unclean.'

'Don't fret, I'll mop you up,' Cormac murmurs.

'Ate mussels. Shellfish,' the young man slurs through his teeth.

Cormac understands, and is filled with rage. Not at Trian; at the Prior, and his rules; at all the makers of rules. 'Of course you did. You were hungry, weren't you?'

Tears leak out of Trian's left eye.

Cormac pulls up Trian's damp robe and starts picking at the drawstring of his braies.

Trian's hand flaps in clumsy protest. 'No. Let me—'

But he's as weak as water. 'Come on, I'm not going to leave you lying in your dirt.' Cormac gets the knot undone and pulls the soaked drawers off. With a goatskin of water and a cloth he does his best to mop Trian's buttocks. (Absently wondering how he'll ever get the soaked mattress clean.) Then—

Cormac stares. In the dim of the cell, at first he's not sure quite what he's looking at.

No wonder Trian's parents impressed on him that he was *made for a monk*—not meant for marrying, likely not capable of getting children.

Cormac shakes his head in confusion. As the apostle Paul

wrote, *Now we see dimly as if in a mirror.* Cormac can't fathom any of this, but he has to believe that God does.

Moving lightly, he finishes cleaning Trian, whose eyes are shut, as if he's being lifted and dropped on the strong tide of fever. Cormac tugs down the hem of Trian's robe, and looks for the spare pair of braies to put on him.

Nothing more that Cormac can do for now, so he goes out onto the Plateau to soap his reeking hands and rinse them in the pot by the cistern. Where the rowan used to grow, a dead stub. The twisted cross of her trunk and two limbs leans against the unfinished chapel, waiting to crown its roof. The mist's thickening. It strikes Cormac that fog blinds all men equally.

He checks on their meagre plot. Finding a leathery turnip, he shakes the earth off it and gnaws on it. He pulls up the last tough leaves (sorrel, spinach, nettle, and fat hen) for pestling into a sour paste. Nothing else to save. Time to bed the garden down for its long sleep. He starts shovelling their midden over the low wall onto the plot, hoping that by spring the clumped, slimy stuff will have rotted down and built up the soil. As Cormac lifts and spreads one spadeful at a time, they flash out at him, the undecomposed reminders of the past half year: the pig bones, bird skulls, beaks and feet, eggshells, feathers, curls of leathered skin; hard cinders from their fires; dry fragments of onion skin; always the reek of the monks' own excrement.

It occurs to Cormac to take the last of his onion sets out of the herb box. He pushes them right into the stinking matter, in faint hopes of an early-summer crop next year, if by any miracle he and his brethren manage to hold out that long.

OVERWINTERING

NIGHT AND DAY now Cormac tends Trian in the beehive cell, while the Prior sleeps outside. He cleans him as necessary; he never says a word about how Trian's shaped.

On the third morning, Cormac wakes to find the young man sitting up beside him. Trian looks ravaged, befuddled, but alive.

'*Deo gratias!*' Cormac hurries to open one of their crocks and mash up the preserved, cooked bird.

Trian seems to regain strength, spoon by spoon.

That Sunday the Prior offers a special Mass in thanksgiving for the recovery of Brother Trian and the preservation of their fellowship. 'Our faith stands like an island,' he proclaims, 'lashed by a sea of doubt.'

For Communion bread they have a pat of soaked raw oatmeal. And when the oats are gone, as they will be in a week or two, Cormac supposes something else will have to stand in for the Host: a leaf? A piece of seaweed? A bowlful of air?

He's altered, he knows; he's brewing an infection of the spirit. These days, when he goes poking around the Plateau in search of anything remotely edible—the last of the bitter spoonwort, campion, dock, stonecrop, spurrey, tree mallow, even flakes of orange lichen, in hopes their colour might carry some vigour—in the back of his mind, Cormac is picking a fight. As he and the Prior keep adding to the walls of the chapel—almost roof-height now—his fury rises too.

One day he finds himself tracking the Prior up the little slope to the North Peak. Their leader stands staring out past the Lesser Skellig, towards the hills of the mainland. Seven, eight miles away, no distance at all. Cormac squints, wishing his sight was sharp enough to let him spot the smoke of a settlement. 'Father,' he begins, too abrupt. 'Would you think again about one short crossing before winter, just for food and fuel?'

The Prior gives him that stony stare. 'Those whom God loves best keep at a remove from the world of men. Remember holy Cóemgen, who lived off the nuts of the wood and the herbs of the earth.'

'I'd love a good nut!' It bursts out of Cormac. 'There are none on this island, and precious few herbs. Look at us, reduced to the state of beasts, clinging to a cold rock and chewing on raw weeds.'

'God will provide.'

'He has,' Cormac snaps. 'He's provided a boat.'

The Prior pulls himself up to his full height. 'The vessel was the means of our voyage, that's all. We might as well burn it now, if it's a fire you crave to warm your hands.'

Is their master losing his wits? 'You'd do that? You'd trap us here?'

'Trap?' the Prior echoes. 'God gave us this Great Skellig. Why would we spurn his gift?'

'But Father.' How can Cormac wake him from this spell? 'Brother Trian nearly died on us, poisoned by—'

He breaks off so as not to give away the secret of the mussels. 'Half-famished! Don't you care whether we survive?'

He means the question rhetorically. But the Prior puts his head on one side. 'Would it matter so very much, in the final reckoning?'

Cormac blinks.

'After all, it's not as individuals that we have any importance,' the Prior muses. 'We three were called to found this holy house, and that's what we've done.'

'Found it, but for what?' Cormac demands. 'I thought we were building for the future, maybe for other men who God would guide to sail after us. But now I see you mean this to be our tomb.'

The Prior doesn't deny it. 'God owns our souls, whether they're dressed in feeble flesh or not. What grounds have we for believing that our living pleases him any more than our death?'

Cormac is staggered. He finds himself thinking of austere Comgall, who one night took pity on his shivering companions and lit them a fire with his loving breath. This man is different; his heart is a desert. 'You called us a family, Father. Your family.'

The Prior shrugs. 'I have no other.'

'Then—'

'But I say, with holy Paul, *Christ Jesus is my Lord, for whom I've lost all, and count it as dung.*'

Dung. The word heats Cormac's face, and he stumbles away.

Time is the problem, as Trian sees it. The days are shrinking, and he needs all the remaining light to work on the Psalter, because in their cell in the evenings he can barely see the page by the wavering flicker of the scallop lamp. But he has to steal an hour or two to find the monks something to eat, by fishing from the rocks or scavenging down by the shore. So maybe the real problem is food. If they open too many crocks and devour their stores of bird meat and fish, they'll starve before autumn gives way to winter. But if they don't eat enough now, how will they be able to work long and hard enough to find more to eat? The oats are all used up. The three men have dark circles under their eyes; they're windy and their breath stinks.

When Trian's belly is empty, he can't get to sleep for its grumbling. Cormac has stuffed their hoarded bird-down into their ticks, but the bristly old leaves still scratch. Then again, sleep is little comfort. When it takes Trian half the night to drop off, he dreams of the rowan, wailing and waving her flayed arms. Or of the grey-fleshed dead scribe (the one the saint dragged out of his grave to finish copying the Gospels), scratching page after page to earn entry to heaven, or even just the quiet of death again.

After such dreams, Trian can't rouse himself at the sound of the bell in the darkness, for Vigil, or in the morning, for Terce. If the Prior has to shout in his ear and rip away the sheepskin cloak, Trian throws himself down to ask pardon, and the Prior will order him to get up and make one hundred genuflections. A day that begins that way…the work always goes badly after, because Trian's tired, and loathes himself, and his hands shake.

So the problem is work, really. He can't form his letters well when he's cold all the time and his belly growls and his eyelids drop and he's distracted by the question of what the monks will eat next, because no problem is greater than that. As he writes, his mind roams the island, probing its crevices, vainly grabbing at the last few birds, who flutter out of reach. If Trian's eyes stray, the descenders of this line's letters will entangle the ascenders of the next. Lack of sleep is the problem, he decides. If he could only find the time to get enough sleep and find enough food and do enough work and...

Trian lurches up in the morning, eats what little there is, and toils on. He's so worn out, he can think of no other way, no deviation from this stony track.

Cormac comes up to him outside the hut and takes him by the sleeve. 'Brother.'

Trian raises his sore eyes.

'You understand we're stranded now?'

He can't think of a word to say. He nods.

'Our master won't let us off the island, no matter what happens. Sooner or later, we'll die here.'

Trian is too tired to be shocked by any of this. What's to be done? They are vowed men. He pulls away from Cormac and stumbles on.

In a cold breeze, alone outside the beehive cell the next morning, Trian is making up more ink for decorating the initial capitals when his numb hands fumble the vermilion. The jar drops and cracks like an egg on the rock, spilling its scarlet powder. Trian falls to his knees but already the stuff's smeared on his shoe, blowing across the Plateau, dusting red on a hummock of thrift. He struggles to scoop some up but he's only making the mess worse. The three fragments of the jar are stained with what they used to hold. He fits them back together neatly, emptily.

He goes to wash his hands with the fishy-smelling soap. Then he seeks out the Prior—eventually finding him in prayer, on the North Peak—and kneels to show him the shattered jar.

The Prior speaks with a quiet chill. 'It's not me you've offended by your clumsiness, it's God.'

'I beg pardon. I've heard a sort of purple can be ground from cockles—'

'Get up.' As Trian does, the Prior fingers the shards; examines a trace of red on his own fingertip. 'This vermilion is ground cinnabar, a rare ore dug out of the mountains in Spain.'

The man knows everything.

'It makes its miners so sick,' the Prior tells him, 'they're known for falling down in fits. Men died to gather this precious red, so that you could make God's words glow.'

Trian gnaws his lip.

'So don't talk to me of cockle shells. Have you no red in yourself that will substitute?'

He's bewildered. Then, 'My blood?'

'Just as Christ poured out his for our sins. There are pagan scribes in the Far East who'll use no other ink.'

Trian bends his head and thanks his master.

'Don't cut your fingers,' the Prior warns him, 'or you could smear the copy.'

'Then—'

'Under your tongue.'

Trian hurries back to the hut to make good his error. In the dim, he lifts his tongue and slips his knife into his mouth. Careful, now, in case he goes too deep and makes a mute of himself. The sting makes his eyes water; under his tongue the hollow fills with a warm trickle. It's salty, metallic, and he has to resist swallowing the delicious, savoury broth. Instead he spits it out into a small bowl.

Trian seizes a clean pen and hurries to begin the inking before the blood can congeal. He places the tiny dots around every curve and sweep of the black initial. All that disappoints him is how quickly the bright red dulls to brown. It seems there's no rare ore in Trian.

He works and waits for the wintry day to be over. The light fades, and it's Vespers again, and a bowl of fish tails to chew with his sore mouth, then Nocturns, the impossibility of falling asleep, and Vigil—the Prior declaiming the Gospel in his ear, *'Why are you sleeping? Get up and pray'*—and sleep so heavy it seems his cloak has turned to lead, and relentless light's return.

The coldest morning so far. Singing Terce in jagged voices, and chewing on seaweed, and here's Trian on his bucket leaning over the Psalter again, pivoting to write in his copy, mouth still tasting like the point of a spear. Swaying, cooped up inside the bounds of an *o* and a *b* and a *p,* caged between the lines, Trian mutters the next words of the psalm as he copies them: *Our souls escape like birds from the fowler's snare.* What he wouldn't give to escape this wearisome labour! To be changed into a bird, now—to wing away over the Skelligs and their sea stacks and little islets. Unknowing, indifferent, freed from duty—from thought itself—needing only the lift of wind.

Trian has made a mark in the margin. Not a blot or a smear but a tiny shape, a round head with a beak. When did he do that—just now? Was he asleep, or in a trance? He can't erase it, so he keeps on drawing, giving it a tiny curved breast and wings and a tail. Feet tucked under because it's in flight.

'What's this?' Massive shoulders in the doorway block out the light, as the Prior leans in to examine the page.

Trian jerks. 'Just a picture.' He struggles for words: 'The psalmist compares the soul to a bird here, and I found myself drawing—'

'You *found yourself* doing it? No one sins by accident.'

Trian sets down the pen on the ground as if it's burning hot.

'Such appalling arrogance, to think the words of God could be improved by your scribble.'

'I'll scratch it out—scrape it off.' Trian has the knife out already.

'You think it won't still show, in the bare margin, the stain of your daubings?' With a lunge, the Prior snatches away Trian's knife by the blade. 'You've spoiled the whole leaf, almost two pages' worth. All that work for nothing.' He folds back and flattens the gathering so the offending leaf of vellum lies on its own on the upturned bucket. He cuts along the spine, which takes him two tries; the knife point protests on the brass edge and rips a jagged piece off the parchment. He grunts in fury.

'Father, shall I—'

'Ruined!' The Prior lurches out of the hut.

Trian dives after him.

'Look what you've done.' The Prior hurls the whole gathering away.

Disbelieving, Trian watches the wind catch the sewn pages and carry them along like some broken-winged, headless bird. He drops to the ground at his master's feet.

'Sloth!' the Prior screams. 'Disrespect for Scripture, pride, disobedience, self-will. You've defaced God's holy work.'

Trian weeps into the turf. 'Let me make satisfaction.'

'It won't undo what you've done.'

'Please, Father! Set me some penance.'

'Go down and stand in cross-vigil in the water, then, until the sun sets.'

Trian runs to the cliff so fast he almost overshoots the path and slithers down the slope.

Down at Landing Cove, he leaves his shoes above the tide line. He wades into the water in his robe, up to his neck. It bites like ice.

Trian plants his feet on barnacled rocks, widens his stance so he won't be knocked over. He spreads out his arms in cross-vigil and turns his palms up to the sky. Watches the white disc of the cloud-masked sun inch overhead. Water to his chin, gnawing his flesh. He tells himself this is not full winter yet; he's hardly going to freeze by nightfall. The salty swell must hold some memory of the summer warmth, surely.

He's already hurting all over. But pain's only a kind of labour, after all. He can bear it. One long day in the water, that's all, and then his master will forgive him.

Pain strengthens the soul, sharpens the mind, subdues the will. This is colder than hell.

Trian deserves it.

Pain's a kind of prayer. Doesn't he owe this aching and more to Jesus, who lovingly suffered so much to redeem all mankind? This should work as surely as a wheel moves a cart: confession, contrition, penance, then absolution. God is landing loving blows on his child, that's all; knocking self out of Trian.

Is this how the rowan felt as the hatchet blows rained down on her?

Pain brings wisdom, Trian reminds himself. The longer he stands here, the closer he'll come to being one with the fish, one with the rocks, one with the sea itself—with all that God's made. He can't feel his limbs. Water in his ears, his nose, his throat; he spits and struggles upright. His hair's loose, red weed floating around his face.

Hours.

Trian dozes and dreams that he's become a featherlight copy of himself, like that kittiwake he found after the storm—that his body has shed all its awkward weight and survives only as pure line.

Cormac watches from the cliffs, and keeps watching, even though all he can make out is a blurred shape in the surf.

He mustn't go down to the shore; he mustn't intrude on this awful privacy. If he hauls Trian out of the water, he knows the young monk will only shake him off and wade back in to begin his penance all over again.

No one could accuse Cormac of being soft. He's seen men writhe in a tangle of their own guts on the battlefield. But he finds he can't stomach this, somehow. Is it maybe because of what he knows—what he saw when he was nursing Trian?

That shouldn't make any difference. So what if the young man's oddly made?

Or part girl, even. Don't women often bear what would break their mates? Cormac's known several who've died with babies halfway out.

Besides, full male or female or somewhere in between, Trian is made of strong stuff. Cormac thinks of the hero Cú Chulainn, with his fourteen sharp fingers and toes and burning pupils; the fierce beauty of his strangeness.

Then again, Trian's been so ill. So close to death from those bad mussels, not long ago.

Still, if he came through that trial, this sea-punishment won't kill him, surely?

The shape in the water staggers, lurches.

No, Cormac can't watch in silence any longer; can't stand by. What's choking him is the injustice. Trian's done no harm. For the Prior to lose his temper so savagely and set Trian to use his own blood to replace the red ink dropped by mistake... and then to send him to stand up to his neck in the cold sea all day for a drawing no bigger than his thumb-tip... It's a kind of madness, it seems to Cormac. The man has to be stopped.

He hurries up to the Plateau, soles slipping on the scree. He finds the Prior on his knees by the damaged high cross, murmuring in prayer. He musters all his nerve to interrupt.

'Father.'

The Prior turns his head stiffly.

Cormac tries a soft approach. 'I'm sure Brother Trian's truly sorry for his errors. Can't you forgive him, as God forgives us for His son's sake?'

'Gladly—'

His heart lifts to hear it.

'—once he has made restitution.'

'But Father...' He wavers. Grasps at words. 'Trian's an odd one, but he wants only to please you, and please our Lord. He's not like other young men.'

'How is he not?'

Cormac's desperate. It's a grave matter to tell a secret. And such a secret. But what else can he try? How else can he shake their master out of his hard-hearted certainties? 'There's something about him.'

The Prior snorts. 'What something?'

'A burden. Or—no, more of a mystery.'

'Brother, spit it out.'

Cormac gnaws his lip. He can't think what else to do.

The Prior demands, 'What *mystery*?'

After all, they're all three bound together on this rock for life. Sooner or later, there'll be no more secrets. Hadn't Cormac better risk telling it in his own words now than waiting till the Prior happens to glimpse it for himself?

Faltering, he does his best to describe as much as he knows; uses all his eloquence to make the Prior grasp the uniqueness of Brother Trian.

The Prior's ash-grey eyes reveal nothing. But he says, 'Fetch him out of the water, then.'

'May I?'

'Right this minute.'

As Cormac picks his way down the cliff, grabbing at the

ropes, his heart's hammering so hard he forgets to be afraid of the steep descent, the rolling pebbles. Relief and dread wrestle in his chest. Has he managed to persuade their master to be merciful?

'Brother?' he calls, approaching the cove.

Nothing.

'Trian!'

Belatedly the waterlogged figure twitches in the surf, staggers a little, lifts his head.

'You're to come out.'

Trian lifts his red-rimmed eyes.

'Your penance is finished,' Cormac tells him, though the Prior didn't say that. Suddenly Cormac's afraid of what he's done. Is he a blundering tale-bearer? Has he only made things worse?

Trian crawls out of the water, skin bluish with cold, as if he can't feel his feet.

Cormac wishes he'd thought to bring him a dry robe, or a cloak. He leads the way back up. Twice on the way up he waits to catch his own breath, leaning on the rock face. The second time, Trian comes up behind him. The young monk has a better colour now, even though he's still soaked, and he's moving rather faster too.

By the unfinished chapel, Artt readies himself. He's trying to fathom how his dream of half a year ago could have led him so wrong.

Hearing footsteps, his head snaps up. He strides to meet

the monks. 'Brother Trian.' He bends down and hauls up the wet robe.

But Trian goes scarlet and pulls away.

'Let down your braies,' Artt orders him.

His arms clamp to his sides. 'I was taught to be modest. Never to let—'

'What I teach is obedience,' Artt growls. 'Bare yourself.'

Cormac hangs back, his face contorted with worry.

Trian stands very still.

Artt prepares to meet a refusal; tightens his fists.

The young monk hoists his robe, undoes his braies, and lowers them.

Artt bends to stare. He's never seen one of these botches that Pliny calls *androgyni*. Not a true male, made in God's image, nor a true female, shaped to bear young. Neither fish nor fowl. It turns his stomach. 'Cover yourself up.'

Trian scrambles to dress.

'Brother—no, I can't call you that anymore,' Artt corrects himself, 'as you're no monk. Unless it's a whole man who vows chastity, the sacrifice is void.'

'I didn't...' Trian gasps: 'I don't know exactly what I am.'

A weed in the flax, that's what; a pebble in the grain; rot in the fruit. It's all quite clear to Artt.

Cormac sputters: 'It can't be the lad's fault, Father. Who but God made him this way?'

Artt speaks as though from a great height. 'Perhaps his mother erred gravely, and the infant was marred as a consequence.' He turns back to Trian: 'Or it could be a mark of some weakness of spirit of your own.'

Trian's face has fallen in on itself.

'Ah, no. Would you look at my hands, for instance?' Cormac spreads them to display the swollen knobs and pearly cysts. 'Misshapen by any measure, but they do their work. How's Brother Trian any different?'

'This case is not alike,' Artt tells him. 'Remember the Scripture: *Male and female he made them*.'

'What if . . .' Cormac is flailing. 'Could that line include some who are male *and* female, both in one? Mixed, somehow—is that beyond the bounds of possibility?'

This commoner, who's spent most of his life in heathen ignorance, daring to debate theology! Putting his finger in Cormac's wrinkled face, Artt warns, 'That's heresy.'

The old monk astonishes him by persisting. 'His parents must have known he couldn't marry—must have given him to the Church for a safe harbour.'

Artt wheels around, pointing at Trian. 'Then it was a plot. You entered the monastery by stealth, like a thief in the night.'

Barely audible: 'I was only thirteen.'

'And these half-dozen years since, why did you never own up, even in private Confession? Why keep it from me, your master and soul-friend, this last half year?'

Tears drop like jewels from Trian's jaw.

Artt must have courage enough to banish all monsters. He quotes, '*Who may live on your holy mountain? Only he who walks uprightly*.' He looks at Cormac. 'We can no longer have him—her—this creature—in our fellowship.'

Trian bends over as if he's been punched.

Artt pronounces sentence: 'You must leave us.'

Silence, except for the stir of the wind.

'How on earth can Trian leave us?' Cormac demands.

Artt knows what God requires, but not the details. His mind's whirling. He takes out his knife and sharpens it on the little whetstone from his pouch.

Cormac lets out a moan at the sight of the blade.

The rattleheaded fool must think Artt's about to do some butchery. But Trian doesn't quiver. Does he too believe the knife is for his throat, Artt wonders? Whatever else he is, he's brave. Artt moves close enough to put the blade to Trian's neck, and cuts through the cord until it's weak enough to sever with a tug of his hand. The wooden Greek cross comes away, and he shoves it into his pocket. 'I release you from the vows you had no right to take.'

He can't confiscate the robe, as they have no other clothes. How to remove the tonsure? Artt starts scraping at Trian's skull, to obscure the outlines of the holy triangle. The bare patch widens under his blade; pink-grey scalp spreads like a puddle around the red-brown triangle of skin tanned by the summer. He finds that nothing can erase the mark. As he works, he prays for further instruction. Should he put Trian out to sea in the boat? He's heard of criminals being set adrift that way. But that might amount to murder. What if Artt gave him an oar?

He wipes hair off his knife now, and sheathes it. 'I expel you from our brotherhood.'

'How can he not be one of us,' Cormac wails, 'when we all have to share this Great Skellig?'

Trian still doesn't say a word.

Artt finds he's come to a decision. 'The person will live out his days here, but apart.'

'How, *apart*?' Cormac asks. 'Like a slave or a prisoner, you mean?'

He shakes his head. 'Separately.'

'Eating apart? Sleeping alone? You wouldn't do that to a dog.'

'Brother Cormac,' Artt says, very low, 'hold your tongue.'

Trian finds himself left behind on the Plateau. Salt has dried in stiff tracks down his face, and his cheeks have cooled. Beyond shame, now, it seems. Even beyond grief. He's weak as water; he remembers he hasn't eaten since dawn. He sits down on the rock. He feels very old. There's a psalm he's trying to recall. *For you are God, my only safe haven. Why have you cast me off?*

The Prior is approaching with a bulging sack.

Trian looks up. He doesn't have it in him to kneel, or even rise.

'I've packed you a share of everything we own.' The man's tone is punctilious. 'Food, salt, one of the waterskins, some tools, everything needful.'

The Prior's justifying himself to God. 'Please, Father,' Trian says. 'Any punishment but this.'

His master—his former master—sets down the sack. 'Choose some part of the island for your own.' Then he makes a cross on the air with the bell. For a moment Trian mistakes it for a blessing, till he sees the Prior's used his left hand. The cursing hand.

Artt goes to find the holy chest in the hut, and hangs his white stole around his neck. Outside, he rings the bell, and keeps ringing it until his one recalcitrant monk comes.

Cormac's eyes are puffed with weeping, as if he's lost a child of his flesh.

'I mean to offer a Mass of special intention, now, to rededicate us,' Artt tells him. Adding, for clarity, 'The two of us.'

But Cormac grabs him by the arm. 'I've prayed about it, Father. This banishment is both cruel and stupid. You call this *fellowship*?'

Artt yanks away. 'You misjudge me, Brother. I have no malice in my heart.' And how does the old man dare to judge him? 'I do only what God bids. As must we all.'

Cormac steps back. 'Then I throw in my lot with Trian.'

Artt stares. 'With the freak? This is revolt.'

The word doesn't seem to shake Cormac.

'Must I remind you that the vows you took bound you to me forever?'

'Then release me.'

Artt shakes his head. 'I cannot. You're the same man you were that day on the riverbank.'

Cormac's mouth works. 'I didn't know I was swearing fealty to a lunatic.'

For a moment Artt can't catch his breath.

'I see now you won't rest till you've made this island a hell on earth,' Cormac says. 'I release myself from my vows.'

'That's not possible. You would be an apostate—a foul deserter.'

He roars, 'I'm not your man, but Christ's!'

Artt breaks away, striding towards the unfinished chapel—his church to come, which rises so clear and perfect in his mind's eye, dominating the island with its twisted wooden cross, ruling over the whole ocean. He steps through the entrance and stands in the unroofed centre. Closing his eyes, he stands very still; makes an offering of himself.

Trian is up on the South Peak, lying on the narrow spar that pierces the abyss. The eagles cry overhead. What's Trian now? A ghost wandering between life and death, earth and heaven, belonging nowhere.

All this fuss. Such a small part of his flesh, what is or isn't between his legs. Not spirit but matter, a little bit of matter, so why must it matter so much?

Trian inches forward on the spur till the stone runs out. Moving like a snake, the creature cursed *above all other animals, to crawl on his belly, and eat dust, all the days of his life.* Trian wouldn't jump, he'd never jump, because then the devil would win his soul. But he finds himself wondering, as he hangs his aching head over the gritty end of the spar, if he were to tumble, seized by that invisible power that makes all things in this world plummet, would God see, God who watches the fall of every sparrow? Would he understand that it was none of Trian's doing? Might Trian's soul escape judgement and float free as his body sank under the waves?

No. The knowledge is a yoke dropped on his shoulders. Life is the weightiest of gifts, and there's no giving it back till the end.

Trian starts edging backwards along the spar.

How to live apart, though, as an outcast? To haunt the edge of their monastery, hiding himself. Can Trian hollow out a little rain-hole up here on the South Peak, for water, or will he have to spend his days skulking around the Plateau so he can steal from the cistern without encountering the men who used to call him brother?

He staggers to his feet. He drifts, he climbs, not really seeing, only covering this shrunken territory. At one point his foot slips, throwing him down, and he clutches the ground as if it's precious to him. As if all he wants is not to fall and be killed. Because even this unbearable life is still sweet to him.

Trian's lost track of the time now. He's back at the eastern end of the island without having found anywhere to hide. He sways, looking out at the Lesser Skellig, which like its greater sister has been deserted by almost all its summer birds. Spots appear in his vision and he rubs his eyes to erase them. Two miles away, at most: on a calm day like this, might Trian just be able to swim that far? An absurd idea, but he can't think of another. Even with this wretched sack of necessities tied over one shoulder, dragging him down? Still, it would be worth a try. He'd be truly *apart* then; islanded, isolate. A permanent exile from human company, from human speech. If Trian were to live alone on the Lesser Skellig, waiting for the return of the spring flocks, would he turn half-bird himself?

The vertigo is probably only weakness, he realises. He rummages in the bag for a crock and pulls the stopper out. He pushes his fingers into the thick fat, finds a piece of cooked puffin breast, and wolfs it down.

Cormac is frantic. He's scrambling down to Landing Cove for the second time today, even though the heavy sack he's packed keeps pulling him off balance. He fingers the fissured wall for grip. Every so often he stops to catch a breath and cry out, 'Trian!'

Only a cormorant replies. No glimpse of the young monk anywhere; no trace of his passing.

How did it happen that they came to this place? Was there a different way the currents and breezes could have taken the boat that would have washed them up on another, gentler island, where spring and summer and autumn might have played out differently? Or have the three of them always carried this terrible tale inside themselves?

Down at the water, the boat lies inverted on rocks surf-spittled and slimed green. Cormac bends his shaking legs and crouches beside its shell. He won't give way to despair. He has to find Trian. This island's become a fortress that the two of them must escape.

What makes him look up? Craning his neck back painfully. The figure on the heights above him is indistinct, but unmistakable. What's Trian doing up there?

'Brother!' Cormac's voice cracks.

Is the young man contemplating the most awful sin? A final casting-off, a cutting of all ties. A single thrust, that's all it would take: those long legs would straighten and spring and Trian would be launched into the glittering sky, his speed searing the air as he dived, legs fused, sack pulling him down, arms winging up. Does he remember the pointed rocks under the foam, ready to smash him? Or will he jump far enough out to drop into open water, sew his body cleanly through its hard blue skin, down down down past weed and fish until he's swallowed up in the eternal chill of the deeps, and the sea seals itself up over his head?

'Trian!' Cormac howls. All he's failed to do, the many ways he's let this young man down...when it's for this, it comes to him now, it's for this that he's been allowed to live so inexplicably long: to save Trian.

All Cormac can do now is bear witness. Hold his breath.

High above him, one hand goes up, waving.

Trian picks his way down to the shore, to where Cormac is straining at the upturned hull. Does the old man mean to cast the boat away, set her adrift?

He goes to help. Between the two of them, they manage to turn over the leathern shell and scrape and bump it down the stones. Both are wet to the thighs already. The hull splashes into the foam. Without mast, yard, or sail, it's as bare as a cupped palm.

Cormac drops a half-full sack and a waterskin into the boat. He picks up two of the three oars and sets them in her too. The rope tethering her to a spear of rock slants stiffly. He throws one leg over the side and clambers in.

In misery, Trian asks, 'You're leaving?'

Cormac holds out two hands. 'Not without you.'

Trian twists away with a kind of shyness. The boat rocks between them. He keeps his eyes on the cove's rock walls, their fault lines, the incomprehensible words they spell out.

'What's there to keep you here?' Cormac asks.

My vows. They're broken, but he still feels them like invisible ropes. They've been broken for him, he reminds himself. Trian's cross has been torn off his neck, his tonsure erased, the very name of *monk* stripped away. The only master he knows has disowned him.

Cormac pleads: 'Get in. We may have no sail, but we can row.'

Trian holds onto the gunnel. To set out once more, banished from his only home...

He turns the question over in his mind. Can he let Cormac set off alone, as solitary as a drop of rain on a curling leaf? This man who—Trian knows it now—has been the truest of fathers?

He asks confusedly, 'Would you be our leader?'

The old monk throws up his hands to ward that off. 'You and I will go in true fellowship.'

'Go where, though?' Where on earth can they take refuge?

'We're God's children,' Cormac tells him. 'I suppose we'll end up wherever his breath blows us.'

The boat's tugging at her leash. The tide's on the turn.

Trian takes that as a sign, for lack of any other. He lays his own sack of supplies and tools beside Cormac's. He wades over and unhitches the rope, gathering it into a coil. He gets over the side. Taking up his oar, he shoves them off the rock.

From his high perch, Artt watches the tiny vessel move out of the bay, the pair of sinners rowing. Thieves, turncoats, demons in human form...

And the Lord said, I will wipe man from the face of the

earth, and the beasts and the creeping things and the birds, for I repent I ever made them.

Then the fury is over; Artt finds it's blown right through him. They're gone, the two of them, so what do they matter? Unworthy from the start, always chafing against his rule. Clearly Artt misunderstood his dream: the two monks were like the boat or its baggage, nothing more than the means of his pilgrimage.

Well, he need be nobody's Prior anymore. His bonds are broken. No more obligation to teach, guide, direct, and chasten. No human babble to clog up his ears. Artt has this whole island to himself and it's his alone. The steep land will be his pristine page and he'll write on it with every step, every prayer, every breath. A bastion of faith, a sentry post where he will man the outer frontier of Christendom: oh, such a place it'll be now! No one and nothing to bar his way to heaven.

AUTHOR'S NOTE

Off the coast of County Kerry in the southwest of Ireland, two jagged islands rear up. The larger has been called Skellig Michael since sometime before 1044. The first record of monks living there can be found in a compilation of stories of saints written down several centuries earlier, *The Martyrology of Tallaght* (c. 790–830). Archeological evidence of human presence there survives from about a century before that. Tradition holds that the monastery was founded even earlier, around the year 600, at a time when clusters of Irish monks were retreating to remote places, so that's when I've set my entirely fictional story of a first landing party.

Out of the more than two dozen Early Christian monastic sites known in Ireland, this was the most isolated (from the Latin *insulatus,* 'made into an island'). The settlement stayed small, likely never growing to more than seven drystone cells on Skellig Michael and a tiny oratory on Little Skellig. Its monks (more pragmatic than my invented characters) seem to have survived over the long term by keeping sheep, goats, and pigs, and trading with larger communities for firewood, grain, and wine. They may have retreated for winters to the mainland at Ballinskelligs, and in the twelfth or thirteenth century they moved their base there, keeping up the island buildings for use only by hermits and pilgrims.

A UNESCO World Heritage site since 1996, Skellig Michael, like so many other secluded, sacred places, is now at risk from over-tourism. The island has been a magnet for *Star Wars* fans since its use in 2014–15 as the location of Luke Skywalker's hideaway in *The Force Awakens* and *The Last Jedi*. The monastic ruins face another threat at human hands, too—the increase in extreme weather consequent on the climate crisis.

My treasured friends Margaret Lonergan and Susan Coughlan, thanks so much for sparking this novel by bringing me and mine along on a boat trip around the Skelligs in July 2016. Almost four years on, I had researched and planned *Haven* and had managed to secure a booking for a landing on Skellig Michael...when the island was closed due to what the monks would have taken in their stride as the latest pestilence to plague humankind. So I've never been there, except in spirit and imagination—the one form of travel that can't be forbidden.

In writing *Haven* during the on-and-off COVID-19 shutdowns, I've drawn gratefully on the work of too many historians to name. I've guessed when I had to. We know of no manuscripts produced on Skellig Michael, for instance, but copying was a core part of the mission of early Irish monasteries. In the archeological record there's no evidence that the monks ate great auks, but it struck me as likely, given that those huge flightless birds were a mainstay of North Atlantic coastal communities till they were hunted into extinction over the centuries between about 1500 and 1850.

Richard Manning, many thanks for survival tips. My beloved father-in-law, David Roulston, caught most of my boat-related errors. One of my monks is named in homage to Irish book-lover and publicist extraordinaire, Cormac Kinsella.

Finally, *Haven* is dedicated to my very dear friends Anne Schuurman and Zoë Sinel, a medievalist and legal scholar respectively, who've been backers of this project from the first day I mentioned it. May all books have such champions.

Read the first chapter of
Emma Donoghue's upcoming novel,
Learned by Heart . . .

RAINE TO LISTER, 1815

My dear Lister,

Last night I went to the Manor again.

I open the door here—I don't delay even to pick up a cape—and step out across the village green. My shoes write inscrutable, fleeting messages on the dewy grass. When I reach the moon-marked road, all I have to do is follow it. In less than a quarter of an hour, at the walls of York, where Bootham Bar has been arching for eight hundred years, here's that antique hodgepodge, King's Manor, hiding our school behind its redbrick face.

The great medieval door with its lion and unicorn opens at my touch, and I find myself in the scented courtyard. I turn right to enter the Manor School itself, where three generations of one family have watched over the better-born daughters of the North. I walk invisible from one familiar, ramshackle room to the next. Through the kitchen and pantry, refectory and offices, and up the footworn stone stairs I float. Through the classrooms on the first floor. Into the north wing, past the mistresses' chambers, and up again, to the second-floor attic. Past Cook's room, then the one the four maids share, then the box room full of trunks and portmanteaus. The fourth door is the Slope's, and it springs open to my fingertips.

You'll understand my wishful fancy; I pay this visit, in fact all these tender nightly visits, in my mind's eye only. In the flesh, I've not passed the lion and unicorn and entered our school in eight years. These days of course I'm prevented, thwarted by circumstances beyond my control. But last year, or in any of the intervening years since I left, although I often passed the lovely old silhouette of King's Manor, somehow—careless, unthinking—I never thought to knock on that ancient door. *Eliza*, I ask myself now, *why didn't you go back while you still could?*

You won't be surprised that I so treasure these old haunts. It was in York that I received my education; where I was stamped like warm wax by a seal, formed once and for all. I know you'll recall the song—*where all the joy and mirth, made this town heaven on earth.* At the Manor School, I tasted *heaven on earth* even as I toiled to pack my poor skull with the knowledge and wisdom I was told I'd need for life. The joke is, Lister, the only lesson I learned, or at least the only lesson I remember, was you.

We two were so young—had barely seen *the change of fourteen years,* as Capulet says of his daughter. Less than a twelvemonth the pair of us spent under our Slope's slanted ceiling, but there are fleeting times in life, especially in youth, that shine out more strongly than all the rest and will never fade: veins of gold in dull rock. For the rest of my life, I believe, I'll be transported back in dreams to memory's private theatre, where our girl selves still move and chat and laugh.

These days I live on words, since my imagination is starved of other stimuli. Not that I keep a diary. The year we turned seventeen, you did your best to teach me that improving habit, but I always found it hard to pluck details from my daily round that seemed worth recording. Without an interested ear inclined towards me, my words dry up; I lack that bottomless spring that bubbles up behind your clever tongue. It strikes me that your own journal-writing has much in common with your other powers—walking, say. Whatever you like, you do with energy and ambition, almost greedily, and with a vigour that impresses us lesser mortals, even if we sometimes find it exhausting. No, only in letters to one sympathetic listener can I open my bosom and speak my pleasures and pains. So I read all day until my eyes are sore, then write to you, though all too hurriedly—two or three pages' worth, I find, is about as much as I can get out under these conditions—before I'm obliged to lay down my pen.

In the night I send out my mind to roam, and of all the places I've lived in my almost quarter century (Madras, Tottenham, Doncaster, Halifax, Bristol), the lodestone to which my restless mind is always drawn, as a compass needle to true north, is York—and in particular to our Manor School. Less than a mile in distance from this house where I sit scribbling, but in time, a yawning gulf: ten years back, to when we were fourteen. And not just any ten years but that vast stretch between raw girlhood and settled womanhood.

Like some old lady, at twenty-four I find most fascination in retrospect. The memories come back to me with the irresistible force of waves striking a shore. It would be absurd to deny how changed I am; in ways I need not list, I am not what I was when we met. But I recall that Eliza so vividly, I only have to close my eyes to slip into her, under her skin. Under the mossy, leaky roof of King's Manor, I was quickened to life from the day I first laid eyes on you, Lister. As the old Roman chiselled on our stone, *Happy the spirit of this place*.

In our Slope I passed my best hours, and sometimes I have to remind myself that they are indeed past. But I tell myself that I'm not dead, not yet. Wilted plants have been known to revive if given just a little water. Could I have you by my side once more, I almost believe

Discover more from
Sunday Times bestselling author
Emma Donoghue

TEACHING MIXED-ABILITY GROUPS

TEACHING SERIES

General Editor: Professor E. C. Wragg

Teaching Geography Patrick Bailey
Teaching Modern Languages David Webb
Teaching Teaching E. C. Wragg

TEACHING
MIXED-ABILITY GROUPS

E. C. WRAGG (editor)
Professor of Education
University of Nottingham

DAVID & CHARLES (HOLDINGS) LIMITED
Newton Abbot   London   North Pomfret   Vancouver

ISBN 0 7153 6865 6

Library of Congress Catalog Card Number 75–31316

© E. C. Wragg, G. T. White, S. H. Miller,
R. W. Seckington, B. L. Cooke, M. Gracie,
D. W. Lingard, J. Darke, M. P. Grant, 1976

Set in 11 on 13pt Linotype Plantin
and printed in Great Britain
by Latimer Trend & Company Ltd Plymouth
for David & Charles (Holdings) Limited
Brunel House   Newton Abbot   Devon

Published in the United States of America
by David & Charles Inc
North Pomfret   Vermont 05053   USA

Published in Canada
by Douglas David & Charles Limited
132 Philip Avenue   North Vancouver   BC

Contents

1 Teaching Mixed-Ability Groups

E. C. Wragg

A few years ago I worked with a group of young teachers in their first year of teaching at local secondary schools. There were eight or nine who came with an air of excitement, a nervous twitch and baggy eyes. These, it transpired, worked in the school which at that time was the only unstreamed comprehensive in the area. They were trying to cope with all the usual problems of a first-year teacher, and in addition were having to learn a new set of strategies about which few of their older colleagues were able to advise.

Since that time the position has changed in certain respects. More schools have experimented with mixed-ability classes and more teachers have accumulated a reservoir of experiences from which they enrich their own teaching and advise their younger colleagues. Yet published acounts of mixed-ability teaching remain few in number.

The central purpose of this book is not to argue the case for and against mixed-ability groups in secondary schools. That has been done elsewhere, and the debate about criteria for grouping children during their education will continue for many years to come. The contributors' prime intention is to describe what they regard as successful classroom strategies. In attempting to do this they draw on their own teaching experiences as well as those of other teachers. Inevitably in such a series of personal statements there are detectable differences between the writers, most of whom in varying degrees are committed supporters of heterogeneous grouping. Consequently a more radical contributor may argue for total mixed-ability classes for five years, and against prizes, mark sheets,

7

whole-class teaching and sub-groupings based on ability, whereas another writer may take an opposing point of view.

What is beyond question, however, is that no single solution can be offered. For many years hundreds of investigators have sought the current version of the philosopher's stone, the answer to the question 'What is good teaching?' Even surveys of such inquiries can run to hundreds of pages. The only commonly reported conclusion amongst those who have sifted the teacher-effectiveness literature is that there is little agreement amongst researchers, teachers and administrators about what constitutes successful teaching.

In the absence of strong consensus it is right that variety in teaching patterns should be constantly explored. The contributors to this book describe a number of possible approaches to mixed-ability teaching. None would claim to be able to offer a series of recipes for instant success. They are, however, attempting to describe practical approaches in such a way as to stimulate teachers to devise their own tactics in accordance with the situation in which they find themselves. If there is any common thread between the chapters it is that teaching mixed-ability groups requires planning, foresight, imagination, awareness of children's needs and a desire to make the experiment work. Without this commitment from a teacher, failure is a near certainty.

Although the main purpose of most chapters is to describe classroom practice rather than engage in polemic, some contributors do attempt to secure commitment by persuasion. Inevitably their own enthusiasms penetrate their descriptions, and clearly if one includes among teaching objectives the development of social skills or the learning of tolerance of others, such aspirations can be given prominence, and the nature of the group becomes possibly more important than the subject matter.

Over the years various criteria for grouping children have been used. For many centuries a single social criterion, the ability to pay fees, was paramount. Subsequently measures of mental skill were used, and children learned all their subjects according to their assumed intelligence as measured by more objective, largely verbal, intelligence tests and total academic achievement based on composite

8

mark sheets. After streaming by general ability came setting, where each child was judged according to performance in the subject under consideration. At the present time all these criteria are being applied in some schools, and in addition there are hybrids such as a mixed setting and streaming policy where only certain subject groups are in specific ability sets. 'Banding', whereby two or three broad bands of ability are identified and children randomly assigned to classes within the band is another hybrid, a combination of streaming by general academic achievement and mixed-ability grouping.

Historically, therefore, mixed-ability grouping stands as an alternative to these other criteria. It rejects grouping by general or specific aptitude or by social class or parental wealth. Its weakness perhaps is that it may be seen to be largely negative, ie grouping by no criterion at all, unless friendship groups or primary school of origin are used. Many teachers are unwilling to operate these latter because they might reflect some of the rejected criteria such as social class or general intelligence. They would only wish to assemble a group of children of varying ability in their school work, no more, no less.

Nor is mixed-ability grouping the sole alternative to setting and streaming. Thelen, for example, has explored 'teachability' as a criterion, and teachers were asked to assemble compatibility groups, that is groups of children whom they enjoyed teaching.[1] Eysenck, who has attempted in his research to describe the differences in learning between extroverts and introverts, advocates personality as a basis for groupings.[2] Indeed the next series of experimental groupings might well explore such alternatives. There is no reason why 'learning style' or 'teaching-style preference' should not be considered to be as important as other elements of children's make-up. One day perhaps those children who prefer a syllabus and clear instructions will work with the more directive teachers, while those who prefer explorations and open-ended work will be in the care of teachers who find this a more acceptable way of working.

This brings us back to the opening statements of this section. The book is not meant merely to persuade hostile teachers to adopt strategies of which they disapprove. Rather it is an attempt to describe current practice in mixed-ability classes for the teachers who already work with such groups and the many more who are contemplating it. No one would wish to underestimate the amount of thinking and planning involved either for individuals or groups of teachers, but the rewards can be substantial. The constant effort of many thousands of teachers to explore novelty in a responsible way, in an attempt to improve the opportunities for learning of the children in their care, is a healthy indicator of the high level of professional concern under what are often adverse or inadequate conditions. Whether or not mixed-ability teaching becomes the norm there is little doubt that a large number of interesting and imaginative teaching tactics will have been developed along the way. They will provide a lasting enrichment of the repertoire of teaching skills of many members of the profession.

THE CONTRIBUTORS TO THE BOOK

Each of the contributors to the book is able to write with some authority after many years of successful experience in the teaching profession. Yet each takes a slightly different standpoint.

Graham White, in his chapter on teaching English, draws heavily on the skill and love of reading. He probably describes more whole-class activity than other contributors, and advocates reading aloud to a class as an important element of the day to day work. He stresses development of language, be this expressive, transactional or poetic, and thinks that flexible classroom layout as well as proper resources is essential to support such teaching. Among many points of social interest is his suggestion that all children's work should be on display, not merely the best.

Stanley Miller concentrates on the teaching of French, but clearly the procedures he describes and the problems he faced in a large comprehensive school will be similar to those in other languages. Rewriting a commercially produced course to make it suitable for the groups in his care was one of the more time- and energy-consuming elements for the group of teachers involved. As languages are frequently assumed to be less suitable for mixed-ability teaching because of the linear nature of traditional presentation methods, teachers will be interested in the use of team teaching, of audio

10

instruction for the poorer readers and of self-correcting worksheets. His description of collectives of six or seven schools whose staffs meet to pool ideas and share material has many possibilities for subjects other than languages.

Brian Cooke, writing about history teaching, gives a good example of multi-level workcards on the same central theme of Roman Britain. Three levels of workcard are described which would enable almost everyone in the class to make a valuable contribution to the study of the Roman wall. Similarly his proposals for mixed-ability subgroups working on model making, drama or similar activities would, if sensitively handled, ensure a respectable role for all participants.

Margaret Gracie's contribution will be of special interest to the many teachers who wish not only to teach mixed-ability groups but to depart from conventional subject constraints and work as teams in an integrated studies area. Although writing about social studies/ humanities teaching, she makes many points of general relevance about resourcing integrated studies, teachers visiting other schools to collect ideas, display and discussion of pupil's work, and the challenging of children to produce for themselves a new hypothesis or question. She extends her area of concern further than other contributors by discussing how children who have learned to study independently might continue to develop their skills of inquiry when they pass the age of sixteen.

Roger Seckington is able to draw on experiences gained when, as a Schoolteacher Fellow at Exeter University, he completed one of the earliest inquiries into mixed-ability teaching. In addition to describing strategies for the geographer, such as the creation of resource boxes, tape/slide sequences, and the use of textbooks and job cards, he considers general questions of timetable blocking, assessment of children's work with their own performance as a baseline, and the establishment of flexible teaching and learning areas in a school.

David Lingard probably moves further away from traditional practices than many mathematics teachers. Both his rejection of a remedial class and advocacy of only rare withdrawal of individuals for special remedial work are based on trusting children to evolve their own curriculum under guidance. Consequently high dependence on national curriculum packages is discouraged, and he discounts the linear sequential argument that certain mathematical concepts can only be learned when others have been acquired. The use of older pupils and college of education students is proposed to amplify the teaching of the full-time mathematics staff. Clearly the level of commitment required for such teaching is extremely high, as the almost totally individualised programme he supports tends to limit the life of an individual workcard to a single usage.

John Darke, writing about science teaching, analyses six different patterns of teaching and describes in detail schemes of work arising from some of these. He has interesting observations about record-keeping in mixed-ability groups, and also raises matters of general importance such as self-directed homework and the use of question time.

All the specialist contributors describe the question of resourcing mixed-ability teaching from the standpoint of the teacher who needs to build up a stock of resources to support his own classes. *Michael Grant,* writing as the director of a large school resources centre, has responsibility for servicing teaching and learning in all subject areas. He is able to give authoritative and up-to-date information on storage and retrieval, and his contribution is full of practical advice about the use of an optical coincidence co-ordinate index, the purchase of suitable furnishings from suppliers and local auctions, and the administration of technological and reprographic facilities.

Some readers may wish to select chapters of special interest and read only these, but all the contributors have attempted to broaden their scope away from narrow subject interests and include matters of general concern such as teaching strategies, criteria for assembling subgroups, assessment and resources, as well as subject integration and team teaching.

TEACHING STRATEGIES
Although the individual contributors describe at length teaching tactics which are subject specific, it is worthwhile considering, at this stage, an overview of the procedures commonly adopted with mixed-ability groups.

Whole-class teaching

For many the shift in emphasis away from whole-class teaching towards small group and individual work is the single major essential modification when changing from streamed to unstreamed lessons. Yet it is expensive of a teacher's time to give or relay the same information up to thirty times. The question is not so much whether or not to abolish activities involving the whole class, but rather in what circumstances and how frequently these should occur. Indeed it is difficult to conceive of a group of thirty children and a teacher, or multiples of these units, being together for a whole year and never behaving as a community.

There are a number of perfectly legitimate uses of whole-class activity. Managerial transactions are often most economical in a whole-class unit. These include setting up a class project, even if it is on an individual basis; giving information which is of concern to every member, such as warnings about laboratory safety, or changes in plan; and communal activities such as tidying away or preparing for future work.

Under the heading of group communion can be included any experiences which the teacher feels help establish a sense of community and sharing in the class. Class discussion in a humanities lesson, for example, enables the small group (the class) to consider the problems of the large group (society) to which it belongs, and every member may have a tenable point of view about topics such as the family, leisure, work, violence or the mass media. Equally important are the occasions when individuals report on their progress. Children engaged in different studies can describe their work to their fellows, answer questions, and relate their own feelings to those of others in the class. Another example would be when the teacher wishes for a certain experience to be shared by all the class prior to individual work. Graham White's use of story reading in English lessons and the showing of a film, video tape or set of slides come into this category.

Workcards

Attempts to devise individual programmes of work frequently involve the use of workcards or assignment sheets of various kinds.

The purist creates individual cards for each child which are based on a sensitive monitoring of his progress. This can involve a colossal amount of preparatory work for the conscientious teacher who must be forgiven if he sacrifices a little purity for the sake of his own well-being. Consequently most teachers like to keep their workcards for future use or else to form the basis of a modified assignment on a subsequent occasion.

Multi-level workcards, as described by Brian Cooke, need a great deal of imagination and preparation, but are well worth the investment. They enable the teacher to maintain a certain feeling of community, as the whole class is more or less concerned with the same area of study, but offer many options within the common framework. Purists would reject this tactic as being a form of hidden selection, streaming by workcard, but many teachers find it an acceptable compromise.

The use of coloured card, plastic film, felt-tipped pens and modern reprographic aids means that an attractive product can be achieved even by those of limited artistic competence. This can be an important factor if one considers the visually rich and varied surroundings in which many children live and the professional finish of commercially produced materials. It is here that a graphics assistant in a school or regional resources centre can help teachers achieve an acceptable and polished product which reflects the needs of individuals in a class.

Subgroups

Although work on an individual basis and whole-class teaching may account for much of the time in a mixed-ability class, the use of smaller groups within the class is also a common feature. Many criteria may be used in the assembly of such groups. They may represent natural friendship patterns, or alternatively membership may be decided by the teacher. Size can vary from pairs of children in a science lesson up to groups of eight, ten, or half the class. Clearly both the size and the constitution of the groups will vary according to the task in hand.

Where group membership is determined by the teacher, the bases for grouping may include the association of children known to work well together, ability groups, and deliberately heterogeneous units. Many teachers would reject subgroups based on children's ability in the subject as being yet another form of hidden streaming, but others who work with such groups justify using them on the grounds that great flexibility is possible, and that a fluid grouping policy permits the existence of constantly changing groups of children who, for a particular task or on a particular occasion only, show a similar degree of competence or experience. Deliberately heterogeneous groups are those assembled in such a way as to ensure a genuine cross-section of ability in each group. The teacher may assemble teams of children which include both able and less able, and encourage an atmosphere of mutual helping.

Team teaching

Partly because of the relative novelty of mixed-ability teaching and partly because it appears to make good sense, teams of teachers frequently work together for a sizeable block of time, perhaps half a day. Many varieties of team teaching can be observed, sometimes adopting the familiar format of the 'lead lesson' for the whole group followed by individual work or small-group activity, and on other occasions operating to a much more elaborate structure involving open-plan areas, teachers and children moving to various parts of the building, and plenary sessions at key stages.

One advantage of team teaching is that it needs considerable planning, and this alone can be rewarding and stimulating for the participants. A disadvantage is that incompatibility between members of the team can lead to friction and discontent.

Poor readers

Strategies for coping with poor readers exist but pose a difficult problem for the teacher. Workcards can be constructed which require only a simple level of reading competence; other children can be asked to read instructions to any small group containing a non-reader; a cassette recorder can be available with the teacher's voice on tape, so that children unable to read cards can play back tape recordings instead. None of these tactics is entirely satisfactory because to some extent they may perform a disservice to the slow reader. In his superb account of work with poor readers, Daniel

15

Fader explained how reading should be made important for children. The boys in his care were constantly reminded that reading and writing were important skills. If they needed a spanner to mend a motor bike they had to write down their request on a piece of paper before it was granted.[3] The teacher with a mixed-ability class containing poor or non-readers faces a dilemma. If all instructions are given verbally by the teacher, by a child who is able to read well, or are on a tape recording, then the hidden message seems to be that ability to read is not necessarily important. If the task is described on a card or worksheet then some children may be discouraged before they have even begun, and their plight may become worse. There is no easy solution, but many teachers do manage to strike a successful balance between signalling the importance of reading skill as a means to certain ends, and helping those in difficulty to surmount certain obstacles. Peter Bell gives a comprehensive and sensitive account of the problems of teaching slower learners, and much of what he describes is of relevance to teachers of mixed-ability classes.[4]

Assessment

If one can learn a great deal about a society by investigating the occupants of its prison cells, it is equally true that a teacher's attitudes to and methods of assessment and record-keeping can reveal interesting aspects of his approach to teaching.

Assessment for some is a taboo subject, felt to be incompatible with the concept of low-profile judgment-making thought to be central to mixed-ability teaching. This view is based on the mistaken assumption that assessment need be a terminal activity and that it must always be matched against a notional group mean. A broader definition of assessment will permit inclusion of any evaluative response to an activity or product. This response might be heavily value-laden and followed by directive action, were that reinforcing or punitive, or it might be of a different nature. Value-free scrutiny of pupils' work is rare if not impossible. Children learn to read the complex mass of signals, largely non-verbal, transmitted by teachers in their daily interactions, and statements from people who claim never to assess are difficult to believe.

16

For mixed-ability groups a wide range of assessment procedures must be considered. The conventional mark sheet of ranking from the top to the bottom of the class is often totally inappropriate, especially if individuals are engaged in a variety of activities. It is not until a group approaches public examinations that some comparative ranking in terms of performance grades is needed. Prior to this it can be regarded as optional.

As an alternative to comparative rankings in the earlier years many teachers prefer using a personal baseline. In other words, a grade C or five out of ten means that the quality of work appears to be similar to other recent pieces of work, and anything higher or lower indicates better or poorer than normal performance. Consequently the brightest child in the class might score D or E, and the dullest can achieve A. This is a difficult system to operate fairly as children can easily become demoralised. The element of patronage invested in the teacher is substantial and should not be underestimated. Used skilfully, however, it can be fair and act as a genuine incentive to all members of the group.

Many teachers of mixed-ability classes prefer to make no numerical assessments at all but rather to keep elaborate record sheets of pupils' progress and, if necessary, include their own appraisal of their work. Similarly children can keep record books which contain both their personal comments and those made by the teacher.

Howard Bradley describes how assessment can be related to proclaimed teaching objectives. He cites an example from a fourth-year English class at Bingham Toot Hill Comprehensive School:

The English department has, however, decided to use not only the traditional teacher's mark-book, but also departmental records of each child's progress in achieving the particular objectives of an English course. These are written up, whenever the English teacher thinks he has evidence from work a child has done to be able to comment on a particular strength or a particular weakness in the child's English profile. Here is an example from a fourth-year English group.

Written – to improve accuracy of observation
and description of things observed

> – to foster creativity and creative
> writing
> – to improve techniques or argument-
> ative prose
> – to improve letter-writing

> *Spoken* – to improve the quality of discussion
> techniques
> – to improve ability to read aloud
> – to make himself understood and
> interesting to children in the group

This might lead to an entry on the department assessment sheet such as:

'Paul has shown promise in the quality of his writing, both of a creative and purely functional kind. He expresses views clearly and sensibly in argument and he has the ability to describe accurately what he sees and experiences. His understanding of the written work is not up to the same standard. He needs to read more books and think more deeply about what he is reading. He speaks well in discussion, but when he reads aloud he pays little attention to the sense of what he is reading.'[5]

The book also contains some interesting examples of record sheets used by teachers in various subjects.

If one accepts the concept of a helpful evaluative response, assessment and record-keeping can be helpful indicators of progress and important factors in the pupil's learning. Self-appraisal by the pupil can be a valuable part of his learning to set and keep his own standards, and consensus record-keeping involving both teacher and pupil can strengthen the contract between them.

PARENTS

Without the support of parents many new developments in education make less progress than need be the case. When a school introduces mixed-ability teaching there will be many questions that parents will wish to ask. Patrick McGeeney[6] has written extensively about the liaison between home and school, and there are several steps which schools may consider taking so that parents remain informed. These include the following:

1   A letter to parents explaining the nature of the changes. This should be full and informative and if possible related to a meeting for parents to ask questions on the lines of those proposed below.
2   A meeting for parents to hear more about mixed-ability teaching and ask questions.
3   A 'curriculum evening'. This can take many forms. For example a room can be laid out as it would be for the class concerned and the parents pick up workcards or assignment sheets and try their hand at some of the tasks involved. This can be an enormous success in, say, elementary science, but is not impossible in less likely fields. Some schools report a good response to a crowd of parents being put through the first unit of an audio-visual language course. Another possibility, if the school has access to closed-circuit television equipment is for a video tape to be made of some of the classes at work. The tape is played back at an evening meeting and the teacher answers questions and explains some of the activities. Similarly some schools have role-played a lesson by arranging the hall so that half of it is set out like a classroom and the other half has seats for parents. The teacher sets up an activity and once the children are working the parents can come into the classroom part and see what is happening, ask questions of the teacher and children, and, perhaps, join in. This is more difficult to mount than other kinds of evening but is often very successful. A key point here is to secure the co-operation of the class in preparing the 'classroom' and the activities. In this way they are more likely to persuade their parents to come and can feel very proud of their own stake in the event.
4   A progress report on lines such as these:

Dear Parent,
    As you know, we have been trying mixed-ability teaching

classes for a year now. Indeed many of you came to the evening we held in February when science and English lessons were discussed. You may be interested to hear our thoughts at this stage.

Next year we plan to extend mixed-ability group teaching to the second year in some subjects but not in others. The teachers in mathematics and French feel that mixed-ability groups were fairly successful but they will operate a 'banding' system in the second year. This means that children will be taught in three groups. Those who have done very well will be in one group, those who did fairly well will be in another group, and those who found mathematics and French more difficult will be in a group where we can give them special attention and help them make better progress.

All other subjects, however, will be taught in mixed-ability groups as the teachers feel encouraged by their experiences this year. We hope to hold another evening in February, and this time you will be able to see what your children are doing in humanities and creative arts.

As ever we very much value your support and I shall write to you again next June to let you know the arangements for the third year.

TEACHER TRAINING

Training for the whole of one's professional life is no longer a single initial event. It may be that teachers in future will need to make a partial realignment at regular intervals and undertake more substantial retraining at intervals of a decade or so.

The adjustment to mixed-ability groups often occurs in the context of school reorganisation and curriculum reform, and there is a need for timely in-service workshops of a fairly substantial nature. At the initial training stage students can gain valuable experience working alongside experienced teachers of mixed-ability groups. They can act as ancillaries, take responsibility for a small group, work in the resources centre, and make a genuine contribution to a variety of activities, perhaps taking an occasional 'lead lesson' during team teaching. For experienced teachers the needs are rather different. They have usually acquired the more everyday skills of teaching and must consider the many possible teaching strategies involved. A simulation exercise can often be used to enable certain basic issues and anxieties to be explored. For example, the tutor working with a group of about eight teachers can furnish details of an imaginary school about to change to mixed-ability grouping. The participants are each given a sealed envelope describing the role they are to play during discussion, eg 'You are first-year tutor and are very much in favour of mixed-ability groups; however, you realise that some of your colleagues are less enthusiastic and your task is to be as fair and objective as possible during discussion', or 'You are opposed to mixed-ability groups and must find as many arguments as possible against the experiment. You are particularly concerned about slow learners and about the school's lack of resources'.

Such a simulation can be either a very successful opening event at a course or a miserable failure, but if the goodwill of participants is secured the former outcome is more likely. An additional bonus is that the role-playing format enables participants to have a safer and more comfortable introduction to the course because they can hide behind the character they are supposed to be and are not under pressure to reveal their own hopes and anxieties at an early stage.

Visiting other schools is also a useful procedure, as is the 'collective' idea described by Stanley Miller, where teachers from a number of schools meet to exchange ideas and materials. In addition a number of quite specific workshops might include topics such as the teaching of various subjects, resources for mixed-ability groups, records and assessment, and a wide variety of others.

FOOTNOTE

No one should underestimate the amount of time and energy needed to make a success of mixed-ability teaching. Nor should it be forgotten that it is nothing more than the current attempt to find the best kind of grouping for children in schools, an experiment from which a great deal is being learned. I find the enthusiasm and ideas of the supporters of mixed-ability groups infectious and persuasive, though I have difficulty in accepting some of the views expressed.

As this book is full of personal statements perhaps I should state my own view, for what it is worth, though there is no reason why it should be taken more seriously than that expressed by others.

I believe that each school should make its own decisions in the light of its own special circumstances: the catchment area, the children, the building and the enthusiasms and interests of the staff, the parents and the head. I believe that newcomers to the secondary school have the right to make a fresh start via mixed-ability groups in the first year. I would then wish to operate a broad banding system for the next two years, enabling a certain amount of mixed-ability work to take place but not involving the full spectrum of ability. Thereafter more or less individual timetables should be possible by the time fourth and fifth years are reached, in that pupils might choose certain options allowing children from the same 'home base' to follow different programmes. As a personal view this is certainly a more cautious one than that expressed by some contributors, but readers should heed the first sentence of this paragraph. Ultimately each community must find its own solutions to the question of grouping for learning and teaching.

For notes to this chapter see p 183

22

2 Teaching English in Mixed-Ability Groups

G. T. White

A large, mixed, urban comprehensive school recently (1972) gave a diagnostic reading test to all of its second-year pupils and found in one of its selected top-stream classes assessed reading ages which varied from seven years to fourteen years and above. The reading tests were given, after an experiment in the establishing of mixed-ability classes had been, it was thought, abandoned a year previously.

We need more study of how teachers arrive at their differentiation between pupils and the criteria they use to infer ability in one pupil rather than another. It could well be that, among other things, differences in a teacher's style and the material that he decides to use with pupils categorised as able and less able plays a significant part in confirming those differences between pupils which streaming assigns to them, and which in turn becomes self-fulfilling to meet the expectations of the pupil and teacher alike. We may be circumspect about the validity of some of the many different reading tests, and Rosenthal and Jacobson, *Pygmalion in the Classroom* (New York, 1968), and others have reminded us that assessments of ability are not simple affairs, but our own attentive observations. Our reading of children's writing, listening to their language and their responses to literature should tell us of the variety of abilities in any class we teach. The psychological differences between individual children in so-called homogeneous groups are likely to be as great as the individual differences between children in heterogeneous groups; teaching English to groups of unstreamed classes makes the assumption that the individual differences are more significant than

23

the similarities and it aims at providing for their expression and use.

One would expect to meet in any class pupils at very many different stages of development in linguistic resource. The University of London Institute of Education Writing Research Team's written samples show the wide diversity of individual skills in writing in its various forms – the expressive, the transactional and the poetic. As far as reading is concerned we should expect that the attainments, interests and needs of the individual children in a class will vary so much that, for example, to impose a 'reader' on a whole class believing it to be appropriate to the general ability-level of that class, could fail to nourish the moral and imaginative literary growth we are hoping to encourage. Early recognition of the diversity of language and reading abilities in the classroom might lead the teacher and the class itself to appreciate the emergence of individual excellence of not only intelligence but all manner of personal and social skills – humour, patience, perseverance, enthusiasm and tact.

In general the provision for remedial work in secondary schools seems to be meagre. Since it is important to avoid the totally random non-streaming of groups and to organise mixed-ability groups so that there is, where possible, a proportional balance, with no marked weighting in numbers of pupils of evident high or low ability (to avoid, for example, including in one class six or more children who need remedial work with three or four of the very brightest children of that year) there is consequent need for more time, accommodation, resources, and a welcoming climate for those children withdrawn from classes for remedial attention. Two rooms are needed, one equipped with cubicles for work with tape recorders, film loops, reading kits and language masters, and another comfortable room where there can be plenty of talk and reading practice to build up confidence. Remedial teachers maintain that to work effectively a maximum of eight children in a group is essential and the greater the number of lessons a week the better; even with a generous allowance of full-time specially qualified remedial teaching many schools will only be able to cope with those whose reading ages are of 8·5 years or below if an encouraging proportion of pupils is to return full-time to normal lessons. Schools which ensure that they have a pervading concern for the individual pupil feel that no separate remedial department need exist, and that remedial work can be integrated with the normal activities in all subjects. It seems preferable for such children not to be 'siphoned off' from the mainstream of the school and they can, I believe, accommodate themselves easily and often very forcibly in some, at least, of the normal English lessons, especially those given over to drama, reading, and discussion.

READING

There is a lot of tired and unoriginal fiction for children, often beautifully illustrated. It is not easy to create something of sufficient imaginative strength to touch those archetypal depths where children feel at home, using an appropriate narrative simplicity, but this is the kind of fiction we should introduce to children in mixed-ability classes. The quality of the imagination and the excitement of the writing in the books must match in some degree a child's own wonder at the world; the books must confront experience with the degree of honesty of which children themselves are capable, and must have a vital though not oppressive sense of reality, instead of a diminution of the world through frivolity, sentimentality, or condescension. Stories which stir and absorb children go to the heart of their real joys and problems. For children of all ages and abilities there are universal themes that appear in fiction of naturalistic detail of a social, psychological or historical kind and in the conventions of myth, folk-tale and legend. Children will recognise cheerfulness, love, bravery, deprivation, moral dilemmas, the search for personal status, in books with an immediate contemporary environment, an alien social setting, or in the fantasy of universal myth. They look for the satisfaction of their own pressing emotional and instinctual needs; this is part of a growth in their capacity to make an objective and impersonalised response. It is precisely in adolescence that one 'misuses' art, personalising it, investing it with one's own frustration or obsessions. Refusing to accept its fictionality one puts oneself in the character's position, treating character and incident as if they were real before being aware of the novel as existing in its own right as an expression of an author's intention.[1]

Instead of using one 'reader' for a class each term some teachers of mixed-ability classes offer three carefully selected novels aimed at the above-average, below-average, and average readers. Neither of these alternatives seems to me to satisfy important considerations: no child should be expected to enjoy any one particular book at any particular time and since children seem to grow psychologically in fits and starts, their reading interests, attainments, and needs vary unpredictably sometimes from month to month. They can move in their reading from a simple, traditional fairy tale one week, to a book about Vikings or about life in a modern, urban family the next, turning and re-turning at all stages of growth; it would be misleading to suggest, for example, that advanced readers won't read fairy tales, or picture books.[2] Too often, perhaps, children are given books that they are too young for, and it may be that in some cases emotional and imaginative experiences missed in infancy need to be gone through later. This may be true of not only backward readers but the average and above-average readers too. In choosing books for a streamed and supposedly homogeneous group it is important to resist the stereotyping effects of streaming and to cater for all levels of emotional and intellectual development, and the same considerations will apply in the choice and range of books for use with unstreamed classes, with the additional criterion that the choice will have to be that much wider and consist of picture books, myths, fairy tale and both simple and more sophisticated children's fiction.

Approximately sixty paperback books form a class library for each mixed-ability class which has the advantage of not looking too much like those school editions which so often symbolise the division between school and real life; there should be one copy of each title, but especially worthwhile books should occur in each class-set for that year. The following lists are an attempt to indicate such a representative library for a mixed-ability class of boys and girls in each of the first four years of the secondary school; in each set there are books of a more reflective, poetic kind and more accessible books with more action, short-term suspense and simpler moral issues; books of poetry and non-fiction (for example, Hamlyn paperback series, Penguin *Connexions* series) and books that the children

26

themselves had written would be added; 'readers' especially designed for backward readers have been omitted since they often lack any intrinsic worth, but there are many good books for seven- to nine-year-olds which are tactfully presented and enjoyed by backward secondary readers.

First year

A Small Pinch of Weather	J. Aiken
The Latchkey Children	E. Allen
A Likely Lad	G. Avery
Flood Warning	P. Berna
A Hundred Million Francs	P. Berna
A Bear Called Paddington	M. Bond
A House at Green Knowe	L. Boston
Children of Green Knowe	L. Boston
The Secret Garden	F. H. Burnett
Alice in Wonderland; Through the Looking Glass	L. Carroll
The Cave	R. Church
Emanuel and his Parrot	K. Craig
Charlie and the Chocolate Factory	R. Dahl
Along Came a Dog	M. De Jong
The House of Sixty Fathers	M. De Jong
Wheel on the School	M. De Jong
The Saturdays	E. Enright
Thimble Summer	E. Enright
The Summer Birds	P. Farmer
The Poisoned Dog	F. Grice
A Severnside Story	F. Grice
Jimmy Lane and his Boat	F. Grice
Oworo	R. Guillot
Sama	R. Guillot
Sirga	R. Guillot
I am David	A. Holm
The Iron Man	T. Hughes
The Incredible Adventures of Professor Branestawm	N. Hunter

Emil and the Detectives	E. Kastner
Stig of the Dump	C. King
The Colour Fairy Tale Books	A. Lang
The Lion, the Witch and the Wardrobe	C. S. Lewis
The Magician's Nephew	C. S. Lewis
A Bookshop on the Quay	P. Lynch
The Laughing Dragon	K. Mahood
A Book of Giants	R. Manning-Sanders
A Book of Dwarfs	R. Manning-Sanders
A Book of Dragons	R. Manning-Sanders
A Book of Witches	R. Manning-Sanders
No More School	W. Mayne
Pig in the Middle	W. Mayne
The Last Bus	W. Mayne
The Fishing Party	W. Mayne
Adventures of the Little Wooden Horse	U. Moray Williams
The Goalkeeper's Revenge and Other Stories	B. Naughton
The Railway Children	E. Nesbit
The Treasure Seekers	E. Nesbit
Five Children and It	E. Nesbit
The Wouldbegoods	E. Nesbit
The Borrowers	M. Norton
The Borrowers Afield	M. Norton
Bednob and Broomstick	M. Norton
Mrs. Cockle's Cat	P. Pearce
Hurricane	A. Salkey
Drought	A. Salkey
Jonah Simpson	A. Salkey
The Silver Sword	I. Serraillier
The Ivory Horn	I. Serraillier
West Indian Folk Tales	P. Sherlock
Anansi Stories	P. Sherlock
A Hundred and One Dalmatians	D. Smith
The Boy who was Afraid	A. Sperry
The Boy from Hackston NE	R. Taylor

We Couldn't Leave Dinah	M. Treadgold
Charlotte's Web	E. B. White
Little House in the Big Woods	L. I. Wilder
Little House on the Prairie	L. I. Wilder
On the Banks of Plum Creek	L. I. Wilder

Second year

Watership Down	R. Adams
The Wolves of Willoughby Chase	J. Aiken
On the Run	N. Bawden
The Origin of Life and Death (African Creation Myths)	U. Beier
The Drummer Boy	C. Ekwensi
The Four Storey Mistake	E. Enright
Black Jack	L. Garfield
Mister Corbett's Ghost and Other Stories	L. Garfield
The Drummer Boy	L. Garfield
The Moon of Gomrath	A. Garner
The Weirdstone of Brisingamen	A. Garner
Tales of the Greek Heroes	R. L. Green
A Book of Myths	R. L. Green
The Rescue	F. Grice
The Lifeboat Haul	F. Grice
The Spider's Palace	R. Hughes
Myths and Legends of India	V. Ions
Bevis	R. Jeffries
Joseph's Yard	C. Keeping
Tales of Troy and Greece	A. Lang
A Wrinkle in Time	M. L'Engle
Prince Caspian	C. S. Lewis
The Voyage of the 'Dawn Treader'	C. S. Lewis
The Silver Chair	C. S. Lewis
The Battle of St. George Without	J. McNeill
The Midnight Folk	J. Masefield
The Changeling	W. Mayne
Summer Visitors	W. Mayne

A Swarm in May	W. Mayne
The Grass Rope	W. Mayne
The Battlefield	W. Mayne
One Small Boy	B. Naughton
A Dog So Small	P. Pearce
Minnow on the Say	P. Pearce
What the Neighbours Did, and Other Stories	P. Pearce
Hero Tales from the British Isles	B. L. Picard
The Little Prince	A. de Saint Exupery
A Fall from the Sky	I. Serraillier
The Way of Danger	I. Serraillier
Beowulf the Warrior	I. Serraillier
The Challenge of the Green Knight	I. Serraillier
Gumble's Yard	J. R. Townsend
Widdershins Crescent	J. R. Townsend
The Children's Crusade	H. Treece
The Horned Helmet	H. Treece
Viking's Dawn	H. Treece
Tom Sawyer	M. Twain
Antelope Singer	R. Underhill
Beaverbird	R. Underhill
Moonman	T. Ungerer
Avalanche	R. Van Der Loeff
Children on the Oregon Trail	R. Van Der Loeff
They're Drowning our Village	R. Van Der Loeff
Wordhoard	G. P. Walsh, K. Crossley-Holland
The Sword in the Stone	T. H. White
Mistress Masham's Repose	T. H. White
Kangaroo Tales	R. Wighton
The Happy Prince	O. Wilde
By the Shores of Silver Lake	L. I. Wilder
The Long Winter	L. I. Wilder
These Happy Golden Years	L. I. Wilder
The Rocks of Honey	P. Wrightson

Third year

The Whispering Mountain	J. Aiken
Nightbirds of Nantucket	J. Aiken
Black Hearts in Battersea	J. Aiken
Grandad with Snails	M. Baldwin
Joby	S. Barstow
Myths and Legends of Africa	M. Carey
Fifteen	B. Cleary
Drop Dead	J. Cunningham
Lokotown and Other Stories	C. Ekwensi
Crossroad	G. Frewer
The Diary of Ann Frank	
Jack Holborn	L. Garfield
Smith	L. Garfield
Devil-in-the-Fog	L. Garfield
The God beneath the Sea	L. Garfield & E. Blishen
Elidor	A. Garner
The Owl Service	A. Garner
The Bonny Pit Laddie	F. Grice
The Oak and the Ash	F. Grice
The Endless Steppe	E. Hautzig
Louie's Lot	E. W. Hildick
Birdy Jones	E. W. Hildick
King of the Barbareens	J. Hitchman
The Mouse and his Child	R. Hoban
Springboard	D. Jackson
The African Child	C. Laye
The Wizard of Earthsea	U. Le Guin
A Kid for Two Farthings	W. Mankowicz
The Experience of Colour	M. Marland
First Choice	M. Marland
Walkabout	J. V. Marshall
Ravensgill	W. Mayne
Sand	W. Mayne
Earthfasts	W. Mayne
Island of the Blue Dolphins	S. O'Dell
The Wooing of Beppo Tate	E. Palmer

31

Tom's Midnight Garden	P. Pearce
The Children of the House	P. Pearce, B. Fairfax-Lucy
The Scapegoat	S. Porter
Jacob's Ladder	S. Porter
Shane	J. Schaefer
First Blood	J. Schaefer
Maiden's Trip	E. Smith
The World of Little Foxy	N. Smithson
Hill's End	I. Southall
Ash Road	I. Southall
The Pearl	J. Steinbeck
The Red Pony	J. Steinbeck
Treasure Island	R. L. Stevenson
Dragon Slayer	R. Sutcliff
The Eagle of the Ninth	R. Sutcliff
The Lantern Bearers	R. Sutcliff
Sword at Sunset	R. Sutcliff
Whichaway	G. & K. Swarthout
Hell's Edge	J. R. Townsend
The Intruder	J. R. Townsend
The Dream Time	H. Treece
Hounds of the King	H. Treece
The Prince and the Pauper	M. Twain
Pudd'nhead Wilson	M. Twain
There is a Happy Land	K. Waterhouse
Billy Liar	K. Waterhouse
The Master	T. H. White

Fourth year

Things Fall Apart	C. Achebe
Collected Stories	I. Babel
Short Stories of Our Time	D. Barnes (ed)
Desperadoes	S. Barstow
A Kind of Loving	S. Barstow
Borstal Boy	B. Behan
Under Twenty	G. Bowker (ed)
Wuthering Heights	E. Bronte

The Outsider	A. Camus
The Thin Seam	S. Chaplin
The Leaping Lad and Other Stories	S. Chaplin
The Guardians	J. Christopher
Hard Times	C. Dickens
The Diamond as Big as the Ritz, and Other Stories	F. S. Fitzgerald
Child of Two Worlds	M. Gatheru
Goalkeepers are Crazy	B. Glanville
Lord of the Flies	W. Golding
My Childhood	M. Gorky
Goodbye To All That	R. Graves
The Taste of Too Much	C. Hanley
Catch 22	J. Heller
Kestrel for a Knave	B. Hines
People and Diamonds	D. Holbrook (ed)
A High Wind in Jamaica	R. Hughes
Sunday (in *Wodwo*)	T. Hughes
The Rain-Horse (in *Wodwo*)	T. Hughes
Portrait of the Artist as a Young Man	J. Joyce
Dubliners	J. Joyce
In the Castle of my Skin	G. Lamming
Odour of Chrysanthemums	D. H. Lawrence
Nine African Stories	D. Lessing
Through the Tunnel	D. Lessing
Member of the Wedding	C. McCullers
The Mystic Masseur	V. S. Naipaul
A Roof Over Your Head	B. Naughton
Late Night On Watling St.	B. Naughton
First Flight	L. O'Flaherty
Animal Farm	G. Orwell
Shooting an Elephant	G. Orwell
The Courage of his Convictions	T. Parker
Unknown Citizen	T. Parker
Modern African Prose	R. Rive (ed)
People Like Us	A. Rowe (ed)
Vertical Ladder and Other Stories	W. Sansom

Little Children	W. Saroyan
My Name is Aram	W. Saroyan
Key of the Door	A. Sillitoe
Saturday Night and Sunday Morning	A. Sillitoe
The Loneliness of the Long Distance Runner	A. Sillitoe
Josh	I. Southall
Short Stories	D. Thomas
This Time Next Week	L. Thomas
Lark Rise To Candleford	F. Thompson
Childhood, Boyhood, Youth	L. Tolstoy
A Working Life	P. Toynbee
Huckleberry Finn	M. Twain
The Border Country	R. Williams
Black Boy	R. Wright
A Precocious Autobiography	Y. Yevtushenko

The books can be given protective plastic covers in a different colour for each year, installed on shelves or a trolley in each class-room, and the class given the responsibility for their care for that year. An exercise book can accompany each class library to act as a simple index and loan system whereby the title of each book being read can be written down under each pupil's name on a separate page of the exercise book. This allows the teacher to see at a glance which books have been read by each pupil so that discussion groups can be organised quickly, and the teacher can refer to books read when talking to individuals. The book can be used as a basis for recommendation for extended kinds of reading for individual children, and it offers a practical means of avoiding squabbles when pupils come to choose or take up their books each time. The books should be accessible to the class at all times; in addition to their more random use at any point in English lessons other staff will be grateful for these books when there are staff absences, wet lunch hours and leisure moments in the school day.

I believe that one period each week should be reserved entirely for silent, private reading – the teacher doing likewise and resisting wherever possible the temptation such a situation offers for helping individual pupils, or catching up on administrative work. Such a period each week is particularly important in the first year when many children find that it is not the soft option they imagine: the novelty, the silence and the necessary concentration make some uncomfortable, but with encouragement, reminders and example the quiet absorbed enjoyment makes it a period they look forward to for the best of reasons. They quickly and eagerly take possession of the books, read avidly, recommend enthusiastically among themselves and settle down to their reading before the teacher enters the room. It is not sufficiently recognised that there is a direct relation between the quantity of reading that a pupil does and the growth of his capacity to handle written language; it should not follow from the proper importance that we attach to the quality of what is read that we inhibit omnivorous reading. The teacher needs to read the books too if they are to be put to effective use and opportunities need to be created for the regular sharing of judgements, opinions and criticisms of favourite books between the class and the teacher and the other classes of the year. Lists, displays, reviews, and publicity material can be put on classroom display. Worksheets or cards to accompany the fiction can be compiled and formulated so as to guide individual writing or group talk where pupils can express, consolidate and share their responses to the book they have read. The sheets should consist of questions aimed at increasing levels of exploration of the book so that, as with a homework assignment or written task, they extend the brightest pupils and the most mature readers, and yet encourage the slowest learners and readers to feel that the task is within their interests and capabilities. Good models would be the suggestions for talk and writing in the teachers' notes for the BBC *Listening and Writing* pamphlets, and the suggestions for close reading in the Longmans edition of *There is a Happy Land* (Keith Waterhouse). The chief aim is clearly to have children wanting to read and discuss books without the need for the crutches provided by such sheets, and if they are used at all they should not be automatic sequels to reading but rather there to be asked for.

The ability to establish relationships is essential for much that we do in English teaching, and for nothing more so than the appreciation of literature. Children can often gain most from a book if at first they hear it, or parts of it, read aloud. The 'reading aloud' lesson is a basic activity and a focal point in English work. A teacher often feels uneasy when he does no more than read a novel or short story aloud, for pleasure, with no questions asked unless the class raises them. It was, perhaps, this feeling that led to the practice of 'reading round the class' and to the equally preposterous practice of giving literary history, notes, and tests to assess retention – anything that could divert the child from absorption in reading towards mark-getting. Reading aloud to a class is a more delicate and subtle process of exchange than we usually realise. The reader has to be intent on experiencing a passage within his own mind in order to convey it to the listeners. There should be no distraction; the listeners do not need to follow in their own books, which can be a distraction in itself. A practised reader will know that a firm, clear contact between the reader and the passage is sometimes lost, and it is at these moments that classes flag, and loss of interest, attention and understanding occurs. If the reading is done sufficiently well, if the book is one that the teacher really enjoys, if the words are animated and read feelingly – and this, of course, requires practice and confidence – then the effect of such reading provides the corroboration of its worth. It is a communal sharing of a felt experience and a unifying activity of a satisfyingly complete kind.[3]

As Geoffrey Summerfield says, in *Directions in English* (Cambridge, 1969):

> . . . our concern for cognition tends to drive the felt experience out of the classroom. So that pupils who are deeply moved by an episode, an event, an encounter, a death, a calamity, have to rush to pull themselves out of their felt response in order to cope with the cognitive orders of the day.

It is easier to understand experience than it is to make explicit that understanding. Stories work on the experience of the reader at many levels and a feature of the worthwhile story is that it reaches depths of thought and feeling within the reader that are not always readily accessible or only dimly apprehended. Books can be read successfully to pupils in mixed-ability groups which they, as individuals, would find beyond them. Once children are aware of and assured by the teacher's confidence in his material they begin to ask questions that are relevant to the passage and their understanding of it. It can be unnecessary sometimes for the teacher to begin to ask questions – a difficult task, for how can we be sure that our questions are their questions, and how sure are they that we haven't already decided what their answers should be? If we lose faith in our capacity to bring a passage to life we are the more likely to fall back on murderous dissection and examination – 'lemon squeezing'.

The reading aloud of passages from a book in the class library can act as a springboard for discussion, creative writing, topic work or drama work, and use can be made of the class library for pupils' 'programmes' of readings with accompanying music and sound effects on tape. A book used for reading to the whole class will need to have all that we require of a worthwhile novel for children and also have something to offer of common interest to children of all abilities in the class; it will need to throw light on an aspect of the pupils' own lives so that the teacher can, if he chooses, explore the relevance and truth of the literature in order to illuminate the pupils' intellectual and emotional experience, extend their range of understanding and widen their experience of the uses of language.

The choice of book can depend on the relationship between a class and a teacher, and can develop that relationship and lead to an increase in the range of material that a teacher can profitably introduce to his class. A teacher needs to know his class and be aware of his own ability to handle the material and the questions, discussions, and possibly the discoveries that may arise during the course of a lesson with a particular class. A serialised reading by the teacher can evoke an excited or thoughtful response, triggering off memories and evoking new experiences for class and teacher alike. A serialised reading of *A Dog So Small* with a first-year class would explore the gap between promise and fulfilment, the necessity of fantasy, and the adjustment to the unaccommodating complexities of reality. A reading of *The Bonny Pit Laddie* with second- or third-year pupils would open up topics for discussion and writing, ideas for improvisation and bring to mind other texts (contemporary ballads and newspaper accounts, photographs, stories, poems, scripted plays, film) as the book worked itself on the collective imagination of the teacher and the class in a collaborative exploration of, in this case, calamity and heroism in a mining community. The lessons would move freely from reading to talk, writing, and drama. Using ballads, poetry, tape recording, and film with a third-year group, a reading of *Walkabout* would explore crises in adolescence and the clash of cultures; *The Owl Service*, centrally concerned with adolescence and powerful love and hate, is a novel that some less able pupils would miss if it were not given a serialised reading. A reading of *Summer Birds* can lead on to an exploration of the Icarus myth via Ian Serraillier's *A Fall From The Sky*, Auden's 'Musée des Beaux Arts', Breughel's painting, Elizabeth Frink's sculpture of free-fall, and bird, insect, balloon and space flight; Rosemary Sutcliff's *Dragon-Slayer* read episodically can be used in conjunction with Edwin Muir's translation of the original and Ian Serraillier's version, *Beowulf the Warrior*.

There are other suggestions for extended work with a class reader in *Reading Together* by K. Calthrop (1971) and *Reading Study Units* by J. Foster (1973), but there is a danger that extensive work of this kind – topic work based on a 'literary core' – could degenerate into a variant of set-book study, with literature used only as a tool. Just as our prime concern in the classroom is with what the book can do for the reader, not how it does it, so the work arising out of a teacher's serialised reading should usually generate from the children's response to the book, and no 'work' at all need take place. As so often with a poem, a good reading may be enough; but the teacher's ability to create, maintain, and extend the enthusiasm rather than merely to impose the activity is crucial if the literature is not to suffer.

TALKING AND WRITING

The aim will be to help children to be themselves, to become people who are able to use language appropriately in the variety of situations they meet. The teacher's own talk plays a vital role: if he is only a question-master or a purveyor of lesson notes, then it is

38

less likely that he will be a person to his pupils and they will not hear his enthusiasms and doubts, or the gestation of an idea, the fresh language of imaginative improvisation, the range of registers for appropriate occasions from the instructional, expressive, anecdotal to the heightened poetic; nor will he be likely to set the climate in the classroom for such presentations by his pupils. The diversity of experience, the variety of interests and different social, linguistic, cultural, racial backgrounds which an unstreamed class of pupils can offer can ensure that the necessary acquisition of transactional language will not, through an obsession with proprieties, be at the expense of vitality and expressiveness. The gains in language acquisition will not be one-way traffic: 'middle class' children will gain from 'working class' children, 'able' from 'less able'.[4]

It is helpful for a class to feel that it has an identity, and a lot of direct class teaching is both possible and desirable to prevent the class from becoming fragmented. There will be many occasions when the class as a whole will come together to share a reading, a discussion or an improvisation, but in an unstreamed class the significant teaching unit will be the small group. The teacher can organise groups of six or so pupils, or groups can be allowed to come together by choice. Conflicts, which may arise whether the groups are planned or not, can be faced by the pupils, who, with tactful help from the teacher, can learn the valuable lesson of working together through their difficulties and making amends for irritating and disturbing one another; they can become more sensitive to each other's needs, acquire notions of justice, tolerance and considerate attitudes towards others, and learn to form close personal and working relationships; but to do so they will need to have the trust of the teacher and the security that a well-organised classroom will give.[5]

There are many different kinds of talk that can be arranged during small-group activity, and conversations need not be heavily mediated by the teacher. Much of the talk will be necessary: social talk; transactional talk, concerned with making decisions, using language to enable them to relate to each other functionally, to plan and organise their programmes of work, visits, play reading, film making and displays; the expositional reporting back to the whole class; and expressive talk, using language to come to terms with experience, to explore attitudes and feelings and to respond to literature and their own writing and drama. The teacher will be listening, encouraging, making suggestions, noting the progress of groups and individuals and helping in the planning and the provision of resources. For the most part talk in groups needs to be structured: a class used to group discussions can initiate a great deal for themselves but merely to disband a class into groups with a few questions is likely to confuse and demoralise, and it is best to use workcards or their equivalent at first to give the group security. The teacher can then become part of each group in turn to help weld it together, encouraging an experience of success and incorporating reluctant talkers. The eventual aim and emphasis, however, should be on the individual and the group shaping their own awareness in their own language, yet making some use of the more mature formulations of the teacher. In group talk one pupil will prompt himself to use language to think more abstractly while another pupil will need the teacher to prompt him to do so. It is important, therefore, that the teacher arrange for discussion and writing in the classroom so that the pupils can benefit from each other and the teacher can in turn offer the help necessary.[6]

The arrangement of work around a theme is a convenient method of framing experiences into a manageable classroom shape. Work on topics and themes, collecting material and forming programmes of work for a sequence of lessons where all the skills of reading, modes of writing and discourse, and drama can be used as the need arises, to illuminate a central topic or interest, provides children with a real opportunity to work on their own and in groups. By having a great deal of material on one theme the teacher has a range of options to present to the pupils and an individual's work can be self-chosen and self-generating, the teacher helping the pupils to develop their capacities for self-management. A number of groups of children of varied abilities can work on a class project under the teacher's guidance, or a group can work on its own topic, or each group can be given different assignments related to a larger topic to be produced in project form in a book, on tape or as a display. Especially useful will be folders or packs of material concerned with a topic and consisting of photographs, pamphlets, prose extracts, poems, newspaper cuttings, advertisements, statistics, prints, facsimiles, broadsheets, tapes, records and children's writing. A flexible classroom layout can be important and desks, tables and chairs arranged around the perimeter of the room allow for group work, whole-class discussion and drama, reading and writing.

Much of this work will mean that the classroom will become more of a workshop with pupils moving from a whole-class unit to small groups and individual study. Reciprocity and collaboration in the classroom means that there will be speakers and listeners, writers and readers and sharing of success and failure. Extended projects and thematic work should have a sense of structure – and for the inexperienced teacher and class a fairly tight structure to begin with – but also a flexibility which allows for choice and discovery, imagination and intuition as the topic works itself upon the class and the teacher. The project should be open to the range of suggestions that the material and the pupils can offer – and the initial structure will be modified in practice in the light of these discoveries and connections.

A fourth-year mixed-ability class worked on a theme entitled 'Loneliness and Isolation' for five weeks as part of their course work for the CSE. Each member of the class was given a copy of the duplicated worksheet which the class teacher had prepared. The worksheet consisted of eight subsections. Each section introduced one aspect of the overall topic in a short paragraph providing facts and opinions, calculated to cajole, provoke and stimulate interest and thought, followed by suggestions for talk, writing, and other activities (use of tape recorder, camera, questionnaire etc) and appropriate references to the resources available in the room (fiction, poetry, magazines, newspapers, colour supplements, photographs, reproductions, advertisements, graphs, statistical tables, case histories and so on). The worksheet was designed to provide a starting point and be sufficiently directive to support some of the students, yet open ended enough to encourage them to form their own opinions as early as possible. The permutations of choice permitted groups of varying sizes to work on any of the sections in turn as they explored the central theme, and the groups could form, disband

and reform as the work progressed; the teacher was freed to join groups and individuals as they were working on their folders, and at appropriate moments groups would report back to the whole class directly or by way of wall displays or edited tape recordings. The groups were self-selecting and allowance was made for individual pieces of work; to prevent the group stifling or inhibiting the personal development, originality or individual inquiries of its members, individuals were allowed to express themselves freely in circumstances where the responses and opinions of others were sometimes irrelevant.[7]

The role of the teacher in a mixed-ability group is to stimulate, encourage, and guide the pupils' learning activities, to provide opportunities for informed discussion and to help pupils to question, listen, qualify, elaborate, collaborate and accommodate themselves to others. This involves children of all abilities, interests and points of view in reviewing their own and other people's responses, sharing in a creative activity, forming new friendships, and valuing and respecting each other in the give and take of the group or class in the interchange of a variety of points of view and diversity of language. The teacher has to have the readiness and ability to encourage his pupils to be no less dependent upon each other than they are upon him. The educational advantage of a group is that everybody joins in the process of educating everybody else, the members of the group being just as liable as the teacher to set one another right, the group taking over what used to be the sole function of the teacher. There is less emphasis on instructing pupils by communicating to them bodies of knowledge that the teacher has already acquired; the teacher is, of course, more expert and knowledgeable in many areas, but he is in collaboration with his pupils, doing work that is of mutual interest, and there will be some things in which they are most expert. He can no longer act as sole arbiter of wisdom and truth, the sole source, sponsor, and assessor of material presented or accomplished. The teacher may sometimes be as much in the dark as, sometimes more so than, some of his pupils – Dickens' aphorism on M'Choakumchild was 'if he had only learnt a little less, how infinitely better he might have taught much more!'

Discussion of one another's work by the pupils will increase awareness of correctness of usage, technical details, competence in spelling and punctuation, and will reveal as well a high capacity for considering ideas and content. If the teacher encourages a tactful mutual criticism by the pupils of each other's work, does not dwell on faults at the expense of gaining the trust of the pupils, and shows a sympathetic and enthusiastic interest in their efforts, the pupils become more naturally concerned with improving the accuracy and effectiveness of their work and more ready and willing to improve their basic skills in writing. The 'polishing' of the work in progress (and much of the writing we ask of children in class cannot be expected to be much more than this until time is given over to its further shaping) is seen to be genuinely necessary before the work is presented to the teacher, the rest of the class, and others outside the class. It is important for children to write for a range of possible audiences – not only for themselves and their teacher, but for their contemporaries in their own small groups, their class group, other groups in the school or another school, and for a relatively more public audience outside school, such as parents and friends. It is also important for them to write across the spectrum of the kinds of writing: transactional, expressive, and poetic.[8] The sharing of writing by small groups through reading and discussion can be helped by mounting displays of writing and magazines; it is important that such displays are not limited to the most competent pieces but should include work by everybody and acknowledge endeavour as well as achievement.

For notes to this chapter see pp 183–4

3 Teaching Modern Languages in Mixed-Ability Groups

S. H. Miller

There can be few areas of the curriculum of our secondary schools which have undergone such changes in recent years as modern languages. The Standing Consultative Committee of the Modern Language Association in its report entitled *Tools for the Job* describes this situation very clearly.

> The organisation of language teaching in England and Wales up to the 1950s followed a recognisable pattern: most of the pupils were in selective schools or streams, the objective for the majority was success in translation and essay at O level and, for the minority, the completion of a literary and linguistic sixth-form course in preparation for a university. The staff were mostly graduates, using an approach adopted from their own school days and from their university. The length of the school language course and the content of the textbooks differed little between the schools. Within this common pattern of limited numbers and familiar approaches success, measured by agreed criteria, was frequently achieved.

We all know that this situation has changed radically with the spread of comprehensive education, leading to an expectation on the part of many more pupils that they will be offered the opportunity to learn a modern language. The spread of primary French has under-lined this expectation on the part of many of our pupils so that the teaching of modern languages across the ability range is fast becoming an accepted part of the secondary scene. To quote from *Tools*

44

for the Job once again, 'One of the most far reaching developments has been the extension of modern language teaching to a large number of pupils differing in ability and attitude from those who have taken languages in the past.' This, indeed, is the very heart of the problem for, unlike the pupils described in the previous quotation, today's modern language learners in secondary schools reflect an enormous range of attitudes, aptitudes and abilities. In order to meet the varying needs of this wide range of pupils, modern language teachers have often adopted the procedure of setting. The aim of this device is wholly laudable – to meet the differing needs of the pupils by offering differing types and levels of language activity within the setting arrangement. After all, experience and investigation confirm that the slower learners in modern languages tend to find it very difficult, if not impossible, to sustain the pace of the abler pupils and to achieve the same degree of accuracy or even oral competence. Above all, they fail to develop that vital skill, the ability to make linguistic analogies and, therefore, to take short cuts in language learning. Thus, what more sensible arrangement could there be than setting, when faced with the problem of teaching modern languages to a very wide range of ability? One or two observations, however, do tend to undermine one's confidence in this approach.

During the academic year 1970–71 a working party of the Advisory Committee on In-Service Training in Modern Languages at the University of Nottingham looked into the problem of the slow learner in modern languages. They discovered that in most of the schools visited there was an important number of pupils who could be said to fall within the category of 'poor language students'. It is significant that among the schools visited was a highly selective independent school, as well as comprehensive and other non-selective schools. Each of these schools indicated that about one third to one half of their intake presented difficult teaching problems. The general feeling was that, despite some good work done in oral French, German, etc, the weaker linguist is usually weak elsewhere in the curriculum. On the question of whether these pupils made progress, it was very difficult to be precise: what indeed is meant by progress? Perhaps the only definite thing to be said about this was that where pupil and teacher felt that progress was being made, the learning of a foreign language continued in a more or less satisfactory way. On the other hand, where pupils and/or teachers were not happy about their progress, achievement began to tail off markedly, particularly towards the end of the second year. It was at this point that most of the real problems began to appear.

The significance of this investigation is not difficult to see: 'poor language students' sharing the difficulties described earlier seem to be present in roughly the same proportions no matter what kind of school or what degree of selection is operative. Mrs Madeleine Lewis, writing in *Modern Languages in Scotland*, puts the problem in what seems to be the correct perspective: 'When teaching is not producing the hoped-for results, the tendency with French seems to be to say that it is not suitable for the slower learners, nor they for it. The crucial question – "What is it that is not suitable?" – seems sometimes to remain unasked. The answer might be "French teaching as it is being attempted".' And again: 'Where results are disappointing, it might be more constructive to look at the mode of presentation of the teaching materials, rather than sadly at the pupil's intellectual deficiencies.'

The setted arrangement is often justified in terms of 'producing the goods': after all, top sets tend to do well; bottom sets achieve little by comparison. But are we not here in the realms of the self-fulfilling prophecy? By labelling a child 'top set material' do not both teacher and learner instinctively adopt a positive attitude to the work in hand, leading to a large measure of success? And is the converse not even more true? How many of us have not set off towards a classroom containing a bottom set with feelings of apprehension and weariness, to be met by pupils showing much the same feelings?

In that same thought-provoking issue of *Modern Languages in Scotland*, which takes as its theme 'The teaching of modern languages across the ability range', there is another most illuminating remark concerning setting: John Linton, writing in defence of this procedure, makes the point that setting is a flexible, subject-based arrangement, nowhere near as generalised in its view as streaming. As he says, 'We can adjust sets at any period of the week.' But then he adds, 'It is inadvisable, however, to do so more than once per term, for fear of breaking continuity.'

Certainly it is beyond dispute that, for whatever reasons, in the last few years there has been a move away from streaming, setting and banding within many comprehensive schools towards a kind of organisation which is based on forms, tutor groups or house groups. In order, it is said, to avoid premature and unsound judgements, and to ease the transition from primary to secondary schools, most or all of the teaching in the early years is carried on within the groupings devised for social or pastoral activities: mixed-ability groups. It might therefore be useful to describe the work done by two groups of modern languages teachers when faced with the mixed-ability situation.

As director of language studies and head of the modern languages department in a mixed comprehensive school with a 6–7 form entry, the present writer had established a pattern of setting within the French department which was very much in line with the collective thinking of that department. It was with some trepidation that we decided to unscramble our complicated banding and setting system in first-year French in order to experiment with mixed-ability groups. We had come to the conclusion that we ought to experiment in this way because the move towards mixed-ability groups, together with other trends in educational practice, had begun to give us a feeling of isolation. If French, for it is most often French which is the common-core language, were not to conform, the timetable makers and curriculum planners might say, 'then let's get rid of French – shove it into the fourth-year options and save ourselves a headache!' Indeed, even such an eminent educationalist as Professor Harry Rée has suggested that modern languages might be taken out of schools altogether and taught only in further education. Because of the blocking of first-year French classes on the timetable, we were able to undertake this experiment in mixed-ability teaching in the sure knowledge that if setting proved to be necessary we would arrange this without further ado.

One thing became apparent immediately we had decided in favour of mixed-ability groups – a further decision on teaching materials was absolutely essential before we could move forward.

Previously we had used material such as Longmans' audio-visual French course for the majority, Stage III of *En Avant* for the able and/or the experienced entrants, and the present author's *Allons En France* for the least able. This pattern was then reduced to an apparently simpler system of Longmans' course for the majority and *Allons En France* for the least able in the first and second years. We were very conscious that the Longmans' course was not really suited to the needs of our middle-ability pupils and that *Allons En France* was not sufficiently structured for the more able pupils in the lower band, who might later perform quite usefully at CSE level. Obviously we could not reflect this combination of course materials in each mixed-ability group, even if it had been desirable; its complexity would have been unwieldy. We took the decision to use our Longmans' material – Stage I – as the common core which all pupils should experience, though we realised that even the Longmans' Stage I was going to present considerable difficulties for our least able pupils if we were to use it as the authors had intended.

Our solution was to use each set of pictures and the accompanying text as the basis for a cycle of work in which the lowest common denominator was *basic receptive comprehension* of the French. To this we would add, according to the needs of various pupils, exercises and drills which would give practice in as many of the 'four skills' as the pupils proved capable of acquiring.

By using the blocking of the timetable mentioned above, we were able to bring several groups together for a mass audio-visual presentation of the new unit and then to split into tutor groups or ability groupings for exploitation of this material. (These were temporary groupings whose composition might change from week to week, and the use of ability groupings was restricted to only a small proportion of the total time available.) What we were really aiming at was to rid all pupils of the limitations imposed by 'lock-step' teaching (ie all pupils following the same instruction at the same moment under the direct control of the teacher). We tried to let each pupil's progress be determined by his own ability and motivation. Thus, the emphasis was on individualised tasks once the initial oral exploitation phase had been passed (and here the oral groundwork done in the primary schools was of real help).

Finally, the cycle of work was devised so as to allow the ablest, the quickest, and the most experienced pupils to be led on to a branching programme of work before returning to the main group for the next mass presentation. In order to use the Longmans' course within this scheme we needed to rewrite and adapt a great deal of the original material. This rewriting was undertaken as a collective effort by all the members of the French department working as a team. After a year of working in this way (adding some M Carré film loops for variety and providing extra readers and other supplementary materials for the more able pupils), we had to make another important decision: to continue with this and virtually rewrite Longmans' Stage II or to resort to setting. The decision to let the mixed-ability pattern continue and rewrite Longmans' Stage II was unanimous, although this would make a lot more work for the teachers concerned. The text of the original is virtually all dialogue and the rate of progression very rapid. (It is interesting to note that the newly published rewritten version of this stage, A2, has relegated the dialogues to a relatively minor role within the pattern of work.) We had been unhappy with the original Stage II in any case, and members of the department were anxious to see it rewritten even without the change to mixed-ability; the demands of the new form of organisation gave us sufficient impetus to want to get on with the job. We agreed that our scheme of mass presentation, together with group oral work and individualised and largely self-correcting worksheets, was worth pursuing.

One of the main changes from our first-year scheme was to reduce the complicated dialogues of the Longmans' course to a simpler narrative which would still fit the pictures. Another change in technique was to use the overhead projector to show a copy of this new text alongside the filmstrip visual. To examine a particular unit of the adapted Longmans' material will illustrate how the system operated. The example chosen is from Lesson 3 of Stage II.

1 The first half (six frames) of the lesson was shown to about 200 second-year pupils simultaneously. After these frames had been

FIG 1

The original Longmans A/V French, Stage II, Lesson 3, Frame 1 and text:

JEAN-PAUL: Ah, te voilà, Claudette. Je vais t'aider.
CLAUDETTE: Tiens, comment vas-tu m'aider? Tu es chef de cuisine, hein?
JEAN-PAUL: Non, ni toi non plus. Voilà pourquoi je vais t'aider.
CLAUDETTE: C'est Hélène qui m'aide. Nous n'avons pas besoin de toi.

The adaptation, using the same visual:

Claudette, Hélène et Jean-Paul sont à la cuisine. Jean-Paul veut aider les filles mais Claudette refuse, parce qu'il n'est pas chef de cuisine!

seen with an English commentary in order to make absolutely sure that the significance of the visuals was understood by all the pupils, they were seen again with the French commentary spoken by the presenter of the unit, the member of the French department whose responsibility it had been to prepare this particular unit. The visuals were then seen for a third time with the revised French text displayed alongside. Figure 1 shows the original text which accompanies the first frame of this unit and also the revision which was devised to accompany the same visual.

Given that each mixed-ability group in this particular year was required to start its cycle of work by seeing the filmstrip, it seemed obvious to bring them together in the way just described and this had the ancillary benefit of underlining the co-operative nature of the team teaching venture. Certainly there is nothing magical about the number of pupils involved; in many ways it would be easier to organise such a mass presentation by bringing together two or three groups of thirty children. An important lesson learned from this mode of presentation was that it was all too easy to confuse the function of this activity with the later exploitation phase where the maximum amount of teacher/pupil contact is required. All went well as long as we kept in mind that the aim was to present and not to exploit the material. Naturally enough, however, there were a number of occasions when we slipped into the 'teaching mode' and attempted to achieve with 200 children what is difficult enough sometimes with thirty.

The basic notion then, was to ensure that all pupils had received the same stimulus and had achieved at least 'gist' comprehension of the basic text. In order to focus their attention upon the written text as displayed on the overhead projector screen, it was sometimes necessary to devise certain novel procedures. For example, on one occasion it was agreed that one of the members of the staff team should remain at the back of the hall and play the part of the clown who doesn't quite understand what is happening. By his calling out a number of questions in French relating to the displayed text and by his being corrected by the presenter and other colleagues present, the attention of the pupils was drawn to this text and, incidentally, a great deal of amusement was generated.

Another incidental benefit of this procedure of mass presentation was that it released a number of colleagues to prepare materials needed for the later stages and allowed for the less extrovert members of the team to make their own particular contribution to the exercise in a way best suited to them.

2 The large audience dispersed at this point, splitting into mixed-ability groups. Here they received a copy of the revised Longmans' text, and reading and oral work – question and answer – were the next activities. At this stage of the work the conventional teacher/class relationship operated.

3 Next came further oral work but this time in groups of five or six pupils within each of the mixed-ability groups. The aim here was to enable as many pupils as possible to be verbally active and they were encouraged to ask each other as many questions as possible, derived from the basic text. Undoubtedly this was not as successfully accomplished as it might have been because we failed to provide sufficient help for the pupils in the form of picture and cue cards. Had we been less preoccupied with the revision of the Longmans' course, we might have been more successful in providing this kind of oral stimulus. These cards could each show, for example, a boy or girl going to a particular place. The cue card could have written on it the question 'Qu'est-ce qu'il/elle fait?' with the answer being, according to the visual shown, 'Il/Elle va à la gare, au cinéma, à l'église, etc'. During this stage of the work the teacher's role was that of a monitor rather than a director of activity. By breaking down the formality of the classroom situation and, indeed, its physical arrangement, the teacher was able to move among the class and to develop this more informal relationship with individual pupils or groups of pupils. The level of noise from the classroom was inclined to rise on these occasions, but we were content so long as the noise was a working one.

4 The work described above would have taken something like two 35-minute periods, with the presentation of the new unit occupying perhaps fifteen to twenty minutes. The remaining time

available for each cycle of work (two more 35-minute periods and homework, if required) was devoted to a programme of work undertaken on an individual basis by each pupil. Within our scheme this programme was initiated by means of a series of largely self-correcting worksheets. In other schools with a larger proportion of slower readers, it might well be necessary to provide a wider range of activities including the use of listening machines, picture- and caption-matching cards and the development of a coded system of symbols as illustrated in Fig 2.

FIG 2

QUESTION: POURQUOI VAS-TU A LA GARE?

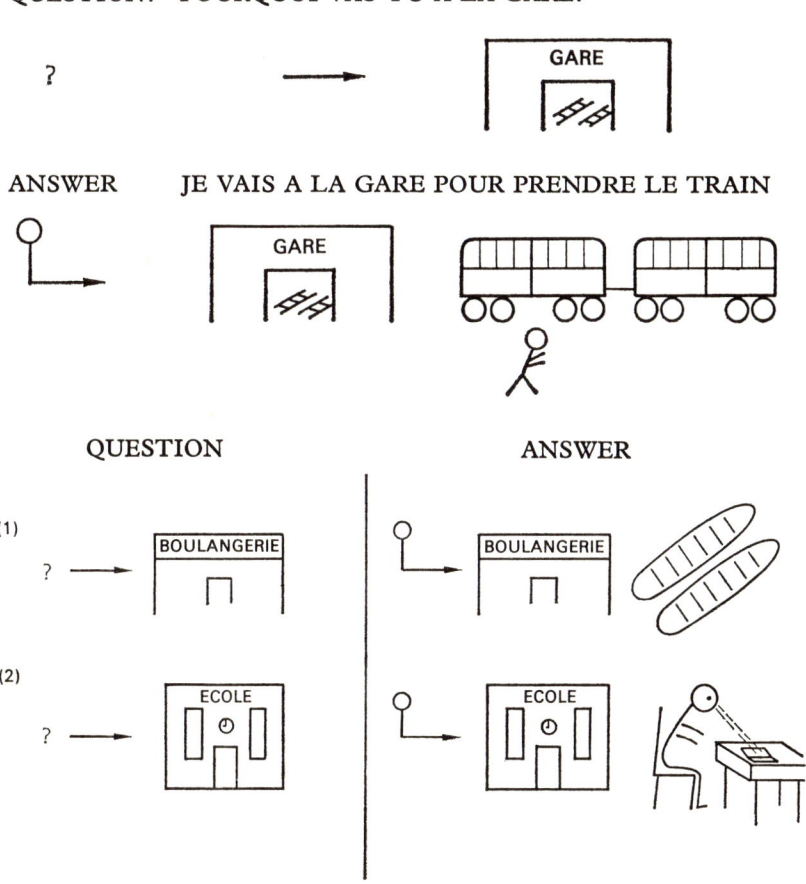

ANSWER   JE VAIS A LA GARE POUR PRENDRE LE TRAIN

The first worksheet issued to the pupils was the same for each child; it consisted of a multiple-choice comprehension sheet and an answer sheet which was available from the teacher upon completion of this work. The aim of this worksheet, and of many of the others, was to teach rather than to test. We hoped that any gaps in the child's understanding of the original presentation material would be filled by the time he had completed this first comprehension exercise. Part of the comprehension sheet in this particular unit of work is shown in Fig 3.

FIG 3

Part of the multiple choice comprehensive sheet used in conjunction with the adapted version of Longman's A/V French, Stage II, Lesson 3, together with its accompanying key.

QUE SAVEZ-VOUS?	WHAT DO YOU KNOW?

1.

i) Où sont les enfants?

  A) Ils sont dans le jardin
  B) Ils sont à l'école
  C) Ils sont à la cuisine

ii) Qu'est-ce que Jean-Paul veut faire?

  A) Il veut jouer au football
  B) Il veut aider les filles
  C) Il veut manger

iii) Why does Claudette refuse his help?

  A) Because Jean-Paul is greedy
  B) Because Jean-Paul is not much of a cook
  C) Because it is too late

. . . .

QUE SAVEZ-VOUS? Réponses	WHAT DO YOU KNOW? Answers

i) C   ii) B   iii) B, etc.

Within each group the speed with which different pupils would complete this first comprehension exercise was variable. This enabled the teacher to check that each individual had successfully completed the work on this sheet before turning to the next activity.

Here the programme branched; those children who had already

given evidence of greater ability or who appeared to be making good progress were allocated a written task. This consisted of a series of questions (largely those already contained in the Longmans' textbook) together with a set of answers given in a random order. The instruction here was that the pupil should write out in his exercise book each question together with the correct answer. We very soon learned that it was quite possible for children to match questions and answers without really understanding what they were doing, so that we were obliged to introduce a further element of difficulty by providing more answers than there were questions. As with the previous multiple-choice comprehension sheet, this worksheet also had its own answer sheet which was obtained from the teacher when he was satisfied that the work had been undertaken seriously and with due regard to standards of presentation, etc.

While the abler pupils were undertaking this work, the slower pupils would have completed the first worksheet and would then be given a sheet marked either 'Ramassez les Morceaux' or 'Les Partenaires', which showed what appeared to be a series of strips of paper torn either at the right-hand end or the left-hand end; each strip of paper contained a number of words forming part of a sentence. The object of the exercise was to match up the beginning and the end of each sentence and to write them out in full in the pupil's exercise book. A variation on this theme was to provide a worksheet which showed not only beginnings and endings but also middles of sentences.

Upon completion of 'Cherchez la Réponse', the written question and answer task, the abler children were directed to a worksheet which involves the use of the expression *avoir besoin*, while the less able were set to deal with an exercise on *vouloir*, both of which points arose from the basic text presented at the beginning of the cycle. These worksheets are illustrated in Figs 4 and 5.

The need for a considerable degree of teacher organisation in all of this is obvious, so that each cycle of work – prepared by a different member of the staff team in turn – is accompanied by notes for his colleagues. This is a very vital element both in order to underline

FIG 4

WHAT DO YOU NEED?   **DE QUOI A-T-ON BESOIN?**

Example:

Question: De quoi a-t-on besoin pour jouer au football?
               (What do you need to play football?)

Answer: Pour jouer au football on a besoin *d'*un ballon.
               (To play football you need a football.)

Notice you have to put DE after 'besoin'.

From the list* at the end of the exercise select the appropriate word to complete your answers.

1 De quoi a-t-on besoin pour jouer au football?
    Pour jouer au football on a besoin d' ....

2 De quoi a-t-on besoin pour aller à l'école?
    Pour aller à l'école on a besoin ....

3 De quoi a-t-on besoin pour manger?
    Pour manger on a ....

4 De quoi a-t-on besoin pour préparer des frites?
    ....

* un cartable - un ballon - une fourchette - pommes de terre - une bicyclette - une douzaine d'oeufs

FIG 5

WHAT DO YOU WANT?   **QU'EST-CE QUE TU VEUX?**

You have a kind uncle who buys you just what you want. All you have to do is say what you want.

Example:

Qu'est-ce que tu veux?
Je veux une glace

What do you want?
I want an ice-cream

Now answer your uncle's questions. Use the words at the end to help you.

Qu'est-ce que tu veux?
Je veux ....
Qu'est-ce que tu veux?
Je ....

une glace - des gants - une robe - des bonbons, etc

the teamwork aspect of the exercise and to provide, for those who have not been directly involved in the preparation of the materials, a clear reference as to the aim and level of each worksheet.

There were certainly deficiencies in this pattern of work. We were constantly critical of our own efforts, but the atmosphere of enthusiasm and interest engendered by this approach among both pupils and staff was most encouraging. Notably, the dread and gloom occasioned by the thought of bottom sets had disappeared and this more positive attitude had spread to the children. Of course, we still had lazy pupils, dull pupils and naughty pupils, but I think it is fair to say that the material that was devised and the approach that was adopted reduced very considerably the overall bad effect of this minority of the pupils upon the majority.

But if this is the situation in one school, how much more effective and worthwhile would it be if a number of schools pooled their ideas, talents and energies to produce, not an adaptation of 'lock-step' materials, but rather some original material designed from the start for use in the mixed-ability situation?

It was with this in mind that the first exploratory meeting was held of what is called rather grandiosely the Working Party on Resources for Teaching Modern Languages, a group which has never exceeded twelve in number but which represents six or seven comprehensive schools in south Nottinghamshire. It consists of those who, either from conviction or as the result of overall school policy, teach French in a mixed-ability situation, and who feel that, whatever may be the advantages or disadvantages of this situation, teachers need materials designed for this type of teaching. Although the group had originally aimed at producing some six units providing supplementary materials for individualised learning in the early stages of French, the total production to date has been one pack of materials which has served as an example of what such collaborative ventures might produce.

The pack contains a unit of work which is based on the theme of the home and family life. It presents a French family in a particular situation – that of a power cut. This situation is presented audio-visually by the use of tapes with appropriate sound effects, and visuals presented initially as overhead projector transparencies.

These same visuals are also reproduced in the form of large flash-cards, and the appropriate captions are available on card for matching purposes and the introduction of reading. Other items available on tape include an aural comprehension test in which the text is very similar to the original 'Coupure de Courant' text – questions in English, to be answered in English, are available on a printed sheet for the pupils. There are a number of reading passages of varying difficulty, recorded first at normal speed and then exploded for repetition purposes. Other items on the tape are a whole range of structure drills, all of them contextualised and derived from the basic text. Finally, the tape contains the text of a short reader which has been devised to accompany this unit, and of which the theme is similar to that of the basic text.

The text of 'Coupure de Courant' is presented to the pupils by means of a booklet printed in jumbo type with the same visuals as we used for the original presentation displayed alongside the text. An example of this mode of presentation is shown in Fig 6. The pack also contains a range of written assignments providing individualised tasks for pupils of various levels of ability. These written assignments are similar to those used at the writer's own comprehensive school and their essential feature is that they provide a range of activity which might well correspond to the range of aptitude represented within a mixed-ability group. The intention is that pupils should work on those which will provide the maximum degree of success rather than work right through the whole set of assignments. Finally, the pack has some brief teacher's notes indicating a possible mode of presentation and the range of material available.

The main problems faced by the working party in the preparation of this pack included those of time and the difficulty of finding an artist – and here the involvement of a sympathetic artist right from the beginning might facilitate the work by any similar group. (The working party was fortunate enough to receive a supporting grant from the Schools Council and this enabled them to enlist the help of a talented artist.) Making the tape also presented problems: assembling enough French voices at the same time and in the same place was quite an achievement on the part of the member of the

FIG 6

GRANDMÈRE AUSSI RESTE

AU LIT

ELLE EST SOURDE

ET N'ENTEND PAS LE RÉVEIL

working party who produced the tape, and the problem of producing and mixing in a considerable number of sound effects also gave rise to some ingenuity! The major problem, however, was not to produce materials but collectively to decide upon the objectives aimed at in using the materials. Possibly the working party has been rather vague in its aims and perhaps it ought to have tried to produce basic course materials rather than supplementary materials. Certainly one grave omission is the failure to provide some objective means of evaluating the pupil's progress with the material. Nevertheless, at least a start was made on something which can be used in schools and it is quite possible that, had the group set itself the larger task of creating a toally new course, it would still be arguing about how to begin.

As with the adaptations prepared within the modern languages department of the present writer's school, the problems here ranged from the purely practical – finding room for all the paper; getting it typed and printed; making sure that each colleague knew what was happening from week to week – to the more elusive problem of training teachers to use these materials in the most beneficial way. It takes a fair effort on the part of an experienced teacher to adapt his style and mode of teaching to the new mixed-ability situation and it demands a degree of flexibility to accommodate the differences of attitude, ability and enthusiasm that are bound to exist in any team of teachers. Nevertheless, a positive step forward has been made in an area where there has been far too much negative response. The adaptations and materials which have been produced in these local initiatives may not be particularly inspiring, or indeed original, but at least they have the merit of being a positive response to a difficult situation. In the last resort, however, the greatest benefit has been that which those involved have derived as modern language teachers from the joint efforts and thoughts given to this particular problem.

As one who was involved in both groups, the need to rethink, not only techniques, but aims and objectives has led the present writer to give serious reconsideration to the place of modern languages within the secondary curriculum, particularly during those years when in more and more of our secondary schools all pupils are obliged to follow a course in a modern language. This reconsideration takes the form of a flood of questions:

Are all pupils capable of learning a foreign language?
What, indeed, is meant by 'learning a foreign language?'
Which form of the language ought to be learned, spoken or written?
Are we to aim for positive achievement in each of the four skills of listening, speaking, reading and writing?
If a modern language is taught as a vehicle of communication are there going to be genuine possibilities for the pupil to use the language in real situations?
What, at the end of it all, is the return on the investment of pupils' and teachers' efforts over a period of, say, three years?

The questions go on, and the comprehensive school modern linguist becomes increasingly baffled and disillusioned, initially at the failure of audio-visual aids to provide a panacea, and subsequently because the mixed-ability movement has increasingly isolated him and his discipline. In desperation he may turn to European or area studies, and instead of promoting this as a serious integrated discipline, he becomes an amateur geographer/historian in an attempt to contain the 'difficult' pupils at the 'bottom end'.

This is to paint the picture at its blackest. There are many modern language teachers up and down the country who have recognised that the mixed-ability situation demands new teaching strategies and a differentiation of objectives, given the differing abilities and motivations of the pupils within the group. The skill of listening is at last achieving some kind of recognition and the notion of a bilingual conversation, in which the speakers understand the foreign language but speak in their own, is beginning to gain ground with a consequent revision of the emphasis on making all pupils expert in the productive use of a foreign language. Nevertheless, this very differentiation of objectives within a set, class or year group creates its own problems. Above all, there is a lack of materials to support the teacher. Furthermore, as indicated earlier, there is a need for a real effort of will to change the style of one's teaching – to change from being the dynamic focus of attention of the whole class and the mainspring of all class activity, to being the quietly purposeful organiser of individual pupil activity. The teacher may sometimes have the disquieting feeling that the very real needs of the less-able pupils are overriding the equally real needs of the average and above-average, particularly in terms of a structured, sequential language course.

In terms of the achievement of the purely linguistic objectives with which we are all familiar by the talented minority of pupils who represent our future linguists, it is doubtful whether there is a better way of organising modern language teaching than in the setted pattern referred to earlier. Yet this is, indeed, where modern languages tend to part company with the rest of the subjects within the curriculum, particularly during the common-core phase. Eventually one has to decide whether a narrow linguistic gain justifies broad educational loss. Is there not, perhaps, a compromise which might be effected? If one were prepared to accept that the abler pupils, the potential linguists, might achieve the linguistic aims which are thought appropriate in a rather shorter span of time than is traditionally considered necessary, then it would be possible to design two kinds of modern language course to be placed end on: a general, non-sequential introduction to the language and its country of origin, followed by a structured and sequential course of language instruction for those for whom it was appropriate, and for the remaining pupils, by either a continuation of the general (topic based) course, or by properly integrated European studies with a minority language component.

If one were to accept the notion of the initial general course outlined above, it would be necessary to accept a limitation of linguistic objectives in this first phase, with more emphasis on the development of comprehension skills and less on the generation of the target language. Perhaps the greatest single advantage is that such a scheme would rid the early stages of modern language teaching of the banal and puerile subject matter which an elementary language course at present demands. Topics of real interest to the pupils could be studied, provided that the objectives of comprehension were kept very much in mind. A course could be provided

62

which took as its theme a number of topics, such as those suggested in some of the proposed 16+ syllabuses, and out of which might come situations where French was relevant. For example, a study of transport in France would necessarily involve the learner in the use of the appropriate French at the moment of buying a railway ticket or travelling on the Métro.

If it is objected that this is what happens already in our elementary languages courses, then it may be useful to examine the typical first- or second-year course-book where, although situations of this type do arise, the French which is used, and indeed the situation itself, has been devised in order to teach a particular point of grammar. What is required is a change of emphasis to a teaching situation where, as one HMI has said, 'background studies become fore-ground studies' and, as far as is possible within the classroom, the pupil has the personal experience of being a foreigner in a foreign situation. This kind of teaching is sometimes criticised in terms of linguistic loss, and of a lowering of academic standards. But when one considers the time spent between, say, the third and fifth years of a typical secondary school modern language course, and the amount of new structure and essential new vocabulary required, then it should become apparent that, given the right motivation and a real sense of purpose, the linguistic skills can be developed to acceptable levels.

Teachers who are concerned with modern language teaching in schools have to be both linguists and educators. If only we were prepared to shed the linguist's cap for a brief period, the educational gain might be enormous and the linguistic loss by no means certain.

For notes to this chapter see p 184

4 Teaching Geography in Mixed-Ability Groups

R. W. Seckington

Geographers have been closely examining their subject for well over a decade now. A new geography has emerged, and although it is by no means universally adopted, it has generated a methodological debate. Traditional regional styles of geographical study are under challenge from the growing systematic approaches; quantifiers are in conflict with non-quantifiers; and the growing use of model building and games play is in dispute with more traditional approaches. Peter Ambrose summarises the main trends as a move in emphasis from regional (form-orientated) to systematic (process-orientated) work; from subjective-qualitative to objective-quantitative handling of information; from unique to generalised explanations; and, often from retrospective to predictive modes of study.[1]

It is in tertiary education that the debate has been most intense and the changes more sweeping. University courses of today bear little resemblance to those of the 1950s. As a consequence many senior geography teachers in secondary schools may have felt themselves on the fringe of the debate relying almost entirely on over-stretched in-service training facilities and any available literature. Secondary school geography has, therefore, tended to absorb the new geography rather slowly and in a piecemeal fashion. Yet important changes can be seen:

> We are all aware of traditional modes of study, and I will not dwell upon them. They tend to emphasise factual learning and empiricism as opposed to theory formation, study by regions rather than by topic, and a concern with the current distributions

rather than the processes by which they evolve ... My main thesis will be that the changes can be summed up as a move from a factual orientation to an orientation concerned with concepts, methods and values.[2]

BASIC TRENDS IN SECONDARY SCHOOL GEOGRAPHY

1 *A greater concern for the learning process*

Traditionally learning has been a very static process with the teacher in absolute control of pace, content, and interpretation and the learner in a very passive role. Any examination of method tended to concentrate on what the teacher must do. 'In short, he dispenses information, a process to which students must submit without choice ... Such a teacher selects the content and delivers it to the students by having them read, listen to, or examine materials he has selected.'[3] There is considerable evidence of a move away from the purely expository modes of instruction. The influence of educationalists such as J. S. Bruner has led to much greater emphasis on 'discovery' methods.[4] The student is placed in control of the data with the teacher asking the questions. Students are being encouraged to investigate, to find out, and thus by implication some of the control of content and pace passes to them. Fitzgerald,[5] himself drawing on Helburn,[6] makes an activity analysis of the stereotype American high school classroom with that of the activities in the American High School Geography Project. In the former, students were asked to listen to lectures, read, take dictation, read simple maps, and memorise data concerning particular places. Only rarely were they required to reach generalisations, and this only by comparing data about one place with that of nearby or similar places. In the latter, students in any given activity were encouraged to use their skills on data in order to develop generalisations which illustrate abstract ideas.

Alongside this desire for direct pupil involvement in the learning process has come a better understanding of the cognitive and affective learning of children.

The curriculum builder and the classroom teacher of the future will focus on relatively few goals, all of which centre around or build upon better understanding of the cognitive processes of sensation, perception, concept formation, and thinking as a means of problem solving, and the relationship of these processes to the affective dimensions of emotions, attitudes and motives.

The same author suggests that

> . . . a renewal of the emphasis on understanding symbolism versus verbalisation should redirect the objectives in teaching and evaluating from what students know to what they can generate, to how well they can leap from learning to thinking to acting.[7]

Heuristic approaches are now much more common throughout secondary and primary education, with the teacher becoming one of the resources available and himself part of the learning process. 'The emerging new curricula in geography, and whatever related research there is, quite clearly favours the investigation-orientated strategies'.[8]

2 What is essential in the geography curriculum?

Most students do not follow a course of study to higher levels of the secondary system. For those who do it might be considered an awesome task in terms of the range and mass of factual material handled. The secondary school teacher has to think of any course devised as one which is terminal for the majority of students, and part of the continuum for the few who will wish to pursue the subject to higher levels. Traditionally the problem has been solved by devising at least two types of courses that differ in content and pace, and measure up to examination and other external requirements. Over recent years with the gradual introduction of common-core curricula, new styles of examination (especially Mode 3) and the major agency of comprehensive reorganisation, teachers have been re-examining what they teach. There seems to be a general trend towards concentrating on a more limited number of goals. There is rather less of the 'we must cover it all' syndrome and more of an attempt to sort out what is relevant and meaningful in the subject. We are, perhaps, less concerned with how much is known and more concerned with how well pupils are building on previously acquired skills and concepts. Also there is a concern that if geography is to make any contribution at all to our society it must be dealing with real problems and not just academic exercises.

3 Links with other subjects

Perhaps the most stimulating aspects of curriculum development in geography in the next few years will be the growth of well thought out schemes in schools in which geographers contribute with historians, sociologists, etc, to the study of problems of common interest.[9]

It is obviously not the place in a chapter of this kind to do more than refer very briefly to subject links. There is, however, a clear trend towards the linking of subjects. Humanities, social studies, environmental studies or similar titles are increasingly found in the school curriculum. Sometimes there are strongly practical reasons for developing faculty areas in schools, which have as much to do with planning and organisation as with developing new learning strategies. At best the development of new integrated courses grows out of an examination of existing curricula, and is an attempt to produce something that is relevant for today. Often new demands are made on school organisation as larger groups of teachers work together (team teaching), longer time spans are required (timetable blocking) and inquiry-based methods are introduced (resource centres). Often these integrated courses have well-planned aims and elaborate teaching-learning strategies. This is not always the case within single subject planning. Geographers have to examine their role and contribution in such schemes and, of course, preserve their essential curriculum within the broader framework. The linking role of geography in integrated schemes is of fundamental importance to the geography specialist.

As well as considerations of aims, objectives, content and method there has been concern for grouping. Yet despite a number of excellent books examining the changing nature of geography very little has been written specifically on work across wide ability-ranges.

P. M. Bailey, writing in *Geography*, drew attention to the range of ability. 'Pupils come from all kinds of home background, are of very varied abilities, have a complete range of interests or lack of them, and will go into every kind of job.' He went on to suggest possible strategies.

> Faced by a total ability range of pupils, geography departments may decide to offer two kinds of course: first, courses with a high component of theoretical geography and much abstract reasoning; second, courses in applied geography which help pupils to understand the more specific problems of their own lives, in their local, national and world setting.[10]

Such a basic organisation into two separate courses would in fact be fairly typical of many schools. Broadly speaking this perpetuates the division of the bilateral system, with the important difference that each teacher involved is much more likely to be aware of the full ability-range rather than just that confined to the grammar or non-selective range. But the problem of the geography department in a comprehensive school is highlighted. All children come to the department, at least in the early stages of secondary education.

It has been long established by educational psychologists that 'people learn in different ways and at different rates'.[11] In spite of this fact, secondary schools' traditional obsession with groups has made it difficult to come to terms with individual needs. 'Ideally, individual differences should be handled (and exploited) through individual instruction'.[12] In the post-war years schools organised their teaching groups mainly by ability and produced streams, sets, bands or other homogeneous groups. In fact all current statistical evidence, notably Benn and Simon, shows that homogeneous groupings still predominate in spite of a growing unstreaming movement.[13] There is considerable research evidence on the relative merits of streamed and unstreamed groups, but it is mainly inconclusive. There is nothing to show that homogeneous groups are more effective for learning, and indeed because of the immensely varied individual differences in learning characteristics it is unlikely that any such group is a possibility. It is doubtful whether any grouping system can cope adequately with the individual differences, but at least the grouping debate has brought teachers 'to the real problem: the learner and his learning'.[14]

Mixed-ability grouping is one attempt to introduce a grouping system that meets individual needs in a more flexible way.

> All of us who teach . . . need to create for ourselves a picture of the capacity of the individual. It is with the best intention that we do this. But unfortunately we enforce our own guesses by setting standards with which he then complies, and also we forget that the child is so extraordinarily sensitive to the evaluation which is placed on him, and records that evaluation and scales down. He becomes under-used if you like. This is why we cannot afford to stream.[15]

Schools that unstream are making a clear statement about their intentions. Among these is the notion of sharing resources (teachers, books, materials and buildings) and making them available to all. No longer will only the more able receive the lion's share. The sharing is carried through to the teachers who themselves now have a common task, and the clear intention of reconsidering methods because the act of unstreaming makes it impossible to continue as before. The teacher, certainly the experienced teacher, has to adjust from teaching groups, which is usually a formal instructional process (didactic), to a situation where he is devising individual work schemes and working in a less formal learning atmosphere (heuristic).

PRACTICAL DEPARTMENTAL CONSIDERATIONS
Rooms

Much depends on the size of the school as to how many rooms are available for geography, and their distribution. Larger schools usually have several which are, at best, grouped together to form a suite. It is surprising how many schools with more than one geography room still have them scattered in a haphazard way. Such an arrangement is often the result of the independence of teachers, their self-imposed isolation in the classroom and the fact that little or no relationship is intended between the activities in one room and another. One of the effects of teaching in undifferentiated groups with a common course is to get teachers working together. If possible the rooms should be adjacent. In some cases it may be possible to remove a wall and create more flexible areas. In smaller schools, with perhaps only one specialist room and some spillover into general subject classrooms, there may be a strong case for grouping rooms on a subject area or faculty basis. In this way a social studies or humanities area may be created with the specialist rooms adjacent to each other and sharing some common facilities.

Discovery methods are very cramped by orthodox classroom layout. Geography is rather luckier than most subjects because it has long favoured tables rather than desks, and appropriate furnishings for practical work such as tracing tables, sand trays and water tanks. Increasing flexibility is required to allow for a variety of activities within a given area, whether this is the suite or a single room. In general the type of furniture that helps is lightweight tables and some movable cupboards with plastic tray racks. It is unlikely that the tables will be set out in rows but rather grouped in such a way as to allow for personal or small-group work. The addition of worktops gives some practical facilities and by using some mobile cupboard/shelf and display furniture there is both an increase in storage capacity and a chance to divide off areas of the room. Thus it is possible to create practical, reference, audio-visual and writing areas within one room. Movement will certainly be greater during lesson time and this needs to be allowed for in planning the layout (Fig 1).

Resource centres

A geography department in an established school will have accumulated a considerable variety of material. The stock cupboard becomes a library, museum, store and security room. Materials including maps, filmstrips, slides, textbooks, photographs, sample studies, magazines, wallcharts, rock samples, fossils, duplicated sheets, models and work packs are available in most departments. The method of storage is usually in piles or boxes on shelves, or frequently on the floor. It is often doubtful whether the 'old hand' knows where everything is and most certainly the new teacher

FIG 1

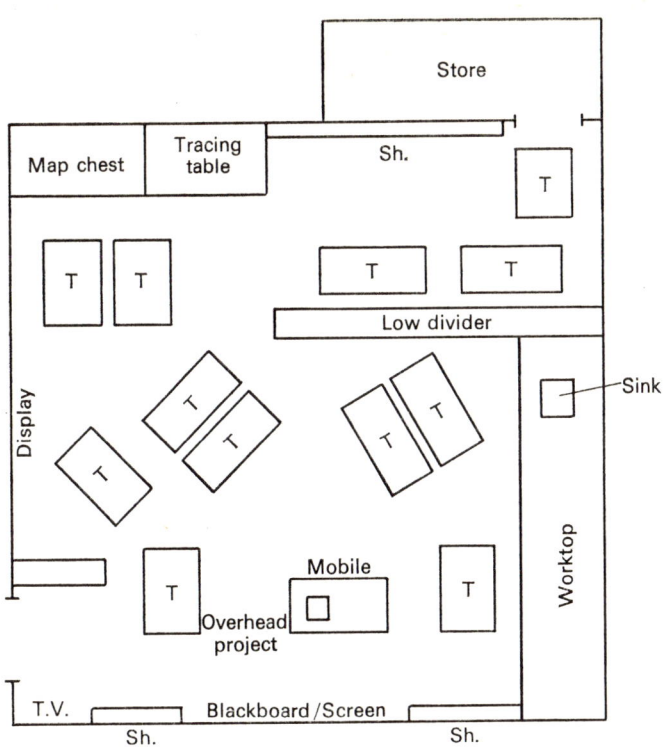

may be unaware of the full range of resources available. Wyatt
describes the result of carefully indexing all the existing materials
available in a geography department of a large comprehensive
school:

1 Even experienced staff, who had been in the department, were
   surprised that there was so much information available that they
   had never used.
2 New staff were for the first time provided with a comprehensive
   index of resource material. This in turn released them to produce
   more by obviating fruitless searches for material which was not
   available in the department.
3 Areas of work that were well served with material could now

71

be selectively supplemented and those poorly served could be concentrated upon annually out of capitation grants.

4 Staff now had easy access to the resource material produced by other staff and this in turn encouraged discussion and the cross-fertilisation of ideas.[16]

Knowing what is there, having a simple and quick means of retrieval, and being able to introduce all new material into the system is essential.

It is increasingly common for all the resources in a school to be concentrated in a resource centre for the whole school, often based on the school library. A school resource centre has a number of advantages.

1 It can be large enough to absorb some children who wish to carry out a particular line of research, thus freeing some of the pressure on the departmental teaching/learning area.

2 It is usually possible to staff the area with either a resource director or a non-teaching library assistant or both, thus ensuring continuous observation of the area and regular servicing of the centre by a specialist. This relieves the teachers of the routine of indexing and retrieval.

3 It should be the case that all departments in the school will have materials in the centre, so children and teachers have access to an even greater range of material. This is particularly valuable where there is some integration, but the advantages to the geographer of knowing, for example, what materials are available in history and biology are all too obvious.

The advantages and disadvantages of centralised and decentralised collections are examined much more fully in *Schools Council Working Paper no 43.*[17]

Even in schools with a well-developed centralised resource centre a lively department will require basic materials to hand. It is important that these departmental materials or resources are classified and indexed by the school resource centre and made generally accessible (Fig 2).

72

FIG 2

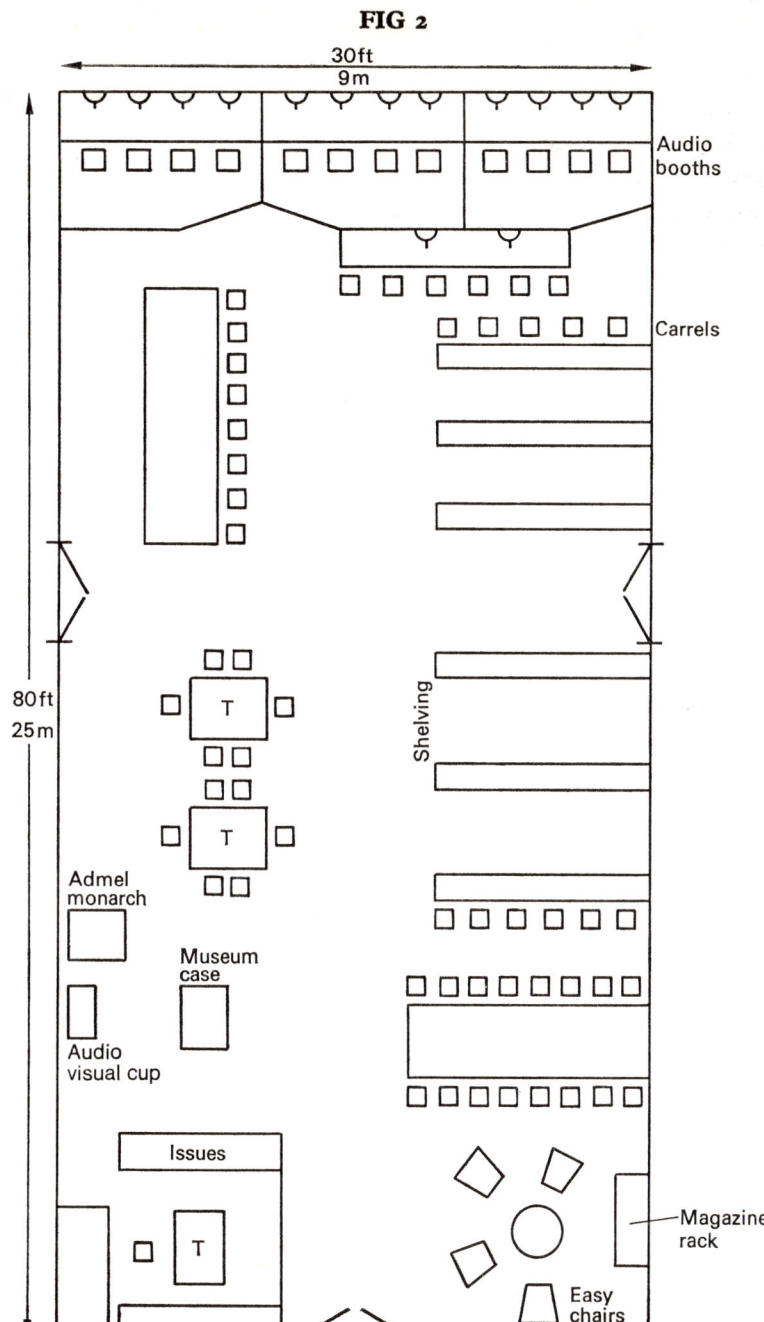

30ft
9m

Audio booths

Carrels

Shelving

80ft
25m

Admel monarch

Museum case

Audio visual cup

Issues

T

Magazine rack

Easy chairs

Reprographic equipment

A capacity for producing printed material is a fundamental requirement. The range of equipment is enormous. Much depends on the size of school and its priorities. An ink stencil duplicator backed with a flatbed photocopier and an electric stencil cutter will give a good range of printed material, including illustrations, at a cost well within the range of medium-size secondary schools. Larger schools with a high output of duplicating may require offset litho.

Audio facilities

Capacity is required (a) for off-air recording (tape recorders in the centre) and (b) for individual and small group work (portable cassette tape recorders). Some teachers have been highly successful in using tapes to bring a more real situation into the classroom, and in recent years there have been significant strides in tape/slide work both commercially and in schools.

Visual facilities

To the normal provision of 35mm and 16mm projectors might be added a video tape recording capacity, and, if possible, a chance for teachers and children to take and process photographs or moving pictures.

A resource centre will be called upon to provide a range of services in connection with display, layout, and mounting of learning materials ranging from mounting slides to graphics and design.

Textbooks

The move from formal class teaching, where the groups were acknowledged to be capable of handling material of the same standard and at the same pace, to the less formal individual approach of the mixed-ability situation, means that the teacher must question the function of the class textbook. There is no longer a case for issuing a standard textbook to whole groups of children where there is a wide range of ability. New schools developing their curriculum around resource centres should have the minimum of class text-books. Books should abound however. The widest range of books and printed material should be available to the children and they should be encouraged to turn to as many sources as possible while

74

investigating a topic. Much of the book material will clearly be textbooks.

Writers and publishers of textbooks are well aware of the changes taking place and this is reflected in their current output of material. The purists are going to produce their own material so that it is exactly tailor-made to meet their particular needs. They will only want to extract from other sources what is relevant to their own course. Many teachers, however, will still place some reliance on a textbook to form a basis to their work.

Textbooks such as *The Developing World* have a questioning approach which assists the teacher in adding colour, information, questions, ideas and activity thus providing a useful resource for the geography teacher.[18] Langford, reporting on the development of approaches to mixed-ability teaching in a Gosport school,[19] stated: 'We have been able to build up stocks of *New Ways in Geography*[20] so that each child can have easy access to all three books and work-pads, and large stocks of duplicating paper were available.' After discussion on teaching strategy two sets of tactics emerged. 'One approach uses the relevant parts of *New Ways in Geography* as the course core which is supplemented for children by additional work-sheets and exercises.' The other approach made much more use of teacher-produced materials and was more self-directed. The type of scheme outlined more fully in this article makes a very important statement about the possible use of a textbook as a course core. Many geographers will enter the early stages of work with mixed-ability groups more confidently with such support. As they continue to build up their own resources there will tend to be less and less reliance on one single source.

Marking, Assessment and Examinations

Marking in a secondary school has tended to be a process of comparing the performance of one person with another. This highly competitive form of marking has often been thought to be justified in the so-called homogeneous group. Indeed competition was once regarded as a healthy necessity for successful learning. With a full range of ability in one group it is not desirable to grade on a 0-10 or A-E scale, otherwise, quite obviously, the less able will achieve no personal success. Marking must be done on an individual basis. This is much more difficult than the often rather mechanical process of class marking in which some kind of norm is assumed and children are graded at, above or below the average. Marking, if it is needed, should be done with the child, whenever possible, building on strength and encouraging self-assessment. A written comment on the pupil's work can be substituted for the grade which may be recorded in the teacher's notebook. This does not mean that good standards are abandoned. Measurement is at an individual level and is based on individual capacity.

Examinations have long been considered a vital part of an assessment procedure. It is perfectly possible to examine mixed-ability groups, but the examination has to be very well planned. Techniques of examining have changed and improved considerably. Multiple-choice questions consisting of the stem and a correct answer with at least four distractors; photographs, models and quantitative material for interpretation, evaluation and descriptive writing; short descriptive paragraphs; definitions; oral or tape work, so very important with the less able – are all useful techniques that can be employed. Formal examinations with children in the 'middle years' can be replaced by a form of continuous assessment. In the upper part of the secondary school gradual changes in external examinations, with CSE Mode 3 involving more teacher participation and control, and much more weight given to course work, are influencing approaches with mixed-ability groups and individual learning situations in the lower forms.

Co-operative teaching

One of the most significant advances in recent years in secondary education has been the way in which teachers are increasingly working together. This is seen with integrated courses such as humanities, or in year bases where teams of mixed specialists spend long periods of the working week with one group, or in departments. The head of department has taken on a new role which includes close concern for in-service training, co-ordination and team leadership. Each member of the team has a vital contribution to make in planning, introducing new ideas and resourcing the department. When a department changes to mixed-ability grouping the isolation of the teacher in the classroom is quickly broken down. The new situation is one of parity, and it is essential that each teacher be aware of what is happening elsewhere in the department, that resources be shared and that each teacher be involved with and contribute to the total programme.

Time

The general experience of geography departments that have unstreamed seems to be that they cannot manage with a fragmented timetable. Children busy discovering information are severely restricted by the conventional single 40-minute period. Time blocking is one answer which can be adopted by any secondary school. Ideally, with more and more self-directed learning taking place in schools, means would be sought whereby children did not have to stop an activity at a high point of interest. In practice the majority of schools find some controls necessary. By accepting the longest span of time available, some considerable advantages are gained. For example, four 40-minute periods could be taken as a single session rather than as four separate periods. More time is thus available for changes of activity and pace. This, I feel, outweighs the often-expressed view that a group needs to be seen at regular intervals through a working week. A small geography department may find it an advantage to be timetabled with another subject, for example history, so that fieldwork or longer investigations can be carried out occasionally.

The geography teacher, when first developing techniques for work with mixed-ability groups, may use as the core of the course a carefully chosen textbook. The following phases may occur:

1 *Textbook* (course core) with supplementary material prepared by the teacher. At this stage it is still the intention to keep everybody roughly together, but to accept considerable variation in depth of study.
2 *Work or job cards* which form the basis of the course, and refer to and draw upon a wide range of source materials. At this stage

the department will have accumulated a reasonable range of book and non-book materials. Depending on the type of job card it may still be the intention to keep a group roughly together. Individual job cards allowing for a much more self-directed approach from the children usually come as a development of the job card technique as the teacher becomes more skilled and practised in their use. The job card system was well explained by Albert Rowe.[21]

3 *Work packs* There are different definitions of a work pack. In some respects it may not be necessary to refer to a work pack as something with a clearly defined identity in terms of size or quantity, but more as a style or method. In its simplest form a box might be used to collect the widest range of material possible on a topic such as volcanoes. Thus the child will find photographs, tapes, diagrams, references from literature, maps and suggested lines of approach and work. The basic idea is to have the richest possible resource base from which the children can select. This means that in terms of work covered there may be considerable variation between each child. Interest will play a significant part, but it is up to the teacher to sort out what he considers essential to the curriculum and to devise the broad outlines of the course. One of the main tasks of the teacher is to put before the children a wide range of data for them to use.

The major problem identified by most geography teachers attempting work through job cards and the much more sophisticated work packs is that of the poor reader. It is a problem, but often rather too much is made of it. My own experience suggests that children who have a reading difficulty prefer this approach because a greater range of material is put before them, much of which is audio and visual, and because trouble is taken to explain what is going on. They can be encouraged to express themselves in a variety of ways, particularly by talking.

It is important to ensure that there is a worthwhile core for all and that the most able can take the work on to really demanding levels. The experience can be the same, but the depth of experience will vary with the individual.

The development of job card and worksheet techniques has made an important contribution to work with unstreamed groups. From this has come the fully resource-based methods being practised today. Other significant developments in the teaching of geography are equally important in work with students of all abilities. Among these is the use of simulations in the classroom. Simulation is fully explained in several well-known sources. Taylor and Walford suggest that 'three major attributes of simulation seem significant'.

1 It is a technique orientated towards activity in the classroom, and in such activity both teachers and pupils participate. It represents an informal and corporate approach to the understanding of a situation.
2 It is usually problem-based and therefore helpful in the development of inter-disciplinary approaches to learning. It also frequently involves the use of social skills which are directly relevant to the world outside the classroom.
3 It is a technique which is fundamentally dynamic. It deals with situations that change, and which demand flexibility in thinking and responsive adaption to circumstances as they alter.[22]

Operational games are a useful technique with undifferentiated groups. Ambrose observed:

If nothing else, it appears to generate a high degree of involvement among participants of all ages and ability levels, and anything that does that is to be nurtured carefully.[23]

Taylor and Walford also consider simulations across a range of ability.

A number of simulations appear to have been useful with both gifted and slow learners at the same time (Gordon, 1968) and in higher education, inexperienced students and seasoned professionals have also seemed able to learn from each other (Abt, 1968).

It is in this type of learning activity, in our experience, that benefits accrue widely. High fliers are motivated to progress to even greater heights without adverse effect on the less gifted who, in turn, learn from their peers and pursue their own course as fits their inclinations. [24]

Peter Hore also felt that games were useful across a wide ability range.

One encouraging aspect was that quite a few children who had difficulties in reading and writing coped with the game adequately and appeared, for once, to be on an equal footing with more literate classmates.[25]

Indeed he felt after several years' experience in unstreamed classes of using various types of games 'that they are one method of successfully involving in a common activity, children of very different abilities and aptitudes'.

Games are one aspect in the developing new geography curricula that has helped towards working in a collaborative way, and are one example from a growing number of methods that give the flexibility of approach necessary in the mixed-ability situation.

For notes to this chapter see pp 184–5

5 Teaching History in Mixed-Ability Groups

B. L. Cooke

We are slowly, very slowly, coming to accept that if history in schools is to have any meaning to our pupils now and later it must involve them actively; it should not simply require them to receive information and ideas exclusively from so-called authoritative sources like teachers and textbooks, but encourage them to participate in decisions about what they study and how they do it, in searching for evidence and in asking questions of it; in reconstructing past events, incidents, developments and lives; in puzzling out problems; and in putting their own findings and views in various ways. They are, in this manner, being helped to realise central aims in education as a whole: the development of skills of inquiry, recording and expression, awareness of themselves, and awareness of the society in which they live, and its evolution. These should be denied no child, whatever his ability and however he is grouped with his fellows. But how is a wide variety of abilities, attitudes and interests among children in one group to be considered when determining what children are to learn in history, how they are to be encouraged to learn it, and how teachers view and prepare their own work? Of course, enlightened history teachers have always seen a class of thirty pupils as thirty individuals, and not necessarily as an homogeneous group to be treated as a whole; but much of school history – having been based on class teaching and class activities – has not reflected this. If we have failed hitherto to see the deficiencies and dangers in such an approach the questions raised by mixed-ability groups are a vital focus for the rethinking of ideas.

Problems of objectives and selection of material confront us whether we teach streamed, setted or mixed groups; differences are of degree rather than of kind. All children studying history, whatever their age or level, should be stimulated to search out information, tackle problems, reconstruct imaginatively a past situation, and express their findings and ideas in various forms. Most topics and periods can be studied at different levels – the Etruscans, Roman Britain, or the development of transport qualify for PhD research and for primary school project work – so that we are not necessarily faced with some periods being intrinsically more difficult or less attractive than others. The widely accepted notion that Roman Britain suits first-year pupils and the twentieth century suits fifteen-year-olds still appears to dominate syllabus construction, but is doubted by teachers who have very young pupils studying recent history.

Much is possible at any stage: it may in fact be more helpful to consider some general principles for what mixed-ability groups should study. On the one hand, they should have the chance to work on a limited number of topics in depth, to follow lines suggested by teachers and to develop their interests and ideas both individually and as members of groups. On the other hand, we should present all pupils with such variety of study that they grapple at secondary school with a range of periods or topics of limited time-span such as Roman Britain, the American Civil War, the Russian Revolution, World War I or the Depression; some selected lines of development across time such as warfare, transport or fashion; and varied scale involving local, British and international perspectives. Historical skills can be acquired and developed within any of these areas; there is no reason why any of them should be less interesting than others if the approach and treatment are right, and with this kind of selection the pupils are exposed to different perspectives and wide contrasts. Such a syllabus arrangement should also satisfy the proper demand for overall intelligibility in planning so that a history course has concern for chronology and evolution, for change and development in time. In the end, many of our pupils may not have that elusive well-developed sense of time, but at least attempts will have been made to place depth studies within a framework of chronological development. So, in order to offer opportunities for probing in depth to all pupils, the exclusively outlines and sweeps syllabus must disappear.

By tradition, whole classes generally study the same topic in history and are required to depend heavily on the teacher. There are some history teachers who can hold a class spellbound for forty minutes with a good story, vividly and excitingly told : such teachers can explain lucidly and can awaken the imagination of their audience. But many, who are not good storytellers, bore and frustrate a class. There are pupils who can be stimulated by a lesson of a teacher's talk; but there are large numbers who cannot concentrate on oral teaching for more than ten minutes at a stretch. This style also overlooks a principle which is becoming more widely appreciated, that children are individuals and that they learn most effectively in different ways. Some children enjoy reading, will do so contentedly and profitably for long periods, and will be able to write about or discuss what they read with intelligence and enthusiasm. But in the same mixed-ability group are children who cannot read quietly for long periods, or who can barely read at all, for whom more varied methods are necessary. Yet why should variety be denied any child? An oral session, teacher-led, with a mixed-ability group should be of limited duration. It has an important purpose as an impact lesson introducing a new topic, or bringing together the activities of individuals or small groups, or dealing with confusion or working problems experienced by many in the class, but we must not overlook the fact that the attention of the less able child will not be held easily – he becomes restless and uninterested. It is most difficult to devise an oral lesson which can bring out the best in the bright and yet remain within the comprehension of the slower learner.

Clearly, teachers of mixed-ability groups must arrange for varied and flexible work in history for individuals and small groups. On educational and organisational grounds the devising of suggestions and guidelines for pupils is essential, and in general this will be most effectively achieved by using worksheets, workcards, and workbooks. Most but not all of the pupils' work will rest on these. As children tackle the work assigned or chosen, the teacher is free from constant oral contact with the whole class and is able to concentrate on particular individuals or groups, encouraging, probing, and discussing with slow learners, plodders and rapid workers as each requires. Those with common difficulties or findings can be brought together for special attention or to share their experiences. The alert, sensitive teacher helps pupils to select or move on to work which is not too difficult yet offers a challenge.

WORKCARDS

How are the workcards, designed for children working as individuals, to cater for the wide variety of interests and abilities of children working on the same historical topic? One possibility is to have a worksheet or workcard which incorporates suggestions, questions and activities for all, beginning with simpler and progressing to more elaborate and demanding tasks. The brighter, quicker worker is able to move at the pace which suits him while slower pupils tackle what is within their capabilities. Here it is important that the card be designed so that the slower pupils can accomplish something worthwhile without having to complete the whole range of tasks. Teachers who have tried to produce such cards know how difficult this is; if it contains a sufficiently wide selection of tasks the card is likely to be lengthy and unwieldy. A more satisfactory pattern is to adopt a common or core card for each topic or aspect of it, which all pupils are required to do at their own speeds, and a number of option cards which provide guidelines for more detailed investigation and specialised activities, and which might include work of different levels. Children are then encouraged or directed to choose options according to their interests and pace of work. A further variation in design has separate cards for different levels of ability (most examples of this practice have cards at three levels as a realistic and practical solution to the problem of producing cards for individuals) which are distinguished by detail and the nature of guidance and activities, by style of presentation and possibly by colour for ease of identification, though the last feature is often criticised since it may tend to reinforce class divisions and harden the idea of different ability levels.

It is unrealistic to think of producing different cards for each individual, and in terms of limitations of time, money and facilities one might consider three or four levels of card to suit the range of abilities within a class. As they come to know pupils, teachers should be fairly well aware of the kind of card to allocate to each individual, which is within a child's capabilities but which contains tasks to stretch him. Where there is doubt, or in the case of a class new to a teacher, a middle-level card might be issued to all pupils and adjustments made as information is revealed about a child's ability and progress. Frequent checks on the work being done will also indicate if the general level of a pupil's work might be raised by more challenging activities.

Whatever the nature of the card, very careful thought must be given to its design and production. In general, it should be attractive and clear so that children are in minimum doubt as to what is required; it should include a variety of tasks and activities allowing for written work of descriptive, interpretative and imaginative kinds plus pictorial and craft work; it should contain information and give some direction to sources (textbooks and reference books, documents, pictures, maps, and perhaps slides and tapes) and encourage children to assemble their own materials from magazines, books and cereal packets. In the following discussion of appropriate style and format for each level, examples are suggested of cards for a topic on Hadrian's Wall, as part of work on Roman Britain, to be studied by a class of twelve-year-olds. The cards aim to provide suitable activities for all in a mixed-ability group, and to involve approximately a common time allocation for working on them – though this is difficult to predict. The variations (between cards) in the types of question, the balance of written and non-written tasks and the nature of guidance and references to books should be clear. Further examples are not needed since the general principles underlying the layout and range of activities are transferable to any topic.

For slower children cards should be especially attractive and carefully laid out, not overloaded with material but incorporating a variety of suggestions and questions generally of a simple kind yet offering some challenge. An illustration might form a heading or centrepiece, directions and information should be clear and unambiguous, and detailed advice to pupils on setting out of work is often advisable. References to one or two uncomplicated books available to the class should include page numbers until pupils are used to working with indexes. Initially a question or two should be of an elementary fact-finding nature, perhaps involving filling in missing words. Although this seems banal and unenterprising it helps the pupil to comprehend a passage and select material, and on the information gathered can be based questions which invite simple comparisons or judgements. An imaginative exercise with some guidance to the information to be used, perhaps linked with a picture, diagram or extract from a simple document, should be included; and the opportunity to draw and use colour is important. A workcard on Hadrian's Wall for slower children might follow these lines:

Roman Britain   Workcard 5
HADRIAN'S WALL

(Picture)

This is a picture of a part of Hadrian's Wall as it is now. You can also see the ruins of the Roman fort at Housesteads.

Have a copy of *A Soldier on Hadrian's Wall* by D. Taylor on your table.

Things to do
1   Write down these sentences and fill in the missing words. Pages 14 and 16 of *A Soldier on Hadrian's Wall* will help you.
   (a)   Hadrian's Wall was built from . . . . in the east to . . . . in the west. It is . . . . miles long.
   (b)   It was made of . . . .
   (c)   It measures . . . . feet high and . . . . feet thick.
   (d)   In front of the wall was a . . . . and behind it was a . . . .

2   Imagine that you are the Roman officer in charge of building the wall. Write a letter to a friend in Rome telling him what the various buildings are on the wall and what they are used for. You can find out about these buildings in your book, pp 16–20.

3 Draw a diagram of one of the buildings in your letter. Label all the parts and sizes of it. If you prefer, make a model of it to scale.

4 Draw and colour a picture showing a scene from Hadrian's Wall, perhaps an enemy attack or soldiers marching along it. From the picture on this card imagine what it must have been like on the wall.

A middle-level card should also be attractive, with a combination of illustration and text, but need not be so specific or detailed in its guidance. Information-searching questions can be framed so as to encourage detailed investigation, and a greater range of books for consultation should be recommended (for which page references need not be so frequent). Guidance towards relevant sections or chapters, or preferably encouragement to use the indexes, is more appropriate. Questions demanding deduction and judgement should be increased, and the use of documentary evidence is of central importance. Most pupils in a mixed-ability group will work at this level, or can be encouraged to reach it, and it is a crucial stage in the development of historical inquiry. A variety of tasks is needed, and suggestions should be made about imaginative work, written or pictorial, giving less guidance than the first level card on what to include and leaving choice of format – eg newspaper report, diary, eyewitness account – more open.

Roman Britain   Workcard 5
                        HADRIAN'S WALL

                            (*Picture*)

This is a picture of part of Hadrian's Wall today.

Read
A Soldier on Hadrian's Wall by D. Taylor
Roman Britain by R. Mitchell

Roman Britain by J. Liversidge, pp 16–33
The Romans in Scotland by O. Thomson, Chapter 3

Things to do

1   Answer these questions as fully as you can:
    (a) Why did Hadrian build a wall across Britain?
    (b) If you were an enemy of the Romans trying to break
         through the wall from the north, where do you think
         its weakest points would be? You will need to find
         information about the various forts and defences along
         the wall.
    (c) Another wall was built twenty years later by the Romans
         in Scotland. Which Emperor built it? Why was it built?
         How different was it from Hadrian's Wall?

2   Imagine that you are the Roman officer in charge of building
    Hadrian's Wall. Write a report to the Emperor telling him
    why you have decided to change the wall from turf to stone
    and to alter the sizes.

3   Draw a diagram of a cross-section of the wall, or of a fort,
    and label it carefully. If you prefer, make a scale model of it.

4   *Either*, as the Roman officer, write an entry for your diary
    describing an incident on the wall.
    Or, draw and colour a picture of the incident.
    Do both of these if you wish.

Finally, for those pupils who work quickly, need less direction
but considerable stimulus in discussion, a workcard should leave
much to the individual initiative and predilection. A wide range of
books and other sources should be recommended, with page and
chapter references only where indexes are poor or unavailable.
More detailed and sophisticated written work is to be encouraged,
with questions requiring a problem-solving or divergent thinking
approach. Here the aim is to develop historical skills and research
techniques, such as the questioning of evidence and the handling

of conflicting accounts, and interpretation and judgement. Pupils should be urged to plan the detail of their own work, and the ways in which they might express their findings and ideas. They should be encouraged to see that in their work non-written activities are also valid. If their training has been sound they will spot the possibilities for reconstructing historical events, changes and personalities imaginatively, and the teacher can emphasise the importance of finer points of historical inquiry in discussion with individuals or small groups, rather than spelling this out on the card. The teacher must be sensitive to the developing requirements of pupils working at this level in particular, and here the use of optional cards is a means of providing for the very rapid worker. But investigation in depth is to be urged for each chosen topic of study, in order to exhaust the range of possibilities involved rather than to rush too hastily to another topic.

Roman Britain   Workcard 5
HADRIAN'S WALL

(Picture)

Consult the books in the class history library on Roman Britain, in particular *The Roman Frontiers of Britain* by D. R. Wilson; *The Roman Imperial Army of the First and Second Centuries* by G. Webster; *The Romans in Scotland* by O. Thomson; *Handbook to the Roman Wall* by I. A. Richmond.

1 Why did Hadrian build a wall across Britain between the Solway and the Tyne? Why were no other routes suitable?

2 Find a picture of a British hill-fort (eg Maiden Castle or Hod Hill) and compare it with Housesteads as a fortification. Illustrate your answer.

3 If you were an enemy of the Romans trying to break through the wall from the north, where do you think its weakest points would be? Why?

4   The Emperor Antoninus Pius decided to build a wall in
    Scotland in about AD 142. Imagine and write a conversation
    between Antoninus and his senior advisor about building the
    wall in Scotland in which they discuss why Hadrian's Wall
    is no longer suitable, and in what ways the new wall should
    be different.

5   *Either,* make a scale model *or* draw a picture of part of
    Hadrian's Wall. Do both if you wish.

While this last example demands thinking of an advanced level
and gives the able pupil opportunities to research Hadrian's Wall in
depth, the nature of the tasks is made fairly explicit. As an alternative one might recommend the books and invite the pupil to
decide for himself a series of questions to ask about the wall –
perhaps taking the form of an interview with the Emperor Hadrian –
and to use various ways to express the answers.

We must now consider other aspects of workcard design, in
particular the materials to be used and the ways in which children
are to record their work. On several grounds the use of strong card
is to be recommended. It is possible for the cards not only to be of
various sizes but also of different shapes, for example where the
shape might reflect the topic being studied. Young children will be
stimulated by cards with the outline of an Egyptian pyramid, a
Roman shield, a Norman keep or a Red Indian wigwam, though the
benefits will have to be weighed against the time taken to make
them. Cards may most conveniently be constructed by mounting
duplicated illustrations, questions and tasks on them and then
encasing them in plastic or polythene covers. They can then be
stored in boxes, wallet folders or envelopes. Worksheets are more
easily produced in large numbers since masters, written or typed,
can be used on spirit or ink duplicators and in conjunction with a
stencil cutter or heat copier can incorporate pictures or diagrams.
But, if speedily made, they are often to be faulted for untidiness
and poor quality of reproduction and, plainly, are not as durable as
cards. Schools which possess, or have access to, offset litho will be
able to produce a better finished sheet.

If attractiveness of format, quality of production and length of life are important considerations then cards are preferable to sheets: but other requirements are also significant. The card does not become a pupil's property, a sheet can; a card provides information, guidelines and tasks but no part of the work done by pupils is brought on to the card itself, but a sheet can be designed so that, where required, children's work can be set under the questions. If this kind of pattern is preferred a variation is to produce a workbook, essentially a sequence of questions and information with spaces of varying sizes for pupils' work.

Where children are being introduced to individual work, or where the teacher wishes all to cover the same ground in sequence and avoid risks of losing parts of the work it is worth producing workbooks for them to complete and retain. If suitable textbooks or other sources are not available a workbook might include substantial information in written and pictorial form, including extracts from archive material and suggestions for further reference. Cover sheets can be of different colours and have attractive title pages either reproduced by the teacher or, preferably, designed by the pupils. But many teachers and children would prefer to have a more flexible format for the assembling of work, with less direction of content and sequence, and for this loose-leaf wallets or folders are better. Loss of items is a risk worth taking in order to underline the individual nature of the pupil's work. Where group work is involved further emphasis is given to the advantages of the loose-leaf pattern.

GROUP WORK

While learning may at its heart be an individual matter the advantages and disadvantages of having children working together in small groups must be carefully weighed. However pupils are grouped the principle that learning should be encouraged by division of labour, collaboration and sharing is strongly supported by many history teachers. Socially and educationally the case is powerful; such arrangements may also allow more effective use of resources, and there are always likely to be activities which are more suitably tackled by several children together than by individuals.

Several different kinds of grouping are employed in history classrooms: it is important to ask if any particular styles are appropriate for history, and others not. In general, groups may be permanent – at least for a year – or temporary, according to the topic or task. They may be determined by the teacher, or by the pupils. Internal setting, the grouping of children within one class on grounds of their performance in the subject, has some support among history teachers because it appears to enable the teacher to identify the requirements of each ability band and organise appropriate work; and for those who have been used to working with homogeneous groups especially in grammar schools it offers an arrangement closer to their traditional practice than other methods.

Unless this form of grouping can be shown to have specific advantages for learning in history it must be severely challenged since it underlines those divisions in selection which many want to reduce, and it ignores the possible benefits of children of differing abilities working together. That each subgroup should reflect the mixed nature of the total group is a persuasive argument for educational and social reasons, though critics or doubters ask if brighter children are held back by not being exclusively with those of like ability, or if the slower are even more confused by having to operate with sharper classmates. Certainly it is likely to make group teaching and the design of group projects more difficult, especially where one wants to have a relatively even spread of tasks among the members of a group, but in terms of work in history, bringing together children with different strengths, problems and interests has much in its favour. There are specific activities in history which are suitable for this kind of group, in particular those which involve practical work. It is difficult to cater for slower children with reading and writing problems if the group task is essentially literary, but work involving a wide variety of activities offers something much more appropriate for a mixed group.

A group of this sort might tackle a dramatisation of an historical event, in which case a script has to be written based on information which is researched. The presentation of the play calls for imaginative ideas; it has to be acted, perhaps recorded on tape in rehearsals if not as an end in itself, and there are various jobs to do – set, props and costume designing, taking responsibility for tape recording, sound effects, and the like. If the format is to be puppetry, then other tasks are created. For a mixed group of five or six children there is much to do: some are likely to produce more ideas than others, some will do more than others, but with sensitive guidance and encouragement from the teacher all can contribute and learn. Similar opportunities ought to be provided for group work by historical model making. Whatever is selected – Hadrian's Wall, a Norman castle, a display of vehicles showing changes in transport – should contain possibilities for division of labour, require historical accuracy and the search for the correct details, and offer chances for collaboration on design and presentation.

The compilation of a newspaper also enables a group of children to take responsibility for different aspects, and it can include illustrations, advertising, crosswords and cartoons as well as reports and articles. This, in fact, may not contain as much scope for variety as a mural or wall display in which painting, diagrams, writing and cutting-out are called for. Such an activity is most useful since it often depends on less complex materials and facilities and can be done in almost any situation. A scene from the past, such as that of a town or village, or a battle, is one popular approach. Another, offering more opportunity for ingenuity, is a mural which shows a sequence of events, or change and development. A story might be told in the form of a presentation like the Bayeux Tapestry, or it might show building stages, or line of development, or an event such as the Armada. In each case a background frieze has to be prepared with a series of drawings accompanied by captions or descriptions and cut-outs to be mounted on it.

The less imaginative or slower child not only has difficulty with written work, but on his own in a group with others of similar ability would never be likely to tackle such tasks as these, or get the same results. And this style of approach also helps to break into the notion that while less-able children should do practical work the brighter should concentrate on work based on the traditional grammar school pattern of reading and writing. The academically able are frequently most enthusiastic about design and constructional work – some of my ablest pupils have produced excellent models of a fortified Tudor manor house, stained-glass windows depicting medieval scenes, and the French guillotine – and ought to be given the opportunity of developing historical skills connected with it. In streamed or setted groups the evidence is that restriction of activities is all too likely.

Such activities for mixed-ability groups do not of course on their own guarantee that the bright and slow alike will be extended and work effectively: the degree to which that happens must depend on the teacher's handling of them, and on relationships and dynamics within the groups themselves. Personality clashes, disharmony and rivalries will hamper the work, and for these reasons, and others, it is important to consider alternative grouping arrangements. So far the groups discussed are formed by the teacher, aiming to balance social and ability mixing with effective learning opportunities for all. But to what extent should group composition be determined by pupils themselves? Pupils should be increasingly encouraged to make decisions about their own work and to take some responsibility for its development, and in groups friends may well work happily together and avert some of the possible disharmony noted earlier. Friendships in early and middle secondary school years change rapidly, and the experience of many teachers is that such groups of friends are likely to be composed of children of similar abilities. How disruptive, too, will a group of difficult children be to the whole class if allowed to be together for much of the time? This pattern is also likely to produce groups of unequal sizes and may make the provision of materials difficult. And what of those few pupils who are isolated, with whom no one chooses to work, and who are not welcome in any free-choice groups? They are difficult to place whatever the grouping arrangement.

For some activities in history it may not matter what particular form of group is created: there is nothing in the nature of such kinds of activity which demands either a setted or a mixed group, or indeed a group at all. In many cases it may be better to see the task tackled by individuals with the teacher at times drawing into groups children who are experiencing particular difficulties, who need remedial attention in history, or who require further stimulus. For other work where a common task involves a variety of activities it may be much more effective to encourage children of differing abilities and interests to collaborate. The composition of each group need not be fixed for a long period, but in the early days at least the teacher is the most likely determinant of appropriate grouping patterns.

ORGANISING WORK IN HISTORY

In organising work for individuals and groups the question of how much guidance or direction should be given by the teacher and how much choice and freedom should be permitted the pupils is of central importance, and not easily answered. Those who argue that our principal aim should be to increase the independence of the pupil in organising and directing his own work rest their case on the assumption that learning will only be properly effective when the learner is encouraged to initiate his own areas of investigation and tasks, and works out for himself what is important. If this implies that pupils, individually or collectively, should make decisions about the overall content as well as the detail of their work, many teachers of history would oppose it. At a very practical level they would see problems in providing books and other materials, and they might argue that the development of the pupils' skills must follow a planned sequence, and that only the teacher can plan it. More would support the idea of pupils being allowed to make decisions about much of the detail of what they do, but only within the context of an education designed to help them to make informed decisions, in which they are brought to see what range of choice there is, and the implications of each particular selection. In this the pupils are led gradually to a position of some independence. So often pupils who are suddenly presented with free choice where this was previously denied them are confused and unable to appreciate the possiblities, and choose on impulse or hunch which is quickly regretted. A skilful teacher may be able to lead such children to a more worthwhile decision, but it is preferable in general to consider how this kind of situation might be avoided by careful preparation in historical training over several years.

It is optimistic but very important to aim for the position where most pupils, when presented with a historical topic or problem, are able to work out the details for themselves with little direction from the teacher. This is where involving pupils actively in history reaches its peak. Whatever the topic they would – in consultation with their teacher – decide what questions to ask of it, search out relevant information, consult a variety of sources of evidence and question their authenticity and reliability, make deductions and judgements, and present their findings and conclusions in different ways. Within the same class children are likely to be going in different directions of study, as they feel the problems take them. This is the essence of historical research; given such limitations as inaccessibility of material and immaturity of judgement, pupils are nevertheless tackling historical problems and conducting historical investigations. This is the kind of activity encouraged – and ability revealed – by a well designed CSE Mode 3, and one hopes by further developments in examining at 16+ and beyond. At this stage of working the teacher might suggest the topic, and offer alternative approaches and references to sources on a workcard, or leave these to emerge in discussion with pupils where possible questions and materials are considered. Here the teacher's role needs to be subtle and unobtrusive, to encourage and guide but not inhibit, and to assess the need for resources throughout the work. In this last respect his task may be the most difficult, for an essential characteristic of this level of working is that, within the general topic determined, pupils will be studying a variety of aspects, and there is not necessarily common ground to be covered. A study of mid-Victorian life, for example, might be tackled at a local or national level, and might be approached by investigation of domestic conditions, the growth of towns, transport, work, leisure activities, education, and so on. At what point the study began would not matter, though pupils would be encouraged to see how their area impinged on others.

Educating children in the methods of historical investigation to reach this level of study is a long process, and not all will progress at the same pace. In order to move towards this kind of independence in both individual and group work, and to provide for pupils who may never reach this stage, one must consider other ways of organising work in history. The teacher whose experience is in more formal teaching techniques, but who wants to engage in more flexible and varied approaches, will also find transitional schemes helpful in becoming aware of the problems, possibilities and practicalities. Those who are introducing individual or group work to children who have little, if any, experience of working on their own and those who prefer more teacher-direction in history are likely to be attracted to other styles and strategies.

To begin with the teacher should decide in detail the overall topic or period, and the various aspects of it, which are to be studied, and give extensive direction for the work to be undertaken. He must plan the time allocation for class teaching, group work and individual work, and provide guides on workcards so that children are introduced carefully to the topic and in particular to the methods of historical study – gathering information from at first a limited but gradually increasing number of sources, answering questions of different kinds, and tackling varied activities. The teacher may decide to have frequent class lessons in order to introduce each new topic carefully, to explain what is required and how it should be done, and to deal with general difficulties. But children can be shown how to set about their work by skilful use of workcards, as the examples for a study of Hadrian's Wall described earlier indicate. At this introductory stage all children in a class are best required to cover the same general ground, though in mixed-ability groups one must be careful to allow for differing speeds of work. Thus, a study of the Middle Ages would involve children in topics such as town and village life, castles, churches and monasteries, sports and pastimes, weapons and armour, or costume.

But the central problems of mixed-ability groups – differing abilities and pace of work – necessitate variations to this approach, and it is advisable as a further development of individual and group work to devise activities so that, firstly, there remains a common topic for the whole class but part of it is central or core study and part is optional, and secondly, the degree of direction can be varied and gradually reduced as the teacher thinks suitable. Class teaching will be a part of the core work but it should be cut down, though never removed, once children are working on their options, with enlarged concentration on individual needs. Thus, a study of the exploration and development of the American West might include among its core topics early expeditions such as that of Lewis and Clark; the pioneers; the origins of settlers; and the coming of the railroads; and as its options topics such as the mountain men; the Oregon Trail; California mining; the Indians of the Plains; ranchers and farmers; various personalities like Kit Carson, Geronimo, Wyatt Earp, and Cochise; and incidents such as the Alamo and Wounded Knee. For Roman Britain the conquest and military occupation might be studied by all children while town or country life, costume, transport, etc would be among the options. In the study of the options pupils are able to work in depth on one, two or more as time allows and their interests guide. It is through the workcards designed for them that the teacher is able to provide for differing abilities and interests, and develop his pupils' opportunity for choice and expertise in inquiry and expression: when he is able to assemble a greater variety of materials, the teacher may be able to produce, for any option, cards aimed at different levels. So, when a whole topic is completed children will have worked on varying amounts at differing levels (unlike the approach described previously where much more uniformity is demanded), and will have become used to greater choice and independence in initiating their own work.

For many children in non-streamed classes this may be the most suitable general approach in history throughout most of the secondary school, and the one which appeals to a majority of teachers. It implies that the teacher determines the overall content and all children cover its essential issues and structure; the teacher incorporates class sessions as he decides appropriate but much more attention is focussed on individual and group arrangements; and optional studies allow for variations in interests, speeds of work and composition of groups. With careful planning the teacher is able to combine his own directions in training his pupils in historical investigation with opportunities for independent activity by the children as they become more familiar with the methods. As some become increasingly skilled at working on their own they can be allowed the greater freedom and independence discussed at the beginning of this section. There is, however, no absolute or comprehensive time-scale for the progression from one stage to the next. It may be organisationally convenient for the whole class to be at the same stage, but this is to deny the principal argument of this chapter, that variety of approach must be central to the teaching of history in a mixed-ability group. In any class, at any time, work may be done at all three basic stages; there will always be those who need close guidance, and those who can be left frequently to themselves. But gradually we should work towards flexibility and greater choice in history so that by the age of fourteen most pupils are well trained in the main features of historical inquiry.

RESOURCES AND FACILITIES

Just as exercises and activities for a mixed-ability group must be varied, so the materials available should be adequate for a wide range of reading and interest levels. There is no need to abandon entirely the basic textbook which provides a common source of information, but it is unlikely that any one book could be written which would not be too difficult for the slower readers yet would contain sufficient detail for the brighter pupils. It may be better, as with workcards, to consider three or four levels and search for basic books for each. This need not mean one textbook per pupil, and for economy enough copies for approximately one half of the class might be available, supplemented by reference books for the work on different levels and options. A class of young secondary school pupils studying medieval topics should be able to use selections from several series such as *Then and There, Focus on History, Evidence in Pictures,* and *As We Were* (Longmans); *People of the Past* (Oxford); *History Bookshelves* (Ginn); and *Life Then* (Hart-Davis). In addition to these, numerous biographies and specialised books on different aspects of medieval life are obtainable – a convenient list is provided in Burston, W. H. and Green, C. W., *Handbook for History Teachers* (1972) – and selections of these might be held in a class or department library. Collections of historical documents, commercially produced or better still drawn from local sources, are important too, though for the medieval period these will need to be translated, transcribed and selected before children can work on them. Facsimiles will be useful for illustration. Pictures for wall display or group work are available from Macmillan's History Class Pictures, Pictorial Charts Educational Trust, Educational Productions Ltd, and from magazines such as *Pictorial Education, History of the English Speaking*

Peoples, and *History Makers.* Where finance and facilities permit the materials on medieval topics should also include audio tapes (eg recordings of *History in Evidence* and *History in Focus* (BBC) and filmstrips and slides which can be used by pupils or by teachers. Paper and card, papiermaché, balsa wood, cardboard boxes, scissors and Sellotape are also important. These are materials which many teachers, especially those with grammar school experience, will be unaccustomed to making available but which must be to hand if children are to tackle all kinds of activities.

Such a range of materials may seem very optimistic to those who work with low budgets and limited facilities, but many history teachers find that their own ingenuity and effort plus changes in policies for accommodation and resources provision are offering improved possibilities. At its most developed stage this implies an approach to learning which is based on an extensive range of materials within flexible working spaces. New purpose-built schools or additional blocks incorporating history areas can be developed along imaginative lines, and much can be done with more traditional physical arrangements.

ASSESSMENT

Much of the work with mixed-ability groups discussed here is with individuals or small groups, with emphasis gradually falling on variety and choice. We must accept that not all of the children in one class will be doing the same work, and this poses difficulties for traditional styles of assessment. Where internal examinations in each year are required it is important that they are designed to test the knowledge, understanding and mastery of skills which are appropriate to the work that has been done in history by each pupil. Where pupils have been covering common ground they may be tested in common, but they must also be allowed to show their knowledge and understanding of their optional studies, and not solely in a literary manner. But several of the objectives referred to in this chapter concern historical skills the achievement of which might be tested by use of a variety of materials. To what extent can pupils comprehend a passage, view it as historical evidence, interpret it and make judgements based on and beyond it, or how far can they reconstruct or suggest possible solutions to a historical problem? These are clearly questions of some importance to examination boards and their history panels. Yet in those secondary school years – the eleven to fourteen age-range – where mixed-ability groups usually exist, or are likely to develop, there is much greater opportunity for assessment of a broader kind, and here a pupil's work can be rated continuously, in terms of his own effort and achievement, rather than set against an absolute standard. The assessment of group work presents, in a sense, the most difficult task of all, especially if the teacher attempts to grade separately the contribution of each individual. It requires a sharp eye to do it, but more significantly it denies one of the major arguments for group activity which is that it should be of a collaborative kind, with – at best – children learning from each other, and contributing their strengths to the common task. Though some teachers and pupils will protest, it is much closer to the spirit of this sort of work for the whole group to be treated as a group so that, in terms of grades at least, each member receives the same irrespective of his own particular contribution. This in no way prevents the teacher, in the course of evaluating group work in general, from reminding individuals of the nature of this way of working, either because they ought to raise their own contribution or because they are taking on too much. Assessment in history, like so many of the aspects of teaching mixed-ability groups that have been considered here, demands on the part of the teacher a fresh and open mind, a willingness to move away from dependence on exclusively traditional methods and to experiment with different styles of working, and a recognition above all of the importance of catering for individual needs with a variety of activities.

For notes to this chapter see pp 185–6

6 Teaching Social Studies/Humanities in Mixed-Ability Groups

M. Gracie

Often the interest and enthusiasm of social studies teachers makes them among the first who want to try mixed-ability teaching in secondary schools. They are not, of course, the only teachers interested in innovation, but their training predisposes them to reject hierarchical organisation. This strong commitment is reinforced by the nature of the long-term aim of their discipline. They believe that the subject can make a distinctive contribution to a young person's social development. They hope that when he leaves school, he may be more aware of the possibilities and constraints of his society and able to take positive decisions to further his ideals and ambitions. Whether or not these long-term aims are achieved, they certainly cannot be tested in an academic sense. It is nonsense to attempt to create ability groups based on potential social awareness, and so the issue of whether to stream in social studies is for many teachers an absurdity. This philosophical position in no way ensures that the social studies teacher is any better equipped to make a success of mixed-ability teaching. He starts off with all other teachers to learn a new attitude to teaching methods and curriculum.

STRUCTURAL REORGANISATION

The social sciences include several highly structured academic disciplines, such as economics, psychology and law, but these rarely appear on a school timetable until the sixth form. By this time the need to stream has never been very strong because groups have selected themselves on the basis of interest, and are in any case small enough to allow for a considerable range of academic ability. The social studies or humanities which are the concern of this chapter are a broad amalgam of all the disciplines which contribute to the study of man's behaviour. The official title on the timetable is a matter of chance; integrated studies, social studies, social science, combined studies and humanities having much the same meaning. The only important way in which this area of study varies from school to school is in whether it includes creative expression and literature. In general, I am speaking of a curriculum which does not. However, as teachers become more accustomed to inter-disciplinary study, they often choose to expand their subject boundaries, and departments either merge or co-operate. The important issues for teaching mixed-ability groups are similar for social scientists and for creative English specialists, and I think that what I say here could equally apply to an area of study which included both.

The introduction of mixed-ability teaching usually involves a distinct change in a school which has been streamed for a long time. Unstreaming is often presented as an event, 'We unstreamed our first year last September'. In reality this event is more a statement of intent. It is but the beginning of a process of change, a change which may lead to a school with an organisation and philosophy capable of liberating the teacher from his role of authoritarian instructor and offering the student the opportunity to develop his individual potential.

My experience of this process has been as a teacher in two un-streamed secondary schools. I have also been able to observe it in a number of other schools as warden of a teachers' centre. I have had a unique opportunity to glimpse many of the stages in the development of social studies departments and some of the patterns of change that they have in common. Eight years ago we were generally unaware of what a tremendous revolution was implied by unstreaming. We began to teach these new groups much as we had always done and the results were discouraging. A number of pupils seem to be able to produce accurate, tidy and even inspired work whatever the conditions, but many more demand a much more sympathetic and sensitive treatment before they are able to commit themselves to learning in mixed-ability groups.

The social studies teachers of the unstreamed school are the history, geography and religious education teachers of the traditional streamed school. They possessed a monotonous teaching technique relieved by the occasional film or visit and by the rare subject enthusiast. With the A stream the teacher offered lectures and text-books to stimulate a series of illustrated essays in the pupils' note-books. With lower streams, the illustrations took up more and more space, until the minimum requirement was a set of captioned cartoons! The science teacher offered practical work; English was enlivened by drama and poetry; only the mathematician competed with the social scientist in deadening technique. Unstreaming high-lighted the need for a change in approach. Eight years ago this need was so urgent that the fact that the curriculum was uninteresting to many pupils and contributed to their boredom, was over-shadowed. We began to evolve more lively and active methods of work, the second stage of unstreaming.

METHODOLOGICAL CHANGE

The simplest changes in teaching technique which have an immed-iate beneficial effect are the introduction of variety in teaching materials and consequently methods of working, and variety in modes of recording or presenting work.

Information can be collected in a large number of ways. Books are vital, the biggest range possible so that the pupil can select one which he is capable of reading and which contains the information he really wants. Textbooks need to be cut to a minimum and the stock of good children's books increased. Schools sometimes manage to exchange their surplus textbooks with other schools and effect some variety this way. Tape recordings can interest some children more than print, and a considerable bank of recordings can be built up in as little time as a year by recording programmes from the radio, by the teacher recording stories and making his own 'radio programmes', and by recording whatever interesting contribu-tions can be obtained from other members of staff and from the local community, for example local history, legend and personal experiences. Too much listening is hard work and all methods of visual presentation are valuable: films, filmstrips, slides, charts and objects. Even if, at first, these are only the old filmstrips cut up and made into slides and accompanied by a tape recording or a short booklet, the fact that children use them on their own, and can take their own time, makes them a stimulating format.

The independent use of all kinds of audio-visual equipment can produce the kind of variety of teaching materials which is required – but of course it is expensive. There were four or five tape recorders in the present writer's first school, but very soon the demand was so great that there needed to be one for each member of the social science and English departments. In some schools there is a more generous pupil-tape recorder ratio than pupil-teacher ratio!

The opportunity for children to record their work in a variety of ways often begins with the use of workcards and with projects. Workcards allow the teacher to programme each child's work without directly supervising it. The least ambitious schemes are rather dull because the cards relate to the book or set of slides and not to the child; more individual cards are prepared for a particular child or group and can be made in discussion between the pupils and teacher. Project work makes possible more open-ended inquiry. If the class is working on a particular theme, each child can choose to work on some aspect that interests him, providing that there are sufficient resources to provide him with the information he needs. At this stage in unstreaming, it is unlikely that the school library will be able to provide enough material, and teachers find that this is an ideal time to start to supplement books with booklets and information sheets which they have made themselves. This too is the moment when teachers begin to reflect about the potential of their subject for teaching the skills of independent research.

Projects have their limitations too. Unless they are carefully supervised, they can lead to prolific copying. This is often hard to detect because a teacher cannot be familiar with all the sources of information available to his class. One way to minimise it is to combine the use of workcards and projects. Asking the child to find out a particular piece of information or solve a problem means that no one book can dictate the structure of his project, and asking

105

questions of opinion increases the original thinking that the child has to do.

A diet of projects and worksheets is a dreary spectacle, even if there is a variety of resources for the child to use. Making recordings, drama, modelling, painting, visits and discussion should all be central to a special studies course, rather than being the alternative offered to children who are 'less able'.

The contemporary classroom has become a more interesting place; one group of children modelling, one group watching slides, another group arguing, and yet other children writing, painting and thinking. The walls and tables are display areas. What about the teacher? His job has become more stimulating because he has had to learn a whole number of new skills. His working day is much more varied and more and more demanding in time. A classroom which gives scope for individuality requires much more organisation, and the teacher finds that his time in school is completely taken up with talking to children about their work, marking work, helping with technical problems, locating books, and so on. At home, he has to give up more time to marking and planning work than ever before. This type of teaching brings teachers into closer personal contact with individual children, and the barrier between pupil and teacher is gradually being broken down as each tries to learn from the other, but the teacher's central role is unaltered. The changes in method I have outlined are ways of taking control of the work of each group and individual in the class. The teacher still makes all the decisions about the curriculum, the topic of work, the range of methods of work, and is still the judge of standards. The pupil is in a far better position than before because he enjoys the variety and choice, but as yet he has no control over his own education and development.

CURRICULUM DEVELOPMENT

Most schools, which began the process of learning how to teach with mixed-ability groups some time ago, chose to begin with methodological change, and considered curriculum change in the next stage of development. But one kind of change demands the other, and schools which have made the change more recently have the advantage of earlier experience, and are able to cope with the challenge of a new curriculum at the same time. One of the problems facing curriculum innovators is that the staff of the newly christened social studies department are in fact the subject specialists of previous years. Even if they are willing to relinquish their specialisms and plan an integrated syllabus drawing from a wider range of disciplines, such as economics, anthropology or environmental study, they are often intimidated by their own lack of knowledge and therefore uncertain about whether they can make a success of the new curriculum.

In some schools, the best solution has been team teaching. There are hardly two schools in which team teaching means the same kind of organisation; in some it means collective planning and shared use of teaching materials; in most it involves the use of 'lead-lessons' to start the work on a particular theme; in others a group of teachers has joint responsibility for a large number of children, and pupils work with the member of staff who can provide most help with their work. All the different models shift the responsibility for planning, research and preparation of materials from individual teachers to the team. This provides reassurance for teachers who are unfamiliar with aspects of the curriculum, gives support to new teachers joining the team, and allows the work load to be spread. Other social scientists have involved themselves in one of the humanities curriculum development projects, and have found in this a way of building confidence and experience in a department. All such projects involve a new curriculum, different teaching methods, and often a fundamentally new role for the teacher. Three of the projects are particularly relevant to social studies teachers.

The Schools Council *Integrated Studies* is an ideal course for schools that wish to base an integrated course on the skills and disciplines of traditional subjects, because it offers a basic structure for a course, which can, nevertheless, be adapted to suit the particular needs of a school. 'Some schools may wish to begin with only a limited form of integration – perhaps no more than two teachers co-operating at points where their syllabuses overlapped. Other schools have taken its introduction as an opportunity to reconsider the whole curriculum of the school.' The course is made up of three units, each of which draws on material from many disciplines – geography, history, anthropology, sociology and the expressive arts. The total course aims to develop those skills which are peculiar to each discipline and to show the interrelation between disciplines which further the study of any topic.

Unit 1, *Exploration Man,* is based on the use of local and personal resources, no materials apart from the teacher's guide being produced for the course. It aims to introduce the techniques and curriculum of the succeeding units. It allows the teacher to introduce the tools of investigation, using maps, reading original documents, planning a questionnaire, recording local people's memories, and so on – all useful experience for future units. It also introduces the central area of the course, 'Man'.

Unit 2, *Communicating with Others,* uses material ranging from street songs to hieroglyphics to focus interest on man's unique ability to communicate and symbolise and to stimulate more effective communication, particularly through personal creative expression.

Unit 3, *Living Together,* is a close study of three societies: Tristan da Cunha, the Land Dayaks of Borneo, and Imperial China. Through each of these studies and through comparison with the child's community, the shared nature of humanity is the important conceptual theme.

Units 2 and 3 contain a package of extracts, accounts, pictures, tapes, slides and work suggestions for the pupils, together with a teacher's book which details the aims and methodology and has useful lists of additional support materials. The course could occupy two or more years at the lower end of secondary school. Some teachers might regard it as a compromise because it retains such a dependence on traditional subjects, but for others its explicit and thorough treatment of each theme makes it an ideal bridge from the traditional to the stage when curriculum development will be school based.

Man – A Course of Study is another course designed for younger pupils. It was developed in the United States for eleven- to twelve-year-olds, and is being used in this country with pupils up to about thirteen. Social studies is a compulsory subject in the United States, and the course was designed in response to criticism that the content of most courses was dull and unchallenging. We are just as familiar with those lessons about the postman, the supermarket and local government which are supposed to add up to a unified picture of society. Teachers who wish to develop a course which challenges children to make their own discoveries about the nature of man and his social organisation will do well to study the materials of this course, even if they cannot afford to purchase them for use in their school.

Jerome Bruner described the aims of the course in this way: 'The content of the course is man: his nature as a species, the forces that shaped and continue to shape his humanity. . . . We seek exercises and materials through which our pupils can learn wherein man is distinctive in his adaptation to the world, and wherein there is a discernible continuity between him and his animal forbears.' The course is purchased as a package of children's and teachers' materials. It divides into two parts, a unit on animal behaviour (the salmon, the herring gull and the baboon) and a unit on man (the Netsilik Eskimo in his historic way of life). Each unit is film based. Most of the films were especially made so that they could replace fieldwork, encouraging children to make their own observations and draw their own conclusions. There are pamphlets, pictures, charts, filmstrips, games and records. The course is sequential, and structured to develop at all stages recurrent concepts which help the pupil to develop his thinking about the nature of man. Such a concept is parenthood, and children examine it again and again in their study of each of the animals, their study of the Netsilik, and from relating this to observation of families they know. The aims and detailed structure of the course are set out in the teachers' guides. These were written to suit a rather formal class structure, but they are packed with suggestions for activities and can be adapted quite easily to suit a more flexible classroom organisation.

The exciting features of this course are the quality of the materials, particularly the film of the Netsilik which is unrivalled in the field of anthropological film, and its explicit demand for a change in the role of both the pupil and the teacher. They are both asked to become learners and to use all their knowledge and powers of questioning in search of answers to questions which are the real concern of mankind. This represents a threat to many teachers at the beginning of the course but it becomes an exciting challenge, one which enables them to handle new materials and experience real learning which was not possible in their previous role.

With older pupils, the Schools Council/Nuffield *Humanities Project* provides the same kind of stimulus and support for teachers venturing into the field of curriculum development. The project materials have been in use in schools for some years and were developed at the same time as schools began to organise courses around controversial issues such as war, poverty, sex, and crime. The project developed a teaching strategy aimed to allow students to develop their own rationally held viewpoint. The first eight 'packages' each related to a different theme: *War and Society, Education, The Family, Relations between the Sexes, Poverty, People and Work, Living in Cities* and *Law and Order*. Each contained several hundred extracts and pictures, printed on loose sheets, which presented divergent viewpoints on one theme; a tape recording; and a teachers' book which was a guide to the use of the materials and a list of further material, particularly film.

In some schools, the materials have added to an existing resource collection, but this is not the use for which they were intended. The teacher preparing to use the materials attends an intensive course to familiarise himself with the materials and to learn and experience the technique of taking the role of the neutral chairman. His main role is to act as the organiser of an inquiry for a group of fifteen to twenty students who makes available such evidence as is demanded by their discussion; he is the chairman of discussions and establishes the procedures for fruitful talk, but he does not try to suggest a particular viewpoint and he does not state his own. This method of inquiry requires a change in role for the teacher even greater than the model in *Man – A Course of Study*. Such a role is indeed a controversial subject for teachers in itself.

Sponsored projects such as the three described above are better financed, staffed and researched than any school effort can be, but they do not contain materials which are tailor-made for every social studies department. They can, however, provide the materials for a large proportion of a course and they help during that difficult

110

period in the process of unstreaming when teachers are uncertain or confused about their best approach. The experience of most teachers is that curriculum materials are never wasted even if they do not warrant a permanent place in the syllabus. They prove the way of involving teachers and pupils in a new attitude to learning and stimulate school or locally based curriculum development. Thereafter the materials may be the basis of a growing collection of resources of all kinds, but they are unlikely to grow dusty on stock-cupboard shelves.

Many secondary schools have now reached the stage where preparing resource materials is a major activity of the staff and where the resource centre is central to the organisation of every department and of critical importance to social scientists. Resource materials are of two different kinds: those which are prepared to service a course and those which are collected to facilitate individual inquiry. Both types, of course, can exist side by side. Resources for a course are usually booklets, photographs, charts, slides and so on which have been prepared in the school to provide the information and guidance for a fairly structured approach to teaching social studies. They are produced in large numbers and are more or less essential reading for students. This is an exciting and thoroughly absorbing stage in development for teachers, but it cultivates the discontent which leads to a further stage of the process of unstreaming, that of independent learning.

My own experience is shared by many of my colleagues, that the most exciting stage in preparing resource material is the research, when we are often engaged in new learning and thinking. It is sometimes an anti-climax to use the materials. This is surely what learning is about, and it is this that our students should be doing. Teachers will find students making this demand for themselves. Every time one of them asks, 'Can I do so-and-so instead?' we have an opportunity to develop this kind of learning. We are not always either disposed to take the opportunity, or even able to, through the pressure of examination work. Most of the factors which make us reply, 'Later', or 'Why don't you do that at home?', or 'No. That is not part of the syllabus', are self-made. We can create the conditions for independent learning if this is what we wish. The crucial

111

question which social scientists must face is whether they think that the essential value of the social sciences can be expressed through a curriculum or whether their value is as a discipline which enables students to form their own interests and viewpoints. Like the decision to unstream, the decision to aim for independent learning is the beginning of a gradual process because it implies a collection of resources, a flexibility in school organisation and another change in role for the teacher, none of which can be implemented immediately. A period of consolidation with a gradual shift of emphasis away from the syllabus is probably a sensible way of handling this change.

INDEPENDENT LEARNING

It is a pity that most teachers only have experience of either primary or secondary schools, and that most secondary teachers are unaware that a model for independent learning flourishes in many primary schools. The atmosphere is very different from most secondary schools. Children are actively involved in project work which has all the qualities of independent or self-motivated learning.[1] What is it that, over the course of a summer holiday, changes a child brimming with curiosity and energy for learning into one who is barely trusted to move outside his classroom, and who needs to be fed information pre-selected by his teacher? Of course the child has not changed but he is in a different institution which demands changed behaviour. However much we have moderated our approach to subjects, the academic university disciplines still dominate secondary schools and the examination hurdles reinforce their importance. Teaching so as to encourage independent learning demands that we study the child and his development and interests, and tailor our contribution to what we see, rather than attempt to force children's minds into ill-fitting academic moulds.

Independent learning does not mean a completely free choice. From the start of social studies, the teacher's role is to continue the development of skills and interests that have started in the primary school. The principal skills that the pupil may have had the opportunity to develop are in collecting information from different sources, training in observation as a prime source of original material,

112

and organisation of all kinds of information into a coherent account, collection or display. By providing stimulating situations and materials a teacher can extend these early experiences of independent learning to encompass skills and interests which were beyond a young child. Independent learning of the quality we must aim for at fourth- and fifth-year level is a culmination of learning experiences, some of which may be highly structured.

Teachers rightly criticise individual 'project work' if similar techniques are employed in every piece of work, whatever the theme. Students have to learn what it means to achieve a better standard in their subsequent efforts. Better standards in the social sciences are achieved when the research goes into a subject at a great depth, when it involves more original research, when the student can command a variety of techniques to elicit information and, most important, when he is able to pose problems and pursue hypotheses. Individual inquiry and independent learning can be seen as the long-term aim of a social studies department. It can be achieved progressively starting from a 'core' course aimed to develop skills and teach any information thought to be essential for future work, and leading to a stage where the core is as small as to be consistent with any external examination requirements.

What are the skills which are the essential content of such a core curriculum? One central skill which is too easily forgotten is reading. There are a large number of children who cannot be categorised as 'remedial' who find library books and even worksheets very hard to understand, and we can help by paying particular attention to the provision of easier reading material and giving personal help with problems. Related to this is a constant need to teach terminology. Other skills fall into three groups. First there are the tools of the discipline, among them the skills of collecting information from maps, statistical tables, films, archives etc; the use of equipment, such as the tape recorder, slide project, map table, camera etc; the use of indexes, tables of contents, and the cataloguing system of the school library and public libraries; and writing letters and making telephone calls to ask for information or to arrange visits. A second set of skills are methodological, the skills of collecting, collating and presenting information and ideas. These include a good knowledge of the facilities inside and outside the school, particularly the resource centre; techniques for collecting direct evidence, such as the questionnaire, the interview, the participant observation; and the most comprehensible and economic methods of presenting research. A way of encouraging students to develop a public form of presentation is to demonstrate that their work has a wider than personal value. A feature of independent learning is that while a number of interesting research projects may be going on in one room, only the teacher knows about them all. A way of encouraging shared experiences is to display, discuss and refer to students' work as a regular feature of classroom activity. In many primary schools, projects are added to the school or class library collection. Many examination projects are quite unique, containing original information researched from local archives, newspapers and local people's memories, and as well as adding to the stock of a resource centre, the habit of keeping projects for other students to use stimulates clear and thoughtful work. It has the secondary function of encouraging a more intelligent use of the resource centre. Students who have contributed to the stock and have helped to classify it will realise in practice what are its possibilities and begin to make maximum use of complex retrieval systems such as the optical co-incidence co-ordinate system.

The third group of skills are intellectual. These are more difficult to describe or evaluate. They are the mental processes necessary to bridge the gap between collecting data and making observations to hypothesising, questioning and drawing conclusions. Not every student will ever develop to this stage, but there are ways in which they can be encouraged; by comparing situations, by deliberately presenting diverging evidence or information, by teaching the discipline of discussion, asking questions of opinion, and by demanding that the plan for every piece of work includes either a question which is new to the student or a hypothesis.

Much will depend on the strengths and interests of the team of social studies teachers when the core curriculum is planned. Almost any curriculum can provide the vehicle for teaching basic skills, but the best policy with young children must be to capitalise on areas that interest them. There are some well known 'winners' with this age group, such as topics to do with prehistory, social history, family history, anthropology, exploration and travel and local and environmental studies. A selection from these and other topics allows an understanding of basic background knowledge to develop, an historical and cultural perspective on present events, behaviour and organisations, and also allows enough scope for pupils to pursue individual inquiry with reasonable choice. In schools where children have had this experience in the early years, the area of choice can be much broader in the fourth, fifth and sixth years and results in a remarkable quality of work.

The teacher's role varies with different types of student. Some need many suggestions and encouragement to choose a topic and others may be able to select and plan a project with little guidance. Teachers will find that projects selected by students, even when they may not appeal to the teacher at first, will always be more satisfactory than themes inspired solely by the teacher, but discreet supervision can ensure that projects are varied and stretching, as the example below shows.

A village study

The present writer worked recently with some sixth-form students beginning an A level sociology course. They were asked to read John Berger's *Portrait of a Country Doctor* and Ronald Blythe's *Akenfield* in the hope that they would become interested in making a village study. The group decided to try, and chose a village about four miles from the school because it was small and geographically distinct, and as we already knew the head of the village school we hoped that he might act as our introduction to the village. Before starting the study we discussed methods of inquiry, trying to select those which would reveal the quality of life in the community, rather than the familiar techniques used to elicit geographical and historical information. We decided to try to build a composite picture of village life by structured interviews which, we hoped, would develop into open-ended interviews. The first time we visited the village, we walked about and recorded our first impressions photographically. The key institutions appeared to be the several pubs, the four shops, the church, the manor house and the school, and we expected some of the people connected with these to give us information about the unseen structure of the village. The students planned an interview with the head teacher, and as a result of this interview approached and interviewed the retired head teacher who lived in the village, the vicar, a farmer, a retired farmer, the 'lady of the manor' and her companion, the butcher and the postmistress. This is how the interview with the butcher was written up:

The butcher appears to be a man with a continual grudge. He claims his trade has been ruined by television and radio which has turned his customers away by convincing them that meat is too expensive. He said that as soon as he got the chance he would get out of the butcher's trade, and recalled with regret that he has turned down an offer of £45,000 for his business and property. He complained about the view opposite his shop. The deserted house in question had been bought by the council ten years ago. He exclaimed that business was so bad that his profits had dropped by £40 a week.

When he had first left school he had intended to be a carpenter but because no jobs were available he was forced to work in his brother's butcher's shop for 'five bob a week'. He said that one week his brother had given him 'seven bob' and 'feeling like a king', he had gone into Leicester for lemonade and a bag of chips.

He butchers all his own meat (bought locally) every Wednesday night but when he had opened his new slaughterhouse only a few people (including the vicar) had been to see it.

As this type of information began to accumulate, members of the group who were less interested in interviewing began to research the background information needed to put the interviews in context. One student collected historical information from the museum archives and from local histories, another collected the history of the railway which had served the village, and another collected population statistics from up-to-date and historical census material. Each time the group met for discussion we challenged them to take up the wider issues that had arisen and produced material from other studies to give more evidence on which to base opinion.

116

Towards the end of the study, a paper was written on the major questions, themes and problems:

Change in a Leicestershire village, 1900–73

In many ways this is the question which interests me most. We have already hypothesised that this century has seen a transformation in the village from a rural to an urban (or it might be better to say suburban) economy. I mean that most of the inhabitants now work, not on the land, but in factories, offices and elsewhere in towns many of which are relatively distant – Coventry, Rugby, Lutterworth, Hinckley, Leicester. (One minor but interesting line of inquiry would be to plot the extent of work in these various towns and to see if any explanation can be found for favouring one rather than another). As a matter of fact we have already discovered certain facts which cast some doubt on the original hypothesis, notably the fact that even before the turn of the century the majority of the working population were not in fact working on the land. Nevertheless my own guess would be that there has still been a substantial change in the nature of occupation in the village, although this may turn out to be not so much a change from rural to urban occupations as a change from local factory or semi-industrialised production to urban occupations in other places . . .

The paper went on to outline the areas in which further inquiry was indicated. The students decided that a house-to-house survey was the appropriate way of obtaining further information. The two teachers were keen to start on this at once, but the students put off the survey for a period because they were not sure how much time they wanted to give to it.

The village study above is an example of how independent learning yields a high standard of work given the right school environment. The first requirement for such work is that the school organisation should be flexible, particularly the timetable. The students were allocated one half-day each week but they had to be able to negotiate other periods of time during the week in order to interview when it was convenient to villagers. The entire staff of

117

the school is committed to this type of work and made it possible. The school timetable is largely made up of blocks of time allocated to broad study areas and teachers are prepared to make last-minute alterations to facilitate a student's personal requirements. This flexibility allows a large variety of long-term projects to develop without the disruption of bells, room changes and lack of time.

The second important prerequisite for such a study is the availability of resource material and good reprographic facilities. So many good ideas are wasted without them. All social science teachers know the frustration of being unable to supply the materials to help a student answer a really important question, and know that this will discourage him from asking that kind of question another time.

Examinations

Independent learning can only reach a primitive level if it does not operate within a school environment which offers a flexible structure of a first-class resource service. It can then become a mode of learning which begins to offer each child an equal opportunity to develop his own interests and potential. Most social science teachers would recognise that they are only part of the way through this process of change and that the foremost structure on this development is the dictate of academic discipline, represented by examinations.

The normal requirements of GCE and CSE Mode I examinations frustrate this style of learning. The examinations were developed to be the culmination of a very different type of education and tested particular skills and knowledge. It is no proof of a failure of modern methods that old standards are not achieved. They are outdated standards and a new form of test is required, if indeed one is necessary at all when many students choose to join a study or activity out of interest rather than from a desire for any qualification. Many schools already assess their pupils with a Mode 3 examination; that is, a school-designed syllabus, a paper set and marked by the school's teachers, but which is open to outside moderation. Unfortunately, the degree to which they reflect the new approach to learning varies, but it is here that there is scope for change. Some Mode 3 examinations seem to be as rigid as the Mode 1 they replaced, but others place as much emphasis as possible on the student's individual contribution. A number of examples can be found in *The New Social Studies* by Denis Lawton and Barry Dufour. I quote below from the East Midlands Regional Examination Board CSE Mode 3 Social Studies at Countesthorpe College.

The syllabus is intended to help students to understand themselves as individuals and the society to which they belong. The students will be encouraged to explore each topic through the expressive arts – poetry, drama, the novel, music and art – as well as through the discipline and techniques of the social sciences but the major emphasis is on the development of a rational understanding of the individual in society. Much of the work will centre on the students' own environment, both locally and nationally, past and present, but they will be encouraged to study contrasted environments and societies also. The syllabus is divided into a number of themes or topics:
1   *The Family* . . .
2   *Education* . . .
3   *Work and Leisure* . . .
4   *Social Class* . . .
5   *Social Stability and Change* . . .
6   *The Political System* . . .

It is proposed that the examination should take three forms:

1   A written paper – four questions to be answered out of twelve in a two hour paper taking 40 per cent of the total marks for the examination. The paper will include essay questions, questions concerning the interpretation of photographs, tables and passages of writing, and questions involving imaginative writing or drawing . . .
2   Project work (40 per cent). This work should include not only 'finished' pieces of writing, illustration and documentation but also descriptive notes on the aims and strategies of the project and on how they were carried out in practice . . .
3   Oral (20 per cent). The oral examination will be based on

both the students' special project and on the rest of the syllabus, but chiefly on the project. It will be a discussion between the student and one or two teachers . . .

CONCLUSION

In this chapter, I have divided the process of change towards mixed-ability teaching into four overlapping stages: structural reorganisation, methodological change, curriculum development and the stage of independent learning. Many social studies departments have developed in this way, and I wonder whether it is a necessary evolution or if some of the stages could be telescoped. It is likely that any established streamed school will choose evolutionary change because the change in teaching role is so great. Teachers have been trained to operate in a classroom where they direct and control the process of learning. A mixed-ability situation demands that they consider new objectives, learn how to work in co-operation with other teachers, learn the role of learning catalyst, and become learners themselves.

In the future, it may be possible for the rate of change to accelerate. Experience of mixed-ability teaching is becoming available to all teachers. The most valuable help can come from prolonged visits to schools which have been unstreamed for some time, where discussions between colleagues can identify areas where mistakes and progress have been made. Teachers' centres can arrange facilities for a continuing dialogue between teachers in one locality and can accumulate examples of the kinds of materials which have been used with mixed-ability groups. Once teachers in training have themselves been educated in comprehensive schools, and when colleges of education provide a training for this type of school, the problems associated with the change in the teacher's role will be far fewer.

Of course, new schools have the greatest chance of leapfrogging some of the stages of this change. It is then possible to recruit teachers committed to the ideals of equal educational opportunity, some with previous experience of mixed-ability teaching. They are able to draw upon the experience of many other schools in planning their organisation, curriculum and teaching methods, but will need time to accumulate sufficient resource materials to make independent learning really successful.

I find it difficult to dissociate the questions confronting the social studies teacher from the larger issue, the aims and organisation of the whole school environment. There are schools in which an otherwise banded or streamed organisation is deliberately rearranged into mixed-ability groups for social studies lessons, but it is difficult to imagine change beyond the stages of methodological and curriculum development taking place in such conditions. The way in which the school formulates its role in society is the crucial change which facilitates or frustrates fundamental change within departments. All schools are involved in teaching the social conventions of society and in providing the qualifications needed by their students, but schools which are committed to their educative role can do more: they can offer the opportunity to evaluate and comprehend the implications of the educational system and can help a student to decide on the part he wants to play in society (or out of it). Such a school is one in which the social science teacher can make a direct contribution to the development of independent thinking in young people.

For notes to this chapter see p 186

7 Teaching Mathematics in Mixed-Ability Groups

D. W. Lingard

BACKGROUND

The teaching of mathematics to mixed-ability groups is uncommon. Mathematics, together with modern languages, is notably more difficult to handle in an unstreamed situation than, say English or science. These views, which are supported by what little evidence exists,[1] are widely held amongst mathematics (and language) teachers and often shared by their colleagues. Many so-called unstreamed schools set (ie group pupils by ability) for mathematics and there is a feeling among teachers that this is both reasonable and natural.

Two reasons are generally put forward to explain or defend this situation, to which I would add a third. The main argument hinges upon the linear nature of mathematics. That is, if mathematical progress is to be maintained, then concept A must be acquired and practised before concept B, and that in turn before subject matter C has been digested. To oversimplify, mathematics may be considered as a straight path along which pupils make progress. Diversions are discouraged, except for the most able children (who can easily catch up later) or the least able (who are not expected to get far anyway). Those who are unfortunate enough to miss, through inattention or absence, one stretch of the path will find the next stretch particularly hard going.

All this presupposes that there is a certain clearly-defined body of subject material which is important and has to be dispensed, in a prescribed order, to pupils. Practice suggests that most mathematics teachers subscribe to this second argument and certainly public examination syllabuses reflect this attitude. Mixed-ability groups, which require pupils to work at their own speeds, often on different themes or topics and frequently in pairs or small groups, make the teacher's job (or recording the individual pupil's progress along the path and ensuring that his next step is the right one) difficult – and many would say impossible. In addition mathematics teachers – perhaps because of their training and the nature of their discipline – have tended to be a relatively reactionary group, frequently behind their colleagues in curriculum reform and development. These factors partially explain the reluctance of many mathematics teachers to teach their subject to mixed-ability groups.

The unpopularity of mathematics itself, however, is not in dispute. To revert to the previous analogy, it is a path that few enjoy walking, and the majority have little or no idea where it leads. For many pupils in school today it is an academic excursion unwillingly undertaken, and much that is 'learned' is forgotten as soon as the final examination has been completed. Mathematics teaching has been notably unsuccessful in the past, and it is only within the last decade that real attempts have been made to remedy what has been rightly described as a crisis situation. It is perhaps too early to judge the effects of recent curriculum projects and the introduction of modern mathematics into school syllabuses, but because most developments in this field still adhere to the 'body of knowledge' theory (the linearity theory is axiomatic to most of them), when the dust settles I fear that the old problems, including the un-popularity, will remain.

None of the above suggests that heterogeneous grouping is some kind of panacea that mathematicians have been seeking. Many schools have unstreamed not primarily for academic reasons, ie to increase the efficiency or effectiveness of subject teaching, but rather, rightly, for social and more general educational reasons, or else under political pressure. As a result mathematics teachers have found themselves timetabled to teach mixed-ability groups of varying mixes and at different levels. This may have been the direct result of school policy, agreed department policy, or, perhaps worst of all, the whim of an individual head of department. Of the teachers who have faced this situation only a few have met with success. Many have reverted to banding or setting where this has been possible (or allowed), and many more have struggled to cope using traditional methods and with an outdated philosophy, complaining bitterly that unstreaming doesn't work. This is the key to the problem. As L. C. Taylor writes in *Resources for learning*, 'It [unstreamed teaching] requires new properties and new skills . . . To use inappropriate old methods of teaching in unstreamed classes is . . . to embrace frustration; to urge ill-defined new methods is to invite exhaustion or confusion.'[2]

The real advantage of being asked to teach mathematics to mixed-ability groups is that the teacher needs to rethink not only how he is going to teach mathematics, but also what he is going to teach and how he will organise his teaching. Hopefully this will lead him to question his own philosophy of mathematical education, resulting in a restatement of aims and objectives. Those who have accomplished this agree that it is a most rewarding, stimulating and worthwhile exercise, and when translated into practice results in far more effective mathematics teaching. Of course, those who do not accept the case for unstreaming may argue that this rethinking can take place in any case and does not require internal reorganisation into mixed-ability groups to initiate it. However, this is rarely borne out in practice – certainly many of the more interesting curriculum development projects and other interesting innovations are taking place within the context of mixed-ability work. What follows is an attempt to show that a solution to the crisis situation mentioned earlier lies in the combined strategy of mixed-ability mathematics and a radical approach to the philosophy of mathematical education.

AIMS
The Newsom report[3] provides a starting point:

> Few . . . of our pupils are ever likely to become mathematicians, but some may well come to find satisfaction in mathematical work . . . Our aim in the teaching of mathematics to all pupils, to those of average and below-average ability *no less* than to those with marked academic talent, should be to bring them to an interest in the content of mathematics itself at however modest a level.

124

What is needed is work that is meaningful to the pupils and work that they feel is worthwhile. It is not sufficient for the teacher to decide that a particular topic ought to be taught, a certain law learned or a skill acquired; what matters is whether the work is relevant to the individual pupil's needs, interests and experiences. This is not to say that the knowledge or skills acquired must be useful. Too much has been made of this aspect of relevance and has often meant that the 'How long will it take to fill a bath with ten inches of water if the plug is out?' type of problem has been replaced by an only apparently more meaningful exercise such as 'Calculate the area of the discotheque floor in square decimetres.'

Teaching should stimulate pupils to produce fresh, imaginative and creative work, at the same time ensuring that the mathematical structure and ideas involved are genuinely understood. How many ideas or concepts are acquired is of secondary importance, for contrary to popular (particularly parental) belief, very little of the mathematics taught in schools between the ages of eleven and sixteen is of use to, or even remembered by, the majority in later years. The feeling, shared by teachers, parents and examiners, that there is x ground (concepts, theorems, laws) to cover in y years needs to be dispelled once and for all.

We must be concerned with the broader aspects of mathematical education. Our aims should be to encourage pupils to think logically and help them to reason – in a sense to teach them how to think like mathematicians; to assist them in the communication of their ideas, both in written and spoken form; to help them generalise from the particular; and to bring some measure of success to all pupils. At the same time we must ensure that their intellectual demands – at whatever level – are satisfied; and be especially concerned that they enjoy their work in mathematics. Teachers anxious to pursue this last aim may well find themselves hindered by the puritanical view held by many parents even today, that if their children are enjoying their work at school then it is either a soft option or a waste of time. This view reflects sadly upon the parents, their frustration and perhaps their own lack of job-satisfaction. It is regrettable that this is allowed to permeate the curriculum, and teachers must be prepared to oppose it. Paul Goodman puts it this

125

way: 'Fundamentally, there is no right education except growing up into a worthwhile world . . . our excessive concern with problems of education at present simply means that the grown-ups do not have such a world.'[4]

STRATEGY

If the key to successful mixed-ability mathematics lies in a reassessment of aims then the realisation of these aims centres upon the provision of the right motivation for learning. It is here that there is a shift of emphasis, for the mixed-ability group teacher needs to be concerned primarily with learning and far less with teaching. His role changes from that of a communicator to that of a promoter. He must strive to provide the best learning situation, generate an equable climate for learning to take place, and use every available means to foster and encourage learning in whatever shape or form.

Children are innately curious and naturally keen to acquire new skills and develop new ideas. Mathematics teachers, particularly when dealing with older pupils, seem to have a knack of first ignoring and subsequently destroying what should be their greatest asset, for it is upon this natural motivation that we should build. Children may want to learn or do some mathematics at, say, thirteen for a variety of reasons: because they find the work interesting and enjoyable; because they can see that it is useful (in science for example); because they have been successful at it; because they like the teacher; or because their girl friend likes doing it. None of these reasons should be deprecated. They all provide foundations upon which to build.

Pupils must be given far greater freedom if their enthusiasm is to be harnessed. This should include the freedom to study the aspect of the work that appeals to them, to choose their own approach within a specific subject area, and also to choose the people with whom they work on a task. Where possible they should be allowed to consult whichever available teacher they prefer. At a later stage it will include the freedom to choose what type of mathematics course they wish to follow or whether to study mathematics at all. This necessitates similar freedoms for the teacher, and rightly so. He must be free to determine what materials and resources are available and what syllabuses, if any. He must provide the most suitable course, or be given the freedom to write his own, including the choice of appropriate methods of assessment.

These freedoms are obviously interrelated and in some cases interdependent, and all demand considerable responsibility on the part of both teacher and pupil. For pupils there will be degrees of freedom and guidance dependent upon age, maturity and experience. Pupil-teacher relationships founded upon trust and respect are essential for the success of individual- and small-group work within a mixed-ability framework. Respect must be mutual, not only for the teacher as someone prepared to share knowledge and ideas, to help and to listen, but also for the pupil as an individual with a valid contribution to make. Discussion between pupils and between pupil and teacher, and conversation (not monologue) are an essential of mixed-ability mathematics. A relaxed informal atmosphere, where children feel free to question, debate and argue mathematical points with their teacher and each other must be fostered. If this occurs then exchanges like the following example may become common-place in the classroom:

Class: Twelve-year-olds   *Topic: Triangles*

William   You said yesterday that the angles of a triangle always add up to 180°.

Teacher   Yes. You agreed too.

William   Yes (*hesitating*), but they can't always.

Teacher   Why not?

William   Not sure, I don't think they will . . .

Teacher   Did you demonstrate that it worked with one triangle when you cut out . . .

William (*interrupting*)   Yes, but suppose we didn't draw it on card?

Teacher   OK. What do you suggest?

William   Don't know. Paper would be the same.

Teacher   What about the wall, or the board . . .

William (*interrupting*)   They're all flat!

William leaves the group and disappears into the resources/equip-

127

ment room. He returns with a cylindrical tin.

William   What about on here?

Teacher   What do you think?

William   Bet I'm right!

William disappears again and returns a few minutes later with a football, on which he has chalked several triangles.

William   The tin wasn't any good, couldn't draw on it, but I'm right anyway. On a football the angles [of a triangle] can add up to anything!

Teacher   Anything?

William   Yes.

Teacher   OK. Can you draw one with the angles adding up to 1000°?

Five minutes later . . .

William   No. You can't have more than 900°.

Teacher (baffled)   Why not?

William   Well. At this point [*indicating one vertex of a triangle chalked on the ball*] there are 360° and the same here [*second vertex*] and here [*third vertex*]. That's 1080°. Right? But you can't have less than 180° inside a triangle so this triangle [*indicating the 'major' triangle on the sphere's surface*] can't have more than 900°.

Teacher   Is this a triangle?

William   Yes, of course it is, it's got three sides and three angles.

Teacher   Why can't you have less than 180°?

We are interrupted here by another pupil and William leaves to investigate further on his own.

ORGANISATION

How can the mathematics department of a school be organised effectively to achieve the aims and objectives outlined above? The unity of purpose of the department's teaching members is vital. The problems associated with the staffing of a department or team in which all are committed to mixed-ability teaching are numerous and complex, and success will depend as much upon good fortune and individual personalities, as upon any skill exploited by the head of department or any amount of in-service training. How and when departments decide to begin mixed-ability teaching will vary enormously and will be influenced by a variety of factors including several discussed below and some extra-departmental ones. It must be clearly understood beforehand (because of the extra demands, mental and physical, made upon staff teaching mixed-ability mathematics), that if this work is undertaken unenthusiastically or with only half the staff genuinely in sympathy with the approach, the consequences are likely to be even more disastrous than the perpetuation of the present streamed and setted situation.

Physical unity is easier to achieve. Many schools tend to group rooms together for subject purposes and in newer schools purpose-built accommodation may be provided (not that this is always ideal or even suitable; far too many schools are still being erected with inadequate facilities for mathematics). Inevitably physical provision will vary. There seems to be some reluctance on the part of mathematics teachers to ask for or demand the facilities they require; many accept the status quo however unsuitable. Advisers, planners and architects can only advise, plan and design the sort of departments that mathematicians want if they are adequately briefed. Until recently there has been little such briefing, and so while science, craft, home economics, languages, drama and music have been generously provided with specialised facilities, mathematics teachers have had to be content with a few traditional classrooms with rows of desks 'equipped' with a solitary visual aid – a blackboard.

Ideally a suite or block of rooms is required, containing a workshop, a resources area, an office, a few small open work-spaces surrounding or adjacent to the resources area, and an appropriate number of classrooms. Flexibility of room usage within the department and within each room is important. The layout should facilitate movement of pupils around the department, especially to and from the workshop and resources area, both of which should be open areas – not only to allow for freedom of access but also to enable staff to exercise a greater degree of control over the use of equipment and materials. The workshop will need running water, electric power points, good lighting, a woodwork bench with a vice, and Formica or similarly topped workbenches with adequate drawer and cupboard space for equipment. The work areas and classrooms should be furnished with tables (rectangular and/or hexagonal) and chairs, and at least one classroom should be fitted with full blackout and projection facilities in addition to any central facilities of this sort that the school may possess. The resources area is essentially an open-plan book and materials store which can in addition house a mathematics library and reprographic equipment. Finally, and frequently forgotten, the pupils will need plenty of room to work in, generous pin-board areas for displaying finished work and adequate storage space for work not yet completed.

This is an ideal which must be aimed at, and given time, patience and constant badgering a great deal could be done in many schools to come near this happy situation.

The organisation of the pupils will, of course, depend upon school policy, certainly in terms of how they are grouped upon entry, but I will assume, and would hope, that we are dealing with genuine mixed-ability groups with no remedial stream, and withdrawal of pupils only in exceptional circumstances. In many smaller schools (up to six forms of entry) it is possible that for the first time eleven-, fifteen- and seventeen-year-olds will be scheduled for mathematics at the same time. This can generate its own special advantages, both mathematically in the cross-fertilisation of ideas and socially with the increased responsibility placed upon older pupils to help their juniors – especially if the department is on an open-plan basis as was suggested earlier.

The composition of learning groups within a class will vary from teacher to teacher and from topic to topic, and will inevitably be dictated by the available facilities. It is important that each teacher should be free to determine which method of classroom organisation allows him to develop his talents to the full. (Though certain methods may not be suitable for mixed-ability work.) Some teachers will feel a need for class teaching some of the time, others never at all, although no class teaching may mean that several of the advantages of having a heterogeneous group are wasted. Douglas Barnes has written about the value of learning in small groups, and this should be an essential ingredient.[5] Grouping is likely to be in threes or fours, either friendship groups or, for certain topics, more highly structured arrangements. Others will prefer pupils to work in pairs and all should allow for pupils to work individually whenever appropriate. The precise organisation is not important but a blend of all the above is probably both right and necessary.

The deployment of the staff presents fewer problems. As all groups are, in one sense, equal, the streaming of teachers, an indefensible but widespread practice in mathematics, is avoided.[6] But in an open-plan mixed-ability situation continuity of pupil-teacher relationships becomes increasingly important. One possibility is to keep one teacher with each class for the first three years (ages 11–14) and then another teacher for the following two years (ages 14–16). The problem of personality clash when pupil and teacher fail to get on is alleviated in the open-plan department, as pupils will come into contact with other teachers during lessons fairly frequently.

I am often asked 'How do you deal with thirty-five children in a 35-minute lesson? – That's one minute each.' This type of question underlines the difficulty that many teachers have in appreciating the consequences of their role change. In the right circumstances pupils are capable of working on their own, (ie without the direct supervision of a teacher), often for long periods of time and far longer than many teachers realise or are prepared to allow. When teachers interfere too frequently many pupils resent this just as much as others resent lack of help. The right circumstances include freedom of access to materials, equipment and books (books that are readable – one of the real problems in mixed-ability mathematics is the lack of these) and the teacher's willingness to trust children to work even when not directly supervised. When pupils need help much of each lesson will be spent talking to them, individually or in groups, encouraging, suggesting, cajoling, inquiring and in particular observing, listening and assessing. In such groups pupils may help each other and should be encouraged to talk and listen to each other. On the whole teachers will spend longer periods of time with pupils, but less frequently.

When pupils have previously been streamed or are used to more traditional methods, they too will take time to adjust. During this period it may be necessary to increase the staffing ratio in some way to overcome the problems created by large numbers of pupils demanding attention simultaneously. One solution is to have two teachers with each class in the first two years for part of the week. Another possibility is to have three teachers spread between two classes blocked together, the third member acting at a floater or trouble-shooter. Both methods have advantages but the latter offers the opportunity for some measure of team teaching if this is felt to be desirable. In either case the increased staffing ratio can be attained by using a proportion of the otherwise remedial allocation (only possible in a fully unstreamed school) or by departmental staff accepting fewer free or non-teaching periods, or both. Older pupils, particularly prospective college of education students, can help children with reading difficulties, advise on use of equipment or discuss problems with other pupils. This can be a considerable asset and of mutual benefit, if undertaken seriously and as a regular commitment.

TEACHING METHODS

Departmental organisation dealt with so far has largely concerned rooms, staff, pupils, furniture, etc. Although these will present problems, solutions can often be found or effective compromises established. Far greater difficulties are likely to be encountered in the structure and passage of the lessons themselves.

There are at least two distinct approaches each offering a variety of possibilities.

1 *Theme or topic common to the whole class*
   (a) *Teacher directed* Not solely class teaching, although it is likely to start this way and then to recur at intervals with usual class discussion. Pupils use text books and worksheets, both suitably graded. Teacher maintains overall control of rate of working and depth of coverage of material. Well structured – teacher has clear picture of syllabus to be covered.
   (b) *Teacher initiated* Theme/topic introduced by teacher using blackboard, film, discussion, display, demonstration, TV programme, worksheet, etc. After brief initial coverage

of any underlying concepts, rapid diversification of work dependent upon pupils' interests and aptitudes. Variety of books, worksheets, workcards and equipment needed. Teacher intervention and direction as appropriate. Teacher uncertain beforehand as to how the topic will develop.

(c) *Pupil choice* Pupil makes initial choice of topic (perhaps within a range determined by the teacher) and follows his own pattern leading to highly individualised work with little or no structure. Suitable reference books are essential as well as other resources.

2 *Individual themes or topics*

(a), (b) or (c) as above but with (a) being feasible only occasionally.

'Theme' and 'topic' need clarification here. A theme will encompass more subject matter, a greater number of mathematical ideas and therefore of possibilities than will a topic – which can probably be more sharply defined. Themes might include number, shapes, measurement or relationships, whereas topics might be networks, aids to calculation, triangles or area.

Of the two approaches I prefer the first only from a practical point of view. In an ideal world with ideal staffing ratios the second must be preferable. But the administration involved when thirty to forty pupils are all engaged on different themes or topics and not just on different aspects of or at varying levels within each theme or topic, as would be the case in (2), is prohibitive for all but the most experienced and dedicated teachers. With the first approach the teacher must decide when the class should switch to another theme or topic. (When the most or least able has reached a certain stage? When the class is generally anxious for a change? When a new topic has appeared out of the old one?) Most teachers adopting this approach will use their professional judgement to make this decision.

The teacher will always need a ready supply of work and ideas up his sleeve, particularly for the most able and imaginative pupils, for whom there must be more challenging tasks than the mere repetition of more difficult exercises. Equally, there is little point in extensive and unremitting practice of the same elementary concepts with the less able pupils for the entire time span of the theme or topic in the hope that 'something will stick', a procedure which is too readily adopted with the bottom streams of many of our schools.

Whether themes or topics are chosen will naturally vary from teacher to teacher and from term to term, and the time-span will vary accordingly, but as a rough guide I would suggest a minimum of one week per topic and maximum of six weeks per theme. The combination of (a), (b) and (c) used will depend largely upon individual teachers' preferences and experience, with newer teachers graduating from (a) to (c) as they gain experience.

Homework is frequently seen as a problem with mixed-ability mathematics, but with a little thought, anticipation and an awareness of what each pupil is engaged upon in the lesson, appropriate homework is easily determined. Homework is the natural extension or completion of work undertaken in class, and provided pupils understand the nature of their work and their immediate objectives they will determine their own, and the formal setting of homework will disappear.

The following outline of the development of one boy's work, taken from notes made at the time by the present writer, will give a little of the flavour of the theme/topic approach.

Mixed-ability group of eleven-year-olds

Theme: Number   Organisation of theme: Method (b). A duplicated handout suggested six possible starting points. Michael's time (just over five weeks) was spent as follows:

1 *Number patterns* Investigation of various number patterns including series of numbers. Triangular numbers led (accidentally via a cross-reference in the index of a library book) to Pascal's triangle.
2 *Pascal's triangle* Number patterns again and situations leading to the formation of the triangle. A little about the life and work of Blaise Pascal and therefore the invention of the mechanical calculator.
3 *Desk calculators* Michael wanted to learn how to use one (hand rotary type) and did so by trial and error and assisted by a large

134

wallchart. The wallchart also indicated other modern methods of calculation including the use of computers.

4 *Computer programming*   I was doubtful when Michael asked about this but agreed, under pressure, to let him have a go! As the school was already making use of a postal computer service, using the programme language Algol, this was not difficult to arrange. Michael wrote two short and simple numerical programmes. One worked, but his interest flagged before the other was completed, partly due to the time delay and some unfortunate data preparation errors.

5 *Punched cards*   I intervened here and directed Michael to some work with punched cards, relating it to the binary number system and the previous topics. From this Michael moved on to number bases in general.

6 *Number bases*   A little of the history of counting and number systems and then calculations in any base. Use was made early on of the Dienes multi-base blocks. The wheel had now turned full circle as topic (6) was one of the other starting points on the initial handout.

CURRICULUM

In the last decade many schools have adopted highly developed courses or packages as the main and often only ingredient of their mathematics curriculum. This has been especially true where schools have unstreamed, and although understandable it is regrettable. Faced with the strangeness of the mixed-ability situation and the problems it poses, teachers have presumably felt that at least as far as the curriculum is concerned they could lean upon a ready-made prop and rely upon the security of a respectable nationally or regionally recognised recipe for mathematical education.

Where the dependence upon such a package is total the policy must be mistaken, for it assumes the acceptance of the 'body of knowledge' argument discussed at the beginning of this chapter. The absurdity of this is highlighted by the substantial differences in approach and content, adopted in the numerous schemes and packages. It seems unlikely once a department has formulated its aims and objectives that a single set of books, slides, workcards and

135

overhead transparencies will be adequate. It is too easy to accept a nationally produced curriculum package and hope that it is in accord with both the teachers' objectives and the children's needs. This undiscriminating adoption of, and in some cases slavish devotion to, mathematics courses, schemes or packages should give teachers considerable cause for concern.

What policy then should a mathematics department adopt when designing its curriculum? Teachers should, I believe, be eclectic, selecting the books, materials and ideas that they consider to be suitable, worthwhile and most appropriate to their aims and relevant to their pupils' interests and aptitudes. They should not assume because a scheme or a book treats its subject in an attractive, practical and acceptable way that this necessarily implies any recommendation for the same scheme or author for either a different topic or a different age group. They should ignore the modern *versus* traditional maths argument, accepting that both have an essential part to play in any school curriculum, and that a successful policy will blend the best of the old and the new.

The curriculum must be open-ended and allow for diversification at all stages. Teachers should not organise their classes to complete various topics in set periods of time and indeed should never feel under pressure to cover ground or finish the syllabus. Any syllabus or outline plan of work must be open to modification and alteration by the pupils themselves; here is real curriculum development, a dynamic process reflecting the moods and interests of the recipients and satisfying their thirst. At no time should a teacher feel the need to say 'No, I'm sorry, you can't do that now because . . . we haven't got the time . . . it isn't in the syllabus . . . you won't be able to cope with . . . we haven't done quadratic equations and you'll need them . . .' Doors must be left open, and as children progress in their own way they will evolve their own curriculum and the teacher should take note of it.

Curriculum planning should take into account the fact that departmental staff may themselves be rightly regarded as a mixed-ability group, if by ability we mean here teaching skill, experience and interests. Individual teachers' strengths must be exploited and called upon to support or complement others' weaknesses. Perhaps most important, the planning must allow theory to follow or evolve from practice. With depressing regularity school syllabuses announce, for example: 'Autumn Term: Indices. Theory and use of logarithms.' At a recent meeting a teacher asked me 'How can you teach logs. without doing indices?' Is this an example we follow in our own lives? How many of us take a course in telecommunications before learning how to use the telephone? Imagine the frustration of an unmechanical and not very able eighteen-year-old denied a driving licence because he couldn't follow the theory of the internal combustion engine. Logarithms are an aid which can open doors to mathematics hitherto unattainable, as can the desk calculator. (Do we teach pupils how that works?) This is not to deny that there is some intrinsic, some would say academic, value in studying the theory of logarithms; but this may not and probably will not be appreciated by the majority of pupils at the time when their use is taught. Motivation to learn more about a theoretical basis may come later – if so, good; if not, no matter. Motivation for practical experience will probably come first.

The implications of this style of curriculum planning are that pupils will follow a variety of syllabuses or courses and that the approach of individual teachers will vary considerably within the broad framework outlined earlier. This will create organisational problems which can only be resolved by constant discussion between staff, both formally and informally.

RESOURCES

It will have become apparent that successful mixed-ability mathematics is dependent upon the provision of the right sort of resources, all of which are readily available. Availability is the keynote here. Departments and schools often put too many of their books, materials and items of equipment under lock and key or out of bounds. Of course an open policy presents the problems of theft, damage and increased temptation, but these matters will not be the sole concern of one department but of the school or community as a whole. Unless the school has a meaningful policy of social education, and until the majority of pupils develop a real sense of responsibility, departments may suffer financial loss. Even so, this is likely to be a small price to pay for the increased freedom of operation. The alternative is illustrated by a remark made by a lecturer a couple of months ago when the present writer was visiting his college. 'The students use this building in the evening,' he said 'so the library will be locked.'

Mathematics teachers have fallen a long way behind their colleagues in the development and production of suitable resources largely because, until relatively recently, mathematics was considered to be an academic (ie theoretical) subject rather than a practical one. An active department will require many of the combined facilities of art, craft and science. In addition to conventional tools such as compasses, rulers and protractors, the mathematics department will need string, glue, mirrors, dice, playing cards, coins, counters, wooden cubes, adhesive tape, peg boards, pin boards, dominoes, geo-strips, wire, drinking straws, weighing scales, needles and thread, scissors, rice, marbles and matches. An essential supply of paper will include plain, graph, cartridge, squared, tracing, isometric and dot lattice, together with sheets of card in a variety of colours and thicknesses. Telephone directories, rail and bus timetables and motoring guides all provide splendid source material cheaply, as well as the more commonplace newspapers and magazines. Departments will only determine their precise requirements once mixed-ability teaching is under way. These requirements will not be met overnight and so, inevitably, a list of priorities must be established. This will be influenced by local factors, as well as personal interests.

Homemade workcards and worksheets must be easily, cheaply and readily produced, and a spirit duplicator together with workcard blanks and transparent protective envelopes (colours allow for grading or topic differentiation) are basic resources. A question frequently asked is whether one should keep worksheets and use them again. Despite the obvious savings such worksheets are often so specific to a certain group or class that to run off copies of a previous sheet for another group on a different occasion and perhaps employing a new approach, does little for the worksheets and nothing to assist spontaneity. Workcards and worksheets decrease the teacher's dependence upon textbooks, although the latter remain a valuable asset if carefully chosen and sensibly deployed. The number of copies required is drastically reduced as sets of books are rarely distributed to entire classes, and thus a far greater range and variety of textbooks may be purchased. All of the above requires the added support of a well-stocked library, housed in the department and supplementing the school library. In addition to the usual works of reference this could contain books on the history of mathematics and mathematicians, books of games and puzzles, topic books, activity books and books on associated subjects such as astronomy, logic, philosophy, circuits, surveying, computers and design. In all lessons pupils should be encouraged to seek out any relevant literature; and if space permits an area where they can sit, read and discuss this in comfort, that is an added bonus.

ASSESSMENT

A small number of schools take mixed-ability work in their stride for two or three years, but few continue in this way with pupils over the age of fourteen. It is undoubtedly examinations that cause teachers to set who are theoretically in favour of unstreaming. The vast majority of external examinations in mathematics in this country are designed to perpetuate the 'body of knowledge' theory referred to at the beginning of this chapter. They ensure that pupils with good memories are guaranteed success. The absurdity of the traditional pattern of teaching and learning mathematics, the handing down of knowledge and this dependence on memory is made strikingly clear by Gattegno in *What we owe children*.[7] Others have shown that there should be far more to assessment than examinations, yet the majority of teachers have chosen to ignore this.[8]

The role of assessment also demands careful analysis. I cannot see any intrinsic value in assessment, most forms of which (especially examinations) are obstructive to the real activity, eg the learning of mathematics. In a meritocratic society some form of external assessment may well be a necessary evil, in which case teachers should attempt to mitigate the effect of this upon their pupils and develop methods of assessment that allow it to be only an incidental activity.

How then should teachers approach assessment within the context of mixed-ability teaching? Internally there will be no need for specific assessment assignments (half-termly tests, yearly examinations, etc). With considerable individual and small-group work and thorough regular discussions with each pupil the teacher will be in a position to assess individual pupils' progress and attainment continually throughout the year. How the teacher records his observations is largely a matter of personal preference. The present writer prefers to keep a large, stiff-backed notebook for each class that he teaches, with a double-page entry for each pupil. Observations recorded here may result from a conversation in class with a pupil, listening to a discussion between pupils about their work, or reading a piece of homework. Notes written in this way are confidential, but may well form the basis of a report to a form teacher, tutor, parent or youth-employment officer.

Externally, teachers obviously have to accept a responsibility towards their pupils with regard to examination success for as long as the present examination situation continues. Where assessment is of a divisive nature (as with GCE and CSE at present) and until some form of common assessment is introduced, some compromise may be inevitable. A form that this is likely to take is the introduction of setting for the final year before examinations, if only to tie up loose ends and make sure that all candidates have covered the syllabus – no easy task after several years of largely individual study.

Only a minority will be capable of following existing GCE syllabuses, and the majority will get much better provision when schools are able to present their own syllabuses and methods of assessment for nationally recognised qualifications, as is now the case with CSE Mode 3. In this case course content should not be rigidly defined. A general statement of intent may be all that is required, outlining aims, objectives, methods of assessment and some indication of the likely areas of study.

Continuous assessment over the two-year course seems to offer more advantages at less cost to the learning. Over this period each pupil would be required to submit pieces of work for the purpose of assessment. Preferably this work should be undertaken by the pupil as a result of his or her own interest or involvement in a particular topic, but specific assignments of an investigative nature,

140

for example, can also be set. Methods of assessment will vary but a variety of methods is essential so that pupils who display a measure of creativity, powers of deductive reasoning or independence of thought all have the opportuntiy to demonstrate their ability. The precise nature of the assessment will obviously depend on the objectives specified, and for guidance on this I would recommend both *Examining mathematics at sixteen* and *Exploring achievement.*[9]

For notes to this chapter see pp 186–7

8 Teaching Science in Mixed-Ability Groups

J. Darke

INTENTIONS IN SCIENCE TEACHING

As teachers we are always concerned with the general educational development of our pupils; at times we focus on more specifically scientific ends. General intentions include increasing the pupils' self-respect and helping them to learn to value others, to establish high personal standards of attainment, to co-operate and to increase their self-control. Science teaching is well placed to help here since laboratories are dangerous places where order and self-control ensure safety and where co-operation is obviously more fruitful than dissension. Scientific intentions are generally directed at tacitly recognising science and getting an idea of what it feels like to be a scientist: becoming aware of acting and thinking scientifically instead of working in other ways. (Like historians or artists, for example.) This involves learning how to ask appropriate and productive questions, how to design ways of answering them, how to record and present observations and how to evaluate records. We are also interested in recognising patterns, ordering and simplifying what we see and learning the limitations of measuring equipment. (For a fuller account of scientific aims and objectives see *With Objectives in Mind,* a booklet in the Schools Council/Nuffield *Science 5–13* project).

Quite obviously a teacher's specifically 'scientific' intentions may contribute to a pupil's general education. Although acquiring information or scientific knowledge is not stated as an intention, it is nonetheless impossible to carry out any sort of inquiry without learning a number of facts, acquiring new skills and practising old ones; but learning facts for their own sake seems pointless. If the subject matter is selected according to context, the required facts will simply be tools to be used in the course of investigation.

PATTERNS OF TEACHING

There seem to be six distinct teaching patterns that one must evaluate when deciding on classroom strategies for mixed-ability science teaching:

1 Teacher directed, with all pupils studying the same topic.
2 Teacher directed, with several topics being studied.
3 Teacher directed, followed by pupil choice.
4 The teacher dictates the end-points, the pupils find their own way to them.
5 A combination of (3) and (4).
6 Completely independent choice by groups of pupils.

Pattern 1 is the traditional class-teaching pattern where everyone apparently goes through the same routines, with varying degrees of success. This pattern produced the need for streaming in the first place, since theoretically all pupils move at the same pace. The teacher acts mainly as an instructor, and there is very little opportunity for pupils to develop originality or creativity, however skilful the teacher. In this teaching pattern, the role of the pupils is as passive receivers. Since many sets of apparatus are required simultaneously, this is an expensive pattern for the science teacher to adopt.

Pattern 2, which is sometimes called the 'circus method', usually means in practice that a number of exercises involving the use of apparatus are carried out by the pupils, who move from one set of apparatus to the next. Often this pattern involves the use of worksheets. This pattern makes science teaching less dangerous, since danger points are static, and it is easier for the teacher to watch them. As with *pattern 1* there is little or no chance for the pupils to show initiative, since the instructions on the worksheets still come directly from the teacher. It does, however, have the advantage that the expense of apparatus is reduced, there being fewer identical sets in use at any one time; on the other hand, the presentation of each session may involve preparing a wide selection of items carefully integrated with the worksheet. This can be extremely time consuming.

Pattern 3 still has the teacher directing the class initially, but later in the lesson the pupils are allowed a certain freedom of choice. For example, the teacher might introduce a topic such as water. He would then direct investigations by the whole class of boiling and freezing points, and then allow the pupils to choose which further aspects of water they wished to study. Some would choose to study water as a solvent, others might decide to investigate the effects of detergents, the percentage of water in organisms, or density in relation to temperature.

Alternatively, pupils might be given instruction in the use of a particular technique, and then allowed to choose from a range of investigations all requiring the use of the technique. For example, the class might be given instruction in the use of the line transect, and then allowed to use this either for vegetation analysis or to find out how a certain factor influences the distribution of a particular species. Another variation on this pattern is to limit choice to a number of worksheets all of which derive from the initial theme.

The teacher using *pattern 3* has to change his role during the lesson. He starts as a director, but as choices are made he becomes more of a consultant, discussing the problems that arise as the pupils set out on the investigations that they have chosen. The pupils begin to see the need for someone better informed than they are, but there is room for them to display and develop constructive initiative.

The use of this pattern calls for considerable skill on the part of the teacher, who must select apparatus and materials very carefully. The teacher with a syllabus to follow may have some difficulty in deciding when to stop the pupils' investigations and go on to another topic, and the topic itself must be chosen with the greatest care if it is to give the pupils sufficient opportunity to choose their own subsequent investigations. If the pupils respond unenthusiastically to being allowed to choose their own investigations, this may be because the topic has been chosen with insufficient care, and does not in fact offer the pupils a real or interesting choice. Sometimes a discussion with the class may avert this kind of situation.

Pattern 4 requires the teacher to indicate to the pupils the direction their inquiries will take, but ostensibly leaves them to choose just how they will conduct their investigations in order to reach the conclusions that the teacher has indicated Often they are given a certain amount of time during which they are relatively free, and are expected to produce their results at the end of this period.

Usually the teacher acts as a consultant, helping pupils to get started and helping them with problems that may arise during their investigations. Since there is a set of common end-points, pupils quickly begin to exchange and modify ideas, and although the framework is obviously controlled, there is scope for a considerable amount of originality. During the pupils' investigations the teacher will be a needed and hopefully a welcome group member, but at the end he will return to a more traditional role as he summarises the work of the class, comments on the various approaches taken by different pupils, and makes sure that no essential facts have been overlooked. This pattern is a useful compromise for the teacher who has a syllabus to cover and a definite amount of factual material to convey, but who wishes to give his pupils the opportunity of making their own decisions and learning to ask original questions.

Pattern 5 uses the teacher as starter and summariser, but in between pupils have far more opportunity to attempt to work originally and creatively, and to become involved in taking the decisions about what they are going to do as well as how and when they are going to do it. The Schools Council/Nuffield *Science 5–13* project is ideal material for this approach to science teaching.

Pattern 6 requires the greatest amount of organisation and awareness on the part of the teacher. Where pupils are allowed to choose their own field of study, there is a risk that conditions can become chaotic and disorientating, which will result in both a lowering of the standard of work and a feeling of irritation at the apparent lack of progress. If this teaching pattern is to be used with any success, the direction in which the class is moving must be made very clear to all the pupils. As with the first pattern, the whole class will tend to be working on the same topic, the difference being that it will be a topic that the pupils have chosen themselves. During the investigations of each topic, there are a number of possible variations and directions that the class may take, with all the risks and benefits that this entails.

GROUP SIZE

Children may be organised individually, or in groups of various sizes, which of course can include the whole class working as a group. But generally when a whole class is being taught one is forced to make the completely unacceptable assumption that the class constitutes a homogeneous group. The teacher either has to address principally the pupils at the middle of the ability range, which will make the other pupils dissatisfied, or he has to alternate between teaching the quickest and the slowest, which generally will mean that the pupils at the middle of the ability range will suffer. The wide range of abilities in many mixed-ability classes makes either of these methods impossible. Consequently the teacher usually divides the class into groups, and generally it is wise to give a great deal of thought to this division. Important factors are:

> The teaching pattern to be used.
> The importance of discussion of the work being done.
> Whether worksheets are being used.
> How easy it is to get pupils started.
> The number of groups the teacher can attend to.
> The possibilities of co-operation or friction in a class.
> The degree of danger in the work to be done.
> The availability of apparatus, gas, water etc.
> The ability of the children, especially reading ability.
> The nature of the room; its shape and working surfaces.

The group should be small enough for pupils to feel that they are part of it, and small enough for each member to be actively involved in discussing, planning and carrying out the interesting operations. It should be large enough for the teacher to be able to focus on a sufficiently small number of reference points.

Individual work in a large class has several disadvantages. It will usually mean using worksheets or workboxes, but one cannot assume

146

that all the pupils can read well enough, or that the teacher will have time enough to deal with the problems that may arise. Preparation of both equipment and worksheets is also very time-consuming; the writing of the latter in particular taking an almost disproportionate amount of time and skill.

To divide a class into pairs immediately eases things, although a worksheet system is generally necessary, as the teacher may have fifteen pairs working in one class. For pupils to work in groups of three or four presents fewer difficulties; groups of this size are far more manageable, and it is easier for members of such groups to gain access to the teacher and to equipment and services. The fact that there will be fewer groups in any one class will mean that the teacher need not rely so heavily on worksheets, but on the other hand the larger the group the greater the likelihood of friction between its members, particularly because there will be fewer chances for each member to do the more interesting parts of group activities. This is probably outweighed by the advantages of groups of this size, one of the most important of which is that it is probably the best size of group to accommodate non-readers and to encourage a fertile exchange of opinions between all group members. The dangers that are always present in science laboratories are minimised, and the teacher can probably communicate best with groups of three or four pupils. Three pupils is probably the best number, as there is a slight tendency for groups of four to split into two pairs. The teacher will probably be happiest with groups of three as the norm and groups of four or two on occasion.

Having decided on the size of the group, the teacher also has to decide upon a basis for grouping. The rationale of mixed-ability groups is that exchanges of mutual benefit take place between group members of differing backgrounds and abilities, and in particular stimulating exchanges of ideas. One should therefore aim to create genuine mixed-ability groups. preferably with minimal interference from the teacher. Friendship groups seem to work best, as one might expect, but of course this can sometimes lead to the reverse of a mixed-ability group, if all the friends in the group are of high ability, for example, or if they are all non-readers. If this happens it is probably best to intervene and disperse the members of the

147

group, even if this causes some friction or resentment. Ultimately the teacher has the responsibility of organising a class in the interests of the pupils, but if this organisation can follow the natural friendship patterns this may provide a useful sanction.

Whether pupils should be allowed to move from one group to another will depend on the pattern of teaching. If one was teaching in the style of pattern 6 it would not be wise to permit this as a newcomer to a group would lack the necessary shared background.

In the first year at a secondary school children usually group themselves according to two criteria. Either they choose other children known to them from their previous school, or they choose those with whom they happened to be sitting in the first registration in the new school. These groups tend to stay together during the first year.

The teacher may wish to group children according to their previous school reports, perhaps taking into account such factors as sex or IQ. In practice such groups, which are imposed by the teacher, will almost certainly prove unsatisfactory, mainly because of friction between group members. This is undesirable in any subject, but particularly so in science, where uncontrolled or aggressive behaviour can quickly lead to injury.

PRACTICAL PROBLEMS
Starting the lesson

In science teaching the two major problems are (1) making sure that all the pupils understand exactly what is to be done, and (2) organising the supply of all the necessary materials, apparatus, etc.

1   Where the teacher is acting as the director of activities, as in teaching patterns 1–5, the best method of ensuring that all the pupils understand exactly what is to be done is to use either worksheets or an oral introduction. If one is following teaching pattern 6, on the other hand, one will often find that most of the pupils manage quite well. When they are allowed freedom of choice, the work that they have just completed often leads on to the next topic, and pupils seem to have much more of a sense of direction when they are allowed to assume more responsibility

for the direction that their studies take. If occasionally a group seems to have difficulty in making progress, the teacher who is allowing his pupils freedom of choice is himself able to spare the time to give the group the help it needs. If homework is expected to be done, then the group can formulate its intentions in class and give them more detailed expression as a homework exercise, which allows the teacher to learn in advance what is likely to happen during a particular lesson.

Whether the teacher uses pattern 6, giving his pupils real freedom of choice, or whether he prefers the more gradual transition from teacher direction to increased choice, as in patterns 3 and 5, the following classroom strategy seems likely to be successful.

(A division into groups of three or four is assumed).

(a) The teacher enters the classroom with a set of ideas or topics already prepared. For example:

Metals.
Life in water.
Myself.
Paper.

(b) The teacher invites suggestions about the kind of areas of study the pupils wish to become involved in. If the response is poor, he falls back on the list as in (a) above.

(c) After a discussion between members, each group is asked to prepare a list of possible studies, based on the previously agreed topic.

(d) The teacher asks each group to read out its ideas, and assembles the ideas in the form of a blackboard summary. This summary can often stimulate fresh ideas, and if the children are given a free hand it can sometimes grow embarrassingly large.

(e) The teacher assesses the suggestions and eliminates those that are undesirable from his point of view.

(f) The teacher requires each group to choose a topic from the list of acceptable topics that results from (e). They may select their own suggestion or any other, as they see fit.

149

(g) The group then writes its own programme of possible investigations or activities, often with the teacher's help. Often this can be usefully done as homework, and hopefully the opportunity to make their intentions explicit in this way helps pupils to give order and direction to their work. Their own part in regulating their own behaviour and activities increases their self-control and gives them the feeling of having a large personal stake in their own education.

2 The problem of practical supply tends to diminish as the teacher gains experience. In the more teacher-directed teaching patterns the usual methods are often adequate – for example, trays prepared beforehand, and pieces of apparatus assembled in trays containing the right equipment for the work being done. It is then quite simple to make sure that everything has been returned at the end of the lesson.

When pupils are allowed to choose their own topics for study, the problem of supply of equipment becomes more complex. If the pupils' choices are based on existing worksheets a box can be prepared for each of the activities that are likely to develop from the worksheets, with each box containing all the equipment for a particular activity. This method has the disadvantages that preparing the boxes adds to the time already spent on the worksheets; each box needs to be carefully checked at the end of a lesson; and it is necessary to duplicate a lot of items of equipment.

If the teacher is using the more pupil-based teaching patterns (3–6) two possible techniques exist. The teacher can be given a list of requirements by each group, preferably at the end of one lesson in preparation for the next; or the children can fetch their own equipment from the shelves. Neither system is perfect; if the teacher spends too much time carrying equipment he does so at the expense of talking to the pupils about the work in hand. If the children take the equipment themselves, the teacher will have to devise procedures to prevent theft and to prevent accidents with poisonous and dangerous or expensive materials and equipment. It is worth mentioning in passing that if the teacher is using teaching pattern 6 a lot of these disadvantages are eliminated; this may be because the pupils feel that they have a greater stake in what is happening, or it may be because this way of teaching science makes it necessary to have less equipment in use at any one time.

If ancillary assistance is available this can remove much of the load from the teacher, but it does not remove the responsibility, and care should be taken that all the activity in the room is under the teacher's direction and that his assistant is not accepting responsibilities for which he is neither qualified or paid.

SEEING EVERYONE

The whole educational process in schools depends upon the personal contact made between the teacher and the pupils, and on the pupils being able to make this kind of contact between themselves. How much this actually happens will depend on the teacher-pupil ratio, the amount of lesson time, and the size of the group. Thus those who teach with larger blocks of time available, as in the four-session day, stand more chance of establishing this kind of contact with their pupils than do teachers who only teach for periods of thirty-five or forty-five minutes. On the same principle, teachers of science (as opposed to biology, physics or chemistry) will be at an advantage because they will have more teaching time with each class.

In an eighty-minute teaching session the actual time available in which the teacher can be in personal contact with the pupils is usually no more than sixty minutes, and if the pupils are working singly this allows only about two minutes per child. Two minutes is not much, especially if that is all the time available during the week, and this makes no allowance for times when the teacher will want to discuss matters with the whole class. If pupils are in groups of three or four, much more time will be available to each group. After five minutes with the teacher a group rightly feels that it has had a good deal of attention.

It is worth discussing the problem of finding time to make personal contact, and constantly bringing the subject to the attention

151

of pupils. If the teacher can establish the idea of himself as a person whose advice and experience are needed, the more willing will the pupils be to apply themselves to the work, but this depends entirely on being able to make all the members of the class feel that they are getting some of the teacher's time and personal attention every lesson.

It is a sound practice to encourage one member of each group to take a note of the points raised during the group's discussions with the teacher. This record can later be written up by all members of the group, and this will give the pupils both a useful reference point and a feeling of continuity. The practice of keeping records of transactions between teacher and pupils is generally to be recommended, but with fourteen- or fifteen-year-olds it will probably be more difficult for the teacher to make regular contact, especially if they are being continuously assessed for examination purposes, and therefore it will be even more valuable if the teacher can keep a diary of points raised with each group of pupils. If pupils also keep a record of these exchanges, they will be able to work more independently and fruitfully at times when the teacher cannot spare much time to talk to them.

HOMEWORK

Homework should always be the completion or the consequence of work done in class; it should not be set for its own sake. If pupils are being allowed to play an active part in the direction of their studies, they will also have to set their own homework, and the teacher must be prepared to accept very little homework one week, when the work in class does not give rise to much that must be finished off at home, and in return to receive more homework from pupils during a week that is more productive. If homework is the logical extension of the pupils' work, and is not merely a routine, and if the teacher is sympathetic when the amount of homework varies, then pupils are less inclined to evade homework. The homework that is the result of this increased choice by the pupils will be more varied, and consequently more interesting to pupils and more productive of group discussion.

152

WORKSHEETS

Worksheets are time-consuming to prepare, and after they have been in use for a while they are usually found to be unsatisfactory in some way, and therefore to need modification. This does mean that they can be made to suit the requirements of the teacher and the class, but often pupils working with worksheets come to rely too heavily on the teacher's directions.

Two kinds of worksheets are useful in science teaching. Some are suggestions and directions for practical work, and others are descriptions of techniques in constant use in science classes (eg, 'How to use a voltmeter'). It is useful when writing worksheets to note the following points:

Use a simple vocabulary.

Start with a clear statement of objective.

Be positive.

Use as few sub-clauses as possible.

Keep punctuation simple.

Give only one instruction at a time.

Present a clear and complete list of the equipment needed.

Give instructions on the kind of results table that will be needed before giving instructions on how to start the practical work.

Use diagrams that are as close as possible to the actual equipment that will be used (eg, if you have a particular type of voltmeter, make sure that your diagram is of that particular type too.)

Give instructions on how to conduct the inquiry.

Give clear and explicit warnings of danger and details of precautions.

Instruct the pupils to refer to the teacher at certain points, not only as a safety measure but also to increase the teacher's control (eg, 'Ask the teacher for acid'.)

Instruct the pupils to replace equipment and to clean up afterwards.

Refer back to make sure that any results tie in with the objectives.

Make suggestions on the next step to be taken when the worksheet has been finished.

STANDARDS

When mixed-ability work is discussed, even by those who are in favour of it, the most commonly expressed fear is that it may lead to 'a fall in standards'. It is therefore very important to consider what sort of standards are applicable, and also how these standards are to be arrived at. This applies to streamed and unstreamed work alike, although implicitly traditional standards apply to written work.

The basic criterion must always be either the child's actual or potential performance. Since the teacher will apply the standard, it must be his estimate of the child's performance and potential that is used, rather than the child's own. (Many teachers will have had the uneasy feeling that what children do is usually well below their capacity: which is in other words placing a higher value on their ability than the children would put upon it themselves.)

The teacher, then, has his own idea of the performance that a child is capable of, which he may have acquired in a variety of ways. But when a teacher evaluates a child's performance, he must always compare it with the child's best performance. Once a new quality of work has been achieved, this must become the new standard.

A teacher should not openly compare one child's attainment with another's. The differences in their backgrounds and personalities are so complex that they invalidate any such comparison. Thus children should not be subjected to marks, class lists or prizes. Marks should be replaced by remarks. Not only is the expression 'six out of ten', for example, an inadequate way of summarising the complexities of evaluating a piece of written work; it is also quite illogical to evaluate only written work, and to neglect to evaluate oral work, behaviour, or ability to assemble apparatus. The meaning of evaluation to both teacher and pupil should be made clear as a result of personal contact and communication. Interviews should be used as much as possible, and a running commentary should be used when marking a child's written work; this commentary will challenge the child's motive, for example, or question the effectiveness of his method and comment upon his results and interpretation of them. Appropriate summaries of these comments should be recorded in the workbook and when the workbook is full the teacher should keep it as a record. If the teacher uses a numerical marking system, he should keep it confidential from the child except when marking for direct examination purposes, as in CSE Mode 3.

QUESTIONS FROM CHILDREN

Questions are an essential part of scientific work. All experiments start with questions, and if pupils are to attain any sort of success they must work in an atmosphere that encourages exploration. Children's questions are particularly important if they are being allowed to choose their own topics, and if a teacher is allowing this kind of freedom of choice he must do all he can to establish the right sort of atmosphere and the right sort of questions. One useful technique is to pursue the idea that some questions are more productive than others. If the pupils are to be able to find their own answers to questions that crop up, then they must learn the importance of asking sufficiently precise questions. If a question is imprecise children can become confused because they cannot handle the amount of information involved. They may lack the background and equipment to answer the question. For example, a child cannot answer the question 'Why do nettles grow near walls?' experimentally because too many considerations are involved. The question which is used to start class or group activities must be refined in a dialogue between the teacher and the group until a realistic question leading to a limited and attainable aim has been formulated, so that it becomes possible to gather information with some sort of chance of providing an answer. Examples include 'Which mixture of sand and cement makes the strongest concrete?' or 'Does the depth of a bubble alter its size in water?'

One way to encourage an exploring atmosphere is by the use of a question-time. Few children have access to an informed adult who is willing to answer questions about the things which intrigue them. Many are discouraged at home since a question is often seen as an attack on the authority of the parent. If the teacher is willing to accept the role of receiver of questions, and if he makes an honest attempt to answer them, he can alter the whole atmosphere of a class for the better. This can often be used to fill an awkward gap before the end of a session, or when a class is unable to use the laboratories.

155

It is particularly successful with nine- to thirteen-year-olds. The questions will not always be about science, nor will the teacher always be able to answer them, but the fact that the teacher allows pupils to ask questions on their own initiative has the effect of putting a value on their questions. Here, too, it will be important for questions to be carefully framed if they are to be answered properly, which will reflect on the starter questions for free-choice work mentioned above. Sometimes this question-time may lead to a really productive discussion, where the teacher will perhaps take a minor role and allow the children to take a constructive part in the discussion. Where children's contributions are seen to be of interest they become increasingly willing to take part in the general swirl of conversation in the room.

One class in its first week in a comprehensive school asked the following questions, and went on to ask hundreds more during the year:

Why is money worth changing value?
Why is there one World Cup competition every four years?
What is plastic made from?
Do you have to have a good degree to be a scientist?
What makes your teeth ache?
Who invented the bridge?
What makes your ears stick out?
How can you make a continuous flow of static electricity?
Why are some people rich and not others?
If you drive fast do you use less petrol?
Why does copper turn green when rain falls on it?
Where does wood come from?
How do trees make wood?
Why don't bricks break when put in an oven?

Many questions naturally stimulate some sort of demonstration and allow the teacher to introduce ideas which he feels are important. Some will occur during discussions about the work that is being done, and it is often useful to encourage pupils to write down these, forming a supply of questions for future use. Other questions that are asked by pupils when working together in groups, and which simply form part of their conversation about the work they are doing, may play an important part in the learning process.

LANGUAGE

Language is often a problem in mixed-ability work, especially in science, where teachers often assume that a special terminology is necessary. But the problem is really much more complex than the problem of vocabulary. Douglas Barnes of the Leeds Institute of Education discusses the problem very fully in an unpublished paper called 'Learning in small groups'. On terminology he writes:

'The instructions relating to the Air Pressure apparatus contained the sentence: "Remember to give an explanation using the correct words." One can understand, of course, that a teacher of science might be concerned to encourage his pupils to use the terminology of his subject. He will, however, be more interested in whether they can use the scientific concepts for thinking with than in whether they can say words. The difficulty about telling children to use the "correct words" is that they may interpret it as an instruction about words rather than about concepts. If so, it may seem to them equivalent to telling them to make noises which sound scientific. We have seen how some of the children use "vacuum" and "air pressure" as vague labels which absolved them from thinking more analytically about the process referred to. It is conceivable that the instructions encouraged this. If we emphasise the use of stylistically appropriate language before pupils have sorted out how to use concepts, we may actually inhibit development (Piaget made this point in his comments on Vygotsky's book).'

And again:

'If teachers insist too soon on the so-called "language of the subject" they face the pupil with two tasks at once, organising thought and guessing what language is acceptable. Some able children can do this easily, but for others this demand is the death

157

of exploratory language, in speech or writing. Learning to play teacher's wordgame may be necessary to future specialists, but for most children it is only an extra barrier, for the word is no use to them until they have some grasp of the concept.'

For teachers who see the main aim of elementary science education as learning the language, mixed-ability work is likely to be an unhappy experience. It will be infinitely worse for their pupils, who are likely to become dissatisfied with making 'noises which sound scientific', and may lose interest and finally give up altogether.

It is much better to use words in general use and avoid the use of scientific jargon unless it is clearly necessary. There is no real advantage in using 'trachea' instead of 'windpipe', 'effervescent' for 'fizzy' or 'transparent' instead of 'see-through'. Sometimes the introduction of a scientific-sounding jargon word may give pupils a quite spurious feeling that they are making progress, and biology is particularly prone to becoming simply a naming activity, thereby deflecting attention from the processes and interactions involved. Some teachers may feel that to use everyday words implies a lowering of standards, but in reality it is only a matter of working to a less traditional standard, so that the interests and enthusiasms of pupils are encouraged rather than the use of scientific jargon. In fact, if one can encourage pupils and foster their enthusiasms, and establish a close personal contact and a feeling of mutual respect, it will actually be easier to introduce difficult terms when this is necessary, since children are only too anxious to do what is expected of them.

Douglas Barnes gives a further account of the importance of written and spoken language:

The American psychologist J. S. Bruner, summarising Piaget and other researchers in one sentence, once wrote: 'I suspect that much of growth starts out by our turning around on our own traces and recoding in new forms . . . what we have been doing or seeing, then going on to new modes of organisation with the new products that have been formed by these recodings.'

And as Bruner pointed out, the most powerful of these systems for recoding, and therefore reinterpreting, experiences is language. The journey from being able to parrot a phrase from teacher or book or imitate a process, or carry out a calculation, to being able to use the idea or the process to solve new problems in new areas is a long one. As Bruner says, an important part of this is turning around on our own traces and telling ourselves what we know. Teachers have become so habituated to thinking of language in terms of communication that many have ceased to consider that it also performs important subjective functions. These subjective functions can be summed up by saying that language is the major means by which we organise experience and make sense of it. If in the classroom we limit spoken language to the teacher telling and the pupil replying to cross examination, and limit written language to getting information from a book and writing it down to show the teacher that the work is done, we ignore and reject the function of speech and writing, as an instrument for reshaping experience, that is, as a means of learning. This is why we emphasise above that through language children can come to terms with new knowledge and relate it to what they already know. But this takes time: children need time to assimilate what they are learning by talking and writing about it in relation to what they know already. Too many classroom discussions and writing assignments ask children to relate strange information only to other strange information. The conversation is carried out but in terms of what the teacher knows while the child's other experience – in and out of school – is excluded. This prevents the children from engaging in significant recording of their experience – to return to Bruner's formulation . . . Once again we find . . . that the kind of learning which can go on in the groups is a matter of using language on the one hand to animate and reshape existing knowledge, and on the other to try out new knowledge as a way of reinterpreting the old. And these are certainly aspects of what Bruner referred to as 'recoding'.

Other less obvious problems arise from the unconscious use of the teacher's own day-to-day vocabulary and speech patterns and the insistence of many teachers that they should do nearly all the talking. The emphasis should be on children's talk because evidence increasingly points to the idea that most of us learn through talking. It is a truism to say that the person who learns most in a classroom is the teacher. This is an important reason why the usual pattern of organisation should be in small groups of three or four children, and talk about the problems and processes under investigation should not only be between the teacher and each group, but also within each group. As for the complexity of vocabulary and speech generally, all children benefit from simplicity on the teacher's part, and there is no reason why highly literate children need find this offensive.

AREAS OF STUDY

Within the limits of space, of knowledge on the teacher's part, and of practical provision, any area of study should start from children's own experience and interests particularly when they overlap with those of the teacher; there is a multitude of local possibilities such as the room itself, water, sand, batteries, air, traffic, which lend themselves to the teaching patterns previously described. Necessary techniques, such as measurement or the use of apparatus, will develop as needs to be filled, instead of children starting from 'measurement' as a topic and then finding ways of applying measurement.

Suitable sources for mixed-ability work include the Schools Council/Nuffield *Science 5–13* project; *Secondary Science* and *Explore and Discover* (Nuffield); and *Science for the Middle Years* by Gordon Hughes in collaboration with the present writer. The writers of the Nuffield *Combined Science* claim that their scheme has been used successfully with mixed-ability groups. The origin of their subject matter lies in the separate O level physics, chemistry and biology projects, so any attempt to use combined science with such groups must entail careful selection of the topic, and also thought about its appropriateness and mode of application.

All the above entail a choice by the teacher, so they can be used to capitalise on local possibilities. They should not be seen as courses in themselves. *Science 5–13* is particularly suitable because of the help given to the teacher in displaying the aims and objectives appropriate to science and correlating them with the developmental stages of the pupils concerned. But any teacher of science to mixed-ability groups will find that *With Objectives in Mind* is perhaps the most indispensable book of all.

The teacher must have the final decision but whatever the course decided on there will be plenty of opportunity to deal with the great natural laws and scientific principles. The more diverse the children's work, the greater the number of occasions when these laws are seen to be operating.

For notes to this chapter see p 187

9 Resources for Mixed-Ability Groups

M. P. Grant

If you asked the young boy who was crossing the playground at 2.15 pm on a Friday where he was going, he would probably reply 'Over to resources, Sir'. A new word has been added to the vocabulary of the writer's present school – a simple word, but, I think, indicative of the change that has come over the curriculum in the past few years.

If you went further, and asked him why he was going over to resources, he might tell you that he had certain things to find out, and hoped that he would be able to track them down in the resources centre. Probe a little more, and ask him how he would find the data, and another new phrase might come to light . . . OCCI! While he might not be able to remember that this stands for the optical coincidence co-ordinate index, he would perhaps tell you that it was the punched card index system standing in the corner of the resources centre and he would probably be pleased to show you how it worked if you accompanied him.

On arriving at the resources centre, a quick inspection would reveal a book library, classified according to the Dewey system, together with shelves containing periodicals and pamphlets, neatly housed in pamphlet boxes; filmstrips and films; audio and video tapes; certain pieces of reprographic equipment; a large table slide-viewer; a punched card index system together with a light box; overhead projector transparencies; and various study kits and arte-facts on display.

A resource, very simply, constitutes anything which serves as an object of study and which may facilitate the learning process. There

162

are, of course, many other definitions, but perhaps the most comprehensive is given in the Schools Council Working Paper no 43 *School Resource Centres*.[1]

> A resource includes anything which may be an object of study or stimulus for the pupil including books, periodicals, newspapers, press cuttings, pictures, diagrams, maps, charts, photo-copies and microforms, worksheets, slides, film strips, film loops, films, records, audio tapes, radio and television programmes, video tapes, slide tapes and film strip/record combinations, multi-media kits, programmed materials, models, specimens and realia, as well as individuals and objects in the community . . .

Leslie Ryder, ILEA adviser on resources, widens the definition still further by dividing resources into four categories:

1 People.
2 Spaces in a school.
3 Existing resources already in the school.
4 Outside resources – from national bodies, centralised bodies etc.[2]

It becomes obvious that all schools have resources of some kind and it would probably be surprising to members of staff if they were presented with an inventory of all that their schools possessed. How much lies dormant in the darkness of cupboards defies imagination! Teachers have a reputation as hoarders and unfortunately, like squirrels, they like keeping their spoils to themselves, rarely sharing them with colleagues. Thus many schools have little idea of what they possess, and duplication of certain materials may be rife.

If all schools already have resources, then why have they become a topic of such importance in the last few years? It is not sufficient to say that changes in the curriculum have necessitated a new look at teaching methods, as new needs have developed. If we are to identify these new needs, we must ask ourselves why there have been changes in the curriculum. The minor transformation that has taken place over the last decade has stemmed mainly from a general discontent among educationists and a sometimes traumatic review of the aims and objectives of existing syllabuses. As regards the

163

content of the curriculum, it is generally accepted that with the mass of new knowledge, no child could possibly learn all there is to know, and that to make available a mass of knowledge to be learned for its own sake is no longer a valid aim of education.

Talking of science teaching, Jevons comments that:

There is a built in tendency for syllabuses to become overloaded, with all the effects that has on *how* they are taught. As is widely recognised, cluttered syllabuses exert a baneful influence on the quality and style of science teaching.[3]

I am sure that his comments apply equally to subjects other than science. There has, too, been an increase in the study of the learning process, and the development of cognitive powers now ranks highly as an educational objective. To achieve this it is thought that more emphasis should be placed on creativity and autonomy of thinking. As Taba says, we no longer can assume that mastering well-organised knowledge automatically develops either autonomous or creative minds.[4]

The 1960s in particular saw the heyday of the philosophy of child-centred education, where children followed an integrated curriculum by means of self-directed activity, with the teacher taking responsibility for the creation of a suitably stimulating learning environment, and abandoning the old role of didactic instructor.

This was a message conveyed in the Plowden Report. During this time, too, comprehensive reorganisation was well under way, which meant effectively that schools were having to open their doors to deal with mixed-ability intakes. While streaming and setting became the two recognised methods of dealing with the difficulties of teaching different abilities, some schools experimented with mixed-ability group teaching.

We must also take into account the great technological revolution. Television and radio provided a most valuable teaching aid. Then came equipment for recording both sound and vision so that play-back facilities were well within the reach of schools. Other pieces of equipment became more common – filmstrip and film projectors, overhead projectors and a variety of reprographic machinery.

Thus we have seen a reappraisal of our existing curriculum structure, starting mainly in the 1950s and developing into the philosophy of child-centred learning. This together with the presence in our schools of children of mixed abilities within the comprehensive system, has led to an identification of new needs, not only in curriculum content, but in the methodology employed, which, in turn, has been facilitated by a revolution in educational technology. Teachers have become far more aware of why and how they are going to educate, and with the help of such bodies as the Schools Council and teachers' centres, a little less wary of innovation.

The major points to be drawn from this summary are: the need to cope in our schools with mixed-ability groups, the emphasis on child-centred learning, and the chances that teachers now have to influence and change the curriculum. Hence the need for resources centres, and not merely the availability in schools of resource materials, which are often there already in abundance if teachers only knew it! Resourcing mixed-ability group teaching involves assembling those items already defined into some form of collection in order that their retrieval by pupils and staff may be facilitated.

Resources are normally classified as either 'hardware' or 'software'. Hardware is machine technology – the tape recorder, the projector, the photocopier. Software is all that material which is either used on its own – books, newspaper cuttings or pictures – or in connection with the hardware – recorded tapes, slides, or films.

If we recognise that resources, both hardware and software, exist already in our schools, and that there is, in some cases, total unawareness of what the school possesses, together with a certain lack of sharing, then it seems reasonable that the resources of such a school should be classified in some form, in order that such facilities can be used for the benefit of the school as a whole. Particularly in software, as we shall see, certain items can be of as much use to the science department as to the humanities department. There are cases where one department orders filmstrips, only to find subsequently that another department in the school already possesses them. In other words, there is the very practical need for classifying resources in order that we stop being squirrels and learn that co-operation improves the effectiveness of our teaching.

In all probability both the curriculum and the methodology employed in transmitting that curriculum will demand certain resources, so that it becomes a necessity to have some form of storage and retrieval system in the school.

One thing is quite certain. If a school decides that its curriculum necessitates the use of an inquiry- and learner-based methodology, and accepts that a haphazard collection of resource material will do, then it could be a costly, time-consuming mistake. Keith Evans has warned of the danger of resource centres not based on curriculum needs becoming multi-media white elephants.[5] Nor is it sufficient for children to spend time sifting through a badly organised collection of materials. A good systematic collection of resources is necessary, and it should have, at its nerve centre, an indexing system which makes successful retrieval by pupils a straightforward operation. The argument is sometimes advanced that a successful indexing system cuts out browsing among the library shelves. How many of us, I wonder, have noted the sense of frustration and eventual disillusionment in our pupils, when for period after period they have sought fruitlessly for information in the school library, and where little has been gained from browsing at all?

If children can locate immediately a mass of information relevant to what they are seeking, and through which they can then browse and select, the educational value more than justifies the hard work involved in indexing the material.

The Schools Working Paper no 43 states that 'A resource library is a resource collection organised and indexed for use, much as a book library is organised.' Indeed, at this point it should be stressed that the main part of the collection will probably comprise the school library, which offers a superb collection of resource material provided that it is open for that purpose.

Many schools use the library as an extra classroom, which may be necessary because of lack of space. In addition there is the question of adequate staffing (a matter which is discussed below). Education authorities are now beginning to realise the value of ancillary help in schools, and it is not unusual any longer to find qualified librarians employed as school librarians. Similarly, it is not uncommon to find posts advertised for heads of resources or directors of resources, and in London there is a new breed of ancillary helpers known as MROs or media resources officers.

There is now a growing realisation that because of the volume of work involved in establishing a resources collection, or ultimately, a resources centre, staffing becomes an important criterion if an efficient system is to be created and maintained.

A final definition from the Schools Council Working Paper no 43:

A resources centre is an agency for stimulating active creation and use of a resources collection including the six elements of:
1 Production of home-made resources.
2 Selection and acquisition of other resources.
3 Classification and indexing for retrieval.
4 Storage.
5 Use, including guidance, lending, etc.
6 Evaluation and weeding.

A resources centre can be many things to many people. It provides for the pupils' needs in that it houses the nerve centre of the resources collection – the central indexing system or systems – together with the main book resource, if the school possesses a library, and collections of other resources that it is found expedient to centralise.

It is a place where some pupils find great stimulus to work, and therefore, ideally, should possess tables or study carrels for individual research. Other pupils might prefer to borrow the material, working in another part of the school. It is a place which, because it stimulates the active creation of resources, becomes invaluable as a staff workshop. It is a place where staff should be able to seek help. It is not always feasible to expect staff to produce their own supportive material; one can argue that all members of staff should have this active experience of creation, but many teachers have a fear of recent technological development, unlike many of the pupils they teach. It is for colleges of education and university departments of education to ensure that student teachers become familiar with the equipment that teachers must increasingly use in their lessons.

Not all teachers are gifted artists, even with such aids as print transfer techniques. The resources centre should be able to provide a supportive role for the teacher, either in a training or advisory capacity, or in the last resort, by producing the work itself. Keith Evans makes the point that the teacher can no longer perform the multiple roles of composer, arranger, conductor, performer, audience and critic.[6] He should be able to delegate a few of these roles to the resources centre.

Once the decision to establish some kind of central resources provision has been taken a plan of action must be devised. At one particular school, where the present writer was involved in the creation of a resources centre, visits were made to the General Studies Project at York University, and the recommendation in their paper on resource centres led to the ordering of an optical coincidence co-ordinate indexing system (OCCI). At the time of my arrival, it had already been decided that this system should be adopted, and this in no way detracts from the first point I want to make – that the first step must be a fairly definite determination of what system of retrieval is going to be used.

I say 'fairly definite' because it is no use carrying on with a system that is obviously not working; and to give the system a fair chance to prove itself, and then have to change it, will waste valuable time. If such a situation is to be avoided, a considerable amount of thought and planning will be necessary. My assistant and I spent our first four weeks in the school discussing the implications of the system, and compiling a 'feature list' which is an operational process of the OCCI system. The decision on a retrieval system determines the type of storage to be employed, the amount of space required, staffing and ancillary involvement, and possibly, at a more advanced stage, the type of technical equipment that will be needed to produce items of software. There can be little doubt, therefore, that it is a priority decision.

There is so much one could say about retrieval systems, but let us remember the prime concern of any retrieval system – the simple location of information on any given topic. In a school the system should be such that no child is incapable of operating it, and procuring for himself a feedback from the system. If a member of staff has to be at hand all the time to find the material for the child,

168

then there is something wrong with the system. Similarly, if it is capable of being worked by those in the sixth form and not by those in the first form, then it is a wasteful exercise that sooner or later will be regretted by its originators. A Schools Council project on school resource centres is considering systems of retrieval most suitable for use in schools as part of its brief.

There has, understandably, been some difference of opinion between librarians and others involved in setting up resource collections, on the use of newer indexing techniques. Some librarians are adamant that the traditional methods of indexing books, such as the Dewey decimal classification, can meet the demands of multi-media resources, and argue that, as the standard practice of classifying books in public libraries throughout the country is based on Dewey, other systems should perhaps not be employed, so as to avoid confusion.

There is another factor in classification, however, that must be taken into account. Many resource items have several applications. A book of poems in a library, for instance, containing poems written by Bushmen, may be of use not only to the English department, but to a humanities department studying Bushmen. Unless a child is specifically directed to that book, or unless the title of the spine mentions the word 'Bushmen', it may never occur to him that if he browsed through all the poetry books, he might find a poem written about Bushmen by a Bushman. Another example is given by the General Studies Project:

> ... there is a book in York Public Library called *History of Football*. It is classified by the librarian very reasonably, as 796.334 (ie sports and pastimes, association football) but the book is not only about football. It is also about history and religion and education and literature and newspapers and many other matters of potential interest to pupils and teachers. And it has in it a picture of a misericord in Gloucester Cathedral, a seventeenth century engraving of the Piazza of Santa Croce in Florence and many other plates that give good evidence about styles of dress in a variety of periods up to the 1950s . . .'

169

It is unlikely that a child writing a project on church architecture would be drawn to a book entitled *A History of Football*, unless in some way he was guided to it by means of a retrieval system. We have found that children, left to their own devices, avoid using the classified catalogue, preferring to go directly to the shelves to browse under the major classification headings. One of the problems a librarian has to solve in any multi-media collection is, that if this is a normal pattern, should and can multi-media materials be shelved together? In other words, at 796.334 (sports and pastimes, association football) should one expect to find all the books, together with cuttings, filmstrips, films, video tapes, journals and pictures, next to each other on the shelf?

If a collection were run on the basis of topics or themes, it would be possible to adopt such a system, with all items on a theme housed in a box, suitable labelled. This has been done to good effect, particularly in primary schools, and I once started such a collection, although it was limited to topics within one subject, and had no method of cross-referencing the items. Boxes, of course, are cumbersome, particularly if they are going to house a variety of materials, and deep shelving or racking becomes necessary. The boxes are usually stored in alphabetical order, and this method probably constitutes the simplest, least sophisticated way of retrieving items.

The major fault with this method lies in its inability to provide cross-references. One item may well have several applications, and unless the item is duplicated it may well be only in one topic box, and not be retrieved by a child using another box under another theme.

It is to avoid this difficulty that a more sophisticated index catalogues all materials held in the collection, and classifies them so that they are arranged according to the nature of the items. If the Dewey decimal system is adopted for the multi-media resources centre then it must have additional support in the form of added entries, if all aspects of the resources are to be covered. Thus a filmstrip on ancient civilisations can only be housed in one place, but it might well be relevant to architecture, and thus to the design department, or to the music department, because there are important frames on musical instruments. The cataloguing will have to include

170

an approach through these relevant subjects. This means a considerable increase in the number of cards in the catalogue.

What of the newer systems? A description of one has appeared in *The Times Educational Supplement*. A small team at the Birmingham Polytechnic School of Art are experimenting with a notched 'fact-finder' card. These experiments stemmed from the need to find a more flexible method of retrieval than that offered by the traditional methods. To catalogue an item in a variety of ways, notches are made around the outside of the card with a special cutter. The basis of the classification is still the Dewey system. To retrieve a card, or cards, the pile is placed inside a box-like machine which vibrates the notched cards downwards. The card itself is a little complex, and therefore, while suitable for tertiary education, may not be quite so suited for primary and secondary levels. This is basically a more refined development of what is often called 'the knitting needle system'.

One other system, the optical coincidence co-ordinate index, deserves some elaboration. Although generally it is agreed that it allows for more cross references, nevertheless it does have its critics. Many criticisms stem from a lack of knowledge about the system itself, although some are justified. These will be dealt with after a brief technical description.

It is, basically, a punched card system which has been used successfully in industry as a method of data retrieval for several years. Its backbone – and this, I feel, has implications way beyond the use of the system – is the compilation of a feature list. This is a list of the categories or features of resources, which are felt to be relevant to the school curriculum, and basically the system provides for an answer to three main questions:

What is it?
Where is it?
What is it about?

Under the first heading, the main question to be answered is the actual form of the resource, closely related to the definition of resources as given by the Schools Council Working Paper no 43.

The question 'Where is it?' presupposes that the materials could be anywhere, either inside the resources centre, or anywhere in the school, or for that matter outside the school. On our feature list, we might note the central library in the town, the teachers' centre, the museum, and even the regional resources centre.

It is, of course, not necessary for a resources centre to house the total collection of resources in one school. Any attempt to centralise all resources would be a mistake, and might lead to opposition from departments within the school. A good system must be based on as much decentralisation of software as is practical, provided that it has been indexed into the central system, so that its availability is known and registered. The index may well lead a pupil to a filmstrip belonging to the drama department, and with the good-will of the head of that department, the filmstrip can be borrowed and used. Decentralisation of software but centralisation of the index is the key.

The next question on the feature list is: 'What is it about?', and under this we have four subheadings each of which should be considered carefully:

What periods?
What places?
What timetable subjects?
What topics or themes?

When we designed our first feature list, it was the final list which took up most of our time. Obviously, one could go on adding to this part of the list. However, we felt it necessary to keep the list short, and therefore our selected words were wide in application. A section of the list appears below:

Ideology	Pattern	Techniques
Industrial Relations	Photography	Technology
Industry	Pilgrim	Television
Infection	Pioneers	Tension
Insects	Planning	Textile

For every word on the feature list (and there are 512 items),

172

there is a card in the index. Each card has on it 5,600 small squares, although this number depends on the make of card, as some cards have an accession capacity of 10,000 items. Each resource dealt with by the centre is given an accession number and a feature list is duly filled out for it – that is, all the relevant applications of that particular resource are noted under the headings discussed above.

There may have been as many as 39 features ticked on the feature list, and the next task is to take out from the box the 39 cards representing those features. Let us suppose that the item we have been dealing with has been given the accession number 1300, then all the cards are punched at square 1300 and returned to the box.

The pupil operates the system in the following way. If he wants to find something out about Tutankhamen, he must first ascertain what cards will be of most help to him in tracking down the information he seeks. This is in itself a valuable educational exercise for he must synthesise what he wants to find out. Thus, he ascertains that the pharaoh lived approximately 3,300 years ago, which is 1300 BC. The relevant card in our system is headed 'Before 499 BC'. Next, the place – most children know that he was an Egyptian, and so the place card for Egypt is selected. Tutankhamen was a pharaoh – but no card is listed under pharaoh. This is where the boy has to think – pharaoh means king or ruler – and there is a card for this.

So, he has three cards – 'Before 499 BC'; 'Egypt'; and 'Kings/Rulers'. He then stacks them together in a light box, and eleven pinpricks of light appear where holes punched in the cards coincide. He jots down the numbers on a piece of paper, and then turns up each number in the appropriate reference volumes. He might find actual material reprinted in the volumes, or be given instructions as to where he can find the material. He will also be able to ascertain the nature of the material so that he can decide whether or not to pursue his investigation further.

In this case the OCCI at the present writer's school would have turned up for him:

One article from the *Sunday Telegraph* of March 12 1972 on Tutankhamen.

Three references to *National Geographic Magazines* of various dates.

One audio-tape from the BBC *Man* series, on Tutankhamen.

One set of slides acquired from the British Museum.

Three books in the library section under obscure titles.

One BBC pamphlet, which has very good photographs.

One criticism that has been levelled at all the newer types of indexing is based on the fact that anything works in the first flush of enthusiastic innovation, and that systems may collapse once the pioneer of the scheme has left the school. It is, unfortunately, true that innovatory situations are sometimes terminated by the movement of staff from a school, but it often depends on how well the scheme has been prepared and how successful it has been. However, the one case I know of where there was a collapse of an OCCI system came about because no one in the school was prepared to take on the hard work of continuation. The originator had carried the system on his own, with very little time allocated to him during his working week. This difficulty may be avoided when there is adequate provision of ancillary help in schools.

Another criticism is that it is folly to run two systems; that a choice must be made in order to provide an integrated approach to information by means of a single catalogue. It is possible to run both with success. While the Dewey system remains for the majority of the books in the centre, OCCI supplements this (by means of its feature list) by accessioning all non-book materials, together with those books noted by the librarian as containing material which is thought to be valuable but unlikely to be retrieved by children because of the nature of the title. The example given earlier of Bushman poetry illustrates this.

A further common criticism is that because accession of materials is sequential, one must physically house all items in a sequential order, which, as we have already noted, provides major storage difficulties. But this is not so, as one groups similar items together – in other words, there are specific places for all the tapes, the slides, the filmstrips and the sets of magazines. A child using OCCI is directed from the reference sheet to the place where the item is stored. For instance, he will be led to an article in a *National Geographic Magazine* by the cryptic note 'Availability – Nat Geog shelves – Resources Centre', having already been given the date of publication, and a description of what is contained in the article.

The criticism that it is too complicated for children to use, we have totally disproved. After an initial period of instruction on entering the school, first year children use OCCI very happily.

Finally, there is the valid criticism that it takes a lot of work to keep going. This is true, and if one person is doing it, then it is a genuine labour of love. But any expanding library necessitates hard work, and punching holes is a simpler and quicker process than typing library cards – indeed, pupils in the school can give a hand with the hole-punching process. Furthermore OCCI enables users to get the maximum out of software, with its fine cross-referencing capability. Thus a systems approach to the recording of resource material must be undertaken if a pupil is to be provided with a more than hit-or-miss chance of successful inquiry. Anything other than a planned scheme of collection, cataloguing and classification is wasted effort on the part of teachers, and generally leads to an unproductive learning situation for the pupil. There can be little doubt that, in a decade, schools will be using a national computerised data-base of catalogue information relating to learning materials, and some schools or groups of schools may well combine in harnessing the facilities that a computer may provide to their retrieval needs. However, this is still some way off, and only a pipe dream as far as many schools are concerned. There is, therefore, a need to examine, very carefully, the retrieval systems that are available, and, having done this, to select one which is not only suitable to a school's needs, but one which that school is capable of operating, maintaining and developing.

Starting resource collections involves deciding what to collect. It is not easy to provide a definitive answer, as the situation will vary from school to school according to the curriculum needs, and possibly the approach of the member of staff in charge of resources. One might not understand why an infants teacher is collecting the insides of toilet rolls until one sees the lovely little snowmen that her class has made, with the cotton wool hiding the mundane cardboard roll underneath! Bearing in mind all the time the definition of a resource as 'any object that facilitates the learning process', one must be constantly vigilant.

Magazines are useful, particularly colour supplements, *National Geographic* and *Geographical Magazines, World of Wonder, Pictorial Education, The Listener,* and many others. While some may be ordered by the school, it is amazing how many other sources of supply there are. An appeal to parents to send in their used magazines, rather than pile them up for the refuse collector, may bring in a great deal of unwanted material but also much that is of value. Teaching staff, too, can be encouraged to bring in their colour supplements.

Auctions provide another productive source of raw materials. At one school we managed to acquire an almost complete set of *National Geographic Magazines* dating back over the last twenty years, many of them in duplicate, and all these from local auction rooms. Spare copies mean that one can extract the relevant material to build up a study pack. Good quality overhead projector transparencies can be made from the later editions (or from any photograph printed on a clay based paper) by a very simple process.

The same school also managed to acquire complete bound editions of Purnell's *History of the Twentieth Century* (original price nearly £30) for £3.50; *The Game,* published by Marshall Cavendish; and Purnell's *The History of the Second World War.* Other purchases included a superb collection of rock specimens and fossils, collected in 1867, which cost very little, and a table slide-viewer rather like a television set, which cost under £2, and which has proved to be one of the most-used pieces of equipment in the resources centre.

Business firms often have a spring-clean, or go bankrupt, and their unwanted stock finds its way to the sale room. This brought about the acquisition of a Copycat ML 3, a fine copier that can reproduce almost anything from colour into black and white negatives which can be stored indefinitely, the new price of which was in the region of £160 and which cost only £15 at an auction. Two large shop fittings with numerous drawers and glass fronts purchased for £10 made excellent storage cabinets. Glass display cabinets from shops are very good for housing display material.

It is not always necessary to get time off from school to attend the auction itself. One can view after school hours the day before the sale, and leave a bid with the auction staff. One often finds that they have a son or nephew in the school and will be only too willing to bid if it means a bargain for the school!

However, if one is going to regard auctions as a serious source of resource material, then it may be necessary to persuade the headmaster that immediate funds should be available to meet expenses. Auctioneers may not take too kindly to delays while the local authority makes up its mind to authorise payment of the bill, and there are ways of speeding up the process. It is extremely useful if heads of resources can have available a fund of petty cash on which they can draw immediately they see a bargain.

Newspaper articles are often relevant to needs, and should be cut out and carefully filed. The method of preserving newsprint depends on the equipment and finance available, but in general it does not take too kindly to excessive handling and it deteriorates with age. Originals should be kept, and a photocopy made to which reference can be made by the pupil. An effort should be made to collect articles which are not of an ephemeral nature, and this applies to all resource material. It may often be the case that it becomes necessary to keep newspaper articles that are ephemeral, and such articles can be kept in a specialist file with only the file indexed. For example, if some pupils are following political events in Northern Ireland, this means that a whole series of cuttings may be accumulated. In a year's time, some of these cuttings could well be replaced by more relevant and up-to-date material. If each cutting has been indexed then there will be an excessive waste of index numbers when pruning takes place at a later stage. However, if all cuttings are put into a 'Northern Ireland' file, which is itself indexed, then it becomes a simple operation to up-date that file by weeding out material which is of a transitory value.

Pictures are best preserved by mounting them on stout manilla. A convenient size for storage and display purposes seems to be about 25cm by 32cm. Captions should not be forgotten. It is all too easy to preserve pictures without captions, and then months later to have forgotten the vital details that go with them. It is also a good idea to quote the date and source of the information, so that if at some later stage there is a reason to reproduce it, matters concerning copyright can be taken care of.

It goes without saying that slides and filmstrips are an essential part of any multi-media resources collection. Many good slides and fiilmstrips are produced and marketed commercially, and most departments in a school will buy their own. However, it may be that the head of resources feels it necessary to buy sets of slides or filmstrips, if they are of a more general nature. There are, of course, other sources of supply – not the least being those slides taken by teachers and children on school trips. They are usually willing to allow copies to be made, and sometimes they will even donate them to the collection. Children are often adept at using cameras, and can take very good slides.

It is extremely useful to house all catalogues dealing with both hardware and software in a central store. Ordinary box-files, suitably labelled, ensure that a member of staff can come with a specific request about the availability of appropriate material, and the information he requires can be retrieved quickly and efficiently. This adds to the image of the centre as a source of stimulus for curricular activity.

Finally, there is the question of what a resource centre should hold. As a workshop for both staff and pupils, it should be able to provide such materials as print transfers, special pens and materials used in the making of overhead projector transparencies, print stencils, as well as the more everyday resources like writing paper, tracing paper and pencils, scissors and rulers. Ideally, the centre should also provide a simple reprographic capability that can be used by both staff and pupils. As far as more complicated repro-graphic machinery is concerned, this is purely a matter of what each individual school can afford. Certain items are essential, if the maximum amount of educational value is to be gained from the use of resources. For instance, every school should have a duplicator, whether it be spirit or stencil, although too often such equipment is regarded as the sole property of the school office and its staff, and getting work duplicated becomes an operation that requires extreme diplomacy or stealth!

At the moment, thermographic copiers are found in a few schools, and only in the larger comprehensives, or a few 'enlightened' smaller schools, are there electronic stencil cutters. Machinery often lies derelict, either out of disillusionment on the part of the staff who are unable to gain access to it, or because of mechanical neglect. Difficulties arising from a school's proclaimed inability to purchase such machinery are sometimes exaggerated, and it is frequently the result of the headmaster's unwillingness to devote part of the school funds to such a cause.

Even the spirit duplicator is capable of producing high-quality material, particularly in colour, provided the staff have a little expertise. Here again there is a strong case for in-service or external training, run by county advisory staff. If the spirit duplicator is coupled with a thermographic copier then the production capability is extended to include copying from originals, making spirit masters from originals and making overhead projector transparencies. This system, however, cannot copy from books, the quality of picture reproduction is poor, and copies can only be made from inks with a carbon or metal base. Nevertheless, it is an economic and fairly flexible system, which can be operated by most teachers.

Copying from books requires the use of a flatbed machine, which is one on which a book can be laid face down. The size of the image varies according to the cost of the machine, but a flatbed copier is extremely useful, and does save tearing out pages from books or periodicals.

There are two other, more sophisticated, possibilities for duplicating. These are stencil duplicating and offset litho. Stencil duplicating is far more common, because most schools already possess duplicators of this kind for administrative purposes. Stencils can be hand-cut by the use of a simple cutting instrument, although it must be stressed that this process requires patience and skill. They can also be typed, and made on a thermographic copier. However, there is another method, namely the electronic scanner, which produces very accurate results.

The most professional method of duplicating is by means of offset litho. Makers of this equipment are becoming increasingly conscious of the needs of schools, and are therefore making smaller, cheaper and less-sophisticated models. The price, however, is still high when compared with many of the items purchased for schools. In the past professional operators have been needed, but now manufacturers have automated the process in such a way that they claim that half a day's training is sufficient. The main advantage of offset litho is the high quality achieved in duplication. It is also cheaper for runs of over twenty, and by using a paper plate, than any other process. The paper plate can be typed, written or drawn upon, or produced on most of the copying machinery, and it can normally be expected to produce several hundred copies of consistent quality.

Audio reproduction must also be catered for, and good tape recording facilities are essential. It is difficult to choose between reel-to-reel and cassette recording as far as quality of reproduction is concerned, but there can be little doubt that the cassette is easier to store, and to use, and is less prone to accidents when used. A very simple operation ensures that accidental erasure cannot occur, and thus the recording can be kept indefinitely. It is possible to buy machines for playback only, at a greatly reduced cost, and these machines are very useful. Headphones are recommended for any playback of sound, as use of these prevents interference with other people's work.

We must not forget, too, that in these days of technological advancement, recording of vision is a comparatively simple process, and is likely to become cheaper. Again, the use of the video cassette, for the reasons stated above, is highly recommended.

Children should have access to cameras. Elaborate models are unnecessary, and Instamatics require very little technical skill to operate. A simple darkroom, which can be used for developing and enlarging, and apparatus for taking slides from pictures in books, and also for duplicating slides, will prove invaluable. Some of this equipment can be made on a 'do-it-yourself' basis, and therefore does not necessarily involve a great deal of capital outlay.

In conclusion, there seems to be little difference, in principle, between collecting resources for mixed-ability groups and collecting them for homogeneous groups. However, two points of difference do occur. Firstly, the retrieval system must be such that children of lesser ability are able to operate it, and therefore, time and care must be spent on looking closely at the operational factors. Learning must be facilitated in such a way that the child learns because of the system, rather than in spite of it!

Secondly, material collected, and hardware used, must reflect the different ability levels of those who are to use it. It is no use, for instance, cutting leading articles from *The Times,* if all the children who are to use it have reading ages of nine years. A greater variety of resource material must be collected to cope with differing intellectual capabilities, and to allow for these capabilities to be extended.

Resources must be collected according to curricular needs, and thus should not dictate to those needs. As writers in other chapters have described, there are many good reasons for curriculum changes, and the setting up of resource collections or resources centres is not one of them. Resources are tools of the learning process, and must therefore facilitate its operation. Their function is to be part of the climate wherein learning becomes an exciting and stimulating process – where the words 'want to learn' become substituted for the words 'have to learn'.

Nurturing this climate should not be marred by half-hearted attempts at setting up resources collections, as happens in so many cases. Commitment should be total, which means taking a new look, not only at finance, but at how we are to provide the manpower. A solitary teacher trying to cope with a full timetable or even half a timetable is not the answer.

Douglas Holly warns of the limitations of resource-based learning:

Resources learning is no panacea. It is *one* element in a variety of strategies required by comprehensive education. Direct pupil-teacher relationships remain fundamental . . . The need is for *more* not *less* humane relations, relations based on the assumption that a teacher's job is to help pupils in their all-round self realisation, not to teach some remote subject – still less to become manipulators of externalised materials. While distant attitudes may have been appropriate for a system which alienated education

181

from the learner, they are quite inappropriate to a system which seeks to transcend this. Resources materials are a means, never and end in themselves.

For notes to this chapter see pp 187–8

Notes and References

1: Teaching Mixed-Ability Groups (pages 7–22)
1   Thelen, H. A. *Classroom Grouping for Teachability* (1967)
2   *Times Educational Supplement* Report (26 April 1974)
3   Fader, D. N. and McNeil, E. B. *Hooked on Books* (1969)
4   Bell, P. *Basic Techniques for Slow Learners* (1970)
5   Bradley, H. W. and Goulding, J. G. (ed) *Handling Mixed-Ability Groups* (Nottingham 1973)
6   McGeeney, P. J. *Parents are Welcome* (1969)

2: Teaching English in Mixed-Ability Groups (pages 23–43)
1   Harding, D. W. 'Psychological Processes in the Reading of Fiction', *British Journal of Aesthetics*, 2 no 2 (1962) Reprinted in Osborne, H. (ed) *Aesthetics and the Modern World* (1968) and Hardy, B. 'The teaching of English: life, literature and literary criticism', *English in Education*, 2 no 2 (1968) and 'The teaching of Literature in the University: Some problems', *English in Education*, 7 no 1 (1973)
2   Britton, James. *Language and Learning* (1970) 267, and 'The Role of Fantasy', *English in Education*, 5 no 3 (1971)
3   For a number of very helpful points on reading aloud and much more on presenting fiction in schools, see Jones, A. and Buttrey, J. *Children and Stories* (Oxford 1970)
4   See Labov, W. 'The Logic of Nonstandard English', *Language in Education* (1972); Rosen, Harold. *Language and Class* (Bristol 1972); Keddie, Nell. 'The Organisation of Classroom Knowledge', *English in Education*, 5 no 2 (1971)
5   For an extensive and quite the best analysis and discussion of classroom group dynamics and disciplines see Hargreaves, David. *Interpersonal Relations and Education* (1972)
6   Professor James Britton discusses particular group conversations with and without the presence of a teacher and considers the kind of learning which such conversations make possible in *Language and Learning* (1970) and *Language, The Learner and The School* (1969)

183

7   For suggestions for work on individual, group and whole-class topics and themes see Adams, Anthony. *Team Teaching and the Teaching of English* (1970); Summerfield, Geoffrey. *Topics in English* (1965); Tottman, S. and Carlen, P. *Projects* (1970); White, Graham. 'Guidelines for Unstreamed English', *English in Practice*, ed. Summerfield and Tunnicliffe (Cambridge 1971); *Penguin English Project* (1971) eg Jackson, David. *Family and School*, and the accompanying *Teacher's Handbook;* Pepper, Dennis. *An Index of Themes* (Holloway Teachers' Centre, London); *New Approaches to English Teaching*, Teachers' Handbook, Inner London Education Authority Television Service.

8   See Burgess *et al. Understanding Children Writing* (1973)

3:   Teaching Modern Languages in Mixed-Ability Groups (pages 44–63)

(a)   The following is a list of useful titles in which the mixed-ability situation is both opposed and defended: 'Teaching Modern Languages across the Ability Range', *CILT Reports and Papers*, no 8 (September 1972); 'Teaching Modern Languages across the Ability Range', *Modern Languages in Scotland*, no 1 (May 1973); Rowlands, David (ed). *Group Work in Modern Languages* (York 1972); *Modern Languages* (Journal of the Modern Language Association): Partington, John. *Streams, Sets or Mixed Ability Groups*, 50 no 3 (September, 1969) and Smith, David. *French and the Less Able*, 54 no 3 (September, 1973)

(b)   Additionally the following publications contain many useful references and hints with regard to the situation under discussion in this chapter:
Tools for the Job, published for the Joint Council of Language Associations by the Modern Language Association (1972); *The Place and Aims of Modern Language Teaching in Secondary Schools* (the 4th Report of the Scottish Central Committee for Modern Languages (HMSO, Edinburgh, 1972); Upton, Leslie. 'In Defence of Comprehension', *Modern Languages* 53 no 4 (December, 1972); Cole, Leo. *Language Teaching in Action* (1973)

4:   Teaching Geography in Mixed-Ability Groups (pages 64–80)

1   Ambrose, Peter. 'New Developments in Geography', *New Directions in Geography Teaching*, ed. Walford (1973) 69

2   Ibid, 71

3   Hill, James L. 'Building and using inquiry models in the teaching of geography', *Focus on Geography* (National Council for the Social Studies, 1970) 305

4   Bruner, J. S. 'The Art of Discovery', in *Readings in Human Learning*, ed. L. D. and A. Crow (New York 1963) 425

5   Fitzgerald, B. P. 'The American High School Geography Project and its implications for geography teaching in Britain', *Geography* 54 no 242, part 1, (January 1969)

6   Helburn, N. *Journal of Geography*, 157 (1968) 278-9

7   McCartin, Rosemary. 'The cognitive and affective learning of children', in *Focus on Geography*, 255

8   Kaltsounis, Theodore. 'An analysis of teaching strategies in emerging geography curricula' in *Focus on Geography*, 420

9   Reynolds, John. 'Curriculum development project', *Geography 14–18 years, Schools Council Geography* 56 no 250 part 1, (January 1971) 34

10 Bailey, P. M. J. 'The organisation and management of geography departments in comprehensive schools', *Geography* 57 no 256 part 3 (July 1972)

11 Gardner, William and Rogers, Vincent. 'Learning Principles' in *Social Sciences and Geographic Education; A Reader* ed. John M. Ball, John Steinbeck and Joseph Stoltman (1971)

12 Gardner, William and Rogers, Vincent

13 Benn, Caroline and Simon, Brian. *Half Way There* (1970)

14 Gardner, William and Rogers, Vincent

15 Himmelweit, Hilde. 'Why we cannot afford to stream', *Comprehensive Education* no 16 (Autumn 1970)

16 Wyatt, H. 'A resource centre in geography teaching', *Geography* 58 no 259 part 3 (July 1973)

17 Beswick, Norman W. Schools Council Working Paper 43, *School Resources Centres* (1972)

18 Crawford, S. *The Developing World* (1969)

19 Langford, Michael, Hardman, Arnold and Savery, Sheena. *It takes all kinds* Times Educational Supplement (May 1973)

20 Cole, J. P. and Benyon, N. J. *New Ways in Geography: Introductory Book; Book 1, Book 2, Book 3* and *Teacher's Book* (1969–72)

21 Rowe, A. W. *The Education of the Average Child* (1961)

22 Taylor, J. L. and Walford, R. *Simulation in the classroom* (1972) 33

23 Ambrose, Peter. 77

24 Taylor, John L. and Walford, Rex. 33

25 Hore, P. in Walford, R. A. (ed) *New Directions in Geography Teaching* (1973) 133, 136

5: Teaching History in Mixed-Ability Groups (pages 81–101)

1   Longmans' *Then and There* series – *The Town, The Village, The*

Monastery, The Castle, Pilgrimages, The Tournament, The Norman Conquest, Magna Carta

2 *Focus on History* series – *Life in the Medieval Monastery, Norman England, The Crusades, Medieval Life*

3 Oxford's *Peoples of the Past – An Eleventh Century Mason, A Twelfth Century Benedictine Nun, A Thirteenth Century Villein, An Archer in the Army of Edward III, A Fifteenth Century Wool Merchant, A Fifteenth Century London Housewife*

4 Ginn's History Bookshelves – Green Shelf: *English Monasteries, Bayeux Tapestry, English Castles, Life in a Manor House, A Port and a Pilgrim, Work on a Manor*

6: *Teaching Social Studies/Humanities in Mixed-Ability Groups (pages 102–121)*

1 A vivid description of primary school independent learning is contained in Dorothy and John Paull, *Yesterday I Found . . .* (Mountain View Centre for Environmental Studies, Colorado, USA)

Further Reading

Bruner, J. S. *Towards a Theory of Instruction* (particularly 'Man: A Course of Study') (Cambridge, Mass. USA)

Goodson, Ivor. 'Developing Contexts for Autonomous Learning' *Forum* 15 no 4 (Spring 1973)

Holly, Douglas. *Society, Schools and Humanity* (1971)

Lawton, Denis and Dufour, Barry. *The New Social Studies* Paull, Dorothy and John. *Yesterday I Found . . .* (Mountain View Centre for Environmental Education, University of Colorado, USA)

Schools Council Integrated Studies, *Teacher's Guide and An Introduction to Integrated Studies*, (1972)

Schools Council/Nuffield Foundation, *The Humanities Project* (1970–73)

7: *Teaching Mathematics in Mixed-Ability Groups (pages 122–141)*

1 Benn, Caroline and Simon, Brian. 'Half Way There', *Report on the British Comprehensive School Reform*, 2nd ed. (1972) 221 Sampson, George. *The Organisation of Mathematics Teaching in the Comprehensive School* – a report on a questionnaire. (May 1971) Smith, S. S. Report of a small inquiry into the teaching of mathematics in mixed-ability groups.

2 Taylor, L. C. *Resources for Learning* 56

3 A report of the Central Advisory Council of Education (England) The Newsom report, *Half Our Future*, 148 paragraph 442, 151 paragraph 459

4 Goodman, Paul. *Compulsory Miseducation*, 55

5 Barnes, Douglas. *Language, the Learner and School* (1969)

6　Allen, Adrian. 'Are Teachers Streamed?', *Where?* (January 1971) 17–20

7　Gattegno, Caleb. *What we owe children.* The subordination of teaching to learning. 1–5

8　Sturgess, David. *Examining mathematics at sixteen.* A report based on the meetings of a working party convened by the Mathematics Advisory Unit, University of Nottingham School of Education.

9　Mathematics teaching pamphlet no 14 (Association of Teachers of Mathematics), *Examinations and Assessment,* 13–34.

8: Teaching Science in Mixed-Ability Groups (pages 142–161)
Bibliography
Barnes, Britton and Rosen, *Language, the Learner and the School* (1969)
Barnes, D. R. *Learning in Small Groups* (unpublished)
Britton, J. *Language and Learning* (1970)
Holt, J. *How children fail* (1969)
Darke and Hughes. *Explore and Discover – Science for the Middle Years* (1974)
Darke, J. 'Mixed-ability Science' *Forum* 13 no 1 (Autumn 1970)
Schools Council/Nuffield *Science 5–13* texts
Nuffield Foundation. *Chemistry Texts* (1966); *Biology Texts* (1966); *Physics Texts* (1966); *Combined Science* (1970) and *Secondary Science* (1971)
Schools Council. *Science for the young school leaver,* Working Paper no 1. (HMSO 1964) and *The Middle Years of Schooling,* Working Paper no 22 (HMSO 1969)

9: Resources for Mixed-Ability Groups (pages 162–182)
1　Schools Council Working Paper no 43 *School Resource Centres* (1973)
2　BBC broadcast. *Resources* (1972)
3　Jevons, F. R. *The Teaching of Science* (1969) 40
4　Taba, Hilda. *Teacher's Handbook for Elementary Social Studies* (1967)
5　Evans, K. 'Multi Media Resource Centres: A Cautionary Note', NUT *Secondary Education* (1972)
6　Ibid
7　Schools Council General Studies Project, York, *Resource Centres* (March 1969)

List of Useful Addresses
Indexing Systems:
G. Anson & Co Ltd, Anson House, Southwark Street, London SE1

J. L. Jolly & Partners Ltd, Westbourne House, Westbourne Street, High Wycombe, Bucks

Storage:

Railex – Frank Wilson (Filing) Ltd, Railex Works, PO Box 19, Manor Road, Southport

Scanex – ADM Business Systems Ltd, King Street, Hammersmith, London W6

Pamphlet boxes – Don Gresswell Ltd, Bridge House, Grange Park, London N21: Lawtons of Liverpool Ltd, Fold-Flat Storage Division, 60 Vauxhall Road, Liverpool L69 4BT

Slide Holders – Diana Wyllie Ltd, 3 Park Road, Baker Street, London NW1

Chart storage – Pictorial Charts Educational Trust, 181 Uxbridge Road, London W7

Further Reading

Taylor, L. C. *Resources for Learning* (1971)

Foskett, A. C. *The Subject Approach to Information* (1971)

Richmond, W. K. *The School Curriculum* (1971)

Hare, Richard. *Know How* (1970)

Riddle, Lewis and MacDonald. *Non-Book Materials* (Canadian Library Assoc.)

Schoolmaster Publishing Co Ltd. *Treasure Chest for Teachers* (1971)

APLET *Yearbook of Educational and Instructional Technology*

Coppen, H. E. *Aids to Teaching and Learning* (1965)

Young, J. B. *Reprographic Principles Made Easy* (NCAVAE)

Periodicals:

Educational Media International (quarterly; ICEM Modino Press)

Pictorial Education (monthly; Evans)

Visual Education (monthly; NCAVAE)

Visual Education Year Book (each July; NCAVAE)

Audio Visual (monthly; MacLaren)

Index